For the Duration
~
Robert F. Jackson, Jr.

Illustrated by the Author

Dedication

For my father and mother, who lived World War II at sea and on the home front; my father-in-law and mother-in-law, who endured it in the Philippine mountains and forests; and all similar survivors and the many martyrs for the cause of freedom in that greatest of the world's martial struggles.

History Soup

I'd like to pour a cauldron
Upon this page for you,
For, I know something of life then
And can feel their yearnings to.

But it was not my place in time,
Perhaps my cup is too small.
Then, to know the flavor of war
You needn't taste it all.

Instead, take just enough
Sipping slowly to be sure
Like those, who being there,
Gulped it scalding hot and pure.

Those who were there of course
Have served it up to me
Of long and lonely hours
On cold and stormy seas,

Cool or lukewarm beer
In steamy island shacks,
And bitter, lonely vigil prayers
So that lovers might come back,

Or a hard and frigid foxhole
In a still, white Belgian wood
Awaiting German panzers
Right where grenadiers once stood.

Now, I can taste as surely
As if I'd gripped the deck rail tight,
Salt spray across a slanting deck,
Fear hanging heavy in the night,

Or the bitter sweet of waiting
Like a father, son, or wife
The way my mother waited, praying
To guard my father's life.

And I can taste that tangy soup
Spiced with all a life can feel
Crushed cigarettes, an empty
 glass, a kiss
Served with brass and chilled
 with steel

This book is a work of fiction, and any similarity or resemblance of any character or person in this story to any actual person, living or dead, is purely coincidental. Events, situations, specific locations, or specific businesses portrayed within are fictional and set in a fictional future. The same can be said for organizations and agencies.

Any copying, retrieval, storage, or transmission of the material in this book by mechanical, electronic, photocopying, digital, or any other means is strictly prohibited, unless written permission is received from the author.

Limited short excerpts for promotion and review purposes or for educational assignments are allowed.

ISBN-13: 978-1723308390

ISBN-10: 1723308390

Copyright © 2018 Robert Jackson
Cover Illustration, Copyright © 2018 Robert Jackson

Contents

Introduction
Essential Notes before Reading

Which way is Paradise?   *1*

A Fairy Tale   *28*

... just at first light"   *65*

...all the tears I have right now"   *203*

"Nothing .. just a hollowness"   *259*

The Searchers   *330*

Map of the Philippines   415
Map of Southeast Asia & East Indies   416

Introduction

In 1941, when the bombing of American territory in the infamous Pearl Harbor raid sent our nation into the cauldron of the Second World War, lives by the millions were changed. For good or ill, almost all American's lives were affected in some way. Most dramatically, other than the obvious sacrifice of young men's lives for the greater good, young women were widowed and young children left fatherless. War invades the lives of the young the most. In taking sons it saddens parents and grandparents as well. In those times, it took mostly men, but it broke the hearts of their women. Those losses were America's burden in order to bring a proper end to it, for winning was the only option. It was a just war.

Our United States, once beloved by almost all its residents, was not the only cog in the allied war machine however, and others gave up not just their men but their daughters too, as civilian victims and as fighters. A total war, there were the civilian victims of our enemies at our warriors' hands, justified or not. And that's another story.

Fought across vast lands invaded by Japan and Germany with a callous evaluation of the lives of those they encountered, the war witnessed the abuse and death and ruptured lives of many a woman, young and old. And the young woman, by virtue of her natural desirability was always at risk. At numerous times and various locations, the enemy seemingly attempted, with some success to turn the use of captive women for sexual satisfaction of their warriors, into an official system, almost factory-like in its organization.

This novel is not about that but alludes to the risk because it was always there, just in the shadows. This novel is about ordinary people placed by life, willing or not, into extraordinary circumstances and becoming themselves extraordinary . . heroes and heroines. It really is one of life and history's most enduring and repetitive tales. Citizens of the world's various nations go from mundane, but perhaps satisfying daily lives, to the types of roles being required of them that novels and movie scripts are later written about. America and other lands are full of Molly Pitchers.

To that end: the reality of life under the pressure of duty, the reader should be prepared for this author to portray the ordinary, everyday, sometimes mundane nature of courage.

Essential Notes Before Reading

Uses of **'crush'** for romantic infatuation are claimed as early as 1599 according to *Merriam Webster Dictionary* and 1903 according to *A Dictionary of Slang And Unconventional English* (8th. Edition), by Eric Partridge. Other slang terms have similarly been checked for validity for the era.

The rank of **Chief Petty Officer** had only one level in World War II. Chiefs enjoyed a strong reputation and still do, stronger even than their counterparts in other services perhaps. Comparable to the highest-ranking sergeants in the Army and Marines, they were charged, among other things, with training new ensigns in the fleet, who would, as officers, outrank them.

Emergency recruitment of Navy personnel during World War II, without basic training, has not been confirmed, but circumstances like those of Jake Pierce surely occurred, which in his case left no other option. Therefore, artistic license was taken with confidence by the author.

Emergency advancement to the rank of Chief more quickly than normal is common knowledge as the rank of Acting Chief Petty Officer has long existed. When in use, it was temporary but could be made permanent.

Enlisted rank pilots were standard in the Navy for many years, including World War II. On planes with a crew and two or more pilots, one of which was an officer and the other an enlisted man, a more experienced enlisted pilot would be in command during flight duty, and a less experienced pilot who was an officer on the same plane would be the superior in command of the crew when not in flight.

Movements and general location of the hospital ship *Refuge* at the proper time frame to be the ship of mercy in this story was found in *Hospital Ships of World War II, An Illustrated Reference*, by Emory A. Massman, Copyright 1999, McFarland & Company, Inc., Publishers, Jefferson, North Carolina and London. Besides much informative data, it contains an enjoyably readable short history of each ship and is apparently the only definitive book on this important subject.

Except in the case of broader historical actions, campaigns, and events, military units, people and operations are fiction in this book; but, for the sake of realism, they are similar to the operations that did take place during World War II. As an example, the hospital ship, **USS Refuge AH-11** was real and her general location and movements in the story are historically accurate, but none of her personnel in the story nor any others portrayed are real people or based on particular real people.

Pan Am Clippers, which at the time the war began were Boeing 314s, were purchased by the government and used for important people's trips and missions. The flight in the novel is fiction but of the type that might have occurred during wartime. One source of information about the Clippers was **Pan American Clippers, The Golden Age of Flying Boats**, by James Trautman, 2007, The Boston Mills Press. Pan Am did not take them back after the war.

Everyday items of known origin, such as a particular brand of drink or make of car or furniture (etc.), used for historical context, were chosen out of respect for their positive worth and contribution to their respective cultures and our lives and/or those of the generation(s) that lived during the time of this story and endured the Second World War.

Atty. Jose Taboada & Dra. Natividad Corrales Taboada, who appear briefly in this story are real. The Nipa house in the city was real as well.

Ny Isa refers to Teresa Magbanua a female Filipino school teacher and military leader from Iloilo Province on the Island of Panay during the revolutionary period in the Philippines in the late Nineteenth and early Twentieth Centuries. Her biography is available online by simply searching her name.

The story of the **Hopevale Martyrs,** murdered by Japanese soldiers on Panay during World War II, is related in Louise Reid Spencer's war memoir, **Guerrilla Wife**, MCMXLV, Thomas Y. Crowell Co. The miners the author's husband worked with helped found and hid in the Hopevale settlement with those who were eventually martyred. Information about the people and events is available online.

Two excellent memoirs recount the experiences of very young military men caught up in the events of the Second World War. Alvin Kernan's memoir, **Crossing the Line, A Bluejacket's World War II Odyssey**, 1994, Naval Institute Press gives an excellent view of life for World War II carrier men, as he was an aircraft carrier crewman and a TBF Avenger turret gunner. He describes early night fighting missions during which his plane used radar to direct Hellcat fighters to enemy bombers.

Three Days to Pearl, 2000, Naval Institute Press, describing Peter J. Shepherd's British experience joins many other good books about the fall of Malaya and Singapore to the Japanese. But his is unique, as he became privy to very sensitive information. The young Malayan nurse he met and apparently had romantic feelings for was the inspiration for Maya in this novel.

Research does not reveal **PBY Dumbo crews** making a show of naming their flying boats, as the *Flying Cloud* is in this book.

The characters in this book commonly refer to their **Japanese enemy in Asia and the Pacific** as 'Japs' and 'Nips' (Nipponese). It would have been a logical short slang term without the anger and resentment caused by the sneak attack and military misbehavior of the enemy. That the words were also used to denigrate the enemy is easily understandable, given the general methods of abuse perpetrated on captive peoples by Japanese forces. This author has heard firsthand eyewitness accounts from relatives in the Philippines, and there is plenty of photographic evidence. The novel's narrator, in attempting to indicate the feelings of the characters and their moment in history, sometimes uses 'Jap' and 'Nip' too. This is **not** intended to denigrate or insult Japanese people today. But at the historical moment, when directed at the active foreign enemy and his behavior, it seemed appropriate.

Richard A. Cataldi, Commander, USN (Retired) assisted with Navy related historical information. If there is erroneous material in this novel, the fault lies not with Richard's advice.

For the Duration

~

Of those whom you gave me I lost not one.

John 18: 9

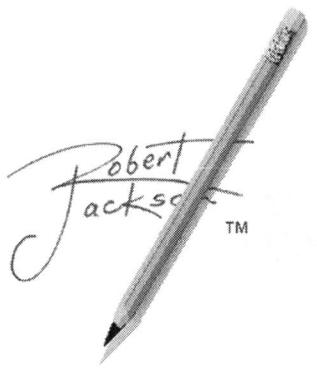

Which way is Paradise?

The sailor knocked the snow off of his boots at the door of the small community hall in the little mountain town of Paradise Ridge, California, high in the foothills of the Sierra. He hadn't figured on dancing anyway, which the boots would certainly hinder, and the cold ached in his still healing bones.

Just as he reached for the institutional style, looped, brass handle, what appeared to be a somewhat petite young woman approached from the winter darkness to his left, and he opened the door for her. The hooded coat she wore hid most of her personal appearance and her identity other than a petite height and weight and strands of dark hair sneaking out from the hood's containment. The coat appeared to be handmade with a hint of Native American crafting and a parka type hood of the North that was not in common use yet. The weathered seaman and flyer smiled slightly within at his perfect timing. For he had observed from the window of his room in the town's one little hotel as the grill lights across the street had gone dark and, moments later, a light had come on in the apartment above followed by the porch light at the top of the wooden steps that accessed it.

Reaching the warmth of the indoors, the chief petty officer immediately offered to help the woman with her coat and turned to hang it on one of the brass hooks on the wall by the door. With his back to her and the room, which contained quite a few people already, he removed and hung his dark, navy blue, wool reefer as well. It was the sailor's traditional, short overcoat, a double-breasted peacoat with the gold buttons of a chief, the top dogs in the enlisted ranks of the United States Navy. In those days of the greatest conflict on earth, there were no senior chiefs or master chiefs. Jake had reached the pinnacle quickly along the most unusual of routes.

He placed his officer's style hat on top of the coat's thick collar where it bulged like a buffalo's hump over the brass hook beneath. It had a black band with a thin gold strap across it in front above a black visor. The top, cap portion, was white and peaked or raised in front. It differed from a commissioned officer's head covering in that it lacked the larger, more complicated metal badge and bore instead a single gold colored metal anchor and rope design of the sailing era with the letters USN in silver placed across the anchor. The three-dimensional emblem, known as 'the fouled anchor', a masterpiece of simplicity, reflected the simple strength and collected wisdom of the men who wore it and the daily problems they faced.

Some few new sailors were there already and a greater number of local girls and guys not in the services. All were of an age that reflected youth except the newcomer who stood out in his more officer like uniform. The sailors were green, just out of boot camp, and their dark blue jumpers, with the traditional collar flap extension in the back, were stark and plain with few markings of distinction. The navy blue, cloth sailor's cap without a bill all the new young sailors in the room had worn when they arrived differed greatly from Jake's in overall appearance.

The chief, in contrast, wore a dark, navy-blue, officer's style, double breasted dress jacket with two vertical rows of gold buttons. His shirt was white, and he wore a black four-in-hand knotted tie. Two small, horizontal bar campaign ribbons were pinned on his left breast. One was mostly blue, and the other, a Naples yellow one, represented the war in the Pacific. Below them dangled two small but distinctive medals each from the ribbons that suspended them about one inch from their pins: a Purple Heart and a Silver Star. Above everything were the gold wings of a pilot. On his left arm, blending into the blue of the jacket, was a navy-blue chief petty officer's patch with three red chevrons, a red arc above them, and small gold threaded aviation rating wings within, beneath the arc. Above the arc, a white eagle with wings spread looked forward toward the front of the jacket. He had no service stripes on his sleeve, for he had not reached four years of service yet. That was unheard of for a chief petty officer, but he had reached that revered naval rank as an acting chief petty officer in the early, continuous, nonstop emergency filled days of the war. For Jake Pierce had found himself right in the thick of it by accident of timing and location. He was young for a chief petty officer, but, at only twenty-five, still older than the other, untested Navy men in the room.

Only a deputy sheriff sitting on a stool at the end of the little snack bar represented the younger end of the older generation, looking reasonably youthful, for specific generational divisions are vague at best.

As the room noticed the two new arrivals, the chief and the girl who appeared to be together perhaps, some two or three other girls exclaimed, "Sarah's here, . . coffee!"

They were just girls a year or so out of high school, as were most of the others in the hall, the sailors and the local civilian men.

Someone else spoke, a guy, "Yeah, there's no beer, it'll have to be coffee."

A soft chant began, "Sarah, Sarah, Sarah...", and the chief beside and behind her saw the dark girl's shoulders sink a little, even beneath long, very dark brown hair. Though brown it almost seemed raven black.

Music was already playing on a Victrola filling the room through speakers with Glenn Miller and his Orchestra's rendition of *"String of Pearls"*. As it ended, Jake was relieved to hear the Tommy Dorsey orchestra's version of *"I'll never Smile Again"* with Sinatra's clear voice floating across the hall. His war weary legs could handle that beat much better.

Turning to face the young woman and placing his right hand on her left shoulder and taking her right hand gently in his left, the bold chief looked over his shoulder, back toward the collected group and declared moderately, "After this song perhaps. It is a favorite and I've been at sea for three years," and whispering as he turned to her, he said, "Shall we."

It was then that he saw the natural beauty of her simple, uncomplicated, dusky face framed by the rich brown hair that ended laying on her shoulders. The man froze a moment as he could not avoid staring, and then, displaying the grace of an officer rather than a rugged noncom, he led her to the center of the room where they began to gracefully dance with some expertise.

Abruptly, after some moments and before the lovely song ended, the sound stopped with the scratch of the phonograph needle on the record.

Pausing and turning, the seasoned yet young naval noncommissioned officer saw one of the fresh seaman just out of boot, like the rest there, step away from the machine and declare, "Stranger,

Sarah makes the best coffee at these events, and we don't wanna wait."

Turning back to the young woman, the noncom said softly, "Please don't flee."

Then he started toward the record machine intent on restarting it. The younger sailor stepped in front of him, and a bigger 'townie' stood just behind the sailor. Both were slightly taller than the chief, and the civilian bordered on what one might call a 'bruiser'.

"Stand down, sailor. You can restart the music or I will," the chief said.

"This is our party, for us, in our town. We're goin' tuh war."

The chief started around him and was stopped by a firm and forceful open palm of the slightly bigger youth placed on his chest.

"You're out of line sailor," the noncom said and maneuvered around again, only to be grabbed on his left arm by his adversary, who spun him around. Expecting to see a drawn fist as his body turned, Chief Petty Officer Pierce ducked it and drove the front, fingertipped edge of his flat, hard and callused, stiffened right palm into the younger man's stomach just under the sternum, and his nemesis dropped to the floor gasping for breath in a fetal position.

In support of the sailor on the floor, the 'townie' of course approached quickly from Pierce's back. CPO Pierce anticipated and ducked the man's fist, cowardly swung from behind. Spinning and ducking he tripped the fool with his leg and shoved him to the ground on his face by simultaneously pushing on his back. Then he placed his knee firmly on the man's neck.

Unknowingly, Jake's inexperienced opponents faced a veteran Navy man who, though a pilot, had killed two Japanese soldiers in hand-to-hand combat.

The deputy was approaching, and Pierce pulled a Shore Patrol armband out and put it on his upper right arm.

"Deputy, I was coming up here to see some friends, and the officer on duty at Mare Island asked me to keep an eye on these new 'graduates' out of boot down in San Diego. Seems they reported to Mare Island for future firefighter training before their leave to come home prior to shippin' out to the fleet, and left less than a good impression. I don't think boot camp quite saddle-broke 'em yet. Since they all came from here and enlisted together, he knew there would surely be a shindig of sorts, and I guess he didn't want them soiling the Navy's good name. I can handle my guys if you can take care of the civilians, but I might need some jail space."

"You want these two locked up, then?"

"Not if they'll settle down."

"You don't boss us," said the sailor on the floor, having recovered his wind. "We're off duty and on leave."

Pierce replied, "Sailor, there's a war on. You're always on duty in a sense and always required to respect the regulations, the law, and the uniform. A military man is never completely off duty. You're close to being hauled down to the brig at Mare Island by the Shore Patrol. They won't relish the trip up here in the cold and snow, and you'll be the worse for it. You assaulted a Chief Petty Officer. That's dangerous in this man's Navy. Didn't Boot teach you anything?"

Looking at the nearest of the new sailors, Pierce told them, "Calm your buddy here down if you expect to maybe ship out together. I can have him locked up for a very long time."

As the chief looked toward the woman he had tried to dance with, she was starting to walk away, possibly toward the kitchen behind the bar. He thought to himself, 'Was she dull and compliant, giving in to them, or just passive yet still strong?' He remembered the latter so long ago. Well, he'd see; time would tell.

He quickened his steps and caught up with her and, catching her by the arm, said softly and privately, "If we don't finish the dance, they win."

The classic plain faced, dark beauty looked at him and turned toward him, having said as yet hardly a word save a casual 'Thank you' when he had earlier taken her coat. Now taking her nearest hand, Pierce looked at one of the other girls and inquired, "Would you start the music please, dear?"

That girl looked a moment with perhaps some smoldering resentment and then complied with his request. The couple, seemingly strangers, danced the song out; and, with a slight smile and brief, "Thank you. I have to go make the coffee now," the woman excused herself to head toward the hall's little kitchen.

Pierce took a step or two as if to follow, but the deputy back on the stool hailed him with a moderate voice. The lawman had soundly admonished the civilian participant in the previous disturbance.

Pierce still wore the armband for the lingering effect it might have, but he intended removing it soon. In spite of age and jurisdiction circumstances, that status was a link between the two men; and, somewhat respectfully, the deputy commented, "All the gals here are pretty young, just out of school, most of 'em."

"She's a year or so older," Pierce replied, nodding toward the kitchen.

"Sarah? . . . She's had it tough . . . doesn't need to worry about a sailor's advances."

"So, is this the 'What are your intentions young man?' talk?"

"I'd rather you have none."

"The young lady is mighty young to be of interest to you, deputy."

"Paternally, son."

"Well, you've no worries here; I don't make 'advances'. Besides, I know her."

"You know her, . . . 'Sarah'?"

"I don't think she remembers."

"Me neither."

"Eric Pierce's son," the sailor said reaching his hand out to shake the deputy's.

"I know him but never met you 'cause I moved up from the valley after you left. He spoke of you. They moved, didn't they, your parents? I haven't seen them lately."

"Yes."

"Whatever your intentions, don't hurt that girl. she's been through a lot . . lost both parents, her mother recently."

"I know," turning away.

"Some fellas here have made things worse."

Jake turned back and looked at the deputy.

"The Robinson boys, the younger two . . they've tarnished her reputation. You must know the rest: that the Indian thing and her good looks have kept friendships few and far between. You saw it . . hint of low respect about the coffee. They want her beneath them, servant folk."

His voice dropped, Jake stepped closer, and the deputy continued, "Some of these girls know that if she was available, their boyfriends would drop them like hot potatoes. People know quality when the see it, even these young whippersnappers."

"And the Robinsons? I can guess."

"'Course you can. They let everybody think they got what she would never give 'em."

"Thanks, Deputy Joseph. You have nothing to worry about with me," Jake replied, and getting up with determination, yet somewhat tentatively, Pierce walked back to the passage into the kitchen behind the bar area where the deputy sat on the stool. It was brightly lit and had a commercial feel to it with shiny steel pots and pans and coffee urns.

The girl had finished making a big steel urn full of coffee and was sitting at a little Formica topped cafe table like the ones in the eating area out in front of the serving bar. The table was small and square, barely able to serve four people around it, and the woman held a cup of coffee in her two hands as it and her forearms rested on the table. She wore long sleeves and the tawny skin the color of coffee with cream only showed in her hands and face. It lacked any of the reddish tint historically associated with Native American Indians. Jake saw slight wetness in her eyes.

"Wanna talk about it, Sarah?" he said softly.

Looking up, she asked, "What?"

"Your mother or maybe their rudeness out there," nodding toward the hall.

"What's it to you? You're prying."

He did not respond and let it go asking instead, "May I join you for some coffee?"

"Suit yourself; I'll get it."

"No, it's fine. You look tired. Have a long day?" He grabbed a ceramic standard white, thick café cup with a thin blue stripe about a half inch below the rim and filled it with coffee. Turning back to the table with it black, he sat down across from the girl.

Nodding toward him, his chest, the young woman inquired, "What are the medals for?"

Looking down at the colorful, cloth-covered, horizontal bars on his left chest he said, "This blue ribbon is for the American Campaign. You know, because it's partly our war. And this yellow one . . that you were there where the fighting was. They're different colors for the Atlantic, Pacific, Africa, and so on, and this yellow one is for the Pacific.

12

Everyone gets 'em. You just have to be there." Looking still to his left chest where the two medals hung from their own tiny drape style ribbons beneath the previously described horizontal bar ribbons, Jake continued, "This is a Purple Heart and this one a Silver Star."

Gazing sardonically at the man she said in a sarcastic tone he missed, "I'm guessing everyone doesn't get those."

Looking up and perhaps catching the end of her sarcasm, the chief surrendered somewhat and continued, "These are for a mission from Australia to the Philippines and back. But we ended up in New Guinea instead. I don't mean to show off; I just wanted these young sailors to have some reason to respect me if it got tense like it did before. Of course, we are supposed to wear them if we have them."

"Well, what are they, what happened?"

"We took a small flying boat the Navy had taken from our company back up to the islands after Pearl Harbor to bring officers with important information out."

"Tell me all of it, but what's it called again?" She was not going to let it go, and he didn't want to brag.

"It's the Silver Star. It's new for the Navy, just approved this past summer. The army already used it. I guess it's approved for us now for all the crap the fellas are goin' through out there in the Pacific."

"You're one of those fellas . . . and you got it. Don't sell yourself short."

He looked closely at her, and she inquired, "What did you do?"

"I shot down a Jap float plane with a lucky shot. The Grumman Goose is no fighter plane. Then I tricked another later and maybe helped him crash. Then when we couldn't fly her anymore, we commandeered a sailing yacht which I was in command of, 'cause I was the only one who had sailed before the mast and been an officer on one too. We got in a fight with a small patrol that almost prevented that last voyage, and I killed two of 'em."

"And the little purple heart with what looks like Washington's head?"

"You're right; it's Washington. You get it when you get injuries in combat."

"And?"

"I got my legs shot up."

"You danced well. What happened? Was it in that fight?"

She was well spoken for her age and spoke like one more mature than her age as well, and that was as he had remembered. It was like talking to a slightly older girl, a real woman in a nineteen-year-old body.

"We were almost home free to Port Moresby and had called on the radio for fighter escort. We had a pregnant woman on board . . an' those important officers. A Jap scout plane jumped us, vulnerable as we were in that sloop. They're slow, you know . . sailboats are. All I could do was get everyone below and try some hopeless maneuver once, hoping for help to get there, and it did. It would have only worked once, but the cavalry arrived on time."

"Well, not before you got hurt. Tell me."

"He came in from astern of course, and I'm right there at the helm in the cockpit. It's in the stern, the back of a sailboat, so the helmsman can see the sails and rigging and watch how the wind affects them. I think he was toying with us, 'cause he didn't open right up. It played into my hands, thank God. There was a strong offshore wind to starboard, the right side. We were on a broad reach with the wind off the starboard quarter, so I waited 'til I heard his guns, the first burst, and spun the wheel to starboard, putting her on a beam reach and losing little if any headway but throwing his aim off. He might have been able to stay with me, but like I expected he shot right over us, going fast, you know. I knew he would likely not expect it. He overshot of course and would surely come around again and destroy us. As he passed low over us and turned seaward to come back around, I looked up and he was flying head-on into three British Hurricane fighters. I was laying on the deck by then, in the bottom of the cockpit."

"You were hurt right then?"

"Both legs broken by his 7.7 millimeter machine guns. I was lucky they weren't shattered. I'd not be in the Navy now. Only one round hit each leg . . lucky he shot low somehow too."

"Oh . . My Go…!" she exclaimed, but not loudly, and respectfully cut off the last word . . then softly, expressively said, ". . Jake?" with a look of concern and a voice full of questions.

With those words she revealed that, despite the more muscular frame, deeper voice, and sailor's tan, she had figured out who he was and remembered.

She had hunted all of her life. Sarah knew about guns. She knew 7.7 mm might seem small but was big enough, and she had never imagined until this moment a lone man against a fast, heavily armed machine . . and one that could fly, thus knowing no bounds.

Pausing, the cup near her lips, and looking at him intently, Sarah added, "Like I said, you danced well. You're a hero. You know that, don't you?"

Jake responded truthfully, "Well, I don't know about that. I use a cane. It's temporary. I left that in the hotel room. That dance was a bit painful but well worth it." Looking seriously at her as, with that revelation, she looked up at him, Jake said, "My most pleasant experience in some long time."

Sarah looked down at her coffee and, after a pause, asked, "Is it really bad out there?"

"For those close to it . . I mean close to the fighting or the action on the ships . . It's only bearable if you can take bein' around death."

"I'm sorry, Jake, but what is it really like?"

"Well, when a plane gets hit, it can just burst into flames. And some carry several men. Then when they land on the carriers, well, sometimes they miss and can sink before the guys get out . . our flyin' boats at sea too. Course sometimes the carrier planes crash and burn on the deck. And of course, the fighting for the marines and soldiers on the land is just crazy."

Sarah nodded sadly, and Jake Pierce said quietly, "It's near eight o'clock, and I'll guess you've not eaten."

"I'm okay, I snacked at work, and we're having food here of course."

"I'm not dangerous."

"So, what did he tell you?"

"About your mom. So . . you still run that little grill alone now. I guess I shouldn't have tried the dinner date. You can eat what you want all day."

"How do you know that? . . But that, gets tiresome, you know, eating in the same restaurant, even your own."

"I helped your mom after the Chief died, you know. We're old friends you and me, but beyond that, you didn't notice me much, and you were behind me in school. You were working in your-all's vegetable gardens and I was rebuilding the barn."

"I remember. I actually didn't recognize you. You've changed . . You're more muscular and darker, and your voice has changed, deeper. Your parents moved."

"And older too," he chuckled. "They are down near the Bay. I've been in the Pacific for five years on schooners and flying boats."

'Wow' To herself she thought, 'That explains the tan.' He touched the back of her nearest hand, laying on the table top between them, but she excused herself and got up and retrieved some chocolate cake and more coffee for them both.

When she looked more intently at him, Jake said inquisitively, "Dinner?"

Sarah smiled and said, "Is tomorrow alright? It's Saturday; I'll close early."

The young woman had always been a bit independent and somewhat of a loner as she was on the fringe of the youth society in Paradise Ridge. She was only nineteen now but, though youthful looking, seemed older. The maturity sprouted up out of the marginalization within the community's youth culture, which resulted from her ethnicity, her minority status. Sarah was one of those girls who wore a peacefully simple, plain face but one that was extremely pleasant to look at, with a charming twist to her smile and subtly sleepy, dreamily soft appearing eyes . . soft brown and extremely intelligent. These were paired with a soft, roundly sculpted, slightly flat nose rather than the strong Roman-like nose of some American Indian peoples. That distinctive feature probably came from her little bit of Navajo blood. Matching that pretty face with her warmth, charm, and tawny Native American skin she stood out perhaps too much with the other girls near her age and thus they did what they could to keep her at bay, at an arm's length distance socially. Most of her blood, her heritage was Blackfoot, a people that was said to have produced some of the country's most attractive Native American women. She was quite Americanized in the sense of the general society, the somewhat white dominate society, but held on to her native roots and knew much of that culture, which came from both parents, a quarter was Navajo from her father, and she was half Blackfoot from her full-blooded mother. Sarah acquired from her Indian background enough of their ancient oriental genetic heritage; and Jake, having been in the Philippines for years now, could almost see a hint of a mestiza Filipina in her face. She was slightly darker than a half white mestiza however.

Often, a common result of social marginalization of an individual like Sarah (personally well-equipped, individualistic, attractive, smart, creative, moral) is a strengthening of the moral fiber already within them. The adversity merely becomes the weightlifter's barbell, the lumberjack's tree.

The greatest hurdle, the strongest weight Sarah pushed against was the reputation a few of the local boys had recently hung on her in the period of Jake's absence. She was a moral girl, but several young men wanted to enjoy her womanly favors as the young, exotic, almost pure-blooded Indian girl matured into a beautifully desirable woman. Those fellows figured that on the margins and with no native or Mexican men around for her to date, the young girl would give in to her own natural urges and become available with a little convincing from them. The woman's answer was a resounding, 'No thanks,' and the men got their revenge by claiming she had freely given them what they had sought. A lingering, underlying negative view of Indians still was felt in the town and surrounding county, though none remembered much about the history fit. There had been a small, old massacre, but one no bloodier than many others during the Western Indian wars.

Chief Petty Officer Jake Pierce did not push to walk Sarah home, as she lived right near the hall in the apartment above the grill her mother and father had owned and she had inherited. Knowing her personality, Jake may have thought she would have been slightly offended, as if she couldn't take care of herself enough to find the apartment. They did not dance again and she left early.

The evening had not yet melted into the slow, lower lit dances where the dancers were equally melded into each other. It would eventually, even in that little mountain town. It was a more reserved time than recent eras, and yet a war was on, a big one, and even such youths could grasp the serious finality of some of its consequences.

Before the romance began and he could be an even greater irritant than he already had, Jake chose a moment when the music was paused and most of the group of revelers were milling around between the refreshments table and the 78 RPM record collection.

Walking over to the group, the Navy veteran was surprised to be welcomed into it, not warmly yet not rejected. Perhaps some of the girls had finally noticed his tough 'been there, done that' demeanor (without any cockiness about it) and the handsome figure he cut in the uniform. Would that they could get their farm boy boyfriends into such nice duds except on Sunday mornings.

Small talk ensued, and questions began to be asked of the chief. And with each reserved yet revealing answer, curiosity grew; and, first the women and then the men (sailors and civilians) began to realize they were talking to a warrior . . even a hero.

Finally enjoying the respect he had sought, for their benefit not his, the Chief Petty Officer finally clued the new sailors in on some behavior expected of them and the consequences they could expect and would regret when they did not comply. He explained clearly that it was not about him but other CPOs they would work under . . about working on tough jobs in extreme circumstances and the necessary discipline needed to complete them . . to finish them in the face of serious dangers and even death . . too often death. And it was about respect, the Navy, tradition, country, and victory.

Finally, as the evening waned and the pairs of dancers each became like one, realizing, after his short, casual talk with them, what they each of them might soon lose, Jake and the deputy talked.

"Chief, Sarah is like a niece to me. When I took this job a few years ago, she was a junior in high school, and that's when several of the worst of our fair young men decided to brag about their conquests of her. Not publicly, just to their buddies. But those things get out. It's been three years now that's been simmerin', and I feel for her, but I don't know what to do. I'd like to bust some heads. Course it all fits in with the lingering Indian hate around here, and then the girls are jealous of her. I'm glad her father never saw it, but I guess her mother knew."

"That's no good. You can't lean on 'em. The cat's outta the bag, even though it's not true."

"So, you believe in her."

"She wouldn't be like that."

"And you weren't trying to go home with her or take 'er to 'ur room? What'd you ask 'er?"

"You're awful nosy."

The deputy shrugged.

"I asked her to dinner."

"Well, you see, she didn't go. How's it look if she goes out with a sailor. You guys have a reputation."

"Not all sailors fit that reputation."

"That wouldn't help hers any. Look Jake, they messed her life up and now she's alone 'cept for a few of us older folks who like the young girl and have faith in 'er. Look how tough she is running that grill alone like she is at nineteen. An' you'll be here and then gone."

"It's more than that," Pierce said, and nodding as he rose from his stool, he walked out the door and back to his hotel.

Paradise Ridge had earned its slightly unusual name from an old trapper, though few today knew it. Sarah knew because her great grandfather knew the trapper. On one night full of drinking, and before the trapper and her Blackfoot ancestor both settled themselves down with wives, the debate over the local name became quite heated. The Indian could hold his liquor better than most of his race. His concern in the argument was that his friend had based the name at least partly on a slight of native women, a suggestion that he wished to rectify.

The trapper, a worldly man like a few of those who ultimately chose that life, had sailed on a whaler and seen the South Seas. He had done a few other adventurous things in other far flung 'corners' of the globe. Basically, his point was that Paradise Ridge had a beauty that rivaled that of the far flung and scattered Pacific islands, called 'Paradise' by many. He further suggested that the American Indian girls were equally attractive, willing, and 'easy' in comparison to those of the Society Islands and the rest of Polynesia. A truce between the two friends was reached and the name made official, as official as two drunken trappers had the power to apply labels, and the name stuck. The truce revolved around the insightful analysis, based upon true knowledge of the historical facts, and the two agreed that the more distant generations of non-Christian young women of both cultures could not be blamed for following the cultural mores they were raised with in societies that made no demands relating to virginity before marriage and even considered practice in lovemaking to be a good thing. Those practices were not true of all Indian cultures but were of some. Believers in the Christian God, but not the best fellows at practicing His rules, just before the two pals passed out those many years ago, they agreed, the Indian reluctantly, that the aforementioned cultural practices could qualify a place as a paradise.

Jake would have liked to have spent the evening talking and getting to know the young woman again and better. She was thirteen when he left, and he had already seen her worth then . . and agonized a bit over the age difference, five years . . turning it over and over in his mind as he was again now. He thought to get a bottle of bourbon or some wine but wanted to remain sharp. Finally, it being winter and cold and snowy, he asked the desk clerk for some cocoa powder and milk from the hotel kitchen. He had learned over the years to travel with a small steel teapot and an electric hotplate. The clerk found some donuts as well.

The next morning the grill across the street appeared closed, and the morning clerk said that was what the yellow flag meant, raised high for all to see. He wondered if it was a way to avoid him, but the clerk said it was because of the heavy snowfall coming down.

Jake went down to Delmonico's and set dinner up with André, a special one with a few frills: a wine Jake had brought and a special chocolate cake André made that he knew Sarah had loved as a child. If she was still going to take him up on it, he and André agreed he would call ahead an hour if the meal was still on. André said to signal if the phones were down, which often occurred in heavier snow. It was a case of one of those technical problems that could never get properly eliminated, only repaired each time.

Jake decided not to be aggressively inclined toward courtship though he had realized that he was as obsessed with Sarah as any man with any girl he thought he loved. It was clear to him now that it was real . . to see her again the night before after five years and with their physical changes over that time . . and he could hardly stand to be away from her. He had felt that way those years ago and, of course, had to make himself leave her. He tried to read through the day with moderate success.
Incongruous for what he had been through and for a man contemplating a wartime relationship, he was reading one his generation's great war novels, Hemingway's *A Farewell to Arms*, even a grotesque chore perhaps, given his circumstances. Whiling away the hours pacing when he wasn't trying to read, he just mused about her. It had only taken the encounter with Sarah the night before to rekindle it all, the old feelings. Could love really work like that . . so mystical and so . . so . . romantic as in a storybook? Deep down he knew it was what he had come back for.

It was not just visual, her attractiveness, but that stood out. She was subtly exotic, and he had been around plenty of such women in Southeast Asia. Earlier, as a young man in his teens, Jake was able to travel his beloved West with his parents and even more with business trips with just his father. He had found Navajo girls to be appealing as well and saw their resemblance to oriental girls and Filipinas in particular after he had spent most of his five years in the Pacific in those particular islands. Some Navajo had never forgiven the whites for the Long Walk and Bosque Redondo incarceration perpetrated on their parents and grandparents and could be standoffish at times. It had only been about seventy-five years before, after all.

Jake knew why he came back and why he had left those years ago. He came back for her. He had left when he was nineteen because she was too young, and now he was back because she wasn't.

A Fairy Tale

Finally, about five in the evening, as winter dusk began, he could have it no more and went up the somewhat rickety wooden steps to her door above the grill she ran as her parents had before her.

Opening the door, Sarah was obviously dressed but not particularly ready to go anywhere, and Jake thought she might be playing hard to get or just wasn't interested. But of course, there was the age thing, and he had to keep fighting off the feeling that he was a pervert.

"Come in, Jake. I've made some coffee. I want to know more about your war trials if you don't mind. Do we have time before dinner?"

Whew, that was a relief to him, though he was reluctant to tell the tale. But, at least she was interested and friendlier than the night before.

"I have to signal Andre with your lamp by the front window or a call if the phones are working. Six or seven?"

"The phones are down. Is it a long story?"

"Seven it is," he said and walked to the window. Then he paused and said to her, "Remind me at five-thirty. That's when he will look the first time."

'What did this mean,' he thought to himself. 'Was she just curious, or did she suddenly, maybe incongruously care more about him.' Of course, he wanted that, it was his goal. But could he be this lucky? He thought of all the lonely guys he left behind in the big Pacific, scattered across it . . some who would never come back to a girl they left or to a storybook romance like the one that seemed to be unfolding for him . . . and he felt so guilty. She had caused this with her request, but it was obviously because she cared . . obviously more than curiosity, and it had to be faced.

She saw it, she was that maturely intuitive, and she said, "Jake, I'm sorry." And she started to get up from their shared seat on the sofa.

"No, sit down. It's okay." They fixed their coffee and smiled at each other. Both had some angst, the typical angst of young single people of the opposite gender who thinks the other may have interest in them or are worried the opposite is true.

"I went to Philippines with by parent's blessing. America owns them you know and we have family there, an uncle of mine. He knew some folks and introduced me to them . . thought it would make a man of me. Maybe it did. I worked for the O'Brian family for most of three years, 'til the war started. I sailed in their schooners first. They had two old ones in great shape, well maintained and refurbished, that had been the first the family had acquired. Then I worked on their seaplanes until the war started. We call them flying boats because they have a boat hull that they land on. Seaplanes have a float attached to them that they land and float on. During that time, I learned to fly. The business was started by a New Englander who went down there and married a native girl. Her sister married his Filipino first mate and the family grew from there. The next generation that I worked for started the seaplanes in the islands. I finally learned to fly and got a license. I had been flying for a year and a half when the war broke out, but they told me I was a natural and flew better than some who had more hours in the air.

When things got bad in early '42, the older folks may have gotten out or hid in the backcountry. I wasn't there because of my duty. They were in their sixties and some near seventy now but mostly still kickin' . . kinda young for their ages. Some could be in Australia now, but most of the families I'm close to are hiding in the hills and probably fighting too. You see, those folks have some other Filipino friends who have Texas roots, and they're my friends now too. There's Navajo in that family."

"Navajo Texans? Navajo Texan Filipinos?"

"Well, they were mixed marriages, and they settled in Texas, and some of 'em went to the Philippines after we conquered the islands. I hope they got all the older folks out, but some of those more capable are in the mountains fighting with the resistance. Of course, they cannot use the seaplanes; the Japs would just shoot them down. They're probably all wrecked now except for the one I got out with. It's wrecked now. The business had two: the Grumman Goose and a Douglas Dolphin. Then there was an old wreck they bought and were trying to rebuild. Such travel is not very common for average Filipinos because of the cost of aviation fuel and thus tickets. Mostly we were used for important cargos or passengers that needed to get somewhere far pretty fast. I told you about the Goose. I'm sure some of the family got out in the Dolphin or the military commandeered it. Otherwise the Japs used it or destroyed it. I am worried about them all."

"You couldn't take any of them out? I mean in the Goose. You said you went back on a mission."

"No. The Navy took it for the war effort, and the mission was only to retrieve essential personnel.

How I got out with Jon the youngest son of the O'Brians is a tale to tell with more time. It is rather dramatic and may best be told with some spirits. I don't know for sure if they're safe, he and his girl."

"What . . oh no, I'm sorry. Maybe this was a bad idea."

"No . . when we come home, it's our duty. I mean to report to you-all."

"I'm so sorry, Jake."

"It's okay. You're the one I wanted to tell." And with that she knew he had come for more than a hometown visit.

She read his face, the pain, and she wanted to stop him, but before she could, he went on.

"I saw them last in Singapore . . right before the fall. We put them on an old freighter bound for Trincomalee off India, but it was a slow boat and we know the Japs went in there . . into the Indian Ocean in force. Can you imagine? That little island country that was feudal less than a hundred years ago sending forces all over the Far East now . . leavin' us snookered and weak?"

"You better signal André."

"Well the Pearl Harbor attack force went into there and I don't know if they made it or not, Jon and his Malayan girl."

His head was down, and he caught himself, brought himself out of it and looked at her with a tense blank stare . . and if he thought at the moment, he probably felt he was losing her. Nothing could have been further from the truth. Here was a real man she had known in youth back now from the war, this great horrendous conflagration, and telling her about it as he revealed his heart . . the heart she had seen when he rebuilt her mother's barn and refused to be paid.

Sarah said softly, taking his nearest hand, "It is painful I know, but the telling of it may help. If you want that, I'm here. We can talk more now or another time."

"We better eat. It'll lighten the mood. I'm sorry I went on so."

"I asked. I want to know. But let's go on at six. Signal André. It's five thirty-three. He'll quit looking."

"Is the phone still dead?"

"It will stay dead. It always goes dead when the snow is this wet and heavy."

They walked together through the soft snowfall, portending more ominous travel in days to come. In the restaurant, sitting down in the great Western mountains in an authentically good Italian eatery seemed a bit strange to Jake, but Delmonico's had been in Paradise Ridge since he was young.

The two had quickly reached some level of renewed mutual acceptance that they understood somewhat yet still perhaps each felt apprehension about, like perhaps almost all potential lovers. And after the exhausting discussion, or rather relation of a tense story, neither yet felt like talking to each other casually, though they did want to be together. So, they just sat and ate in silence for a while. It was not sad or tense, they were happy in each other's company, but his story had been enough for the moment.

Jake suddenly broke the silence, having been caught off guard by the unexpected emotional story from his own lips, especially the end of it about Jon and Maya. Planned comments or any small talk had melted away; and, though he may have realized he had saved these hard things for her because she was that important, he now found himself at a loss for words of any significance or even casual talk. And so, because there was nothing else after those tales, Jake built up his nerve to say it, breaking the long silence.

"I had a crush on you back then. But what could I do? . . you were thirteen . . . . And I was a senior . . five years difference. It's partly why I went away . . to forget you . . but I couldn't. Some people are just special, even when they are young . . you can just tell sometimes what a kid is made of . . even a kid like you were."

He was looking toward her when he started talking and she was looking at her plate. He started with his eyes down but bravely raised them as he spoke and looked at the top of her head. As his words began and the ideas he expressed became apparent, she looked up with some surprise. It was logical, that or to have shyly kept her head down.

They stared at each other for a moment, and then Jake said, "Well, that's it. I don't know anything more to say."

Sarah smiled slightly with that slight crooked twist of her lips that made her unique and alluring, nodded slightly, and then looked down at her plate and continued eating. The rest of the meal was quiet and she seemed not to be angry, scared, or otherwise shocked. But Jake figured he had shot his bolt as he had done what he came to do, though he had been slow to consciously realize it was his main goal. He had also figured he had failed. He felt a similarity, a matched personality and interest with the girl, but he figured that she might not concur . . probably would not concur. After all, they weren't close before and those years had passed.

At some point Sarah looked up again and smiled and asked, "When must you return? Do you want to go? I know you have to."

"I have a month, and if there is no new assignment, it could be longer. They know about the leg of course. When I go back I'll be sent to San Diego and train on PBYs. I was down there before coming up here, studying them and hitting the books a little."

"And they are?"

"Consolidated PBY Catalina flying boats. They are much bigger than the Goose . . an eight-man crew with four gun positions but keep that to yourself. I shouldn't have told you. Our Goose could carry eight passengers, the Catalina many more. I'll probably be a Dumbo pilot and fly search and rescue."

"Like the Elephant in that movie, the cartoon," Sarah mused with a subtle laugh.

"Catalinas have long wings." The tension lessened for him, but all too soon the meal ended, and Jake figured he might never see her again save across the street of the little mountain town they both had grown up in.

Sarah looked at him calmly and said, "Walk me home, . . . but its deep now."

"I'll carry you; your boots are low-cut."

"No . . your leg."

"It's good for short distances. These are tough high boots, though lower than the snow. I'll dry out in my room."

"You'll dry out by my fireplace."

Jake was a slight man, but after several years working the rigging and the helms of the O'Brians' South Seas schooners, the already strong farm boy was muscular and strong. Struggling with the controls holding a flying boat in a strong wind or varying air currents and landing in rough seas made a man out of you too almost as much as working the rigging of a sailing ship. He was not the boy who Sarah had watched when he worked on her family's farm after her father's death. He was more than that, and he picked her up somewhat easily and carried her diagonally across the snow covered street toward the wooden steps around to the side of her grill and up to the apartment above. Almost across the street, either the weaker leg gave out or it hit a slick spot in or under the icy, wet snow; but, whatever the case, his still weak left leg went out from under him, followed by the right. Jake ended up flat of his back in the snow and Sarah was atop him, still being held in the typical way a man carries a woman across his body in such circumstances.

Turning her head towards him with that wry smile on her face she laughed subtly and said, "My knight."

Pulling themselves up, Jake started to pick Sarah up again and she said, "Let's not put more stress on that leg, sailor."

As she led the way, he sheepishly trudged to the steps and up to the apartment, a classic old living quarters above a business that was an icon of American life then and sometimes even now.

Entering, Sarah headed toward her room to change from the wet clothes; and, over her shoulder, she told Jake, "Some clean clothes of Dad's are in the closet in that front bedroom. He was just a bit bigger than you. They'll be just loose and baggy enough to be comfortable."

Jake chose a khaki pants and red and black checkered flannel shirt and came out to start a fire in the fireplace. There was a small pile of wood on the hearth and the tools and matches were there as well. Soon he had a good strong little fire going, the heartbeat of a rural American winter.

The woman could be heard with soft sounds coming from her bedroom. She still owned the farm but chose to live in town near the grill that earned her living. The building housing the grill and single apartment above were solely hers and paid for, her inheritance like the farm. For her age she was well off, and that could have added to local resentments from her own peers and maybe some of their parents. But most of the older generations of Paradise Ridge liked and respected the sweet, hardworking young woman.

As Sarah entered the living room, she said, "I don't have much but real estate. I guess I'm land poor, but the record collection is pretty impressive. Everyone who gives me gifts gives those. And I shop for good new and used ones. It is my one frivolous passion."

"Well some of our songs these days are a bit silly, but in general most are beautiful. The silly ones can be fun. It's not a frivolous hobby, . . . the voice of our age and this war. Too bad earlier eras did not have the ability to do this . . sit and listen like this without live musicians. You're full of surprises."

"I'll put a stack on . . slow, it's evening. Want a drink?"

"I thought Indians couldn't tolerate alcohol."

"I can a little. . . Not full-blooded. I've got coffee, tea, cocoa . . ."

"And ...?"

"Beer, wine, scotch, bourbon."

"Your nineteen!" Jake said teasingly as he turned her to him, a hand softly holding each of her upper arms gently.

Sarah smiled and said, "I'm careful, very moderate with it. I'm alone a lot with my music and mostly cocoa and tea . . mostly, . . seriously. If I was a 'lush', I'd go sit on a bar stool and be a lush."

The young woman of his youthful dreams had suddenly opened up to him, speaking freely and unguardedly as if she cared not what he knew of her, allowing him into her home, her inner sanctum . . accepting him. Well he guessed he would find out if she was too loose a girl soon or if the tales he had heard and disbelieved were true or not. His revelation about his infatuation with her may have been the catalyst. But, for what . . a romance or an affair?

As the now whimsical and graceful girl moved to select and stack records on the phonograph's tall, silver pin changer, she said, "Fix your drink the way you like. It's in the kitchen . . everything. I wanted cocoa but takes too long."

"I can make it. "

"No; heat tea water, a big mug's worth."

He made enough for them both, thinking tea was better than milk before alcohol in case he wanted it later. Coming from the kitchen, Jake carried a tray holding a sugar bowl, a teapot full of hot water, an infuser, a small canister of black tea, spoons, and a cream pitcher he found in the refrigerator in case she used that in her tea. There were two large mugs as well.

Making the tea, letting it steep and taking the first few sips, the two talked casually about his parents and their new home in Hayward by San Francisco Bay. The Bay Area still had charm then. Some moments after finishing the tea, another stack of 78 RPM records were on the spindle, and the warrior and woman were reclining against the sofa back side-by-side.

Sarah had socks on and a light, one piece, cotton housedress that went just below the knees with a short, light robe over it. She sat on the sofa with her legs folded up to the side away from him and wore a pretty, flowered dress.

After drinking the hot drink slowly and discussing the merits of the previous meal and some particular songs, they became quiet and just listened to the second stack, perhaps the most beautiful and sad, beginning with Vera Lynn's version of *"The White Cliffs of Dover"*

She was to his right and leaning against him now, and he held her left hand. He was comfortable in his belief in her, the nice girl he had always thought her to be, and she had a pleased smile on her face and in those dreamy medium brown almond shaped eyes, not Asian eyes, but, like many Native Americans, a little bit of it. She seemed not to be craving him. Through the mind of this now battle-scarred and strongly Christian man (tempered all the more now by the war) went the question: 'If she's what the rumors claim, can I resist it . . how can I possibly resist?'

Then Sarah softly collapsed across the sofa, quickly moving her body to his right more, spreading her dress and robe out smoothly beneath her body with her hands, stretching her legs out away from him, and laying her head in his lap. With a smile she was soon off to sleep. The girl was clearly comfortable with him. Jake brushed her hair back from her eyes and then combed through it with his fingers as she dropped off with a sigh. This girl, this former romantic infatuation from his youth, had accepted him. He was in heaven, on cloud nine. This had been a longing that would not leave him alone for five years in the South Pacific, with beauties all around (especially the native ones he was attracted to because of her memory), a distant dream when he returned Stateside, a doubtful hope when he came back to his hometown and saw her, a hint of reality when they met and talked and he got an idea of the lay of the land with her situation.

Jake listened through the whole sad but beautiful stack of records, songs that were already "war songs" . . that would become identified with it forever . . . and Sarah slept.

Short of actually making love to her, nothing on earth could have made the young farm boy turned sailor, pilot, and warrior happier at this moment.

Ruth Lowe's *I'll Never Smile Again*, was the last one on the stack, the Tommy Dorsey Orchestra version that they had danced to the night before of course. The young Sinatra's clear voice soothed the Navy's tired winged warrior. He was one of those, those winged warriors who had less command of it, the combat . . the vulnerable ones flying slow working man's planes as deadly hotrods of the enemy flew around them and toyed with their prey like house cats with a cornered mouse.

When the music stopped with the last song, Sarah awoke. There was no jolt of surprise at her present state or that her head lay in a slightly older man's lap with just a thin layer of khaki-colored, cotton material separating her from the tools of his love making.

He had always felt somehow . . long ago when she was only thirteen . . that this was an incredibly calm, smart girl who had it all together and would mature quicker than most into a woman of such qualities. She knew what she was doing. Somehow, he had always thought that of her. The responsibilities of being the third, more or less, adult in her family made her that way, that and the partial isolation from the closer-knit clicks in school. Some kids like that become problems or weird. Sarah was the other kind of individualistic 'loner' . . the tough, kind, noble kind. But was she too easy with him, too comfortable with her head in a man's lap at nineteen? Only slightly did he entertain thoughts of the rumors about her. He had faith in the girl.

Jake looked down at her, his right hand softly laying on her tummy and his left gently, almost imperceptibly caressing her brow, softly pushing the flow of lush dark brown hair back that tried to cover her eyes on the left side away from him. He was behaving ever so more easily, comfortably familiar with a woman's body than he had ever thought to before. Sarah looked up at him, straight in his eyes, and said, "So, were you planning to marry me Chief Petty Officer Jake Pierce and take me away from here, . . this little town we both grew up in. That's what you came here for isn't it?"

Her words and the cute, smirky expression seemed sarcastic, almost biting, as if making fun of his earlier deeply expressed feelings for her. He leaned back and looked up at the ceiling, repressing a hint of embarrassment and maybe anger . . an almost unmeasurable hint. Had he misjudged her, even with information from his mother over the recent years while he was gone? The thought even flickered briefly inside that what they said might be true . . that she might have matured through adversity into a woman of loose morals, and he was about to have to decide between just a fun evening or forgetting this all completely. He had stood her on a pedestal in his mind for five years.

She rustled a little, seeking a more comfortable position, and her weight felt good on him, and she was looking up again, reaching a hand up and drawing his head down closer with fingers gently placed around and behind his neck.

She spoke again, audibly but with the soft voice that had hooked his heart when she was still a young woman-child, maybe more woman than child even back then.

"I know it's crazy. I know it is . . but a guy doesn't go half way around the world and stay for five years and come back home to make a date with a girl he knew back when. It just doesn't happen."

He looked at her laying there and replied, "I couldn't get you out of my mind."

"I saw the pictures in your wallet. There are plenty of pretty women where you've been . . dark ones like me. That's what you hoped to find, me still here and single. Well, I've got news for you: You're also my teenage crush that never quite died away. You made those two summers bearable . . even happy ones, what with me missing my Dad so much. I could keep working because you were there to steal a glance at any time I wanted. My work may have suffered for it, for those many glances. When you came on holidays, they were the best ever, except for him not being there anymore. I wanted you to take me away when you left, . . but I was smart enough to know better. You don't know it . . I cried a week when I realized you were gone.

There's nothing here for me, Jake. The last folks I cared about left when your folks moved. They asked me to go with them, you know . . told me I could stay with them."

His eyes widened a bit at the news of her feelings for him and at his parents' action that he hadn't known of, and he said, "We mustn't move too fast . . the years . . we have to get to know each other again and better than before."

She looked up, staring at him softly yet intently, and said lowly but expressively and with that cute slightly twisted smile, "You won, stupid. Accept that it was that easy. Don't throw me back in the stream. I'll die from the wound of the hook. I just had to be sure. Now I am. Here I am, your young, nubile fiancé."

Still sensitive about her age before . . those years ago when his interest made him feel guilty, he replied, "Huh . . what, why joke about that, your youth?"

"That's not what it means, silly. It means the cherries are ripe on the tree."

"Huh?"

"A marriageable girl. It means a girl ready for marriage. Some cultures may just mean the physical part, but face it, I'm legal and I accept what you actually haven't yet proposed."

"Wow, how do you know these things? You're wise beyond your years."

It was meant as a compliment and a joke. He was still a nervous suitor, his uneasiness magnified perhaps by the unexpected ease of the romantic conquest. But the girl, who was still looking up at him turned her head to the front and away, and he could sense the subtle tears.

"What . . . what did I say?"

"What did he tell you?" she said through very soft and subtle crying, really just a hint of it.

"Who? . . Oh, . ." and he paused to measure his words. He was serious now and had overcome the lover's fog of that type of battle. "He told me about the Robinson brothers, the younger two. It didn't bother me. Forget them."

He carefully, instinctually left himself out of the comment, not wanting to say, 'we've got each other now.' That might have carried a hint of '...your past doesn't matter to me' and suggest he might believe the bad things said about her.

He repeated his point, "Forget it, forget them."

"Yeah? You sure?" And she was less careful, perhaps a woman's privilege, as she has more to protect, especially in that era when it mattered.

And looking barely back at him yet really not, just a motion toward it, she added, "Sure you didn't decide you'd get in a couple of nights with your previous dream girl after he clued you in about me . . suggested how easy it would be?"

Her teenager's dream was coming true just as his was. Having been at such a young age blessed but somewhat battered by life already and figuring that such things just did not really happen, the young woman feared it would quickly crash down.

He reached gently down with his right, as his left hand reached under her neck to sort of cradle it, and he gently turned her head toward him. It was awkward because he was new it this. He wasn't an experienced playboy or aristocratic, suave gentleman.

"I didn't give it a second thought, Sarah. You can ask him. I told him so. I told him it couldn't be true, and he knows so too. He said so. He was worried about me . . a sailor, you know . . how I could hurt your reputation. I told him I was interested (hinted it) and that it wasn't like that, like a sailor's one-night stand. Listen, if I get back we'll eventually be holdin' grandkids together. I'm in it for the duration."

He had meant it to reference the marriage but used the official and commonly used war reference, and he saw her tear up again and she turned away, bringing her right hand up to cover her mouth and nose, and this was a real cry, though still softly muffled. He was sorry he said it; but, then he thought to himself, 'She's gotta know it. She's gotta know what she's getting' into.'

Jake let her cry. If this ended it, he'd done his duty, 'full disclosure' and all that. It was high risk marriage now for everybody. She turned again looking quietly at him with reddened eyes and Jake would lay it out the best he could. This was a soon to be very young wife, but there were many in war. War hit the young the hardest, and many married because of it . . *Let's do this now; we may never see each other again. Yeah, I'll wait for you. I'll be true, I'll never marry again it you don't come back,' …and on and on and on, promises kept and promises broken ….*

When she turned to him after such a seemingly long silence and her venting cry, Jake spoke, "Now you forget that, and you forget the other thing. The man who loves you doesn't believe it, and we'll be leavin'. But I'm gonna speak with their brother. But you forget about worry. Life's always got risks. But I'm flying Dumbos . . rescue not combat. There's risk but less of it."

"But don't talk to…" but he gently placed a finger to her lips and said, "Darrell Robinson and I are friends, contentious ones but friends. It'll be okay. Shhhh, sleep now."

She stared at him a moment and then smiled, and Jake nodded softly. After a long pause looking lovingly at the girl of his dreams all those years while far away, he replied, "You figured it right, Darlin' . . I came back for you. I had so many doubts . . our ages and all . . I almost didn't know that was why I did. But I'm for it. I was getting up nerve to ask you. This turned out swell, but we gotta make it last though."

He leaned over and they kissed softly and somewhat passionately . . but the love was there as much as any passion.

She closed her eyes and seemed to soften and melt into the sofa and his lap, like a cat that, though only a few pounds, makes itself seem too heavy to lift when it doesn't want to be moved. Dreamily and very softly, she said, "We know each other .. better than you realize."

They went to sleep in each other's arms, or rather with her head in his lap and her hair caressed as long as he was still awake, which was a while. He leaned back and his feet, warmed by her father's wool socks, were up on the coffee table, which with foresight had a small pillow under them. With just enough tilt to the angle of the sofa's back, he could stay there forever, what with the precious cargo he held and comforted. It was commonly said a sailor could sleep anywhere, apparently a development through the decades of: hiding from off duty demands, living in a rolling and pitching environment at sea, and often being in transit in railway and airport lounges.

It seemed understood that within a day or so they would be married. Not a word more about that after his suggestion and her proposal needed be spoken. The two were finally happy with a long-withheld love in the open between them. Pleasurable consummation of it could wait one more night, especially given the reputation some uncouth local boys had tried somewhat successfully to hang on the unfortunate girl. But that might be solvable too.

As she slept and he couldn't at first, he thought about it and realized she might be right. Two summers together, her in the gardens and him building a new barn out of an old one and helping with other chores. Lunch together every day for those two summers . . sometimes dinner . . sometimes breakfast if he was early enough. He was always invited for holidays, especially Christmas. And then it hit him. He had been manipulated by two women, and neither one was Sarah. Both Valentines days for the last two years before he graduated and left, Sarah's mother had him over for dinner and cake and ice cream, and his mother insisted that he go out of respect. Sarah's mom always joked that he was their, her and her daughter's, metaphorical 'sweetheart' because of the way he replaced her dead husband in helping on the farm. Then there were the pictures from his mom when he was in the East Indies, pictures of Sarah.

As he leaned back and dozed off, marveling at his luck and worry about coming back to her, he relaxed into a restful sleep, sitting upright with her head in his lap. He was a sailor; he could sleep anywhere. He didn't need one of those new Castro Convertibles, and an actual bed would have seemed scandalous to them, especially given the festering issue with the Robinson brothers.

A conversation occurred over a breakfast of Canadian bacon and eggs with orange juice and coffee.

Before the man, contemplative at the moment setting at the little Formica-topped kitchen table, could speak, the occasionally take-charge young woman said, "My mind is firm, it hasn't changed since last night. This is surely meant to be. If it becomes tough, Jake, we must tough it out. America seems to be turning a little bit into a country of broken marriages. I wasn't raised that way. I don't think you were either."

"Let's go to see the fathers at San Miguel."

"Yes, and apply for a license. I believe there is a blood test, and we may have a day or two wait to finally get it. California has no problem with mixed Indian marriages, thank God. He has blessed us that way. I think some states still do. We can come back here for a few days and talk about what to do. What do you see for your future in the Navy, the war?"

"It's not over by a longshot, and there is a lot of rough fighting out there. I think Europe will end first. Those Japs follow their leaders fanatically. We will win this, Sarah. But, honey, its lasting a year or more, probably two. They won't give up easily. I just hope we don't have to go into their home islands. I'm sorry to scare you. I'm not used to having someone who will care so much and be scared for me . . I mean besides my mom."

"Everything that is worth anything at all carries risks. After breakfast, I'll pack. Then we can load up and go if the roads are good enough. Dad made that trip dozens of times in this car on bad roads. I've had the chains on for a while to be ready. I never need it around here. I just walk everywhere, even up to the farm."

"Well, that explains your girlish figure."

"That and that I'm just a girl playing at this adult stuff," said with a laugh to tease him. "I ride my horse sometimes and stable him out back when the weather is warmer. The dogs around here will wake me if a bear or cougar shows up at night."

Later, Jake stood in the snow and bright sunshine as he loaded luggage in Sarah's father's old Buick. The plan was to get a blood test and marriage license, which could take a day or so, and to drive down to Jake's parents' house in Hayward or to the old San Miguel Church. The former old mission, now a normal parish, would probably put them up separately until the marriage could be celebrated. They considered the old Mission de San Vicente Ferrer. It would have been so picturesque, but the Sangre de Cristos were too far. After such a long wait, he did not want to spend his limited time with her on the road behind the wheel of a car, and if they had to wait a day or so for the blood test results, they needed to be closer.

Historical missionaries had long ago brought Sarah's native ancestors to the Christian faith, both her slight Navajo background and her primary Blackfoot heritage had encountered Catholic missionaries. Spain had of course been dominant among the Navajo and the French fur trappers to the north had been accompanied sometimes by priests.

Jake was also Catholic, and the two were headed for the closest church in the area, where the priests knew them both.

As Jake placed the final pieces of luggage in the trunk, Darrell Robinson strolled up. It was one of his two younger brothers who Jake had encountered with the rude, unruly new sailor at the dance two nights before. Jake and Darrell had been classmates who mutually respected each other at arm's length, but were never close friends due to differing personalities, interests, backgrounds and just about everything else. But then again, they were. It was the two of them who spent two nights alone looking for a family of campers surprised by a blizzard years before when no one else dared the temperatures. And it was the two of them alone who stood off a bunch of ruffians from the valley one tense Friday night when they were seniors. It had something to do with football rivalries and silly things, but the lowlanders were serious, drunk, and a few had ax and pick handles. But they learned about real farm boys and the nuances of fists against gang weapons.

Darrell could not help chiding Jake. The latter had stepped on his little brother's neck two days prior after all.

"For you bein' a guy defending a girl's reputation, a fellow's gotta note you dipping into the honey jar thuh very next night."

It was dangerous borderline baiting, but within the history of the two.

Closing the trunk with a bit of a slam, noticeably so, Jake turned and said, "Listen Darrell: she's a good girl, and we both know it. She's been unfairly saddled with this, mostly by your two brothers and their friends 'cause she rejected them."

"She's an Injun," Darrell teased.

"Oh come on now. You don't care, and you know it. And she always treated you nicer than any girl in this town. Hell, she's the friendliest girl here. Just drop all that crap. The few rich, snooty girls around here have tried to hang a bad boy label on you."

There was a pause and then Jake said thoughtfully as Darrell stepped over and leaned back on the trunk, "I never figured the Indian thing in this town. No one can remember the history, and half of the towns out here revel in their native culture, turn it into a tourist attraction."

"You didn't sleep with her and make all the rumors true?"

"No. Darrell. If it is any of your business, we cuddled with our clothes on, listened to records, and decided to go get married today."

"Well how about that. Gonna make an honest woman out uv'er. But, you know, it's hard to believe. She's kinda irresistible, she's a knockout. I mean 'you'?! Maybe she need's glasses."

Suddenly stepping aggressively up to his friend and former antagonist from youthful years, Jake came almost nose to nose with Darrell and said firmly, "Sarah doesn't need that; she **is** an honest woman."

Still face to face the other man responded, "Well, I guess you'll be the one to find out. You'll know in a few hours."

Jake grabbed Darrell's shirt with a hand on each side of the front of it and then, letting go, he sort of comically dusted the area of the material off with his right hand and said, "A little respect, Darrell. Sarah's about to be my wife." He was using her name rather than the pronoun 'she' to bring it back to being personal, demanding more dignity.

And he continued, "We're grown up now. I'm out there and it can be rough, and I know you signed up. If that eye scar doesn't stop you from being accepted, you'll fight like hell. We may not see each other again to ever have that childish fight we never had. Grow up, Darrell. We're leaving, her and me. But do the right thing and make your two brothers clear up the record on all that. Make um tell the truth . . just ease it out that they were teasin' her and it got out of hand. Sarah deserves that. Who knows? We might wanna come back here someday."

Sarah was coming out the door above with her coat and purse, and Jake held out his right hand to shake, which Darrel took as he nodded subtly to Jake's suggestion about his brothers' moral duty.

As Jake held the door of the old Buick and she was getting in, Sarah held her hand out for a passing, casual handshake to Darrell, who was now standing near the car on the passenger side. "Bye Darrell," she said. "We may be back in a few days, but the grill will be down a while. Can you tell folks?"

"I'll put a sign on it for yuh, Sarah."

As the car pulled away and up the snowy street slowly, Jake said to his fiancé, "This won't be a fancy wedding, Honey." Sarah turned and looked at him as he focused on the somewhat slippery road being conquered by his skill, the weight of the old car, and the quality of the tires and chains Sarah's father had purchased.

After a long pause in which she thought about her life and about the man beside her, the woman said, "Jake, a girl has romantic fantasies. Most do like me, I guess . . a prince charming, a warrior, an officer, a prince. It comes closer to real with a schoolgirl crush . . you know the ones who actually marry the football star . . but it seldom happens for real. Later if she waits, she falls in love with some great guy eventually, I guess . . but such dreams are just dreams. The childhood crush, the warrior prince never really comes strolling in to sweep a girl off her feet . . . but you did . . the only guy I ever really noticed or cared about, my fantasy warrior came back to sweep me off my feet. That makes up for everything . . for all of it. Just make it last, please."

"Well, I'm sorry the sweeping off your feet took place in the dark in two feet of wet snow. I suppose that took the edge off of the magic a bit."

In war things can unfold quickly, and true friends are discovered as are false ones. Dear John letters flow, as lonely wives find they cannot wait, so, apparently it wasn't 'forever...' . . . and surely men at war are often untrue as well, 'for tomorrow we may die', and there are occasionally last-minute chances to 'get some'. Wartime loves can blossom fast, and sometimes they are true ones. In Sarah and Jake's case it was probably true. Only a lifetime would tell, but two people of slightly disparate ages had waited five years from their initial, secret teenage crushes on each other to seek any other . . had actually not yet sought another . . what more could speak of or at least hint of true love. It was the stuff of great historical romances and Hollywood movies . . better even than the classic tales of childhood sweethearts.

They drove to the church and were able to convince the priest to marry them . . the war and all, and he knew them. He told them to go to the county seat for a license and that they would need a blood test. Such tests were common then because of the Rh blood factor that could affect child bearing and because some states were concerned about syphilis spreading, perhaps because of the war. So many young men away from home at the same time and in ports and army towns where prostitutes sold their wares, because that was where the concentrations of men were, surely led to an increase of that disease.

These bureaucratic measures took the day, and the priest; an old family friend of Jake's parents, gave them separate rooms in a little guesthouse behind the rectory. He actually trusted them both. The following day they were able to receive the test results, which were fine and had been expedited because it was wartime, and they secured the license. Sarah's predominate Native American ethnicity was no problem; but, in years to come, boys bringing back Asian girls from the war would encounter states that would not allow such marriages. Montana for some reason specifically forbade white-Filipino marriages, an obvious insult to America's former colony; and Maryland would forbid black-Filipino marriages, as if to elevate the Filipino to the level of whites and denigrate the blacks. One can only wonder at what went on in the racist brains of some bureaucrats and legislatures of earlier eras, but clearly the flaw was in them and not those they sought to restrict.

Roads were better to the west, and the Pierces came up from San Francisco to see their son wed the girl they had considered a daughter since her mother's death had left her alone in the world.

When it was all over, Eric, Jake's father said, "I'm going to call Dave and Sarah Butchell. They have a little cabin up in the high valley."

Father Lawson added, "They let us use that cabin from time to time for retreats and such. We can squeeze the six priests for our two area churches in there, so it will surely be comfortable for the two of you for a honeymoon. Give us a moment," he said as he left the narthex with Mr. Pierce to go to his office. They returned with a positive answer from the Butchells.

After a personal reception-like meal at a local restaurant with Jake's parents and the priests, arriving at the cabin in the evening, Sarah searched for the key while Jake unloaded the groceries they had purchased at the general store in the town below. The cabin had two birdhouses on the porch on the corner poles holding the porch roof up. The birdhouse on the left was hinged in the back so that it would swing out like opening a book to reveal the key.

"Sarah, that key also fits a cabinet in here with a rifle, a revolver, and ammo, just in case we want to hunt," Jake said as he carried the groceries through the door. He knew she was a bow hunter and had brought all of her handmade bows and arrows along when she got her most valuable possessions from the apartment. The morning before when they left Paradise Ridge, there was some permanence to it. Jake called his parents to explain things and invite them to the impromptu wedding. The older folks renewed their invitation to Sarah to come and stay with them while their son would be off to the war again. It was something that many families did during the great upheaval, just for the moral support of it. She accepted, thinking that she could also get involved in war work in the Bay Area as well. Therefore, her father's car trunk now held her record collection, Victrola, and some other prized possessions. She would hire Darrell to bring the rest later.

"We should get the revolver out now in case we are surprised up here by any unsavory characters," she replied.

It was nearing dusk and the shadows were falling around the cabin as Jake got a fire going. Turning to the charming natural beauty he had tied himself to so impetuously and quickly, he said with a wink as she looked at him and his fire, "I'm hungry but eating can wait. That's not what I'm hungry for."

"Oh, you naughty boy. Didn't you mother tell you to eat properly and on time? It's dinner time."

"There's all kinds of nutrition, including feeding the heart," he commented as the girl turned into the bedroom.

Moments later as he turned to wash his hands after the fire building, he stopped in his tracks as Sarah stood in the doorway leaning on the door casing to his left, her right. Her right arm was against it and raised above her head, and with her left she played with some of her dark tresses in her fingertips. The only covering was a sheer knee-length housecoat that hid little and barely covered one breast, leaving the other small, well-shaped one glowing in the fire and his gaze. The robe somewhat accented the shape of the breast it covered and was semi-transparent; and, because of the angle of her leaning body, only partially covered the area where her two pretty legs met and a little dark hair peaked out. Her tawny native skin was golden brown in the light of the fire, as it was dusk, and, just to tease, she slowly dropped her left hand down, opening the robe and saying, "Warm hors d'oeuvres?"

Of course, they did not leave that bed for some time, like all new lovers who have finally been able to completely love each other in every way. In their places, who would have? And, especially with their unique love story, who could have? Between moments of passion, of which they were soft and loving rather than violent and athletic, they cuddled and sweet talked to each other. And it seemed that fate had proven how correct had been the waiting and that the two were a perfect match. But time would tell. And yes, both had waited, for Jake's wait was a little obvious, but many a girl not looking toward college in that era would have married at eighteen or nineteen. And, though the young woman had less options in Paradise Ridge, there were those who would have been happy to receive her attention, and who might have been seriously interested. She would have had options as well back where her mother's people were from.

Late in the evening they did eat and talked of more serious things . . the choice they'd made, the path ahead, and more. The room and bed would always be waiting, but there was time to savor it slowly. They had what was left of his thirty-day leave, and he had only used five. During the week in San Diego before coming up to Northern California and the mountains Jake was officially on duty. Of course, the trip across the Pacific and the brief time at Mare Island had been on duty as well. He was home first for medical care and some extra training, a combination which got him home. Neither alone would have probably achieved it.

But the room and bed would really not always be there, for the chief petty officer, an unlikely warrior a year prior, was now a vertebra in the backbone of the Navy in a Navy war. The control of sea lanes in the three most traveled oceans were important in this war as in no other. The duty fell to the naval forces of Britain and the U.S. Land battles in World War II would never have been fought had the Indian, Atlantic, and Pacific Oceans not remained open to the Allied nations. It was the United States Navy's finest hour and work perhaps, and chiefs made it get done. The officers controlled it, the sailors did it, the chiefs made things happen (guiding and correcting both) and were (though outranked by them) even charged with helping train new, young officers in the fleet.

Having never gone through boot camp, Jake Pierce had been as lucky in war as in love. In just a year, through war necessity and his capabilities, he had reached an acting noncommissioned rank that normally took years and was allowed to do what he did best, pilot flying boats. The seemingly slow, intransigent bureaucracy actually was farsighted enough to have allowed for both programs years prior: enlisted pilots and acting chief petty officers. The Second World War required both. Sarah's bed would soon seem empty, even with her pretty body in it, and Jake may never be back.

The next two days dragged happily on the same with pleasant walks between pleasant romps. Hunting was out of the question, the violence of the war on both their minds though they loved to hunt. They also needed no extra food and were not casual hunters. Pairing the thrill of it with the need for game, for them, resulted in a greater reward. They really just wanted the moments close together, locked in the intense emotion of lovemaking or sharing tender moments in conversation or silent thought while embracing.

. . . just at first light"

The third morning, lying in bed after another romantic moment, Sarah said, "Can you tell me about it . . all of it? I won't force you if it is too much, too hard. I know it's hard on you fellas. I realize you guys aren't as emotionally tough as you'd like us to believe. You have to be strong for us. But I'll tell you, I'm strong. I'll be strong for you . . with you . . so let me."

He looked at her calmly with no emotion or angst, and the young yet emotionally and intellectually mature woman explained, "I want to know it all . . all about you. You know about me. Nothing different has happened there . . nothing different about me since you left . . well, except those boys trying to wreck my reputation. I've just been a loner and a book worm when not working. And, of course, I have my records. I have to know all about you in case . . . I want tuh know . . if it happens, I don't want to wonder about this man that was, is, mine . . ."

"In case I don't return?"

"You'll return . . if you can. You'll never leave me, . . but if it happens . . you know . . ."

. . . And of course with that, she cried in his arms . . with that thought rolling off her lips so softly, almost imperceptibly, and it seems melodramatic sometimes in old movies of that era and others, but . . . they died, in the tens of thousands and more they died until the world's numbers, the world's death toll reached unimaginable totals . . tens of millions.

It was not corny or melodramatic to cry before lovers parted, for sometimes there was nothing left to ship home to a broken wife . . blown apart or never found. Where Jake would soon be bound, the big Pacific very often swallowed all evidence of any violent clash of arms, swallowed whole giant steel monster ships with crews numbering in the thousands and including the warriors' remains.

The rest of morning found the young lovers setting very near at the somewhat large country trestle table. It wasn't real big, just big enough for a cozy lovers' breakfast after two days and nights of feasting on each other. More than romantics sharing a table's corner in some small cafe, they were nearly glued to one another on one side of the little cabin's one real eating station, nearest the kitchen for easy access, leaving them separated only briefly.

Settled now with food and drink and nibbling casually to be able to easily talk or pause and kiss without a mouthful, the woman turned pensive and very quiet, and after a long moment of culinary peace, said softly,

"I want too know everything. Tell me Jake. I want to know about my husband. I've not been anywhere; you've been gone five years."

"The central islands, the Visayas, are smaller than Luzon but still quite big. Some in the north around Manila call them the isles of beautiful women."

" Oh . . really now? So did you enjoy that experience . . A young guy right out of high school?"

He paused and stumbled a bit with his words and she noticed, however slight it was and he tried to cover it.

Sarah gently punched him in the ribs saying, "I'm kidding you, sailor. Whatever you tell me you've done is okay."

"Well, . . They're pretty, a lot of 'em, but I wasn't ready for that. I'm a moral guy, you'll be glad to know, I guess . . . an' I didn't want to deal with a baby yet, you know . . if that happened A guy's gotta be more mature for that."

"What about the picture?"

"What picture?"

"The one in your wallet."

Not reacting angrily, but playfully irritated . . . (how irritated could he really be with her . . this angel, his dream girl?) Jake responded softly, "You went through my wallet?"

"No, I looked at the few photographs. I thumbed through those. It was open, silly."

"We're supposed to trust each other," said as he feigned exaggerated disdain.

"I didn't look at it here . . back at my apartment."

"But still . . ."

"You left it laying open, I thought maybe on purpose. We were not married yet. I had to see what I was getting in to."

"Swell, and?"

"They are all of her, your parents and her."

"And you."

"Yeah, fella, where did you get those, you dirty old man? You have every school picture of me since you left, all four years of high school, and snapshots too."

"My mom had 'em, I think from your mom. They were friends. I think my mom knew how I felt."

"...and she figured: when you got back, I'd be legal," Sarah said with a slight grin. "About the gal, buster?"

"We're not quite five years apart, Sarah; my parents are three."

"My parents married when Dad was eighteen and Momma was thirteen, . . almost the same age difference as you and me."

"Maybe I should have just stayed around then and gotten their permission."

She took his hand in her left and patted it with her right, then looked up slightly, as he was taller, . . looked into his eyes with those doe-eyed brown orbs and said soft and sensually, "Had you done that, you would not have this tale to tell your new wife who is starved to know of the missing five years of her true love's exotic, mysteriously adventurous life."

Acknowledging that with a glance, he began, "She is,. . was a friend."

"Well, I know that."

"That's the bulk of it."

"No it isn't. Was?"

"Wha...?"

"You said 'was' and there are too many pictures. Were you in love, did you sleep with her . . ?"

"Sarah, I . ."

"...came back for me . . a girl you last saw when she was thirteen. That's the stuff of storybooks and movies. I'm not upset; I'm in love . . . and curious. You are mine. I want to know what I've got. I don't care if you slept with her, but I wanna know."

This young woman he had come back for, longed for, and now possessed, she was smart . . and mature, nineteen going on thirty when it came to intuition and character. Was she experienced too, like the boys claimed? No. That had been addressed empirically just nights before, on the wedding night. What was her game here now, just a woman's jealousy?

"Sarah..."

"She took both his hands, which she had never let go of, up from the tabletop and between her own and said, "Jake, my mother taught me a lot, about marriage, work, men . . . traditional Indian mothers do that. But I've been nowhere. I'm the weird but attractive Indian girl on the edge of a town that still thinks we're fighting each other or something. That's why those boys . . they could do that to me so easily. Now I have you and the happiness that I lost when they died . . my parents." She paused, looking earnestly at him, an older man (slightly) with travel and experiences under his belt and within his twenty-five year old body . . experiences she could only imagine. The girl said, "My mother told me about it, about what our wedding night would be . . could be like, but that is not doing, knowing is not doing. Mr. you've got some explaining to do," said with a teasing smile accented by that sexy crooked lip. "You played me, my body, like a violin these last few nights. I want to know where you learned that. Boys are stupid about girls, you know. Older boys tell them, I'm sure. But then I'm also sure they fumble around with it, and a girl that gets a pure young man for a husband is his practice dummy. But last night wasn't football; it was a concert. You didn't fumble around. I wanna know, and then I wanna to play some more music of our own."

The young yet weathered and battle-hardened sailor looked back in his love's eyes as intensely as she still did into his. There was a comfortable sofa in the living room of the cabin. It was clean and had been covered with a protective throw. It might yet be the scene of true love's full expression before the week was through.

Jake took her left hand as he stood from the table and led her to the comfortable seat where they sat side-by-side closely with her back slightly towards the right side of his chest and his strong arms around her, enveloping her completely and comfortably. Both were in only a robe, and he avoided letting his hands and fingers explore, which would have quickly ended the seriousness she now sought. As she said, there would be time to play romantic music later. They had the cabin for two weeks if they so wanted. There would follow a room at his parent's house for as long as he was home and as long as Sarah wanted. She was in fact expected to board there if she wanted to leave Paradise Ridge when he was overseas.

His right arm now behind her back and meeting his left draped across her stomach, her head leaned back against his with the dark brown hair flowing everywhere across him, she sighed and he did too, as they savored the moment. In a month or so, the man could be locked in an unusual type of dangerous fringe combat, and before it was all over, he could be dead, ending a short marriage and sending the woman's life into a tailspin and to who could know what or where.

"I worked with the O'Brian family for two years on their interisland schooners. The parents, Jon and Rosario, an Irish American guy and his Filipina wife, founded the business with her sister and her Filipino husband. Originally, the two schooners were Jon's. There's an interesting story or two about that we'll save for later. The children had expanded the business into flying boats, small ones. It was a new and growing business that could get important people or cargo somewhere fast. And so companies were willing to pay for it. I worked for the kids . . the parents were mostly retired from it and are in their sixties now. There's a Navajo woman in the larger extended group of family and friends, and she taught them all something of her natural ways. Seems to keep the older folks healthy, even there in the tropics, and the women hold their looks well.

I worked first on the boats and then in the planes. I got my pilot's license and flew with them the last two years. Then this war broke out."

"Where are they now, the family, and the schooners and planes?"

"We flew down to Borneo with a cargo. That's how I ended up in the Navy, and they eventually confiscated the plane. I believe a lot of them are in the hills with the guerrillas. It would have been hard for them to get out of the Philippines. There wasn't even transportation to get all the important personnel out that might be needed to help plan the counter attack. Some may be in Australia . . the grandparents, who are still quite healthy for their ages, but I believe the military took their Dolphin. They might have used the schooners though. But they're capable. They might be in the hills too. I told Lolo George and Lola Sunny to not stay in the city or their house in the nearby country. Lola and Lolo are grandparents, but we used Tita and Tito too, aunt and uncle, you know, even if they aren't.

'Til the war broke, my most dangerous moment involved Maya, the girl. We encountered her when she was in great danger."

"That's a Central American Indian name, a whole people."

"Yeah. It's Japanese too, I believe. They use it a little in Malaya. Their cultures are mixed and it may have come from India there. They're British controlled there. Well, Malaya and India are."

Jake glanced at his wife and could see that she was in a peaceful place with a pleased look on her face nestled comfortably in his arms. Imagining her hard workdays for the two years since her mother died five years after her father, Jake felt blessed that he had come back to 'claim' her before life had worn her down. Without his return, he realized, suitors would have probably sought her as a wife for her properties. Of course, he knew how smart she was and that she would have chosen carefully; but would any of such men cared for her as he did. Through his mind passed the scene in the little apartment above the grill, a bit dreary for the lack of money for decor and a bit cozy with the phonograph, enormous record collection and the large bookshelf lined with books about the world and its people: fiction, history, travel. This was a hungry, repressed smart young woman, who had taught herself alone at night, absorbing herself in books and music . . . a hungry young woman who could converse as if she was five years older than she was and had been to many a far-flung destination. Jake felt very blessed that he had been able to come back to hopefully take her to those places for real.

And so, the tale of Chief Petty Officer Jake Pierce, USNR unfolded...

In late November of 1941, with Jake Pierce now one of their top pilots, the O'Brians were hired to take a load of general supplies, including guns and ammunition, to some farmers and planters along the northeast coast of Borneo. It had been a bit dangerous for the fact that the planters were stocking up defensively and both the British and Americans might question the whole escapade and call it 'gun running'. There was always a concern in Malaysia and other colonies throughout the East Indies that native populations would rebel. Gandhi had been agitating in India for some time now as the nineteen thirties had been winding towards an end. Jake had taken to sailing as if born at sea and flying was no different. The management of the O'Brian businesses knew a prodigy when they saw one and rewarded him to keep him. That would not have been a problem however. For Jake developed several friendships with several people in the extended family. He became especially close to Capt. George and Kathleen Allison, noted adventurers who had several accomplishments under their belts.

The planters making the purchases were not of the type to support a rebellion, even if one could sympathize with the cause. Jake didn't sympathize with the cause because there were better ways to end colonialism. Nor were the planters likely involved in illegal activities.

Talking things over before the trip was made, Tommy, whose father Manual was another senior partner in the business, vocalized his belief that either the planters were concerned that Japan would someday, in the not too distant future, become a threat or that the planters might have become aware of political agitation among native Malayans, perhaps an influx of Marxist. All agreed: his Filipino wife Erin, his father and mother, and his sister and cousins, even his nephew and Jake's best friend, Jon, named after his grandfather, Jon O'Brian. Jake was the newest member of the close and trusted inner family circle he had been invited into soon after his arrival. He concurred with everyone else. The possibilities seemed obvious and the situation serious. Misunderstandings could develop from shipping weapons.

The flight required both seaplanes, the Douglas Dolphin and the Grumman Goose. Tommy flew the Dolphin and Jake flew the Goose, with Jon relieving him if and when necessary. After delivering their cargo at the assigned small coastal dock that was hardly a port but had an access road into the bush, the planes were refueled, and the men relaxed and ate. The customers had made sure that enough aviation fuel was there. When the refueling was completed, the four men walked up to the ramshackled shack of a store, cafe, and bar for some needed refreshment.

A piano was playing when the men entered the cafe Someone, perhaps the owner played reasonably well, and the repertoire included some popular tunes recently popular in the States. Noticeable immediately was a small group of four shy looking Malayan and Filipino girls along a bench, identifiable by their soft but audible conversation and the differences in the dress each wore. Two Malays were in sarongs and more Western dresses adorned the two Filipinas. Also noticeable near them were some rough looking seadogs who kept shushing the women when they would get loud. There was the appearance that the women belonged to the three men, but the match did not look even, as the women lacked the same hard look as the men. Jake sensed something wrong with that scenario and expressed as such quietly as the group sat around a circular table facing each other. Food was ordered and served, and suddenly Jake picked his plate up and walked to a table alone, just a bit closer to the women.

While eating slowly and enjoying the food, Jake smiled occasionally at the one girl who both seemed more refined and somewhat a focus or leader of the others. Finally, she came and pulled up a chair beside Jake, becoming quite aggressively cozy. When he turned toward her she smiled, and then hidden from the hardened rough men by her position her faced exhibited a pained grimace for the briefest of moments and he thought she mouthed a word something like 'please'.

The other three from the flying boats, jovially continued with their meal and talk, leaving the young man to his pleasurable adventures for the time being. All the while he ate, the woman fawned on him. The men she was with knew what she was doing, and that was okay, for it was clear that this was a business.

Only moments after she sat down and made her first partially inaudible comment she repeated it more clearly but in a hushed tone, "Please hear me, listen." Her words were in clear English with a soft, strong Malayan accent.

Nothing more was said but he became ever friendlier with the young woman, who was charming and behaved both affectionately aggressive and alternately shy. As Jake shared his food with her, feeding her with fork and fingers as playful lovers might do, the impression easing into his mind was that she was enjoying it and forcing it at the same time. That screamed 'prisoner' to the insightful, now experienced, but still green young adventurer. She was playing a role she was forced to play that was out of character for her, but she was also enjoying his company because, he guessed, the rest of her life right now was crap. She was surviving . . doing what was necessary for that.

As Jake leaned in close to her as if to kiss, as he was not avoiding the pleasurable part of the encounter, the exotic, petite young woman said, "Please take me back to a room, pleeaase" . . whispered strongly and almost frantically, as she gripped his hand and the tip and nail of her left thumb dug almost reflexively into the back of his hand. Jake surmised that the woman knew not to talk to him too much because it would appear to her handlers that she was seeking his help rather than his business.

When the plate was empty and the last sip of beer downed, a British one as he could always get San Miguel back in the Philippines, Jake, taking her hand gently, stood up.

"Do you know what you're doin' kid?" It was Manual's son, Tommy, in his thirties and in charge of the current shipping expedition. His father had helped found the O'Brian trading business at the turn of the century.

Trying to appear nonchalant and speaking normally but low, Jake said, "Something's going on here, Tommy. I can't speak now. I'm trying to find out."

Then he turned and kissed the girl strongly and turned back with a laugh, saying, "I might have some fun tonight," then softer and looking intently at Tommy, he continued, "I think they're prisoners . . for whores. If you leave to the planes, leave someone ashore if you can, here or by the docks."

The two men shook hands in a hearty, jolly manner and Tommy walked out in the back to relieve himself.

Jake took the girl to a more private table but a bit closer to what appeared to be her handlers, thus reducing their suspicion about any whispered conversation between the two temporary, commercial 'sweethearts'. It was his intention to reduce such suspicion, for they could converse more freely in a room.

The girl knew what the flyers from Cebu were and that a plane would be a quick getaway. The brave woman had tried that more direct approach the first and only time a nice, respectable looking man had come through. That had not gone well. Now the rough danger surrounding her situation and the men who held her was apparent. They had meant to keep her pure to make a big sale her first night with a customer, but she had to be taught a lesson, which was the job perk that the gang's leader enjoyed.

As a second beer was savored by the couple, one of the rough group of men walked up to the young man and inquired, "Do you like what you see, young fella?"

"....and what I'm feelin'. I like this one in the pretty dress."

"Ho . . that one's from our private stock. She'll cost."

"How much?"

"How much time?"

"I want to savor it . . a girl like this."

"A couple of hours will cost you fifty bucks."

"I look young, but I ain't green. Fifty bucks for a couple of hours with a China whore?!"

"She's Malay with Dutch in 'er. She's an aristocrat. Lotta men wanna play with her. An' she's a virgin. If you wanna be first you better take the deal, she's gonna have to have one trainin' session with me soon. You'll be the first of many."

"A hundred for the whole night. I meant it generally . . she's Asian."

"One fifty."

" . . . twenty-five. All night. It's all I got, so don't try to come in an' roll me. you'll have it all," and Jon handed the man a wad of bills from his pocket.

He was playing it tough and forceful to deflect from his youthful look, which was waning in recent months. He wondered if Sarah would even recognize him if he went back. He also had to play it real and he reached into her bodice, unnaturally loose for a sarong, reaching his left hand through the low neckline and felt across her chest for her left nipple. The he said, "I'm serious that's it. I ain't rich, but they feed me, pointing with a thumb over his shoulder to the group at the table. Now where's the room, an' it better be secure and have a good lock."

The man was surprised at Jake's self-assurance and apparent maturity as he led him to one of the doors on the left side of the larger main room, farther from the side where his friends sat.

Jake had the girl by the arm just above the elbow and wondered how he would best communicate with her and handle this when they were alone. He was sure she wasn't a whore or willingly so. But when he locked the door and turned back toward her she was in his arms instantly and embraced him tightly. Then she stood on tiptoes and reaching her face up, planted a long deep romantic kiss on him.

He was having doubts now about how he had read things, but damn, he was enjoying it. The girl took his hand and pulled him to the bed where she sat and patted the mattress beside her to invite him. She was slowly removing her necklace, bracelet, hair ties and the like. Through his mind passed the thought that if she was a virgin and a prostitute, at least he would not have to worry about infection.

Unsure, because of his faith . . and Sarah, but with strong desires normal for his age, Jake removed his shoes and let each drop.

Then the petite, brown woman turned to him, wrapping her arms around him and coming ever so close, pressing her head to his on the right side and kissing his cheek. In his ear, she whispered almost too quietly to be heard even in the private room and so close to each other, talking as best she could with almost no movement of her lips and jaw. "Can your men help us? We are held for prostitution. They are my friend and new acquaintances. Those men raided our vacation camp on the shore not far from our plantation and killed everyone except us girls so they can use us for income. I'm supposed to say my father had to give me up for debt. The Filipinas were captured from a vessel in a similar raid."

"Yes" came out before Jake could think. What else could an honorable man have said . . or decided. She whispered so softly for the secrecy, and her warmth, closeness, and hot breath were overwhelming.

"Let us plan" she whispered right in his ear as she embraced him gently and caressed his back. "Talk softly, they can hear us through these walls . . . and you'll have to make love to me. I think they may watch."

Maya slipped her fine sarong style dress off over her head and wore nothing now. She was a fine, petite, golden skinned example of her race and had small yet well-formed breasts appropriate to her size. Typical to brown skinned women, her nipples were a dark, purplish tinted terracotta, rather than the dark pink of white women. Jake was feeling weak and choking slightly with a lump in his throat. Only the tension of the surrounding danger could dampen his desire.

His head was swimming now with too much information and emotion. He was in a position most virgin men his age would have paid more than $125 for . . even just most men. But he was strong in his faith, and there was Sarah. Adding to the mental and emotional storm was the danger that surrounded them as well.

"What, you want me to rape you?"

She was rubbing her hand on his chest through his loosened shirt and otherwise being very slowly affectionate. She knew this was life and death for him and regretted involving him. She knew failure was a beating and maybe a rape for her.

She leaned close and whispered, "It isn't rape if you have permission. I'm sorry I involved you. They killed one boy I requested help from."

"And this time you chose me because I have strong companions."

"Yes. I'm sorry. It is my duty to those girls. The boy acted tough, and I thought he was. I thought he could defeat them. But he was killed and they beat me and almost raped me." The woman looked down but kept her hands on him for the appearance of it, "The leader almost raped me for it. That's what he meant, 'training'," and she was softly crying.

Looking up at Jake, she said, "Better you than him."

 "We'll . . uh we'll . . rescue you, get you away from here..."

"What about them?"

"I don't see how . ."

"I am responsible for them."

"Ma'am…" but she pulled him down as she reclined, saying, "They're watching and we're talking to much. I don't want that man on me tonight. I don't want to sleep the night through with him."

"Miss, uh Maya, I . . I don't see how . . I mean, I don't know if the men with me will condone this."

"Then I'll stay too."

"You can't."

"I can. I've steeled myself for what will happen."

"But this . . . "

"We must, or they will suspect."

"But if I can't help, if you won't go 'cause of them."

"Would you leave your compadres out there in a similar danger?"

She looked at him in the darkened room and then continued, "Then I will have one good night to remember with a good man before all the bad ones." She paused and stared in Jake's face leaning over her as he sat on the side of the bed and she lay back now looking up at him. And she said, "When someone is hurting me, I'll remember this night and see your face and forget theirs."

As the plan she had hoped for seemed to be breaking down but her general opinion of Jake remained intact, the endangered little beauty truly saw this as her brief chance for a loving moment, one real meaningful flash of a romantic life and hoped God would understand. Wrapping herself around the strong young American, she prepared to give him his hundred and twenty-five dollars' worth and more.

Whispering in his ear she said, "The light may be just too much to fake it. At least take off your pants."

Jake leaned his head back on the sofa, and took a deep breath, and Sarah was oddly still relaxed in his arms like a well-behaved child during story time. She had not moved during it all or showed any sign of a reaction, but as he kept his head in place on the sofa back and still breathed softly, deeply, and obviously with tension, she reached her left arm and hand back and up and placed her open palm on his left cheek. It was all she could reach in that position; and, in her position, she was quite comfortable and didn't want to move. He was a big boy, he could handle this with her help . . without giving up her pleasant honeymoon seat in his arms just so.

"Well, did you?"

"Did I what?"

"Oh, come on now. Really?"

"I'm sorry, Sarah."

The quiet moment that followed seemed quite long to him, and perhaps she was weighing her words. The point was she knew the answer without his answer, and he was being silly . . at least in her mind.

Softly, with the hand on his cheek slightly caressing it and her right on his arms across her body doing the same, the young wife replied. Her mannerisms lacked the contrived moves of a bad actor, like an inexperienced high schooler playing at life, and her insight was beyond her years. It was a different time with different sensitivities, and she used none of the harsh sailor's or soldier's terminology thrown around so casually by girls in the more modern era.

"Don't be ridiculous, Honey. I don't care if you made love to the girl. The situation was dangerous . . if you're telling me the truth. Why would you tell such a story if it wasn't true? A man would have to have a death wish to do such a thing during his honeymoon." Then, after a brief pause she repeated her interrogative, the question she already knew the answer to, "Did you do it?"

"Well, I didn't make love to her, but thinking of you, then and later, I felt strange. You're just the only girl I ever thought about . . ever thought about being with like that . . 'til that night."

Jake paused and then said, looking down in her face as she turned and looked up at him over her shoulder.

"I . . I guess I wanted her, for a moment I did. I never knew if I'd get back or you'd be here. It seemed silly a little . . us. It just seemed impossible sometimes."

"It's natural, Honey. In that atmosphere. And you can't imagine how you made me feel telling this. That you thought of us even then, of me."

"Well, what happened next was . . .

. . . Jake whispered to Maya, "I'm gonna get you out of here, all of you. Wait here."

"No, you can't…"

"It'll be okay. Your handlers will just see me telling the guys goodbye cause I'm stayin' the night with you. You're not in danger. Stay here; don't come out."

He walked out to the table and leaned over it, talking low, "They're renting these girls out for the night, and they're good girls. I'm doing something about it, with or without help."

"You'll get killed," commented Juan, a Filipino and Tommy's copilot. "I have been in some of these barroom scrapes."

"Then I'll get killed." He still had his shirt off and his small five-inch knife was on his belt still. The heavy khukuri knife Jake had crafted himself in Cebu after the design and specifications of Lola Sunny's and his revolver were on the chair at the crew's table with his flight jacket.

"Well, I may just try to kill 'em all. I gotta think fast. If any of you are in, come up with a plan fast."

Just at that moment, Jake noticed one of the bad fellows who controlled the young women had stood up and walked in the direction of the room where Maya was. It was the one he had dealt with for her. There was nothing else there, and his movement caught the observant young pilot's attention.

Straightening his body and turning Jake looked to the man, wondering if he suspected something as he had now stopped at the door of the bedchamber.

"Excuse me. I paid for the night."

"Well, you shouldn't keep the lady waiting. I'll just keep 'er warmed up, keep the motor running, so's tuh speak."

"Sorry. I paid for the night."

The man ignored him and reached for the knob; and, once inside, he could lock the door and have his way. Jake quickly and smoothly drew his small sheath knife, and in but a moment, with a thud it stuck in the door of the room not more than three inches from the rough character's face at eye level.

Angrily the man turned and strode rapidly across the room toward the now unarmed young American.

Reaching his right hand over and retrieving his khukuri from his kit on the chair and standing, as the bigger man took a broad swing that went over his ducked head, Jake swung hard from right to left and sliced open the man's abdomen. It immediately became a large red smooth wound from which blood, intestines, and what appeared to be yellowish fat oozed, . . a death blow delivered by Jake with his first stroke in his first ever deadly fight. Following through to his left and rotating the hand and knife, he followed with an equally hard, devastating blow with the heavy bladed khukuri to the evil opponent's head on his return stroke. Stunned the fellow fell to his knees and then flat of his face on the floor.

Jake turned toward the area where the bar's owners, the girls' handlers, were sitting at a table, with the women on a bench along the wall in the manner presented in many a place that treated women as a product. Luckily the females were not directly behind the men. Firing lines and angles must be considered and rapidly so. Held in Jake's right hand the exotic powerful blade had already revealed its power, and Jake had also demonstrated his knife throwing prowess. His companions wondered perhaps how many more surprises their new 'family' member had held close to the vest.

In the room, Maya knew something had occurred, but obeyed his request and did not go out at first. Now she slowly peaked around the door she was easing open.

Just at that time, the other two callous men rose from the table slowly with anger on their faces. Sadly, through no fault of the young American adventurer it seemed it was going to turn very violent and more sadly his escapade this night might cost some of his friends' lives. On the other side of the scales, the opportunity for rescue was now in play, and he grabbed it.

The only one standing, a blessing tactically because it mistakenly showed the 'bad guys' that he was in this on his own, Jake had to create a distraction so none of his crew were in danger. The situation, as often occurred in South Seas gin joints, was turning into a saloon standoff and potential shootout reminiscent of the American Old West. He was in a position to draw fire. Now all he had to do was draw it further away from his friends, who appeared to be letting him hang himself.

"Was this scum your leader?" he said with courage he knew not from where. As he did he turned toward the room door where Maya was and walked almost as if nothing had happened. Jake held the khukuri in his right hand and his head turned back over his shoulder toward the two bad scoundrels who would put women in harm's way. He was terrified on some level, like many a competitor in life or death scenarios or in serious competition, yet he hid it. It was a tactical ploy, a bluff of toughness.

"Yeah," the next most dominate in the small gang replied. "He was the boss."

"Well, . . now he ain't," the young, 'green kid' toughened his lingo to respond.

Where did the bravery come from? He was running a rapid heartbeat but was not as uncontrolled as most who believed they were entering a deadly fight as they spoke. Like the boys coming out of the academies, West Point and Annapolis. . . the ones who made the cut and manned the teams, especially the brutal footballers, it came from there . . . from getting your mouth smashed several times a week in the fall and in spring practice. Football, lacrosse, soccer, rugby, whatever young men played there or elsewhere, made men. The academies knew that. It was so with high school football. It had for Jake, the brutal single wing where every back had to run the ball and block.

And only a second or two after he had turned and emphasized his conquest of their leader, he added, ". . and now the girl's mine."

"What?"

Stopping and looking back but not turning, Jake clarified, "I'm takin' 'er; she's mine, permanently."

"Like hell you are," the apparent new spokesman said as he built up a head of steam to follow Jake to the door of the boudoir.

Jake wanted to glance at his friends imperceptibly to see how involved and ready they were, but he could never have done it 'imperceptibly' so didn't try. It must look like he was in it alone, for surely the bad men were keeping an eye on Tommy, Juan, and the younger Jon. Steven was at the pier guarding the two flying boats. But all the while Jake was drawing attention away from them. As he turned back toward the room where Maya was, all eyes, even his own still seated group's, were on him still walking toward the door slowly.

Everyone in the room wore a sidearm except Jake, who had left his on the chair when he picked up the khukuri.

Walking toward Maya, with her sarong back on and in the doorway, trying to calm himself, he prayed inwardly, 'Forgive me,' for he knew that, against his own moral code, he was going to have to be the instigator. Yet he would do it in a way so as to confuse that point.

There was a switch. He knew that instinctively. It turned things on as was his intent, but what would it be and who would click it. Jake only hoped for a sign to avoid being assassinated now by a shot or thrown knife in the back.

He got what he wanted as the other said angrily, "Why you little bastard" . . .

. . and the villain was close, just behind him. it was clear. Enraged at Jake's arrogance, the evil man had strode almost up to him . . within five feet . . wore his knife on his left (as Jake had observantly remembered) . .

. . And Jake, the young adventurer, his back to his opponent, slightly faked a turn to his left, an almost unnoticeable head nod, and followed it by spinning back around right, toward his adversary. And, diving to his left (the man's right) away from the other's knife . . as if diving for the corner of the end zone to score, he reached the khukuri out with both hands for the strength of that, drawing it back and cocking his arms . . . and the instant his left shoulder hit the floor to form a stable platform from which to present the power, he swung up and across and sliced his opponent's thigh tendons of his right leg to the bone just above the knee. The knife was that sharp and that heavily powerful in his hands, and it all happened in the blink of an eye, not the slow motion required for the telling it. The man crumbled in agony, and Jake rose to his knees and drove the point of the big knife into his enemy's throat.

Maya saw it all as she gripped the door almost painfully, herself gripped by tension. And as impressive as that had seemed to her, she had a front row seat as the last bad man drew his revolver and started to point it toward her hero rescuer. As he did, young Jon, reacted quicker than Juan or Tommy, though they did as well. Jon, in his youth was just faster, and, as he stood, the brigand turned to him, they exchanged rapid fire, multiple rounds, and the criminal went down.

The whole incident, the entire encounter after the last word to the first bad man was spoken, took literally three or four minutes and had been a sweet, perfectly executed, unplanned setup that functioned as smoothly as it had clumsily unfolded. Clearly it should never have worked, nor should it have been attempted quite the way it had.

The room was silent, as death filled it. With the speed of the events, the women had only emitted short squeals of surprise and fear as they sensibly dropped to the floor. The men from the Goose and

Dolphin, with guns still drawn, looked around, and Jon calmly said, "I'm hit," and dropped slowly to the floor. His Uncle Tommy caught him before he could hit his head.

Intelligently, Maya had waited for quiet to run out from the door and seeing Jake rising from the barroom floor healthy and apparently unharmed, she ran to the boy on the floor . . guilt rising in her at what she felt she had caused a second time. The woman pushed through the men to see Jon and knelt to him. Unbeknownst to the men from the Philippines, a Malayan of a middle-class family, she had been studying nursing in the big hospital in Johore Bahru before being kidnapped on a family holiday trip to the northern coast and shanghaied away to Borneo.

Kneeling there beside Jon, she called to the other girls, "Susanna, come quickly," for she remembered the Filipina's white petticoats. Reaching under Susanna's dress, she tried to tear off a piece of the undergarment. Struggling to rip it, she looked at Tommy and said somewhat frantically, "Tear it, about two foot pieces, quickly."

By then, Susanna had slipped the petticoat off as discreetly as possible. Many people know how to react in such emergencies.

Taking the pieces of the more or less clean rags, Maya folded each to make it thicker, putting it on the two wounds and putting pressure on it. There were two chest wounds, one high toward the right shoulder and one that surely penetrated a lung. Time would be critical now.

Turning again to the oldest of the flying boat crewmembers, who was in fact Tommy, the boy's uncle, Maya said, "We have to get him to Johore Bahru, to the hospital there. It is not a flesh wound: there can be internal bleeding and maybe organ damage. I'm so sorry, . . I . . I caused this." And she began to cry softly.

At about the same time, Jake, who had walked over, and the uncle said in unison, "No." Then the uncle added, placing his hand on her shoulder, "You are women in distress, through no fault of your own. You sought help. We'll get my boy help. Now, we'll do that."

"He is your son?"

"Nephew."

"We will get him help. I am a nursing student at, Johore Bahru General Hospital. We must go there. It is modern and closer than Manila."

As all prepared to go to the seaplanes at the shore, there was no real choice than for everyone to proceed together to the big British port. The Malayan girl touched Jake's hand and said, "I'm sorry, but thank you for your bravery. My duty is to your friend now, but I am here if you need me."

Jake noticed the slight British accent blended with the Malayan one, but he knew she had Dutch in her as well.

It was almost as if she were purposefully demonstrating an obligation to each man, but Jake felt a relief, saying to her, "He needs you and your knowledge. I don't mind."

Thinking to get something out of the whole escapade in his bar, the less criminally inclined partner of the dead brigands started to whine about the gunfire damage to his walls.

Turning fiercely, Tommy barked, "My nephew is injured, an' we got rid of your riff raff for you. Shut up. I know you're just barkin' 'cause you lost your cut off these girls. I oughta plug you."

Dawn was breaking to the East toward northern Borneo, and as the group worked to get Jon comfortable and a stretcher of sorts rigged, the chatter of machine guns followed the roar of a light plane somewhat low in the sky. A loud, significant boom followed.

Sarah was crying almost imperceptibly and Jake stopped the story to inquire why.

"It's so sad but it ended well if the young man lived. You are such a hero Jake. I know it is all true. I don't doubt it. It's as if I married one of those movie actors. But this is real."

What went unsaid was her feeling of security in knowing her new husband had encountered such a chance for romantic adventure with a petite, café tinted, exotic little beauty . . for she had seen the photos . . and was relieved that he had avoided entanglements to return to her . . wanting and waiting to return to her though he knew not if she or the opportunity would still be there.

There was a sound of a low-flying plane, more or less the distinctive sound of a small single engine plane making and then recovering a dive, and they heard the rapid gunfire of a machine gun. Dashing out the door, the group all saw a seaplane that had not been very low climbing for altitude and heading northward off the coast. No one could make it out, but everyone could see the damaged dock and burning aviation fuel drum that had been hit and was aflame.

The drum had been set apart to load the two O'Brian planes, and the shellfire intended for them caught it as well. Dashing to their treasured planes the crews examined every inch, finding only a few holes in the tail of the Dolphin Tommy had been flying. The control cables and everything else were quickly checked within the planes as both were hurriedly prepared.

Everything had been completed with the smoothness of a trained military operation as the two planes were loaded with some food and drink, and Jon, the Grumman's wounded copilot. Then the group stood on the dock contemplating their emergency, and Tommy took a hard choice in his hands and wrung it like a wet rag needing drying.

Everyone looked at him, waiting for instructions, and he spoke with some controlled emotion, "I can't go with Jon. It hurts because we don't know when we'll see each other again."

The entire group registered some surprise as they listened and searched his face for more, some realizing the ominous change of their world that the strange plane's diving attack had heralded, some perhaps not.

"That floatplane attack means somethings up. Now, even if it was some nutty pilot or something or a prank, what's a warplane doing here . . right here, right now?"

"It's the Japs, I'd say," commented Jake.

"Well, we couldn't see markings, but what else could it be," Tommy continued his original thought. "Now we all know what all the talk has been, but maybe nobody believed it. But one thing's sure, it was somebody, and we cannot afford to not take it seriously. If it is them, they might come marching down this way from where they are now in China . . where they've been fighting for years. The thing is: they may hit back home . . the Philippines, and I've got to be there. Now Jake: we'll take these two

Filipinas home, and you and Maya and the other Malay girl get my nephew to that big hospital. Steven, go with 'em and relieve Jake when necessary. You've got enough hours now."

The rugged man, Son of one of the schooner captains who had started the transport business decades before had a hint of tears in reddened eyes, and none registered it more in their mind than the girl who was now guiding them to Jon's hopefully lifesaving treatment.

She, boldly for that era, stepped over and embraced the man, as if she sensed something, a bond maybe, and went into the plane where his nephew lay.

"I already told him this was how it had to be. There's no more time. Let's get going. Now you watch for more planes, especially 'til you get further south down the Malay Coast. I think that plane was just taking a potshot at us, trying to get lucky and disable us or destroy our fuel. I think he didn't stay around because the fight's not quite on yet. But be careful."

The flight down the coast was uneventful, and, staying on the radio constantly, the crew and two new passengers learned of the air raids on Hawaii and Manila.

There was no reason for Sarah to disbelieve his tale, for she knew his character and that he had always been an honorable man in youth. Many men could fabricate such yarns, the blow-hard types, and they were often the wild types that lived it. But Jake had won her, and no one else was there to hear. Who and why could he be trying to impress, and what would be the point with her. She was already his and he knew it. Besides, certainly such a tale, if false, was counterproductive for a man to tell his wife on their honeymoon, even with the part concerning his restraint. Last of all, there was no need to brag of his heroics? The uniform he wore when they met again after all those years and that he stood beside her in at the altar at San Miguel . . that uniform with those two medals? Well that said it all. He told her simply because she asked.

It followed that Jake related the experience in Johore Bahru to Sarah, describing the feel of bustling Singapore and the exotic markets with the colorful sarongs on the petite brown women with cheerful faces and their cargoes on their heads held by one arm extended upward and occasionally steadied with two as they maneuvered through the crowds and the sounds and exotic spice smells. Many Malayans were Muslim, but the women did not cover their faces. They did wear head scarves that were as colorful as their sarongs, and these were beautiful in their own way. The East Indies was like a cultural theme park or smorgasbord with each nation or colonial region bearing its own unique ethnic and cultural atmosphere and flavor variation on the same basic theme of an exotic tropical paradise full of good, friendly people.

Smitten by the East and its beauty and beauties, Jake knew it wasn't for everyone nor the women appealing to every man. But he knew as well that until the sun baked and wrinkled them in old age, their cherubic faces always lit into a pleasant smile when treated properly.

"Sarah, he added. I'll give you some beauty advice from the matriarch of the Jefferson family. She was the Navajo woman from Texas. She advised all of the girls in her family and the O'Brian's family to restrict their time in the open sun. Somehow, she figured out it caused more wrinkling. She must have been right. Wait 'til you meet Lola Sunny, her daughter. She's a picture of loveliness in her sixties."

But most of all, what Jake remembered of the Malayan visit was the news of the campaign and his worry about Jon's slowly healing wounds, needing to be cleaned and drained too often . . lingering unhealed too long. He told her that too, holding nothing back. She had asked, and maybe it was so bad then that knowing of it would reduce her worry for him now. So he related the constant angst and the sense of doom as the people awaited the

Japanese march down the Malay Peninsula to Singapore.

"Well, we were there for several weeks while he got a little better. The climate is rough on a wounded man, so hot and humid. A fan can cut into the heat but not do much but move the moist air around. All he could think about was Maya because she genuinely fawned over him on the flight and they seemed, in their own places of worry, to get closer and closer. I think she had escaped such a danger without being violated and was so relieved and still scared, especially scared for Jon. Then she sorta disappeared for a time. Little did we know she was back to her nursing, her studies reduced and her on the job training forced by the emergency. You know, the war was in full swing, and I guess you know what happened in Malaya and to Singapore. So, she was actually in the same hospital but not that ward. But she started popping in when she could."

He paused, and she responded softly after a moment. "You know how it is like this. You know I wish I had been there . . had shared it all and known them all. We only know the basic news. You'll have to recount it all someday. I mean your past with them, growing to know them."

He was still looking down . . remembering, and he looked up and nodded, continuing, "Well, you'll *never guess... Just days before we're leavin', she shows up with an evacuation order list with him on it, not knowin' if he was still there, nor Jon expecting her. See, she hadn't been in there for a day or so."*

"I knew it."

"Yeah . . . they were running out of boats and planes were coming in less. And the doctors didn't want him moved quickly. Then I woke up one morning and went out from under the camouflage coverings, and there was some U.S. Navy lieutenant and a petty officer guarding the plane. I asked him why and who sent him, and he said I'd find out soon enough. That's when I met Lt. Commander David 'Buck' Shaw."

"God's work . . her being the one, all of it, His hand." Then thinking ahead, the insightful young wife said, *"But you still had to get him outta there, papers and all . . visa and passport. Those wouldn't have been needed before. Who was going to ask you fellas for that up in Borneo out on that deserted coast you described?"*

"Yeah . . well in Singapore and Johore Bahru, bombs were fallin' every day and sometimes at night. Rumors had the Japs on the island already, but they weren't. People were just panicky. But it was down to the nitty gritty for sure. And we just decided to go. But then the doc said he wanted Jon on a ship

evacuating wounded to Ceylon. It got really scary because we could get trapped there, and we knew it was going to fall to the Japs. The British planes couldn't handle them. I was responsible for him, you know, I told the doc I would fly him out to Australia, and he said it was riskier that way . . more Jap ships and planes. He said the only risk on the Indian Ocean was German U-boats, and the ship would be marked with big red crosses. He said the plane ride with no doctors and many fuel stops was bad for him with a fever and all. There was some infection of the wounds.

Then we met US Navy Lieutenant Commander David 'Buck' Shaw, who was down there observing, and he wanted to requisition our plane for rescue, reconnaissance and such in the Southern Philippines, which we still held. He heard we'd come in and came looking for us in the hospital. Some thought, things weren't so bad yet, and the British thought they were still gonna win. Buck was the one who had put the guard on the Goose.

We resisted, but getting out and getting Maya out was going to be tough with British red tape. So, Lt. Commander Shaw said to me. 'Listen son, this war's going to play hell with all our lives. Give in to it and to God's will. Surely he wants you to do your duty.'

Then I said, 'We have to get back to family in Cebu.' But he replied, 'They won't be there son; they'll be in the hills, left for the Dutch Indies or Australia, just suffering through it all, or dead. But the thing is, you can't just fly in there like you normally would and help them. Those Jap fighters will cut your little slow flying boat to pieces.' And I saw his logic of it."

"How did you work it out then?" Sarah asked.

"He swore me and Jon in right then and there in the US Navy, right by Jon's bed. Then we went to the hospital office and asked to use a typewriter and paper. He typed up a reasonable facsimile of the proper forms and we signed up for service. He said it might not stick with the Navy later, that they'd send us back to basic training, but Jon was military age and the argument was presented to the doctor that he needed to get out for future U.S. Navy service. Then Lt. Cmdr. Shaw got busy trying to get Maya assigned to the ship Jon would be evacuated on. He was now officially in the military and arguably injured on duty in the war's first moments. There had been that plane attack at the dock you know. There were plenty of natives in the Philippines in the US services, so there was precedent for it. I'll tell it all later. I'm tired of talking right now . . not this . . just the throat is dry."

"Let's take a walk, eat something . . then maybe see if that old generator works and listen to some romantic music," Sarah responded. *"My whole collection's in the back of the car. Then there's that other thing we came here to do,"* said with a sweet innocent smile.

"Yes ma'am, sounds good to me."

And the day went just that way, with 'that other thing' periodically following various mundane activities and chores of life . . the stellar 78 rpm record collection aiding in the romantic mood that really needed no help . . she finally with the handsome and admirable older hero crush of her childhood and he with the pretty young nubile love of his life, who he could finally legally, ethically, and morally be with.

After dinner, as they curled together with some wine on the sofa, Jake related the rest of his adventures into the wee hours. Far back from when he had left off, intense pain had begun, and war now raged on the battle lines of the Pacific and people began to suffer quietly yet horribly under the captivity of the brutal, feudal, warrior controlled Japanese Empire. Women especially suffered, but it was shared by all. In Europe, across the Caucus and the Urals, and in North Africa dying was going on wholesale . . dying and suffering, rape and starvation. And by now

America was war driven too there at home, humming with production of the weapons that would arm her and the world.

The story continued to unwind from Jake's lips, and in the office of the hospital administrator, the naval officer had explained his plan stating that since Maya was not a nurse yet, the hospital could do without her services and the ship would need caregivers. Thus, he was going to try to get her aboard it.

The hospital chief replied, "We're going to need everyone we can get in the coming days right here."

"I understand, sir. But Malaya and Singapore are going to fall. Many are going to die here and many on those ships and planes leaving. But the ones on the ships will have a chance, especially those going west toward India. The biggest risk there is U-boats, and the German Navy still has some honor."

"We cannot give up our duty to these men here, these brave wounded soldiers who cannot be moved easily. Some cannot be moved at all."

"I understand that, sir, but the time will come when you will stand beside some of their beds in one of these wards and be shot or bayoneted, and then they will as they lay in their beds. Your pretty nurses will have to choose duty or to run and abandon them. We know how the Japanese have acted in China, especially in Nanking. Your wounded will, when that day comes, urge them to flee. That was their duty after all: to save the flower of British colonial womanhood, even the coffee colored ones. Those brave men wouldn't dare ask those girls to stay where they would have to lie in their beds and watch them being raped multiple times. We're fighting monsters, doctor. Why not get one heroic girl out with her equally heroic guy? Maybe one story will end well."

"I will ponder on this, Lt. Commander. We will need personnel on the *Star of Calcutta*. I had thought to send the most experienced nurses, but I need them here."

"Early this afternoon then, Doctor? We're flying out tonight. I'd like to see his disposition for that. Then I can take them both."

"I told you: he should not be on a small bouncing plane for hours and enduring takeoffs and landings for refueling."

"Well, ultimately that is my call, since he is not in your military. So please consider my request about the girl. I'd feel safer about it for him. If you send her with the patients, no one can argue about it. You have to send someone."

"One this afternoon Lt. Cmdr. Shaw. I'll give you my decision then."

After leaving the hospital office with the Malayan nursing volunteer's situation hanging and Jake in tow, Lt. Cmdr. Shaw went straight to the Goose that had been well guarded in the harbor. A day before he had placed his assistant, Lt. Alexander at the plane in uniform and armed. It was sort of a sign that he had already requisitioned it in his mind knowing that Jake, Steven, and Jon knew it was inevitable and logical for the benefit of them all.

Aviation fuel was hard to come by, but they had scavenged to top off the tank, having begged to be the ones to salvage a Dutch plane that had crashed in the harbor for the rights to the fuel. The Goose had been gassed when she arrived and only needed topping off.

In shallow water to begin with, the part of the plane containing the fuel tank was lifted to an old barge with a winch after all unnecessary parts had been cut off. A small plane, the tanks were not in the wings, and removing those helped reduce water resistance.

After leaving the hospital on the day Lt. Cmdr. Shaw expected an afternoon decision concerning Maya from the administrator, and moments after arriving at the dock near the Goose's mooring, troubles began. The small flying boat had been pulled out of her protective cover from view of bombers just a bit. It had been disguised as much as possible to look like lumber under randomly thrown tarps. This protected it somewhat from bombing or those who might want to steal it to get out of Singapore ahead of the Japanese invasion.

"We'll have to requisition this flying boat gentlemen," snapped a spry, skinny, Brit with a swagger stick and all too old an English diction and demeanor as he strode quickly down to the dock where the whole group of Americans and the other Malay girl stood. A literal caricature was the little man, and he exuded experience and perhaps heroics as well. He wasn't a paper tiger.

The yanks had assumed they were being watched for the weeks they had been in Singapore, and they knew the dire needs.

Lt. commander Shaw responded, "Sorry Major, I already have."

"Well, I'm sorry too, but this is our imperial lands right now and there's authority and rank and all that."

"Major, I believe we might be about equal in rank. As to authority . . I don't doubt it . . but not over us. I'm here in your waning 'imperial' area of authority as an American observer, and you cannot intercede in my legal actions…"

"But the plane is another thing, and civilian owned…"

"The plane has been requisitioned by me and its owner/operators recruited into the US Navy for duty back in the Southern Philippines with rescue and supply runs and such."

"Now see here, this won't do. This is British Singapore," and turning to the sergeant leading the little three-man detachment with him, he called out commandingly, "A guard down here Lewis!"

With that, Shaw drew and cocked his 1911, not yet pointing it at the major and shouted up to the British sergeant, "Belay that order Sergeant if you want your major breathing when you drag him off."

Focusing again on the officer, Shaw started to speak but was rebuffed by the other, "You're outnumbered by a whole army, navy, and air force sailor, you'd better stand down before you miss this whole war being locked in a British brig."

"No major, it will end here; and we will leave as planned or die defending US Navy property from a misguided ally. But before we do we'll destroy it. Your army is pretty occupied, your navy has no ships, and the air force no planes to chase us. And the Japs are about to change your precious authority rights here, just in case you aren't paying attention."

At all that the Brit huffed up speechless, while Shaw looked up toward the little army detachment and inquired of the red-faced major, "Who are the folks up there, the woman and child? Running out with your, family? I never heard an 'every man for himself' order being given out."

"And I never said I was leaving," the Brit, stated rather firmly.

"Is that all you wanted?" asked Lt. Commander Shaw, and the officer nodded solemnly.

Turning to Jake, Shaw inquired, 'Jake?'"

With an affirmative nod from the adventurous and experienced pilot, the American naval officer turned back to the major and said, "Okay, we can do it. We can take your family out, but I've a request."

The British officer stared at the American with a mix of emotions, residual anger, relief, and thankfulness.

"This patient, Jon O'Brian (showing a copy of Jon's newly typed 'Navy' papers with his photo attached) and there's a Malay girl working at that hospital, Maya," stated Shaw.

The British officer took the paper in his hands and Buck Shaw said strongly, "Get them on the *Star of Calcutta*, that hospital ship headed for Trincomalee. It's a tramp steamer, but they're painting her white and painting big red crosses everywhere: both sides, top fore and aft decks, and even the bow and stern. She's not a nurse . . one of those nursing student volunteers. She was on duty when we left moments ago. Use your boys there, order her. Don't leave the hospital without her."

With that the major started to protest, worried perhaps of the time or getting back to the argument of red tape, visas and such; but Shaw put up the hand not holding the gun, holding the free hand open palmed to stop things in their tracks. He placed his gun back in its holster.

"Get them there quickly. When we get to Darwin, we will get your wife and son to the right people and if there's a problem . . any criticism of her getting out . . I'll set them up at my own expense. My wife's in Sydney, and I have some money there. We're not rich, but we can help your family. I'll tell the authorities that it was my decision to get them out."

As he looked in the other officer's eyes, they were reddened and moist. The man looked straight back into his with that strong, brave British jaw jutted out, and each reached a hand out almost simultaneously, them shaking firmly, officer to officer.

Then the British Major said firmly, "They will be on the *Star of Calcutta* . . the two of them, Lt. Cmdr."

He then snapped to attention and gave Buck Shaw a smart very British salute, which was smartly returned.

Dusk was upon the newly formed intrepid little group of refugees, and that was the plan of the commanding officer: traveling at nightfall and through the night to best reduce the risk of encountering the enemy. Not overloaded, what with the reluctant change concerning Jon and Maya, the ship carried some extra small tanks of aviation fuel making the cargo compartment quite a bit more dangerous. The hope was that, if necessary, they could make a dangerous open sea landing and add that fuel to the plane's tanks. Jon and Jake had been a team flying the Goose for a year now. Jon, the namesake grandson of the business's schooner captain founder, was a bit younger and less experienced than Jake, and he didn't mind being the copilot. He and the smart, tough American had become close friends rather quickly and did everything together. They had finetuned the Grumman Goose's engines as long as they had been flying her, and the Goose just might make it to Australia without having problems finding fuel. There was at least one dependable port of call along the way.

There were six of them and one just a child, a crew and passenger manifest the Goose could easily carry. She was designed for a crew of two and a passenger load of eight adults. Besides Jake, Buck, Steven, the woman, and her child was a young Malay woman. Steven had missed the fight at the gin bar in North Borneo as he had been tasked with providing security for the two flying boats. The British major's wife had wisely left everything behind of any weight, bringing only extra, lightweight clothing, her jewelry, the family's personal documents, and a quite a few precious photographs. In such troubled times, the only mementos that really matter are the ones that show a loved one's face and form, loved ones perhaps to never be seen again. She had plenty of the major. The Malay woman was the one rescued with Maya and the two Filipina's and had not sought her family but remained with the group of the Goose. On a whim, Lt. Cmdr. Buck Shaw decided to take her out of danger out of compassion. He would claim her as an employee whose safety he felt responsible for, and maybe she would prove helpful as well. This act might have cut into the weight limits and reduced the amount of extra fuel, but the girl was quite petite, as was her people's nature. Helpful too was the lack of significant luggage any of them carried. Buck had uniforms in the apartment in Sydney. When not relieving Jake in the cockpit, Steven was tasked with constantly, on a tight schedule, checking for gas fumes in the cargo compartment. The lieutenant assistant of the commander while in Singapore and the petty officer that had accompanied them were assigned there and Buck prayed the two would get out or survive a Japanese occupation.

The Pratt and Whitney radials were warming up as the Goose and her refugees sat in the harbor of a doomed Singapore, and over the sound of them, Jake turned to look at the Lt. Commander as they sat side-by-side in the cockpit, speaking a bit passionately to match the atmosphere cast by the dark rose sky to the west and the darkening indigo easing in from the east.

"I can't abandon him sir. He's my responsibility; he's a brother in a way."

The younger man was quite emotional in a sort of stoic controlled way, and the officer, now the younger's superior replied firmly yet with compassion, "You have other responsibilities Jake, Seaman Jake Pierce. We all have many responsibilities now, and we have to choose. Being military helps as we don't always get to choose. The choices are taken away from us. By the way, I may get my butt kicked and be reduced in rank myself, but I have to lift you to petty officer first class, like an experienced sergeant in the Army or Marines."

"But I didn't just bring him, I was sent by the company and his dad, my boss. I was sent with instructions to do my best by him."

"And you have. He is in the best situation possible. You heard the doc: he needs care we can't give on this plane and may not find in Darwin. It's very rural, just an outpost town. It's "Old West'. He is her duty now, and we did ours to keep them together and give them the best chance. I think those two will stick together for a long time. This crucible of war will meld them together."

"They might get sunk out there. I don't trust the Germany Navy."

"And you could do what? Die with them in some lifeboat?"

"I might could get them to shore somewhere."

"Not in his condition. There is no 'somewhere' in the Indian Ocean. The only speck I'm aware of is Diego Garcia, the most isolated place I know of . . miles from anywhere. You have other duties now. Let her do hers. This war is bringing us together, you know . . different people's . . like her and him."

"But my duty to him an' I guess her too?"

"You have your parents. You told me of them. They're your duty too. The damn Japs may still invade the West Coast where they live. Like the rest of us now, you have many duties, and sometimes they conflict. You did the best for them, him and her. With my help, I might add. Now pay the Navy back and do your duty to the U.S. and your parents, sailor. Let's go after these Japs . . keep 'em busy in the Philippines as long as we can and away from America."

"Yes sir," Jake said sullenly, with his head down.

"When we're on the ground, give me a snappy salute at attention when you say that. I don't care that much, but you have to do it right in front of others."

"Yes sir."

Then the officer said, "Steven and the women are situating things. He's helping them with weight, balance, and such. As soon as Steven can get up here and relieve you, let's you and me get some coffee and discuss plans."

The two sailors, officer and noncom, sat with some freshly brewed coffee at the little fold up table in the plane, much like those in small floating craft.

"Now Jake, I'm gonna advance you to acting Petty Officer 1st. Class, which usually takes a few years. But I'll tell you this little open secret: In the air, as the experienced pilot, your superior to me. I can still have a say, and the final say as to strategic issues, destinations and such . . that is if it doesn't violate plane and crew safety in a way you are more knowledgeable about.

I was able to beg a *Blue Jacket's Manual* 1940 Edition, the new one just in time for this war, and it's yours. I got it from that Navy destroyer in the harbor. Now this is the new seaman's bible and good for all enlisted men except Chief . . Chief Petty Officers. I'm going to break some rules here maybe, but as soon as you demonstrate proficient knowledge of this book and can pull off acting like a sailor in public, I'm advancing you all the way to Chief. That usually takes years, and they think themselves the cocks of the walk, and I guess they are. They're the ones that get anything done in this man's Navy.

Now you'll be challenged if anyone finds out about this advancement, but it's legal. At least the rank is, 'acting CPO', but the speed I'm doing it probably isn't. They allow for it, enlisted pilots and acting chief petty officers. I went over it all with the destroyer captain. His main concern was only how fast it would go, after I described your experience and capabilities, planes and schooners and all . . and that bar fight. That you had validation on all of it from Jon, Steven, and the two girls, he was quite impressed. That's why you saw me questioning them all so seriously days ago. While we're airborne, as long as it's safe and we see no other aircraft, you turn things over to Steve and start reading and memorizing this manual. You told me you were a good student. You've got to become the best damn sailor in the navy real fast for us to pull this off. And it's important. It'll give you the respect you need when we get to Darwin and up into the islands again. Otherwise, they'll just take your plane away from you if anything happens to me. If I was a pilot, it would be different. Now last of all: no hesitation, no doubt . . self-doubt. Not only are you an experienced pilot, but a seaplane pilot. There's fewer of those and water landings are hard. Some jackass Army Air Corps pilot would crack her up the first time he tried. And you're a true seaman, before the mast and first mate too and all that. You can use a sextant, take sun and star sights. You are almost officer material. If you had college behind you, you would be. Bottom line, Jake: command the ship to Darwin, even if we get jumped, and study like your life depends on it because, as corny as it sounds, it does."

"Glad she's with him, not here."

"Good for him. That little gal is a true nurse in the making. But you meant more."

"Yeah. If she was here, a man couldn't study very well. Not this book anyways," said with a sullen expression and an almost imperceptibly wry smile.

Having learned much about Jake in the recent days, as he had grilled him for this recruitment and the job ahead, Buck said with a teasing smile, "Well, keep your mind off your little Indian maiden back home too, if you can. You'll be serving her best if you can."

"What a dramatic story, Jake," Sarah mused softly and with a level of emotional and intellectual depth discernable to her husband. He had held nothing back, even his musings about Maya.

Continuing she said, "I want to know about your moments in action of course. You know I do. I suppose it may be harder though. You know, it may be hard for you to tell. I just want to know all about my adventurous husband who has been through so much more than me."

"You've been through a lot, Sarah. You are a heroine to me . . how you handled yourself through everything . . both parents so close together and all that crap around town. And you still managed to have a popular business with all that. You have to know: it is going to get harder when I go. You know that. You're not a kid."

Her head was down, and she looked up at him with an understanding passing between them, and she responded, "Well, you're my hero beyond my wildest dreams all the while I hoped and waited for you to get back . . because your mom said you would. If you can do it, if I'm not hurting you with the asking, tell it all."

"Tomorrow. Let's hit the sack. I'm tired from the hike earlier and too much talking. But not too tired."

Continuing his tale to entertain his new wife after the next morning's breakfast, Jake related his tiredness taxing the Goose to the dock in Darwin, He was tired from reading as much as from monitoring Steven during the flight and taking his own turns at the controls. Once on the dock he was a bit moody and stared off to the west from whence they had come.

Recovering his composure from the somewhat cramped plane ride and the bouncing boat to shore, Lt. Cmdr. Shaw slapped the new petty officer on the back and said, "Focus on your duty, son. You're in it now."

"I almost read that manual from cover to cover twice, but I can't get them off my mind."

"Like I said, we did what we could for them, went farther than most might have. Pray for them, don't lose sight or concern of them, but turn your gaze to another horizon, one where an enemy lies hull down just over the edge of it."

He looked at the younger man, Jake *(who relating it all now to his wife, was not ashamed to show his soft side, his weakness).*

And the naval officer said. "Son. This is real life. And it's bigger than any of us have ever seen or contemplated. Grow up fast and put aside some of those emotions. Be a man and face doing what you don't want to do because you must. Because people will depend on you to. You're in this for the duration. We all are."

Lt. Cmdr. David Buck Shaw later found his two-man Grumman crew in a small pub. He had reported and told what he knew about Singapore's conditions and spoke by radio to his superiors in Sydney.

"Well boys, they approved my mission," Buck said to Steven and Jake as they all sat in the little pub. "Nothing else they could do, really. My command is independent of them, directly from U.S. Naval Intelligence. But we need their support, and I got it. I can't discuss it here. Too public. But they gave me what we'll need. They wanted the plane, but I stood my ground."

Then Buck bent down across the table low to its top and in toward them both, and they emulated him. He spoke just above a whisper, saying, "This is all I'll say now: It looks like we're headed back up to your neck of the woods. We've been assigned, on my request to my superiors, to make a supply run to the men on Mindanao and to then see who we can bring out with information before coming back for more. We'll be ferrying out men in my line of work, Navy or Army, men I know about and how to contact. Your Goose could be helpful in moving some commanders or vital personnel around . . or equipment . . or, if they're still flyin' rescue downed fliers. But really, I suspect we'll get in and get out. They can use natives in their bancas to move themselves around for guerrilla action. No need to risk a valuable asset like the Goose."

They all looked at each other and nodded solemnly, knowing they were needed and there was really nothing left in this world at the moment but war service. Nothing else mattered but family and those who were like family.

To that end, the latter concern, Jake inquired, "What about the folks in Cebu. They're like my family? It's their plane."

"It's not anymore . . not their plane. But it is their contribution, and it's been duly noted and recorded. They'll be compensated of course and given a chance to buy it back for surplus after the war . . first choice before others. But…"

"They're my family, like family, and I said we'd be right back. No one knew…"

"…that the war was coming, I know. But, as I started to say, we cannot use family as an excuse to lose an asset like that seaplane."

"Flying boat . . she's a flying boat." There was a pause, and Jake continued, "We cannot just abandon them. How will the girls fair under Japanese control . . and Lola Sunny . . she's strong and healthy, but can she handle hiding in the hills?" And with the last words he looked hard at the officer.

Steven put in, "I believe Lola Sunny can handle anything, 'til she gets older and feeble. That family has good bloodlines. Look at her mother. She was so strong 'til the last, at what? . . 90."

Lolo George and Lola Sunny Allison were in-laws to Jon, whose sister had married their grandson.

They were in their mid to late sixties but still healthy and active. It was an era in which many that age were fading but others like them, with their good genes and ruggedly healthy lifestyles, kept chugging onward with near full steam.

The naval officer spoke again with authority, kindly expressed though it was, "You'll have to do what we're told, to follow orders. You're in the Navy now, and you accepted it. I told you then there was no turning back, that is wasn't just a patch on things. You're in for the duration, and if you don't obey orders, you'll be disciplined. Now, that's just the way it is, and you accepted it. It got Jon and his girl out of Singapore and getting treated fair now . . for a native, you know. That's a blessing too. The Navy also kept you from being commandeered by the Brits and losing control of your flying boat."

"I accept things now, but they're still at risk."

"They have a chance. That's all any of us have out here where the fighting is."

The next pause was longer and more solemn, and then Lt. Cmdr. Shaw spoke again and more softly, "You did what you had to do boys. I would have had to commandeer your plane either way. Joining got Maya out, and her friend here with us. This way you may get to keep flying your plane. Now when we get up there to the Philippines, we'll ask around and try to find out as much as we can. And maybe our duty will find us up in Cebu. It's a central hub, you know. If I can, I'll make sure we get up there. They're letting me lead on this because you swabbies are still wet behind the ears Navy regs-wise. I contacted my superiors high up the chain right in Washington. I finally decided to live dangerously and spilled the beans. They accepted and approved your ranks and will cover for us with the Bureau of Naval Personnel. Naval intelligence sent a direct order to the people down here to honor your rank. It's all very tedious, what with everything having to be coded."

All three sat quietly once again, Jake and Steven relieved at the offer to try to get to Cebu, Jake especially. Finally, after many tips of a mug or pint glass, the officer spoke again.

"To the latter point, you fellows have been hitting the book haven't you . . the ole *Bluejacket's Manual*?"

"Yes sir, Dave."

"Well hit it harder; I've gotta get you some rank if you're gonna keep flying the Goose . . or anything. Not too many pilots are lower level enlisted men like Steven, but I didn't want to zoom both of you right up to 1st class right off the bat. They might think I'm irresponsible out here. They give us leeway but expect responsibility. Now I took the liberty of advancing you to 1st and 2nd class petty officers, but I want Jake, with the most hours at the controls to be a chief, CPO, and that's holy ground .

. . especially to all the other CPOs. That's top noncom in the Navy . . . can't go any higher . . like a Sgt. Major in the Army."

"Can you do that? You've been talking about it, but really?" asked Jake.

"Like I said, my bosses have authorized to that point, to CPO. The thing is: we have to deal with the people here and not bruise egos or get in a situation where we end up at the end of the food chain when it comes to fuel, ammo, spare parts, and the like. It's a long way over here to Darwin from the ports those things come into, Sydney and Brisbane. Like I probably mentioned, there is an "Acting Chief Petty Officer" rank, and we're using it. There's some Army Air Corps major flyin' out here somewhere I heard about . . in China maybe . . was a Navy CPO in the last war. They made him a major straight out because of service, age and experience, and he can fly. These things happen, they get done in war."

Over the coming two days and out of sight of anyone else, David Shaw drilled the fellows and ran through one practical test after another from typical boot camp drills: target practice, rope climbing, knot tying, uniform rules and inspection, seabag, landing party pack and equipment, and on and on. Actually, an old salty weathered chief did it, sworn to secrecy by the officer and bribed with beer.

Dave gave them little time and periodic tests of their readings, and he secured chief petty officers materials, including probably rarely used tests. He had secured as well the enlisted man's naval uniforms they were now wearing from the stocks slowly drifting in to Sydney from the States. Two men were not hard to do this for. Had it been a larger group, he might not have succeeded.

Buck Shaw was a legend in his line of work, subterfuge, and he found old friends to help him. Just what was needed, Buck discovered the CPO he had met in the Great War when a young ensign and the chief then a seaman. They served together and remained friends after the war as each advanced. He was able to convince the fellow and commandeer him from his assigned duty and placed him in charge of the two young sailors in training. While Buck waited impatiently, the chief put the two through an intense week-long boot camp and petty officer training.

Living close every moment for that time, Jake confided in the chief about the two girls in his life. During one of the more casual moments of talk he summarized the two and added later, in a moment of stressful training, that it would be so much easier if the chief looked like or even actually was either one of them.

Even in its condensed, concentrated intensity, the training needed two to three weeks; they had one and stretched it to another three days, ten days in all.

The two sharp new sailors learned fast and thoroughly, experienced young men of the South Seas, one born and raised there and one there for over four years now. They were both flying boat pilots and experienced as well as officers on schooners.

"Both of those swabbies are good material and pretty well formed now, Buck," the CPO commented to Shaw at the last evaluation report.

Such very close friends and former shipmates the officer and noncom could speak with friendly familiarity without rank, when in private.

"I'd like to take the credit and I guess I can a bit," the CPO continued. "But them being merchant seaman before all this and island pilots already an' bein' in an out of these beach bars has helped. Some of 'em out here are capable but bums. One's out here like these two with good character and upbringing and thuh experiences they've had are petty officer material. That Jake though, he's a rare breed."

Less than two weeks after arriving in Darwin and after a whirlwind course of study, having secured the materials needed to take to fighting men in the Philippine Islands, the three men were flying in the dark of night over the Arafura Sea.

Steven was in the pilot's seat and Jake the copilot's. Dave came up and stood behind them and announced, "Well, I had to do a little cajoling with those I asked for advice on this matter from Chief Barnes that has been working with you and the Navy personnel commander down there, but it wouldn't have mattered anyway . . since I'm on my own out here far from the ones who sent me and turned loose by them, given the state of things. So, here it is: it's official, to give you enough rank to squeeze the authority to fly naval aircraft, especially without too much interference from those we encounter should something happen to me, I'm appointing you Acting Chief Petty Officer, Jake, and your 1st Class petty officer status is formal now, Steven. It's legal, official.

I've got working duds for you back here and the caps. The dress blues and khakis will be in my apartment back in Sydney. I gave my wife your measurements. You won't need 'em on this jaunt and weight and space will be premium on the return. Get us back there and you get to wear them and impress the ladies. Our little Malayan, Sophia, will be impressed, I'm sure. By the way, Jake, my wife was in Brisbane before the hostilities. I didn't get a chance to tell you, but she's come up and met Sophia and the Brit's family last night while you fellows were loading the plane. We three had dinner and the gals hit it off swell. I don't know how she pulled it off, way up here. She's been a Navy intelligence officer's wife too long I guess, and we've been in Australia for years. She knows 'people' now too. Left the little girls with friends who're like family and hitched a ride in a C-47 all the way from Brisbane. Ann will make sure Sophia is treated fair and square . . says she intends for them to be inseparable. You never know, the Aussies can be a bit crude to natives too."

The two turned and looked at Dave, and he added, "These'll be good for quite some time, usually six months to a year, or as the need arises. Certainly, the need has risen, so who knows. If need be I can recommend permanent CPO rank, at least for the duration . . unless yuh screw up."

"Never saw myself in the Navy and now I'm top sergeant to use Army lingo? Guess I better get it right. What do we say, 'top chief'?"

"No, just 'Chief' or 'Chief Petty Officer' or 'CPO', Jake. If you find yourself later in different circumstances, don't be timid. It'll show weakness. But if another chief is around you can defer to him if his knowledge seems greater. And hash marks, service stripes, years of experience, mean a lot in that rank.

Now if we get up to Cebu or Panay, you fellows there can't go running off in the hills up there looking for his family. This is bigger than us; this is a war for us all."

"Yeah," commented Steven, looking over at his best friend, "think of Maya in the middle of the Indian Ocean now and Sophia back there in Australia. They've lost everything and maybe for good. And Sophia, she'd be alone now in a strange land if it weren't for Dave's wife."

"I need sharp eyes and minds right now, for the next few hours," Jake said suddenly changing the subject and the tenor of the conversation.,

"Understood, Chief. But that's true for the whole flight," responded the Lt. Commander.

"Yes sir. But until we make the rendezvous with the tender there can be no more distractions," the chief pilot, CPO Jake Pierce, said slipping into his role as commanding officer of the flying boat.

"We're still far out," Steven commented.

"I know, but this is likely a one-shot maneuver with little chance if we miss the rendezvous point due to any reason. We need to start now preparing ourselves mentally and physically. Without that fuel, we likely will not make land and will have to be picked up in the morning if they can find us. If the Japs find us first, it will mean a strafing."

"What do you want from us this far out from the position of the ship, Chief?"

"First, Sir, remember the seriousness of it. Secondly, study the coordinates and know at all times how far we are from the tender's location.

Third, turn all lights out except map lights and your flashlights when making notes. Fourth, help me monitor all radio transmissions.

We're instructed to send the coded signal when we're twenty miles out, and at that point, we should see their beacon when they flash it. They are supposed to answer our coded message with their coded reply confirming their location or giving any variance from it and then flash the red beacon twice every five minutes. Prepare yourselves now for those actions later. Periodic viewing of the dark sea to adjust to it would be a good idea but don't stare at it continuously."

"You requested those procedures, Chief. Why?"

"Lt. Commander, the procedure limits exposure of signals to anyone else in the area, short and sweet. That's why the tender captain agreed without question. Once we connect and they confirm their location through audible code, if we stare at the correct location, we'll see two blinks close together no matter how tired the eyes."

The Grumman with its crew of three cruised on through the pitch of night and encountered no problems. Night flying, long distance cruising was common, as the big Pan Am clippers and their British counterparts had done for a decade or more, but night fighting was rare to nil before radar would be perfected in the coming months. Flying low or high made little difference because the Goose's engines would be heard either way. Thus Jake, as flight commander, chose to fly higher in the thinner air for better economy and farther from any ship's guns or those on any island they flew near, lest a gun captain guess that they were the enemy. It was thought that any islands south of Mindanao down to Australia were still in good hands, but a gun emplacement commander might guess wrongly that the Goose was a Japanese plane, and a forward reaching enemy ship's captain might guess correctly that the plane was American or an ally.

Good relations and a working relationship with the developing Allied headquarters groups in Australia now paid off. Those organizations being set up would lead the way back into the Southwestern and Central Pacific that was in the process of being conquered by the Japanese as the Goose flew north into the teeth of it. Her brave crew first had to rendezvoused with a tender south of Maluku Island in the Banda Sea to refuel, and Jake's natural talents and sometimes unexplainable expertise for one so young were called on to land in the slight chop of the open sea and taxi close enough to the tender for the refueling to take place. This was one of the hallmarks of World War II, the attempt and completion of tasks that would not have been tried in peacetime except during emergencies. The War was one big, giant emergency.

The refueling finished, the Goose then headed across the Celebes to Ternate off the West coast of North Maluku to top off the tanks. The distance of the trip was such that one refueled when the opportunity arose, whether fuel was needed or not, because there may be no fuel source when the tanks became empty. Urgency was imperative, for on the return, these very places might no longer be in Allied hands to acquire the precious aviation fuel. As the Japanese marched southward across the map of the Pacific, the crew of the Goose needed to complete the round trip to the Philippines and back to Australia as quickly as possible.

Seeking shelter from view as the sun would rise before they could reach the Southern Philippines, the intrepid travelers flew across N. Maluku to find a sheltered cove or harbor on its eastern shore to wait out the day as far from Japanese forces as possible.

In the evening of the next day, the little Grumman plunged forward through the night over the seas where the Celebes Sea met the Pacific Ocean just south of the Philippine Sea portion of it.

Allied military men had laughed at the supposed pin point Japanese strikes outlined on many a map now in Allied offices and strategy rooms. But they were blows, not pin points, and any narrow points of incursion were now made by men such as this brave trio. There would be no support. There was no U.S.

aircover. For Japanese forces had now landed at Davao in the southern Philippines. The three Navy men were on their own when the Goose came in for a landing in the very early morning on Lake Lanao, in northwest central Mindanao in Moroland. No great carrier fleet would be cruising out to the east toward the dawn in the Philippine Sea. America was a little timid at the moment. Just in January, the carrier Saratoga had been torpedoed by an Imperial Japanese Navy submarine four hundred or so miles out of Hawaii.

Among allies on the lake, the crew of the Goose was tasked with flying to Cebu to pick up several men with information and combat experience against Japanese planes and ships. They were the intelligence officers Buck Shaw came for and they were pilots and a PT boat (patrol torpedo boat) executive officer who had engaged the enemy in the fight in in and around the islands. Their reports would be needed urgently in Australia, where Allied counter attack efforts were being staged. Perhaps there would be too many for the Goose. Time would tell. She would be loaded on the basis of the importance of the knowledge they carried.

Looking at Buck across the small table where they were grabbing a good meal, Steven inquired, "Well, sir, are we gonna have time?"

"To check on them? Perhaps."

Looking at him with wide eyes of surprise, Jake's head rising quickly from the well apportioned plate, the two transplanted 'Cebuanos' listened intently to his elaboration.

"If they're waiting by the docks, no. I mean our official passengers. But our important human cargo may not know we're coming . . well they do and they don't. According to the skipper here at this impromptu base, they've been notified to expect it but don't know when. They should be there, but the skipper says they haven't found two guys who they really want to get to Australia. These fellas are, or were, up in the hills with captured documents and maybe a captured Jap. They're important, as is their prisoner, but communications are bad. We cannot radio very much around here and be discovered. The bottom line is: no one knows for sure who will be there when we get there."

"So…"

"Wait a minute, I'll lay it out. If we come in and they're ready, everything's shipshape, we refuel and we're gone. If we have a wait of over an hour, Steven can try asking around. Chief Pierce, I need you by this plane 24/7, guarding, babying, preparing. It's not just the plane. I'm going to make you the best damn flying boat sailor in this man's Navy. And . . . I cannot afford to lose you. Now if the wait is longer, Steven can go up to their house and attempt to find them, find out their plans, check on their situation. If they are heading into the hills as you think . . capable people that they are, they could be valuable assets. I do not believe the Japs are on Cebu. If we find out different when we get there, Petty Officer First Class Steven Ericson's going nowhere. We need him too."

As with the approach and landing in Mindanao, the flight up to Cebu was riskier than in the Celebes, what with the enemy generally in control of sea and air. Most escapes, supplying, and infiltration of new fighting men were being affected by the undersea route with submarines. Now, however, no new men were coming in. The United States had given up on holding the Philippines, and her sons and daughters were on their own save for the supplies trickling in and the few taken off, mostly civilians, military nurses, and essential personnel with essential knowledge. Those, the latter, were why the Goose and her crew were there. Again, the short hop from Lanao to Cebu, where Buck had now learned his important human cargo was, was made in the pitch of night, as the crew waited a day for the moon to wane more, going sooner than they wanted but necessary due to the urgency. Of course, the boys from Cebu were excited about this turn of events.

The Goose came into Cebu in the early morning hours to enable a visual landing in the channel between the big island and little Mactan opposite Cebu City, where Filipino hero Lapu Lapu had killed Magellan. At a moderate height and a bit out from the coasts of the islands, they hoped to avoid night patrols. Impromptu waist gun ports had been fashioned when the crew found guns shipped from Brisbane to prepare planes for such missions. These were made in each side and thirty caliber machine guns were mounted with a clear acrylic window above them. Two had been mounted in the nose too, controlled by the pilot. All this work had been done in Darwin with parts shipped for such purposes from Sydney. In a fight, Jake would pilot alone, and Steven and Buck would each take a waist gun. The Goose was not fast or maneuverable but might be able to take care of herself against a lone attacker in the dark of night. The difficult problem was the tail, where enemy fighter pilots always loved to attack from. Most slower planes were vulnerable to an attack from that position. And in the early days of the war, even Allied fighters were slower than the now iconic Japanese Zero. Some naval bombers had a rear directed tail gunner position in the cockpit behind the pilot. The new TBF Avenger would come out to the fleet with an actual rear-facing, clear, ball turret mounted with a machine gun.

Coming in to the channel between Cebu and the little island of Mactan, Jake actually briefly thought of Magellan's death there as death was becoming a part of his and the lives of others. He himself had killed now, after all.

Dawn was barely reddening the Eastern sky as the Grumman came in over the southern end of the channel. After flashing recognition lights toward the area of the beach that had been indicated by the command in Lanao, Buck took his position by one waist gun. Both pilots were in their seats and Jake was in control, but Steven now went back to the other waist gun.

Suddenly, all hell broke loose as machine gun fire could be heard and flashes seen out of the dark, high to the Northeast. It was all in Jake's hands, as he was the lone pilot and the events were unfolding rapidly as they always do in air combat.

The luck was that the enemy was forward and not on the Goose's tail where air combat pilots were able to attack without being shot at unless the targeted plane had a tail gunner. In the darkness of the morning, the Japanese floatplane pilot cruising across Mactan to learn what he could of American held Cebu City probably was as surprised to see the Grumman as Jake was to be fired upon at that particular time. The enemy had no time to maneuver for positioning for the attack and had to take the opportunity that had been given him by fate.

The Grumman crew had known this could happen; but, as luck or God blessed them, in his surprise, the enemy had fired and missed. And Jake Pierce, a unique man that his parents had raised from the material God had given them, had flipped yet another switch in his life. A reluctant recruit weeks ago, he was now the consument warrior the Navy and his country needed, a professional. And people would soon notice.

First and in an instance after the Nip's machine gun burst and after he could just see the Aichi 'Jake' come slightly into view as the dawn's glow coming over the eastern horizon hit its long canopy and upper fuselage, Chief Pierce pushed the Goose down and to starboard (right) as quickly and safely as possible to order throw off the enemy's next burst. He took the Grumman down and to the northeast off his northern heading (but only for a moment like a boxer's fake in hope of throwing off an opponent's fist), as the enemy had seemed to be bearing just a bit toward the west . . Then he quickly climbed back at full throttle and turned to port and straight back into the Japanese Imperial Navy floatplane. That was seemingly suicidal for the slow, small, charming passenger/cargo plane that the Grumman Goose was. But a physically and mentally blessed man, Jake was a quick minded, quick studied, and quickly reflexive pilot now . . and with a long burst from the twin forward thirty calibers in the Goose's nose, Jake burst the Nip plane and the dawn into yellow and orange splendor and woke up Cebu City.

The Grumman was quickly taxied to a chosen spot up the coast a bit and camouflaged under unassuming greenery. Her importance made it one of the more important jobs at hand. Word had been sent into the back country for the delayed or missing Army officers of some importance, and Steven and Jake relaxed, knowing they would have a chance to try and locate the family. On their commanding officer's request, the anxious former employees of the O'Brian Transport Company sent word to the O'Brian estate with a local they knew and trusted.

Relieved of the need but not the desire to go visit the comfortable, embracing O'Brian home themselves, the two men checked every detail of the Goose, as they would at each point of every mission. Wartime conditions left no room at any time for any error or miscalculation. Already important in the art and business of flying's teenaged developmental years, aircraft condition and maintenance were ramped up many levels now that flying was an integral tool in wartime.

Late in the afternoon, at the little shack that served as an aircraft workshop, makeshift galley, and tiny aircrew barracks, several visitors appeared.

The older Allison couple, whom Jake revered now as he had gotten to know them, came down the coast from the O'Brian estate to see him. Both were in their mid-sixties and looked at least a decade younger. Often away from their home base in the Philippine Islands, the world traveling couple stayed with the O'Brians in Cebu or the Jefferson's in Iloilo on Panay where they had rooms of their own, apartment suites really, at both locations.

With them were Rosario O'Brian, now sixty-seven, and her youngest daughter, who was thirty. All warmly greeted the two sailors with handshakes and hugs seasoned with tears. All knew the hard days ahead that might see them never again meet, that might see several of them dead.

They were all heroes to Jake, a mountain boy who had grown up to be capable in the wilds but had never tasted the dangers these new friends of but a few years had in their daily lives at sea and in the air, surrounded by a beautiful tropical region full of risks.

Explanation was offered for the lack of presence of the others, who were now busy hiding valuables or preparing for a flight to the hills and other counter actions to the rude and brutal invasion of their land. All were quite bright and knew the Philippines was about to be conquered; for, if not, the Americans would be putting up a greater fight with larger amounts of war materials and sad quick meetings like the one they were engaged in would be fewer and farther between.

Looking at Jake, whom she had long ago picked out as a special man in the family company, half Navajo

Lola Sunny Kathleen Allison laid a soft left hand on his shoulder, saying, "We're proud of you in that uniform Jake, even if it is a working one. I'll bet you cut a fine figure in a dress Chief Petty Officer's uniform. Those Aussies fighting in North Africa should be worried for their girlfriends in Sydney when you get there." And as she said it her words revealed much knowledge of military things and current situations. The woman had always liked the look of a man in uniform, and both of her husbands were soldiers.

"I wouldn't do that, Lola, steal another man's girl, especially a fighting man doing his duty."

"I suppose you wouldn't. You're a straight arrow, Chief Pierce."

He could sense it, had for such a long time now, that he was a favorite of the woman just as if he were blood kin, a younger son or a grandson. It was no coincidence that she and her husband, the former Capt. George Allison, U.S. Army, were the ones who had come to see him from the now furiously busy members of the several connected families.

Placing both hands on his shoulders and looking him kindly in the eyes, the woman said, "What of that girl? Have you heard from her?"

"No ma'am, but I didn't expect it," Jake said with his eyes looking down now.

"That's right, you said it was a casual relationship at the current time. It's been so long, Jake; what makes you think . . I mean…"

"…she'll still be there," he finished it.

"I'm sorry, yes, you said she was your mother's friend. I suppose you know."

"My mother . . She says she is still unmarried. And it's the people there, and Mom thinks . . Well, she believ…"

"…you are meant for each other," said softly with a certain weird, soft firmness as from an oracle, one might imagine.

He had never told all of this to Lola, and he looked up to her quickly, as if in slight surprise.

Then he confirmed his view on it, "Yeah, I guess."

"And 'the people' there? What . . because she's an Indian?"

And as he nodded slightly, Lola evaluated it, "Well maybe that keeps her safely saved for you. A silver lining of sorts."

Lola Sunny took his two hands in hers, which would have embarrassed a weaker man in front of his friends. But then he didn't realize either how stunned the onlookers were at her combination of beauty and age. With a pretty woman, a guy could get away with many things without being harassed, or at least knowing it was harassment born of jealousy.

The woman said to him, "Jake you speak to that girl. If this mess is short, you get to her when you can. If you're stuck out here too long, cable her, call if there are connections, or just write. Tell her how you feel. It's hard. I know. But if you don't come back from it; she'll find someone someday. But at least she'll know, and she can carry that with her forever. You owe her that. Cable, it has more drama and thus more impact."

Then she reached her right hand back to Rosario's daughter who was holding a small canvas string bag rolled up around its elongated contents. Taking it the graceful lady turned back to Jake commenting with the soft, full strength for which she was known, "It's time for you to have this . . from one adventurer to another." And she leaned over and kissed his left cheek. There followed a deep embrace between the two, he now holding the bag, of which (instinctively and from the feel of it) he knew what was within.

Her husband stood back smiling with arms folded across his torso, and the young Navy Chief took a step toward the former Army Captain with his hand out to shake. But the man saluted him instead. It wasn't protocol of course for an officer, even former, to salute an enlisted man first, and Jake thought perhaps the former soldier was just caught up in the moment, this pregnant moment filled with so much emotion, duty, pride, and fear.

And yet, as he returned the salute and the two shook, George elaborated, "I just figured you're going into the teeth of it. You deserved that salute."

"Thank you, sir. But Captain, you folks are too. An occupied land can be the worst. They won't let me take you out. The government's confiscated the Goose."

"We wouldn't go, but you knew that. We figure folks here will need morale lifting and moral support and detailed leadership. You know, real ideas, not just platitudes."

"Sir, I wouldn't stay among 'em. They're brutal. Surely, you've heard of some of the stories out of China, Nanking especially."

"I realize it, but these people?" Lola spoke, "We have seen some of these Japanese here and talked with small store keepers and farmers who have dealt with them. I sense in some of them a certain duplicity, though I believe many are innocent and good. Others? I believe there is some arrogance, a racist superiority. Look at what they've done: a modern navy in just a few decades. Why, when we were fighting our Civil War, they were still medieval and feudal."

"In the hospital with Jon, we heard brutal tales from wounded British troops."

"How is Jon? His Uncle Thomas said he was badly wounded."

"Yes, and, where is he?" added George.

Feeling responsible and looking down, Jake then lifted his head and said, "We arranged for a ship to Trincomalee on Ceylon, if they can make it. They said it would be boldly marked for a hospital ship, but I don't trust the Nazi U-boats."

"'They'? You mean the ship's compliment. Then he's alone."

Still avoiding eye contact with Rosario and Melba, who were standing behind the couple he addressed directly, Jake said, "We couldn't bring him. He needed the doctors going on that ship. She went with him. The girl we saved, one of 'em, she went. She, Maya, a pretty Malay nurse . . she feels responsible, and I think they're in love."

And he looked down again. Rosario O'Brian standing just behind Sunny was Jon's grandmother and Melba was his aunt.

"Look up, sailor," barked George, but not harshly. And meeting the younger man's upturned gaze, the Captain said, "It was not your fault, sailor. You get it through your head. You are about to experience hell on earth and none of it will be your fault . . not as long as you do the best you can, even in the mistakes you make."

"It just… I mean, it…"

"It just happened," spoke Lola Sunny, echoing her mother's words to her years ago.

Bravely and firmly holding up the gift still in its bag, the young, tough American looked at her and said, "I'll consider it a loan. You'll get it back, Lola . . when we meet again over some cold calamansi juice or some Tanduay."

Even at sixty-five years of age, the 'halfbreed' American Indian woman, what the Old West had once negatively referred to as a 'breed', still looked stunning, just as, over several decades, many a man had whispered to himself when she would walk by. In spite of the bigoted eras stacked on top of each other since before the Civil War, one might still wonder how many white men would have pursued her romantically had she been unattached and available. She had been for some time, some eight years: unattached but not available after the Cuban Campaign widowed her at a mere twenty-two. But one thing was for sure: had such occurred, not one of them could have used her minority ethnicity to dominate her as a wife.

A few more words were said in private between the two warriors, Jake and Steven, and the visitors to the little impromptu seaplane base, after they had formally taken their leave of Buck. Tears were shed, and words of encouragement all around, and finally more hugs from all of the O'Brian Company who were present.

Rosario held both of Jake's forearms after a warm hug of greeting and before the one of goodbye. Gripping them strongly with encouragement and love, the woman, who as a young scared girl once ran away to sea and found love, spoke strongly to him as she looked straight in his eyes.

"You did not cause it Jake. Whatever happens to my grandson_ it is not your fault. You get that in your head. Those were young women in danger in the worst way a woman can be. I have been there like them. Two times I have been close to such risk. You men that day had no choice but to try to save them. Otherwise, other behavior . . choices, would have left you less than men. Some duties cannot be avoided even if failure seems certain."

Jake was emotional and trying to hide it; they all were of course. As they broke the last embrace between them, first from Rosario, whose story he knew, and then from Sunny, the goodbye embrace, Lola Sunny said to him, "When we were going back to Turkey in '22, we received word that my mother was very ill. We sought to rescue friends working there in Anatolia who were worried about the attacks against Christians by Muslims becoming ever worse. They were Armenians and Greek Catholics and other Christian sects. We rushed to my mother's side in Iloilo on Aaron and Pilar's estate. We had stocked the ship, Manual and Teresa's two masted-schooner *Isabella,* and people were expecting us: friends there in danger, archeologists who were Christian and of course endangered. A terrible slaughter was raging in Anatolia, a massacre of Christians at the hands of Turkish brigands. But we stayed a week with her, and I would never have left her side. She was more than 'mother' she was everything: mentor, teacher, spiritual guide . . even model for myself. You know the stories. But after those few days, those too few days with her, she said to me, 'Kathleen, your duty?' And before I could reply, she said, 'Stay with me as long as you can, but no longer than you can. Lives are at stake.' We sailed eventually, sooner than I wanted . . we arrived just when the fires were at their worst in Smyrna, the terrible heat driving the people down to the docks and the long concrete quay there. It raged for days, ten days, and we took so many children from their mothers' arms willingly given up . . We would put them on boats going to Greece and go back close in for more. You could not dock for the people would swamp or capsize your vessel. We stood off a few yards and sent the boats in close enough for them to toss the little ones safely to us, and the heat was searing. Manual and Teresa and their crew had to struggle to hold a sailing ship just right in the winds at such risks. Go, do your duty, Chief Petty Officer Jake Pierce. George and I and the others will serve in some capacity here. When we returned from the Mediterranean, my mother was alive and lived another fourteen years to die at ninety. There is hope we will meet again, Jake."

Later, just after the company group had left, Lt. Cmdr. Shaw sucked in a deep breath and said, "That is the most beautiful older woman I have ever seen. What is she, fifty-five or so?"

"Sixty-five and still handles a horse better than anyone I know," replied Jake, opening the bag and taking out Jóhonaá's khukuri.

Glancing up he saw the officer's surprised look blending with the previous one of awe at the woman's beauty. It was a time in which sixty-five could be considered old, even elderly; and yet, with good genes and healthy living it became more like the upper half of middle age or literally just middle age. Lola Sunny pushed it back even more into early middle age.

"She is the 'Jaguarundi'," an unassuming Filipino worker stacking supplies for the Goose put in without invitation. "You in your family never speak of it, but we know. Many of us know."

With that, the Navy men all looked at the man who had interrupted a discussion that he was not a part of. Buck noticed the weird shock on the two sailors' faces, as if shocked and not.

The dock worker, who had been preparing to load the Grumman, stopped and looked up. And with arms down to his side, said with some hint of pride,

"She is the Jaguarundi, and she will fight. She is old but strong and 'still young' . . and Filipino now. She brings the warrior of her American native people here to blend with ours, like Lapu Lapu and Nay Isa. They will go to the hills, she and her soldier husband and their children and grandchildren. They will fight, and I will ask to join them. I leave to see them tonight."

Then he bent to his work.

Looking back at the two sailors, Buck inquired, "What did she give you in that bag, Jake? Let's see it."

Stepping over to Buck and joined by Steven, Jake showed the Nepalese Army knife with its right side facing up and then dramatically rolled it slowly to reveal the left side, where carefully and delicately in small script, 'Jaguarundi' had been carved into the rosewood handle by the not prideful woman's husband. Khukuris in British Army service usually had buffalo horn or rosewood handles, and this one was rosewood and had been easier for Capt. George Allison to carve carefully.

The officer took another deep breath and said, "Well, we've got to get on the ball if we want to get out of here so you can tell me some of the stories this knife portends and all be alive for the telling. We may be one of the last planes out. The Japs are in West Borneo. We'll soon be cut off. But right now, we have to see if our precious human cargo has been found."

The two Army officers finally arrived just before the decision to leave without them was to be made. It cost two other men their chance home, but the seat for the enemy captive was still available, as it was decided to leave him to local U.S. military intelligent officers. He was talking some and the change of scene to Australia might scare him enough to shut him up, and it was felt that his knowledge was such that they may have gotten the most important of it, which was now in the report that the Goose's valuable passengers would carry on the long flight ahead. His seat was filled quickly with another American with valuable new lessons from the raging campaign in the islands. He was one of the two almost left behind.

Refueling would be somewhat a dangerous guessing game on the return. The only possible plan was to get to unthreatened Allied territory which meant essentially British territory, as it was becoming clear that, if Singapore fell, the even weaker defended Dutch East Indies would as well. With the enemy encroaching from the West already, the brave naval aviators must soar across the eastern edge of those East Indies, exotic to the white American and tenuously held by England and Holland so far away in Europe. Whenever Jake was around his new female Malayan friends, he could not help but dream of Sarah, who didn't look like them but . . well looked similar or . . at least they were reminiscent of her, of his time with her . . a time of feelings that had to be withheld just as with them now.

The spreading new Japanese Empire was edging much too rapidly southward toward Australia and eastward as if to cut off the Philippines. In lieu of aviation fuel, high octane gas could be used in an emergency but with poor results in engine and plane performance. But the danger was ever closer as Darwin had been bombed by some units from the Pearl Harbor attack. An attempt would be made over the Celebes to contact the seaplane tender as before. Coded messages sent just before landing to hide during daylight would set up the time and night for another rendezvous with the seaplane tender in the Banda Sea. The alternative would be to fly down the southern coast of Papua New Guinea to Port Moresby, hoping to find fuel sources along the way.

The young war wife, Sarah, knew her 'man' got out. He was sitting there cuddling her and entertaining her with these ever too close and scary tales. But she wondered: Did he alone survive each chapter? For she was bonding, as listener to character, to these friends of his. And they represented real lives. And the story wasn't over, even her husband relating it did not know the outcome.

In the darkness along the Mindanao, coast not long after becoming airborne, there was a burst of gunfire from below, antiaircraft fire. The Grumman had just left Lake Lanao on the big island, where her fuel tanks had been topped off, and the crew expected no Japanese naval units there. If it was a Jap, it revealed boldness and the weakness of the American air and sea forces; if the ship was American, it unmasked a weakened strategic and tactical position in the Indies (of which the Philippines were a part) that had bred carelessness out of fear.

Swerving away and seaward to the east, Jake looked down and saw the flash of a second burst coming from off the coast, from two closely positioned sources, and concentrated. He guessed it was a small craft but large enough to have multiple AA mounts. To Lt. Cmdr. Shaw, the sense was that they were twenty-millimeter rounds, and he said so. Jake filed it away in his memory for future reference.

One round had gone through the fuselage in the rear midsection with no apparent damage, having not been explosive or not exploded if it was. Steven went back and worked with Buck on a patch to prevent wind ripping at the hole. Though aluminum, not fabric, the crew was precautious in every detail. A round of the significantly destructive 20mm also went through the tail supporting the rudder, near the top and near where the rudder attached but the actual support and the control cables were not currently affected; and thus, not being able to see the hole, the crew was clueless about it. The Grumman charged at cruising speed southeastward away from the coast and the danger and then bore on a more southerly heading toward its new, temporary home. But on the route, food for the engines would become the new, unavoidable, passive danger; for, the brave men, crew and passengers, could become marooned in unfriendly territory surrounded by a growing enemy presence.

There ensued a long uneventful flight for some hours and measured nautical miles, and as if they weren't in control of the story, the lovers, storyteller and his audience, would break as if waiting for the next action to occur like it was happening to them. With such breaks, they would eat or snack, depending on the time of day; and they would make torrid love, no matter what time of day. That hunger always led to a full course meal.

She teased him with a maturity beyond her years, standing once at the bedroom doorway leaning on its casement, ankles casually crossed, left arm reaching up and holding her weight against the frame, completely nude, dark hair flowing and said, right hand on her hip as if impatient, "Come on, sailor, I got customers." And of course, he was all of them. And why the boldness, the worldliness and where did it arise from within the strong, shy, inexperienced young girl he had left behind?

Well, the somewhat cloistered but learned only child of a hardworking small family and farm and of a denigrated people had grown up while he was gone, grown up all by herself: had read everything she could and listened to every hit song that enculturated as did the movies and newsreels and radio . . and the social abuse she endured and innuendos from local men as well . . knowing she was a young, nubile, orphaned, marginalized Indian woman, fair game, a target. . . . . Hard work honed her too: the farm and the grill, the breakfast and lunch rushes, working alone as her mother's health faded . . and knowledge: breeding sheep and cows and horses and attending to their births like a midwife . . . more a woman than all the town girls all added up together with a tidy pink bow on the bunch of them for good measure.

Now? Now she would grasp the moment . . . this honeymoon that might become the defining moment of her whole life, maybe the only one that would ever matter.

Her schoolgirl crush had been on target . . correct. Her prince had come home from a quest to the young princess. Her prince charming was right here right now . . . vindicating her socially, but that didn't matter. Those people weren't there. He was there. That's what mattered. He was there now and then he wouldn't be . . and might never be again, blown to little pieces thousands of feet above the big blue Pacific that she had often driven down to Point Reyes just to see . . and sometimes all the way to the rocky coasts at Big Sur, over two hundred miles away just to look out at, . . knowing his mother had said he was there, out there somewhere. Driving on a Friday night after closing the grill, she would grab a room in an inn, staying through Sunday and imagining life with him. His mother had encouraged her after all, said he'd be back. It wasn't crazy. Sarah wasn't stupid, she could sense where Ann Pierce's concern was. It was transparent.

Those drives were the young teenaged woman's only respite from the mountains she loved, a complete change of scenery and a ray of hope for a future life. Someday she would break out from her past; she just wasn't ready.

The story came true, the fairy tale, and how often did that happen in these modern times? He would soon be off to some crusade, and how often had that ruined the story through the ages?

Given it all, the circumstances, she would be what he wanted . . just as sweet and loving, slutty and teasing, and raunchy as he asked. It was legal, they were married, and she figured God wouldn't mind. Those were a bit classier times in some ways, people actually thought about such things, about what God might think. Beyond that she thought about the happiness she had found . . they had found . . and that this might be their only time together . . . ever.

The Goose flew south as if one of its namesake Canadian Geese fleeing winter, which of course it actually was, though not fleeing the threatening cold . . . these people struggled for survival in the warm, storied South Pacific.

In the morning glow from the eastern horizon the little flying boat flashed recognition signals above and off the coast of Waigeo where the crew knew there was a temporary allied British presence in the Dutch Celebes . . and fuel. It was just for such needs as theirs for as long as it could be maintained and still had the precious liquid.

Sitting beside the tethered plane at a table on the little wooden dock, sheltered (as was the flying boat) by real palms and banana trees and by fake ones as well, the crew felt reasonably safe as the mooring was a bit away from the recognizable town as seen from skyward. Little did the allies know how deep and thorough the Japanese intelligence ran, and that they knew every anchorage and inlet intimately throughout the Southwest Pacific and Southeast Asia . . the Indies.

To Buck, Jake stated, "Sir, I believe our greatest threat is scout planes. We're on the leading edge of their push to Australia, and Darwin below is the logical desolate prospective beachhead far from our forces in Australia. Float planes and those fast fighters of theirs, alone or in pairs are what I expect. Like when we arrived at Cebu thuh other morning."

Marveling within at the new acting chief's analytical skills and learning curve, Buck replied. "I concur, well said. But if they plan to land there, they have to take Port Moresby first or they've let themselves be automatically outflanked. We'd be, I mean our forces would be behind them. To capture Port Moresby, they have to come down into the Coral Sea or across the rugged Owen Stanley Mountains."

"Well, we know it now; we'll be waitin' for 'em. I mean our troops. But as to our situation: we're gonna need more fuel to get anywhere from here." We'll be a few miles short of Darwin after topping of here."

Each time the Goose was put down on the water, fueling was immediate to be prepared for any emergency that might arise. Then Jake would take a banca or small skiff out and check the takeoff channel for the next liftoff. It should be done right before flight, but that was a luxury that they did not always have time for.

A little beer to relax with some tall tales and then sleep, followed in the dark wee morning hours with coffee to burn off its effects after a few hours of sleep. And morning saw the three Navy men and their full load of passengers, eight military men with valuable information, ready to take off across the dark bay. The stories the night before were mostly what little Jake and Steven knew of the legendary Jaguarundi as Buck had previously requested in Cebu. The two transplanted Americans knew quite a bit about the American expatriate matriarch of the Allison family and her equally adventurous and courageous American husband. All the passengers joined in and listened with some belief more than doubt. All had been stationed in the Philippines quite a while. Some had heard of her.

What reached into Jake's chest into his heart and into his mind as well was how much Lola Sunny (secretly and not so secretly, known to many as the Jaguarundi) looked like his Sarah. The resemblance leaped from the older woman's more youthful photographs. He imagined, though one was half Navajo and the younger one only a smidgen of that but mostly Blackfoot . . he imagined Sarah aging ever so gracefully into a near twin of the elegantly beautiful Sunny Kathleen. What a pleasant lifetime that could present. Since both shared the same pleasantly rounded, moderately flat nose that hinted of the cute 'pug nose' of the typical Filipina, Jake attributed that to their shared Navajo blood.

The Japanese scout pilots knew their job and what they could get out of it beyond scouting. If their presence did not have to remain a secret because of their Nation's greater forces in the region than the Allies, these experienced air warriors knew how to squeeze out a victory here and there for their empire and themselves, even though combat pilots in only a secondary role. One way was to peruse allied coastal bases and inland towns for planes sneaking in and out in the darkened hours, catching them in the deep early mornings and late evenings (each with reddened bloody skies) when the target crafts' commanders and pilots felt safer to take off or land.

It was still dark when the Goose stood up on the step, and they had to hope nothing had floated or blown into the harbor each time they did this in the darkness. They hadn't the luxury of the big Pan Am Clippers before the war of having a second boat visually, and if necessary, physically sweep the takeoff channel each time.

She reached enough speed and, as she lifted off the water, Jake said a little prayer. The first leg to safety was behind them.

The little cove was misty, and as the Goose climbed for altitude a lone floatplane off a Japanese cruiser just north of Papua was hovering near, another floatplane with a pretty large pontoon float beneath rather than a flying boat with a hull like the Goose. Again, as in Cebu harbor, the pilot made the mistake of being a bit to high so as to be farther to mask his engine noise to the little flying boat's crew on the water before takeoff. When taxying, taking off, and flying, the twin Pratt and Whitney engines would drown out any small attacker at some distance away.

The Nipponese pilot put on speed, as he had stayed just a bit away, but Jake had seen him, having learned in Cebu to scan the cloud tops as soon as he was airborne and the slight hint of dawn till glowed quite high.

The passengers gulped and gasped as the little hybrid amphibian vessel made the sharpest roll and descent its designers had drawn into her (and maybe pulled a few more G forces than the blueprints specified). Jake was headed for the harbor again and the overhanging jungle at the far end of it, where the Goose had spent the night. Ever the mental multitasker, the supposedly 'green' Navy pilot was already cursing that he had agreed with Buck to make this leg a day flight. It had been because they were among the Celebes and would be looking for fuel stops to top off before the long leg to Darwin.

Making a quicker than normal roll, turn, and descent, the Goose dropped into in the low mist that began again to surround them, the air graying.

Following, but having briefly lost sight of the Grumman, the Japanese pilot glimpsed it in that mist below and saw that he had almost gotten too close to his previously hidden target and was almost upon it, overshooting it. Nipponese pilots, at this point in the war, were among the world's best, but anyone can make a rookie-like mistake in an early morning with a cold thermos of whatever Japanese pilots put in them, and after a long, lonely, fruitless, night mission.

This fellow was in a Nakajima 'Rufe', a float plane for scouting based on the Mitsubishi Zero. Perhaps that encouraged him and he forgot the big float that his plane dragged around below it.

Rather than accelerating and getting ahead of the flying boat and then coming around for the attack or slowing and coming behind, he went into a steep dive like a dive bomber, almost straight down. If the pilot had seen the harbor in daylight and knew of the enormous tree cover where the jungle crowded the shore, he must have been afraid of losing the Goose under that and then having to strafe the area blindly and being unable to confirm a kill.

Down the Japanese dove, and the Navy plane below was now a defenseless sitting duck, slow on its only logical course, luckily not yet lit by the dawn and unluckily with no gun that could be trained on the Rufe. But the enemy pilot was having one of those days that even the best, Ruth or Gehrig, could have, and he daringly trusted his highly maneuverable plane, forgetting the warnings of its frailties that made it so . . perhaps forgetting the pontoon factor as well. This particular pilot was in fact a substitute on this particular morning and usually flew fighters.

Recovering from the boredom of a long night mission and the overconfident glee of the ending moments of it now, the pilot now became professional and realized he must pull up quickly, a maneuver the Zero airframe wasn't made for. As the Jap pulled back on the stick at relatively high throttle and the little racecar of a plane responded smoothly to level off over the bay it was so low because of the late recovery that it dragged its float (not part of the planned maneuver). There was a cracking sound from without heard in the cockpit and a shudder through out the plane . . and the right wing began to fold back followed by the left, and then both partially detached from the plane and dragged in the water of the bay. The float was digging in and the plane nosed in and began to cartwheel end over end at initially over a hundred miles an hour. In this process, the Nakajima A6M2-N disintegrated across a hundred yards of the water. The destruction of the enemy seaplane might have happened without the pilot getting too low and dragging the float at such high speed, for the Zero had a design weakness, probably due to the desire for a very lightweight fighter. American pilots would later, when they learned of it, try to use this flaw to their advantage if they could engage an overconfident or inexperienced enemy pilot.

The Americans spent the day under the protective green canopy, hoping the Nip pilot did not get a chance to message about their existence. Finally, after some coffee and a plane check for stresses after their own specification challenging turn and dive, all of them napped until it was late enough for a sip of beer to steady the nerves after the morning's experience. Deep into the evening they took off again, thankful for night's protective darkness and coffee.

Night fighting was not the standard yet but it would develop as radar sets did and became small enough to fit in airplanes. Now, two days later and farther, to seek fuel from civilian docks, the small crew in their Goose would continue in daylight, hoping they were farther from the enemy's influence. They flew in early spring, but the cold of death north of them was not unlike a bitter winter. Their countrymen in the Philippines were experiencing that metaphorical winter as their Goose flew from it for now.

Lt. Cmdr. Buck Shaw had been correct though, and the enemy had begun to take control of the air in the vicinity of the Grumman's flight, at least with advanced reconnaissance. With the crack of dawn, they had all discovered what they had feared.

Float plane pilots from two Nipponese cruisers knew their squadron mate had not come back the previous day and that Americans and British had to traverse the Celebes Sea by water or air to get home. Thus, two Japanese seaplane pilots had taken off as early as they dared, knowing they were unlikely to encounter competent allied competition, but not knowing they only faced a tired little old American Goose.

In flight, the Grumman crew tried to contact the ship that had refueled them south of South Maluka on the flight up. There was no reply. These two rendezvous were not random, which would have been ridiculous, but they were part of the original plan of operation. It was one of the blessings of dealing with seaplane and flying boat operations, the ability to rendezvous with ships at sea, weather and seaway permitting.

After repeated attempts, alternate plans were absolutely necessary. Darwin, the crew and plane's temporary home was now out of the question, a distant dream.

"The Goose's range would put us a few miles short of Darwin, had we last refueled in South Maluka. Of course, we refueled north of there. Darwin's out of the question, Buck, uh Sir."

"An attempt to find fuel along the southern coast of New Guinea while steering a course toward Port Moresby, is our only viable option, Chief," Buck replied formally. It indicated to Jake the latter's respect and that the Lieutenant Commander wanted to be businesslike even enclosed in close quarters with friends. But these weren't just friends; other officers were present. Significantly he did not admonish Jake for addressing him more casually.

Confidant of their command of the skies for the moment, another Japanese seaplane appeared to patrol the Eastern Celebes near Papua that shared the island with New Guinea, taking up the western half. The previous two prepared to retire, and the lone one patrolled.

The crew of Goose had experienced a run of good luck that had run its course yet had one last gasp before retiring. And it was the twin plane patrol, low on fuel and with no time to spare that discovered the migrating Goose. Staggered one after the other like the fighter pilots they perhaps longed to be, the two seaplanes dove out of the western sun around two in the afternoon when they saw the Goose hugging the Papua coast and the water as the sun became too bright to hide anymore. All eyes aboard the Grumman that could fit near a window were looking downward, seeking a place that looked like it might have aviation fuel, or any fuel. They were desperate. From behind and high, yet diving fast, the two seaplanes roared down, and there was no chance for the crew on the little flying boat to react toward what they did not know was there. By the time the Aichi E13A 'Jake' floatplanes were heard, it was not important. 7.7 caliber machine gun rounds from the rear seated gunners peppered after the pass over of each plane; but, on the initial pass those from twin 20 millimeter belly canons on the first plane tore through the aluminum fuselage roof of the American plane as if it were a tin can.

The Americans' luck had run out; metaphorically and literally, their Goose was cooked.

Ripping across the length of the plane diagonally from the tail toward the nose and left to right, the last rounds of machine gun fire struck Steven through the back of his seat, and he slumped forward on to the controls, forcing a dive. Jake pulled his seemingly lifeless body back and took control, pulling her up and then taking a controlled dip toward the coastal waters.

None of the controls were cut or disabled; but, as the first fighter had been followed closely by his wingman, the latter had poured 20 mm rounds into the starboard engine which almost immediately stalled and burst into flames.

In the cabin, Buck and two others had wounds from the machine guns but not the canon rounds. It was a lucky break for friend and foe and was almost as if the setup had been so easy for the two Jakes that they had been able to make such a precise attack so as to choose which guns to fire at which point. They had filled the plane with machine gun rounds and it and one engine with the very damaging 20 mm.

Actually, the first plane used both rounds profusely and the wingman laced the tail and starboard engine with the larger rounds. Their work done, their fuel getting low, and the American flying boat, if not the men in it, a definite loss, the two Nipponese planes turned for home. With a last stroke of luck, then, the Americas were spared a finishing off death blow from a brutal uncaring enemy. Luckily, Buck's wounds were superficial.

Immediately, Jake knew he had much less power and control and he had to set her down or lose her and her passengers. Struggling to keep the Goose level, or nearly so, a controlled crash landing of sorts ensued near the shore. Jake had lost all hope of the Grumman flying again and just wanted her near the shore to retrieve injured personnel and necessary equipment. He prayed some unseen debris beneath the surface would not turn a soft crash landing into a devastatingly deadly one. The shallower the water and the nearer to foliage and inhabited land, the greater the chance for debris and a greater volume of it.

The flying boat landed reasonably well, its engine lighting up the dull dawn morning and reflecting orange off the waves; and then the starboard wing tilted down and dug in, spinning her to starboard toward the sea. There was a realization of much reduced rudder control and no starboard engine to fight the starboard turn, so Jake throttled up and let the plane bring herself around back toward the beach. Then, fighting with all his might, he forced a centered rudder as he slacked off of the throttle; and, now pointed toward the beach, he throttled up enough to head more or less straight for the shore.

Satisfied and low on fuel, the Jap pilots made no second attack. Surely, they were aware of their success.

Taking little time to notice such fortune, Jake, now the only totally unscathed member of the plane's crew, started off loading the wounded. Luckily most had superficial wounds, including Buck, and Steven was still alive.

A passenger, who was a major became a bit critical and attempted to take a commanding manner.

"Now, see here, pilot, we'll get ourselves off how we see fit."

Jake would have none of it and replied firmly, "This is my duty; I'll see to it sir."

Buck, as a Lt. Commander, the ranking man among them, also replied to the major, who had perhaps thought the naval officer's wound put him out of command position. The arm of his shirt was red from a minor grazing round.

"Stand down, major; on a naval aircraft the most experienced pilot is always in command no matter how low his rank. With all due respect, I'm still in commission and reasonably healthy, so I'll assume command ashore as your equal but in charge of our transit. I'm sure we'll all get along. We're gonna need your jungle experience, Major Whitmore."

Each wounded man was helped ashore. Luckily all of the passengers except Steven had only flesh wounds. Steven was alive with a reasonably serious yet possibly survivable bullet wound through his upper right torso in the upper chest. Obviously, it had punctured the lungs, but it must not have damaged his vascular system or he would already be dead. Time would tell if the internal bleeding would be a problem or heal itself. Buck had taken two hard grazing rounds in rapid succession, slowed only buy the roof of the plane's cabin. Perhaps that saved all of the injured so far, because such wounds, straight on in the open field of battle, could be devastating. Buck's wounds were near the shoulder; and, with the bleeding stopped and the shoulder and upper arm wrapped and immobilized, in only remained to be seen if there would develop a devastating infection or not and if the shoulder would heal reasonably well.

"Major Whitmore, would you do whatever you need to do concerning or military situation: assign weapons from our supply aboard, set a watch, scout inland if you think it necessary, etc. You would be in command if we are attacked, and I would like you to see that we know the best defensive positions in case of that.

Of Jake, Buck inquired, "Chief, did you see that coastal village we flew over just at first light?"

"And the sloop in the bay?"

"Yes, exactly."

"What's your plan sir?"

"Major," called Buck. "What do you know of the war situation here?"

"As far as we know the Japs aren't this far east . . not into the Celebes yet, sir. Obviously, their damned planes are."

Turning back to Jake but obviously speaking to all, Buck stated, "We'll get back up the coast and beg, borrow, or commandeer that boat, and you'll be in charge again, Chief. In command of your own craft again, as it were."

"Let's get everything out of the plane," suggested rather than commanded Maj. Whitmore.

"I suppose the further from the salt water the better for firearms and such."

Jake said, "Yes sir, I agree on that. Meanwhile, there's bancas and such craft all up and down these beaches. I'll see if I can borrow one and head up the coast to see about that sloop. Which one of you officers wants to go along to help convince 'em and deal with 'em?"

Before any could answer, he added, "We might need some army intelligence back up that way too if any of you soldiers want to tag along. I'd be willing to bet there are Jap scouts or advance units close, Major, . . maybe spies at least among the locals."

"What do you sailors think about just using these canoes?" asked Maj. Whitmore.

"They might draw less attention," added another officer, a captain.

Buck replied, "That is a thought, gentlemen, but it's a long way to Darwin or Port Moresby. Both are in danger of invasion but safe now."

Jake added, drawing from his years now in the Philippines, "Port Moresby it will have to be. A slow sloop sailing across the Arafura Sea will be cut to pieces. Here we can hug the coast and duck into shore if attacked. Paddling bancas will wear you fellas out, what with those wounds. I've used 'em for years. I don't know where these islanders find the strength to go all day in 'em."

"I see," said the major. "Lt. Commander, I agree with the chief here; I wouldn't try Darwin in a sloop . . to slow and too visible."

"That's true. We could hug the coasts in her to Moresby and run her ashore if we see planes. Then when they're gone, if she's too damaged, we could switch to bancas then."

Capt. Langford commented insightfully, "The only risk that way is if Jap intelligence learns of us from the folks back there that we secure the sloop from. . . . And, of course, that any plane that spots us is more likely to think Europeans than natives in the sailboat. It's a Western craft, not Oriental."

"Are you sure you can handle that craft, Chief Pierce?" inquired Maj. Whitmore. He was over any rank issues when he learned the way the Navy respected enlisted pilots. He had been in the Army quite a while and new how important master sergeants and sergeant majors where; and he had been in the Philippines a while and knew the esteem the Navy held for their chief petty officers.

"Yes sir, Maj. Whitmore. When I got down here over four years ago I jumped right in and cut my teeth on a seventy-five foot trading schooner. I was eventually second mate and then acting first mate when the man with the job had a long recuperation."

"Lt. Commander Shaw, you got the rank, but I say, take the bigger boat as far as we can along the coast close in. Maybe we take some of those canoes, those bancas, and strap them to the deck in case the damn Japs sink us along the coast where there are no fishermen to get 'em from." Maj. Whitmore, the ranking soldier summed up a logical plan.

Buck outlined things with some finality, "The first order of business is to get away from the plane, for it'll draw further attention if the enemy already has a presence in the Celebes this far east. Major, unless you feel it necessary to scout back where that boat is anchored, you take the men farther east to the next headland and watch out for our return. That will get us all away from this wrecked plane if anyone comes to check it that we would not want to meet. If you stay and do that, the Captain can come with us as our military analyst. His injury is minor, and he can help work the boat. How many people do you think she can hold, Jake. I would say all of us and maybe three or four more. Wouldn't you?"

He had dropped formality briefly, using Jake's name. The Chief answered, "I agree. She's a pretty good-sized sloop. We may have to take them too if we take their boat. It's only right, and they'll be at risk. But we better hurry. We don't know their concerns and situation. They might emigrate from here before we get there. They may have heard our recent battle."

Each group went their opposite directions, taking as much weaponry, ammunition, medical supplies and food as the could haul. Each took one extra banca to tow filled with supplies. The intrepid warrior survivors never knew when they might have to go inland for safety and fight their way the length of Papua New Guinea to Port Moresby.

Thankfully, just hours later, back up the coast to the west, northwest, Buck, Jake, and Capt. Langford stood arguing with the boat's owner, a somewhat well off half British half Dutch man with a Javanese wife bearing a beautiful exotic look and calm, quiet nature about her and appearing similar to Malayans.

Discussion raged over the need to leave and the urgency of the regional political scenario in general. And it came to a screeching halt when Jake said bluntly, "After we left and the city fell, they bayonetted the wounded in their bed's in Singapore. We heard a report or two by pirate radio and some that somehow managed to get out."

All stopped their arguing and just looked at him, a noncom who had respectfully stayed out of it so far, . . stayed out until he felt it urgently necessary to break a certain dam in the conversational river.

Then Dorfman, the owner said, "We're not military."

To which Buck replied, "But civilized men don't do it; what else will the damn Japs do? Do you want to risk your wife with them in charge here?"

Dorfman replied, "They won't dare hurt us here we are peaceful and…"

"They'll kill your baby in the womb and laugh as they watch you lay there knowing it," Capt. Langford said, turning to the petite, exotic coffee-colored Mrs. Dorfman. "That is after each has raped you repeatedly, pregnant or not."

"How dare you!" shouted the husband as he had to be restrained from going after the captain.

Struggling with the other two men who held him, he continued, "You don't dare talk to my wife like that!"

"I'll talk as I see fit if I must to save the young lady and her child. And be damned with you and what happens to you. And if you step toward me again, I'll deck you, restrained by my injury or not.

I've a friend, my former commanding officer who was in Nanking observing secretly in '37. The damn Japs tossed babies in the air and caught them on their bayonets. They tied young women to chairs, sitting up with their legs spread apart for sex vending machines. They beheaded girls holding their babies in their arms, killing both at the same time. Their racist about their own neighboring Orientals. They treat them like animals. Your women here will be their livestock penned in camps . . corralled like in a Kansas stockyard . . for their sexual appetites rather than real hunger."

The half-breed English-Dutchman now seethed, still full of himself and angry at the graphic descriptions addressed to his wife, and Langford continued, "We don't have time for this, for bargaining with you. Death is just across the straits. She'll damn well go with us, and we don't need your permission to take your boat in wartime with both your countries engaged on our side. You threaten me one more time, and I'll end your involvement in this because

I'll end you!", said very strongly but not with a particularly loud voice.

Then staring coldly, the tough young army officer made one last statement, a sort of rhetorical request, "Let him go boys, and I'll settle this quickly."

There followed a long pause and the Dutchman really had no reply. For it was clear to all that the officer intended to kill the man if he attacked him.

The silence was broken by the formerly seemingly passive wife as she said in her sweet exotic English seasoned with a Dutch Javanese accent, "We will gather some few things, necessaries and papers if you think there is time."

Calmed, the husband said of the boat in a stewing subdued voice, "I'll get her ready. She's already stocked."

To this, Buck replied, "We require your seamanship, and the boat will remain your possession with your cooperation, but Chief Petty Officer Pierce here will be in command on this voyage to Port Moresby in every way, except if I have to make some strategic decision. I'm pretty sure the military authorities will not need the vessel in Port Moresby unless they ask you to do courier service. We're all in this together, Dorfman."

Capt. Langford, trusting the woman more than her spouse, had earlier spoken to Ajeng and ask of her who were her most trusted and capable young plantation workers. Knowing his time constraints, he had then sent them out on reconnaissance to the west by land shortly after the group of Americans first arrived. Two others he sent together, westward down the coast in a canoe. The latter scouts found nothing along the shore and of course could only go so far. For they might have encountered a power landing craft or patrol craft and not be able to out run it. The captain knew that they might give up information about the Americans under torture and told them such honestly, cautioning them.

The overland scouts came back within three hours with disturbing news. Being careful bushmen of their region, they had avoided discovery as, from a safe distance, they encountered an advanced enemy patrol, validating the Allied forces fears of a continued advance eastward toward Port Moresby. Accounting for the distance, the current movement of the enemy, and the time the scouts took to return, both they and Langford estimated the Japanese were an hour away. The boatmen returned with news of a small, almost hidden enemy presence on the shore about the same distance away. There were two canoe type boats with outboard motors. Enemy units were obviously advanced scouting parties.

Both groups were sent back a few meters out in the directions they had gone before as sentries to give warning. Meanwhile, all the while that these men had been about their work, the sloop had been prepared. Everything usable from the Goose that the small group had brought to the sloop was aboard and the machine guns had been mounted: one on the port shoreward side, one forward, and one aft.

The islanders did not want to leave their homes and were capable, so they were advised to blend into the rugged parts of their land if possible and warned of the typical Japanese military behavior. The Americans and the Dorfmans boarded the sloop.

As they were weighing anchor, they could hear a distant small power motor, and the military minds among them got a bad feeling. Whether the enemy knew of the little port and boat or just guessed, after machine gunning the two fishermen who had gone back west along the coast in a canoe, the two powered canoes were making a run toward the American's location. Perhaps they had known they were being scouted and watched.

Momentarily, shots came from the bush behind the plantation house, and rifle rounds struck the sloop's hull and low superstructure. No one had time to guess about the overland scouts' fate, loyalty or cowardice.

As the powered dugouts rounded the point, Dorfman, in his clueless confidence in the political situation, stood in the boat's cockpit at the stern and waved both arms back and forth across in front of him in the air in a gesture of friendship. A machine gun mounted in the first boat made short work of him with the ample target his overweight torso presented.

Just as quickly, Capt. Langford, sensibly crouching next to him, forced the wounded arm and, grabbing the grips of the mounted thirty caliber, made short work of that first dugout canoe and its crew. While he similarly engaged the second enemy boat which turned and stood off a bit, Jake had hopped off the sloop to retrieve a small girl. She was the daughter of the Dorfman's maid and was running after Ajeng, who the little one apparently had affection for. He knew not where the mother was, but the girl was followed by Japs who were firing rifles as they ran.

Bullet whizzed around them and bit the ground, kicking up dust, but running and shooting a long, somewhat heavy military rifle at the same time was not an easily mastered skill and that fact saved the girl and her new hero.

As the girl reached the Chief the first soldier did as well, charging with his rifle butt presented forward toward Jake. Drawing Lola Sunny's khukuri as he pushed the child down to the ground protectively, the Chief ducked beneath the rifle's butt and swung toward and across the man's crotch area with a powerful slicing stroke. Then standing, Jake immediately found himself (as his adversary fell and cleared his field of view) facing the second of four charging soldiers with a long, bayonet-tipped rifle pointed right down at him. Jake fell off to the right and swung the massive khukuri blade into the Jap's leg just behind the knee. In his peripheral view, registering the third and fourth soldiers go down from rifle fire from the sloop, Jake chopped the neck of the one just disabled and quickly turned back to the former one (the first), who still alive, started to rise in his agony. Chief Pierce, half standing as he rose on one knee, from behind, swung the khukuri for the enemy's neck, as that man tried to rise, and almost decapitated him.

Reaching for the little girl, who was tenuous about it at first from his initial shove, thoughts went through his mind of long talks with Lola Sunny well before the gift of the knife. Once in particular, she had just shown it to him and teased that it must taste blood now before it could be put away. "I've seen you handle rigging in a wind, Jake. You will make a good khukuri fighter."

Stillness filled the air, and Jake stood holding the girl and surveyed the scene. The soldiers were dead and no more came from the trees. But he was concerned and wanted to be less conspicuous. In the bay the sloop's stern thirty caliber had fought the second powered dugout to a standstill and with a damaged engine the craft was limping away. That couldn't be. They could get back to a camp with a radio, and then planes would find and destroy the sloop at sea. Now, with no witnesses to survive, the enemy might not know the cause of this defeat. They might not readily know of the sloop until they forced information from the locals. He set the girl down and pointed to the sloop to which she readily ran. Grabbing the nearest Jap's rifle, he worked the bolt and test fired it into the man. Then he stabbed him with his own bayonet for good measure.

Running out to the stone jetty where it rose out of the surf he waded out and stood where the wall of it was chest high. Laying the long gun out across the jetty and carefully aiming, he could see three figures left moving of the original load of about ten soldiers, and he fired and watched the first fall. Repeating it again and again the others did as well. The damaged motor was still chugged erratically, and Jake put several rounds in it and heard it slow to a coughing idle.

Jake jogged back over to the sloop and said to the Captain, "Good work, sir. We'll make you a naval gunner yet."

"I believe you're an Army commando in the making after that little display ashore there, Chief."

"Capt. May I request that you take our skiff and run over quickly and set those motor bancas aflame. I don't want to take this sloop with her big light brown sails around the point there just in case. I also don't want to take time maneuvering her over there when the skiff is faster with its motor."

Remembering the complicated and everchanging command structure the group was working under, Langford jokingly gave an exaggerated salute and half laughingly replied, "Aye, aye Cap'n."

Moments later, lines cast off the pilings and the sails unfurled and filled with wind, the voyage began and the mission to pick up the Major and the others to the east was the next duty.

The little vessel named for Ajeng handled well in all winds and they soon learned of it as a squall blew up a day later. Jake took her out to sea to ride it out safely in the open, safe from being blown ashore and running aground.

Almost immediately after they were underway the first day, Capt. Jesse Langford had become very attentive toward Ajeng. It was duty the Navy men supposed, and the captain cared for the little girl, Ling, as well. A rifle bullet to the right thigh during the battle at the dock was thought to have cleanly exited without hitting bone but his help sailing the boat was now hindered. Later as the pain became worse, Jake and Buck deduced that the bone was damaged and splinted the leg. All aboard noticed that not only did Langford help the woman and girl in every way, but he was talking to them quite a bit. No one minded.

As the squall developed on the second day, Jake explained to the Army men and native girls, "We'll take her offshore. You have to ride these things out at sea where there's fewer obstacles. We can't make quick, tight maneuvers like a car or motorboat. We might not avoid a collision with the land in big winds. I know it may sound silly, as small as this vessel is, but that's the truth of it. If we're too close in during a storm, we can be blown ashore."

As Jake went to his work, Jesse pulled Buck aside and spoke to him, "Lt. Commander, I know we don't wanna be off shore in high visibility. This storm might be our only time, and we're under cover a bit with the clouds and all. I have a request . . . uh, well Ajeng and I do."

"Sure, what is it, Captain?"

"Well sir, this is not kosher I guess, but what is these days. The world's upside down now."

"Okay, I'm listening."

"Well, you being my commanding officer and Jake a ship captain . . I mean of an official Navy vessel as it were . . well the international waters limit may not matter. But, well I figure it would just make it harder to challenge, a marriage, that is. Nobody could say it was in their jurisdiction, you see."

"You two want to get married. And you've known each other two days?"

"It's like this, sir: she's in a spot, and I'm attracted to her I'll admit . . and of course, she isn't white. Who knows how she'll be treated in Port Moresby."

"But marriage just overnight almost. Forgive me, Captain for the comparison, but it's almost like those fellas who sleep with a girl they meet in a bar on leave and then go get married. Now don't hit me; I've seen your temper. I don't mean it's exactly like that. I mean the longevity of it."

"Let me be honest with you sir. I'm trying to help the girl. This war's gonna ruin enough lives. I've got feelings for her, but we'll just see about that. But for now, I'll just be totally honest with my commanding officer who I suppose has to approve the marriage to a foreign national in a war zone. This is partly a marriage of convenience, sir. When she gets down there, the British are like as not to stick her in a refugee camp and commandeer her boat, though they'll likely not need it. Then she's pregnant and likely won't get proper care in a camp. She might lose the baby and even die."

"I'm not sure you can avoid that by just getting hitched. And she's agreed?"

"She knows the spot she's in and scared about the unknown. And she's got the girl and the baby coming. I think she likes me too, but of course she can't show it too much what with her husband just dead.

Now, with my leg broken and my arm wounded too, I will be off duty and will be able to live with her on the boat. They aren't likely to take it from an Allied officer and his wife, whether they like her color or not. Then when I get sent to duty, she should be pretty well established here, I mean in Port Moresby of maybe Sydney. She should be okay 'til I get back. Then when I return . . if I do, we can work on the marriage or go our separate ways."

"You might be frowned on back home, as a couple."

"Might not go, sir. Might stay in these islands. Up in the American Philippines though."

"I'll approve the marriage and ask Jake to perform it. Well do it as soon as we reach international waters, for the extra-legal strength of it like you suggested. Go down and see if they have a typewriter aboard. Ask her. Type up an approval letter from me and a general marriage license with the name of this body of water, the Arafura Sea. If we do it later we'll be in the Coral Sea as we approach Port Moresby."

"Thank you, sir. I figure with me laid up and on leave a while, we can set up housekeeping and get her some respect and legitimacy while I'm gone later."

"We probably don't need to go that far out for the storm, but planes can't find us in this and a sub won't waste a torpedo on the likes of this little boat. We'll record it as official. Don't worry."

When the time could be taken, right in the boat's cockpit in the wind and rain, a most unusual of weddings took place and all noticed that in spite of all that had happened and was occurring, the bride smiled. Maybe Ajeng had feelings for Jesse too. Her husband had seemed quite the sourpuss the little time the American men had known him. Out of sadness came renewal for her perhaps.

Jake lashed the helm, and for the health of it, the pregnant bride and little girl stood just inside the hatch, under the slight cover of the roof as one would enter the hatch from the cockpit forward into the cabin. All was accomplished quickly, and all returned to normal, and yet another family unit was set off on an adventure in the midst of the turmoil of the world's greatest war in its history. And the whole small compliment of the little sloop proceeded under sail through the storm to yet another destination, Port Moresby, clinging to the southern edge of big, mysterious, mountain backed and jungle covered New Guinea . . Port Moresby, the next major targeted jewel of the Imperial Japanese Navy and Army.

A nearly one-sided cat and mouse game ensued, one sided because, as the unusual party neared their destination, no enemy craft of any kind appeared. The sloop and its diverse crew were on the edge of a wartime frontier but on the friendly side. Only submarines and aircraft dared cross such barriers until actual attacks made large incursion necessary.

The final taste of danger and death came while some ways out from Port Moresby, when a daring pilot far from his cruiser on an obvious long ranged, lone scouting mission discovered the sloop in clear weather off the coast. Jake had her as close in as he dared. The Japanese pilot was in another Nakajima Rufe floatplane version of the Mitsubishi Zero, maybe an unauthorized patrol this close to danger. However, one could not easily be catapulted off of a ship without the captain's knowledge, so it was most likely an official flight, reconnaissance of the area around the British port perhaps.

Probably from a cruiser in the Banda Sea to the west or just north across the tip of New Guinea, daring to attack because of the weak Allied aircraft around that area, the long-ranged scout plane made a diving strafing run on the sloop.

Jake had, within the last hour, notified the port authority of their impending arrival and reported their position, requesting any cover possible if planes where in the air. Hearing one such plane's droning sound followed by the sound of a dive, the worst logically went through his mind. Looking over his shoulder at certain death off the stern, for he was the first human target topside and in view that the rounds of a stern to stem strafing run would encounter, he thought briefly of Sarah and felt death grab him almost as if from within.

He heard the Tommy guns and rifles of his companions, military men who had been fighting this war for weeks or even months, as they attempted to deter or even bring down this new tormentor.

As the Jap's heavier rounds struck the sea and peripheral parts of the cockpit and stern, the new chief petty officer in this man's modern Navy, fighting an old school craft in a modern battle, stood his post. And as the plane's hot fire found him, as the fear within had predicted, prompting the woman's face in the streaming video of the mind, he had just the moment before spun the helm over so sharp to starboard that he feared she would lay over on the water to port and capsize. On a broad reach, the sails were full and, through the searing pain in his legs as he fell on his knees, Jake steered a new course from almost due east to southeast so quickly the sloop seemed to briefly shudder as she otherwise smoothly complied. It was the only quick course change logical and feasible with no crew topside to work the boat.

As luckily, the lowly directed rounds tore into his legs, knocking him down, the *Ajeng* swung sharply to starboard, biting into the offshore wind and stayed upright and, due to Jake's courage, swung out of the line of fire, but ever so briefly of course. The low flying plane swooped across the top of the boat frighteningly close and pulled up to go around for another devastating strafing run. With throttle open and the stick back and climbing, the Jap navy pilot pulled his plane to starboard and seaward, leveled off over the water pursuant to coming back around over the *Ajeng,* and never saw the three British Hawker Hurricanes skimming the wavetops and rising to meet him, stitching the vulnerable belly of his ship with death. They had flown out from their combat air patrol duties over the nearby port and come in low from the seaward side to position so as to not be seen or strike the sailboat with errant friendly fire as they rose to meet the higher, climbing Japanese plane.

Jake lay rolling in agony on the deck; and hearing his screams as he became aware of the pain, notably the woman was first by his side. It was the instinct of a woman and thankfulness for all he was doing for her.

In endangered Port Moresby, British New Guinea, leaning on crutches and looking at Steven's body lying there, Jake said, "I've got to get him home."

"Chief, you have; you brought him back from the mission."

"I got to get him to Cebu." It was obviously not going to happen, and it seemed his grief had made Jake delusional. Steven had died shortly after they had reached safety in the British port. Had it happened earlier, he would have been buried at sea. A body could not be transported long in that climate, and Capt. Langford had simply, in the heat of battle and more impending danger, just pushed Dorfman's body into the harbor back at his home port. Jake saw it and wondered at the fact that Ajeng held no anger or other bad feelings for her now new husband over it. In the brief time they had known her, she seemed not shallow, loving enough of her previous spouse, and normal in most ways one could ascertain in such a short period of time. Shoved together in such emergencies people could learn a lot about each other. But women were mysteries, and women of another culture were just complete enigmas. The only summarizing thought that went through Jake's mind, as he dealt with his pain and remembered his own unusual romantic situation, was that the Captain must have given the little Javanese beauty one hell of a sales pitch.

"Get a hold of yourself, Chief. There's a war on. And you know there is no way to preserve a body for only God knows how long. Buck up, Chief. You brought him back; that's what counts."

"I promised them when we split up and we went to Singapore. I told them I would bring everybody home. Now only me, only me . . ."

"Jon and Maya may be safe. But this world is full of dead and broken people right now. Hell's set up camp on earth at the moment."

"But Steven . . dead . . . ?"

"He's going to be buried here in New Guinea, Chief. That's the best we can do. You brought him back; you did your best as well."

"This ain't home. He's never been here."

"You brought him from that hell that is the spreading Jap culture now and back to our world. That's somethin'."

"They're devil people," Jake said through gritted teeth.

"Well, I've been there, and there's a lot to admire in them and their land. But their warrior culture, yes: barbaric . . like stepping back in time. But you know, that little Indian gal you're hoping to get back home to? We weren't as bad as these Japs, but we did it to her people, some of them less than a hundred years ago. People learn. After we beat the shit out of them, maybe these Japs will lose this Bushido way."

There was a pause, a long pregnant one, and then Buck put his hand on Jake's shoulder, "There cutting off captives' heads. Stories are slippin' out of Malaya an' Burma, Jake. We did some bad things back in the Indian wars, and I guess it had to do with race, like we thought we were dealing with savages. Sometimes they behaved that way, but it was their land. We were never this bad, but we did some bad things in the Philippines too. The thing is, what these Japs and I've heard the Germans are doing is beyond the pale. We have to stop it. Some of us will get killed, but nobody's got time right now to worry about where we bury them."

Again, they were quiet as Jake took his words in. Finally, the officer slapped the Chief on the shoulder firmly and with a bit more upbeat tenor to his voice, saying, "You're in it now, son. We all are, right up to our necks and treading water. This is bigger than all of us: that fine family you work for in the Philippines, your heroic Lola, apparently right off the pages of some adventure novel, your girl back home, you, me . . . They're important. They're why we're here, what we're fighting for; but it's bigger than any one of us and bigger than how you define 'bringing them home', the ones we rescue and bring out and the dead heroes we bring out."

Jake's head turned and his eyes followed the officer. Looking back at Jake as he walked away to some duty or rest, it being late in the evening, the Lt. Commander said, "You do what you can in this mess; we all do what we can. You brought Steven 'back', and that's all you could do."

Sarah could not hear the whole tale of her new hero husband, for he didn't know everything himself. No one ever does. There are always the events and the talks behind our backs that we aren't privy to and may never know of.

"You want to give this fella a Silver Star? He lost his plane and it wasn't even a combat mission."

"We'll lose a lot of planes, Sir. Are already. He was in combat then and earlier and wounded. Rescue missions and retreats under duress are combat, sir. Everything is combat in a war like this."

"I know that. But this is early into probably a long war. This is early to be giving out medals . . and a Silver Star already? It's just been approved for the Navy."

"There're all combat missions up that way, sir."

The commander looked at Buck Shaw.

"We may have been the last plane out, sir. We're damn near cut off . . the Philippines are pretty much surrounded. This is when heroes are being made, right now in the confusion of the beginning of it."

The commander looked sternly with resigned disgust and shaking his head bent it down, His arms were folded across his desk with his hands clasped together.

Without looking up, he said, "Sit down, Lt. Commander."

As Buck took a seat in a reasonably comfortable chair to the side of the other officer's desk, the other man said, "You've been through it, as you have related. We'll have a scotch. Something the British can do right, even if they can't hold their 'Fortress

Singapore'. Of course, I'm one to talk. We'll lose the Philippines. They'll all demand independence you know," the insightful man said. "All these native populations are going to say after the war, 'You couldn't protect us; we don't need you; you've no right to stay,' you see."

Buck was quiet and just listening intently. It was becoming a cordial and comfortable evening meeting after the hell he had been through. He patiently awaited the scotch.

"They'll be correct, you know. Their women will be abused terribly. We've seen what the damn Japs have done in China, Nanking especially. Maybe it won't be as bad down here. The Nips hate the Chinese. But I believe they feel racially superior to other Orientals, so who knows what they'll do to girls here. When it all comes out afterwards, there'll be hangings. Just China will earn them that. Hell, we might even hang their emperor."

Buck did not interrupt. The man before him was becoming educational and was a deserving commanding officer. He'd let the conversation flow. The man turned around to an old glass front cabinet and retrieved the bottle of scotch and two small glasses. Turning back, he filled both almost to the brim.

"Now I'll grant you he got your men out of the Philippines and all, and he got you all home. What did you see, what'd you see in the man that put you out there at risk: takin' a man like that without basic training and then making him an acting chief?" said with expression but not loudly.

"He had a plane, could fly, and had a copilot. I was stuck in Singapore, with information of course . . a lot of intelligence about things there and what they, the British, were doing and not doing. And it was a flying boat, invaluable down in all these islands. They needed me and I needed them."

"How did you assist them?"

"The Limeys wanted their plane. I recruited the two pilots and told the Brits so and that the plane was requisitioned U.S. Navy property. They needed help getting their other man out too."

"Oh?"

"The third crewman was a scion of the family that owned the plane. They needed to get him and his girl out of Singapore. I made a trade with a British Major. We flew his family out with us and he promised to get the kid and his nurse on a ship headed for Trincomalee."

"His nurse? How old is he? By the way, you still haven't explained how you saw a chief in such a young man."

"They told me how they got to Singapore. Delivering goods in Borneo, they got into a barfight rescuing two Malaya nursing students and two Filipinas who had been taken by bad types for whoring. Chief Pierce is the one that pushed it to save them, and he killed two of their captors. There were three in all, and the other was killed by his companions, company superiors, who were there in another plane with 'em. The older fellows went back to Cebu to take care of family because they had just learned of the war. Chief Pierce was tasked with getting the young man, who had been injured, to a good hospital. He, the wounded one, and one of the nursing students became close, as she felt responsible."

"Killed two bad hombres huh? Bars can be tough places to do battle. Sure he wasn't just bragging?"

"No, Petty Officer 1st Class Steven Ericson told me the details. Pierce killed both with a knife."

"And then there's all this in your commendation," waving an open hand backhanded across the papers on his desk.

"Yes sir."

The commander had heard the main points but now scanned the commendation fast but somewhat thoroughly.

Looking up with an expression of serious contemplation and of a man who seemed to have been impressed by what he had just read, he said, "The man's like one of these damn matinée idols, Brian Donleavy or Bogart. Is he for real?"

"I was there every step of the way, sir, except for the barroom brawl and the flight with the wounded boy to Singapore. Sir, I wouldn't be standing here talking to you, or anywhere, if not for Chief Petty Officer Jake Pierce."

. . . all the tears I have right now"

The drive down to the coast was solemn at first until the father broke the ice with fatherly wit for such occasions, cracking some slight joke no one remembered but allowing now for casual, nervous banter. All were close, the daughter-in-law a near 'daughter' and thus she unabashedly leaned into Jake, griping and embracing his nearest upper arm. Her eyes were red, as she had finally lost composure and cried herself softly to sleep in his arms the night before.

Weeks before, he had gone down to San Diego for training, and she went too. They drove her car and managed to get a little place, a reasonable flat that a couple of flyers headed out into the Pacific sublet them for the weeks he would still be stateside. They asked that the two try to find a new sublet tenant and, if not able, to turn the chore over to the willing landlord along with the keys. He knew how it was. She figured the rate was reasonable enough because the landlord would surely get in trouble for gouging military men in wartime. Eric and Ann insisted on paying for it. Maybe the hotels and inns were grateful when Navy wives came along because, without them, the men might as well avail of the free housing on the bases.

Both Jake and Sarah felt so blessed for the time his training had given them, if only partial days. But now it was all over, and, as always, the hours and days get eaten up by some seemingly horrible creature called fate. And now, back in the northern part of the long West Coast state, Sarah longed for even those partial days.

At the pier in San Francisco the four stood, and the mother did the motherly things: straightening his collar and patting the Purple Heart and Silver Star . . fighting back sobs to reveal instead just solemn tears of a mother's love, concern, and pride.

Eric, more stoic yet warmly close to his son, offered a hand firmly taken, and then the two men hugged affectionately yet in a manly way, a convention somewhat uncommon for the era perhaps.

Turning to his wife, Eric leaned in and whispered, "Let's leave them alone." Thus, the two walked back toward the car from which they, eventually, obviously observed the younger couple while otherwise leaving them their privacy.

Sarah leaned into his chest with both forearms against it and fiddled with the top button on his jacket. His reefer was under his left arm and, without looking down, he dropped it on his seabag and then brought that arm up to join the other around her slim waist. Somewhat incongruously, because of her wiry strength that he had seen around the grill stockroom and on her farm, she was a mere wisp of a girl, and he held her close. A group of weathered sailors, about four or five walking some distance away, gave a soft wolf whistle, seeming to know just how to do so respectfully enough to not incur the wrath of the chief petty officer whose woman she was. The mere act of it revealed both the experience and the courage of said sailors. None of their 'club' ever knowingly angered a CPO.

Jake said, "We knew this was coming; nobody can handle it better than you. I believe that."

Sarah looked up into his face and eyes and said nothing.

"We'll be together again soon . . just not soon enough," and as he said it she was still quiet and just looked long and lovingly.

"Look, Sarah . . Darling . . I know you can handle this, and I know it's hell . . . we know I'm going to get shot at . . into 'harm's way' as they say, but at least it's not combat."

"Yes it is, she whispered . . be honest, it is . . and you can't shoot back, you'll be too busy."

"My crew can."

"You listen, Jake Pierce: you don't lose that crew for one man, you hear. I know you; you won't give up on anyone. You have men that count on you and the skipper of that plane to bring them home. You and him think of them. They have girls waiting at home too. Don't lose them all for one man."

"Yes ma'am. It's always a judgement call."

". . . and their girls," she almost whispered, leaning her head on his chest.

"What?"

"Their girls and children . . they count on you guys . . you know . . to bring 'em back."

"It's..."

"It's war, Jake . . a numbers game. Just try to help your skipper make the right call." She was looking straight ahead at his chest. Her forearms were resting there and her fingers fiddled playfully and perhaps nervously with the gold buttons.

He looked deep into her eyes as she turned her face up to him again, and he knew she had absorbed every nuance of his stories and understood as much as possible for someone in her position of the workings of the Navy plane crews he had told her about.

Jake knew that she understood that anytime they landed for a downed flier or circled until a ship came for the survivors of a sunken ship . . that anytime like that they could become victims too . . understood that they focused on their goal, the victim. Rescuers were always among the most vulnerable during war, and the young wife understood that.

Looking back into her eyes, he said softly yet firmly, "I won't lie to you and make promises, statements of certainty, I mean. I'll just do my best."

"That's what I meant," Sarah whispered softly in his ear as she hugged him just before the long kiss that followed.

Releasing each other as he indicated with his body that they must, the girl said just as soft and resolutely, "I know we're not in control now."

They were still loosely in each other's arms, close and holding each other's arms with their hands. She looked up at his left jacket breast and said, "I want these, can I have them? They'll connect me to you physically. When some guy makes a move, I'll point to them and say, 'Shove off buster, I'm his.'"

Smiling as he 'pinned' her, Jake said, "Here, Darling, they're yours. I meant to give them to you when I came to Paradise Ridge to propose, so I bought another pair to be properly in uniform."

"You were awfully sure of yourself, weren't you, sailor?"

"Hopeful," Jake said with a smile and a wink, and then he smiled and turned to walk to the ladder.

As her eyes followed him, it was the unspoken truth, sometimes vocalized softly . . sometimes in anger . . sometimes unsaid by so many young people in those years. Young men on the cusp of their adult lives had always fought wars and young wives and girlfriends waited and, in a way, fought too.

As Jake walked away from her and to the gangplank, his parents left her to bear it alone, knowing she would want it that way, to savor the moment that way and remember it that way. And then as Jake disappeared into the interior of the ship where he was to report, the parents joined her and the three walked solemnly back to the car.

Strolling slowly beside each other three abreast, with the daughter in the middle for unspoken moral support, Eric spoke matter-of-factly and somewhat seriously, "The Navy isn't paying to fly him out, and these ships take a bit of time. Perhaps they aren't desperate for his services, you know: to put him in harm's way. And, well, even if they need him, the ship is quite a bit slower. Then well, he's got to get to a forward base, and . . that's probably where they'll want him, experience and all . . and then he has to get a squadron. What I mean is, Honey, he's not gonna get shot at tomorrow."

She acknowledged it with a slight head nod of agreement and kept walking.

Ann said, "Let's eat here somewhere. You decide Sarah where. You might not want to go anywhere the two of you've been."

"Alright, let's look around. You know the area, Dad, right?"

Then as he replied to the affirmative, she said, "I don't know what I would do without you, what with my mother gone. I won't get through this alone. I don't see how some girls are. You two are a blessing. I just wonder if it's hardest on a younger or older wife . . or a mother. Oh . . I'm sorry, Mom . . . I..."

"It's alright, Dear. We all feel it; we can't ignore it. You and I can compare notes when we can talk about it. We'll have to talk about it eventually. It is what helps . . the only thing that does, I suppose. We can compare without competing with each other for sympathy."

Jake would lose himself in his work when he finally could, but for now, for the voyage there was the tedium of long hours with nothing to do, no assignment. It wasn't his ship. He was a passenger. Luckily, he had brought some books and could try to read. A novel full of emotions would have been impossible. He had Gunther's 1939 edition of *Inside Asia* and 1938 edition of *Inside Europe*, a flying theory book, and a PBY manual that he had to requisition and sign for.

For the wife and parents staying together in the parent's home it would be months, if not a year or more, of tedium, of tedious waiting and trying to keep one's mind from worrying too much, of trying to stay occupied on anything that they could make themselves care about enough to actually do it.

For Sarah, unspoken to the mother and father to spare them, there was a deeper concern, beyond the war fear that she held in her heart alone. It was one brought on by knowledge. Knowing can be a kind of curse as can depth of insight and understanding. And she had all these. And, as much as the two lovers were perhaps always meant for each other, somehow ordained to wed long before time, so were their minds matched, as were their hearts and souls. She understood his tales of the first year of war more than he knew. He had transferred the story of the Pacific War all too well: that, as in Europe and beyond the patriotic and moral right of it, the goal was just to stay alive and survive it. Somehow in it all, that came through the clearest because, even in noncombat scenarios . . training or maintenance . . a man nearby could be alive one moment and dead the next. They were dealing after all, under duress, with big, fast, dangerous, and explosive machines and equipment . . without sleep, in the dark and the worst weather . . always with the threat of violent conflict nearby. One did not need the actual conflict to occur to meet his final moment. He just needed to be in or near a bad landing.

Paradise Ridge, a little mountain town, had been many things through the decades, but whether the fur trade, Indian wars, lumbering, or mining was involved, it had remained a far outpost. Given the nature of its history, perhaps the characterization of the local paper as a 'dispatch', a simple message system was appropriate.

PARADISE RIDGE DISPATCH   March 22, 1943
Decorated Favorite Son Returns to War

Chief Petty Officer, Jake Pierce of our fair town and close-knit community has represented us well in the early months of our nation's most dangerous trials. Wounded and decorated the young man returned home to recuperate and take a bride, Paradise Ridge's own Sarah Willowood.

Jake, son of Mr. And Mrs. Eric Pierce, formerly of Paradise Ridge, was in the South Pacific working on sailing ships and seaplanes when the war broke out. He willingly jumped to his country's service and, using his skills with sail and wing, saved several people, some very important. For this he received and wears a Purple Heart for being wounded and the Silver Star, the third highest honor a sailor can earn.

According to Mr. Eric Pierce, Sarah will live with Jake's parents, now living in Hayward, near the Bay and work with various war campaigns. Rumor has it that Sarah has delegated the reopening of the grill to Darrell Robinson, who must hurry and find someone who makes coffee as good as Sarah before he also leaves for the Navy.

The Navy had accepted Darrell Robinson in spite of the scar on one eyeball, but both he and the government were waiting for his broken left arm and leg to heal. He had properly laid his bike down when he rounded a curve and saw a truck accident in his path, sparing it for the most part. But he did not as successfully disengage from it so as to avoid injury.

Darrell had become Greenridge's lovable tough guy, the biker, mechanic, hotrodder in a white tee shirt and black leather jacket that would become the icon of the decade after the war. Trends begin somewhere, and maybe at some bike rally, the guys from LA saw his look and were impressed. Darrell's was a brown flyer's jacket and meant more to him than his bike and almost more than his girl. The undamaged memento had been his older brother's and was sent home to him with David's belongings from the wreckage of a Curtis P 40 and a sparse barracks locker in North Africa.

The girl, a serious flame burning in the now more settled man, was Eloise Sanderson, one of Sarah's former nemeses. His brother's death, Jake's return as a man of the world and war hero, Sarah's exit, and the marriage of the two . . all these things had matured Darrell Robinson, who had manifested a new sense of responsibility by offering to kick his younger brothers' asses if they didn't straighten out things concerning Sarah's reputation.

What was even more earthshakingly transformative was the romance. Eloise was near the top of the social scene of clickish young Paradise Ridge females. She was friendly, even to Sarah, but underneath she was one of the latter's detractors in subtle ways. . . . But, Eloise grew up too. It all comes out from small town folk, the curious inquisitive ones, especially young and eagerly hungry ones, when their peers come back from the world. Her talk with Sarah when the couple returned briefly to town before the move to Hayward and later talks with Darrell captured her fancy and schooled the young woman who was no longer a shallow high school girl. Names like Hawaii, Honolulu, the Philippines, the Dutch East Indies, Darwin, Cebu, Port Moresby, Singapore . . images of people in colorful sarongs . . all from Sarah's lips echoing small snippets of Jake's tales . . all of it, the whole of it rang an exotic gong for Eloise and echoed from the war-laden newspapers and cinema newsreels.

Eloise realized three things. There was a world out there, and Jake and Sarah had discovered it and would relish it. Secondly, Sarah was perhaps her most intelligent, mature, and insightful friend . . and the least shallow. And thirdly, Paradise Ridge had its compliment of young men farming, lumbering, or off soldiering. But among them all, Jake Pierce and Darrell Robinson, two slightly older guys, weren't 'boy's anymore . . they were men. As luck would have it, though generally unacceptable within the social boundaries of her circle of friends, Darrell was **her** secret, high school, older 'bad boy' crush. Well, he and Sarah, both of whom she respected more now, needed help, and she could make damn good coffee, just nobody had ever asked her.

~

"Chief Pierce, come right in and have a seat."

The commanding officer was standing beside the window looking out at the line of Catalinas next to the tender. He turned and returned Jake's salute and then directed with an open hand to the seat in front of his desk.

After he sat, Jake inquired, "You wanted to see me sir?"

"Well yes, Chief. I always meet new pilots and officers. But this time I have something sensitive to bring up. Maybe it's nothing though."

"I'm new here as you know and new to PBYs, but if you think I'm the man you need to see, here I am, sir."

"It's about that, your recent introduction to the Cats. You have a lot of experience, but not a lot of hours, and only training hours in these PBYs."

"I have no ego issues, sir. Assignment will not bother me. I'm here to contribute like everyone else."

"Then I'll ask the big question right out. It's not your call of course, but I want to deflect trouble in crews before the chance comes, you see."

"Of course, sir."

"Well, here it is son: Will you be willing . . not offended, to be the third pilot on your plane until you get a little more familiar with Cats? You would still fly, but not in action unless needed. I just want every man to know their role and equipment."

"As long as I get some hours out to our patrol areas and back, that would be fine, sir. They gave me as much as they could at San Diego and Pearl, but I want to be able to do everything blindfolded if I'm at the controls in combat, sir."

"I have read about you, Chief Pierce . . your files and the letters in there. Your decorated, and one thing sticks out. You're not a hotshot or risk taker. You did daring things, dealt with 'em when they presented themselves . . did what you had to do, as they say. Your former commanding officer makes that very clear. This has nothing to do with that. It is simply a flight hours issue. But you've always been in command of the vessel during your short Navy career. Can you function, when you are not?"

"Yes sir."

After that short meeting with the squadron commander, Jake went down to see the flying boat he was assigned to and meet the crew, all of whom were working on the plane.

"Well, Chief, that's bum luck," the skipper of his PBY said slapping him on the back after the required exchange of salutes.

"It's okay, sir . ."

"Just 'Skip' after the first salute of the morning . . 'less the brass is around, higher brass than me or Chuck, our copilot over there . . or Davis over yonder We're usually on mission together, my wingmen when we can.

You know how this works, right Chief? The most experienced pilot on the plane is in command in the air, regardless of ranks. On the ground Chuck's the boss on the 'Flying Cloud' here, as in the old Clipper ship. He's a captain, I'm a lieutenant. He applied to flight school 'late in his career' as I like to remind him. You don't have to worry about that yet."

"Alright, Skip. I need the hours in her. I guess they need pilots; so, after that, who knows where I'll be."

"Probably right here. We lose some even if the plane gets back. I guess that's why we've got a third pilot onboard when we can."

The squadron was based near conquered Guadalcanal some months later as the struggle for the Bismarck Barrier was underway, the next battleground on the march to Japan after the storied struggle for Guadalcanal. Jake figured that, with the threat from the air gone that far south, the heavily patrolled and confined waters were safer for a tender than the open waters of the Solomon Sea between the Solomons and New Guinea. Jake was now the third pilot as the extra man had found a berth as a copilot. On a bright, clear morning the *Flying Cloud* was in route to its patrol area over the Northwest Solomon Sea, Southeast of New Britain. It was early October of 1943. Combat patrols were always in the air and the PBYs were always out searching for the enemy or downed Allied flyers. The struggle for Guadalcanal, so long and bloody and exhausting, had only moved up the slot to the small islands near Bougainville where ships still clashed at night as the Japanese still were always trying to move troops, either in or out and the Allies were trying to stop them.

"I'd rather be flyin' one of those Black Cats when it gets dark than doin' this," commented Chuck.

"Well, I don't know about getting' shot at," Jake replied from the pilot's seat, as he was getting needed hours and familiarity under his belt.

"We're getting shot at now, aren't we?"

"Quite often. Maybe the Black Cats have fighter escort."

"That's my thinking . . those new night fighters."

Such chatter droned on during such flights until nothing happened but strained boredom and strained eyes looking at the sea below, blue or gray depending on the weather and green near islands. On other occasions the boredom could erupt into a flurry and a fury of activity, lifesaving and life-threatening fury.

Search for the enemy or a downed pilot or survivors from a sunken or damaged ship could always turn to terror and a real chance of death in the skies if the hated Jap Zero fighters turned up. Unable to maneuver with the little hornets with a powerful sting, the Catalinas could only climb for the clouds that seemed often so far away, especially when the pursuer was so much faster and often in swarms. With their own multiple stingers, the Catalinas took their toll on the enemy; but, like the B-17 bombers in Europe, it was often a dying gesture for freedom and democracy.

It was October seven, and the naval *Battle of Vella Lavella* had occurred the night before just northwest of Vella Gulf off of Vella Lavella Island. A small yet deadly clash of steel saw the 'tin cans' (as destroyers were called) slug it out in darkness with guns and torpedoes. The Japanese had attempted to withdraw several hundred men from the northwest coast of the island in an operation that was interrupted by the American force. The Japanese rescue was successful as they took the troops off at Marquana Bay on the northwest side of the island. Hundreds of men were dead, wounded, or missing. So, the crew kept their eyes peeled for survivors as the traversed the area.

With more in his life to lose now, Jake could only think, at the waning of such missions, that he wished they would all be this easy. But another part of him regretted missing *Midway*, which was now becoming apparent in its importance. And he regretted missing the early 'meat' of the *Guadalcanal Campaign* and rescuing fliers after the blood, fire, and fury of the *Battle of the Eastern Solomons*, the *Battle of Cape Esperance*, and the *Battle of the Santa Cruz Islands* . . carrier battles in which neither fleet saw the other but their fliers died with great heroism and big gun battles between steel ships manned by iron hard men. And he could save 'em . . that was his role, and now he reveled in it and in the danger of it. He was back on the field at Paradise Ridge High and the game, no . . lives were on the line.

During recent months throughout late 1943, after Jake had returned to duty in the Southwest Pacific, the Imperial Japanese Navy and the United States Navy clashed in several smaller night naval engagements like the larger cruiser and battleship actions during the struggle for Guadalcanal. The little destroyers took center stage now, those little scrappers with their 300-man crews and powerfully dangerous and deadly torpedoes that had played their important role in those large nighttime clashes such as *Tassafaronga* and *Savo Island.* They were the ones sent into the center of such large naval melees, small as they were, to run out in front of a massive enemy force to lay smoke to hide the valuable big gun assets of their own force and to launch, in the teeth of death, the stealthy torpedoes that a man never saw coming until, often it was too late. Now through the summer and fall of '43 these little, pugnacious, unarmored warriors slugged it out with their Japanese counterparts at *Lavella, Kolombaranga,* and *Vella Lavella* in the Northern Solomons, and the result was no less vicious. The numbers were less because the crews were smaller. There was only that.

So, on this day, flying to their patrol area the crew looked down at the scene of the carnage the night before and scanned meticulously for any of the missing thirty or so American sailors. Even such a little battle had cost the Americans around sixty dead and forty wounded, and the enemy over one hundred dead. Skip, at the controls took her lower and circled in ever broader arcs a few times to no avail. No survivors were found.

"Those damn little Nips won't surrender, you know," he said over his shoulder to Jake crouching behind him, to help look, and Chuck at his right. The boss says he read in the reports they refused to be rescued, many of 'em, and just drowned right in front of our guys, the guys on the destroyers who tried to pull 'em in. I guess the fellas have to stay and watch it. They can't steam away and leave a live enemy to maybe get some second wind and swim ashore to fight another day."

Enemy air forces were weakened through attrition now, nevertheless, the enemy pilots remained active if fewer, . . and out of nowhere two zeroes slashed across the Catalina's nose on a left to right path angled toward the PBY, which was, at the moment, on an easterly heading. They had come low over the treetops from the northeast across Bougainville and had surely come down from Rabaul, making that low loop eastward and then back west across. It was daring of the two Zero pilots and an attempt perhaps, like the PBY crew, to assess the previous night's damage.

Roaring across the front of the PBY with all guns blazing, they exchanged fire with the bow turret gunner, Jerome, injuring him. Coming in diagonally, one after the other, to lay some fire back into the plane's cabin, the Japs killed Skip immediately and put Chuck in a bad way.

Chuck struggled through blood in his throat and chest to call out to Jake who was checking on the waist gunners. In only a moment the radioman, Zeke, caught the gist of it and screamed, "Jake, get up here. We got no pilot." Luckily Jake, seasoned as he was, knew it already . . knew the cockpit had been raked with fire, and that was all he needed and, in a moment, he was in Skip's seat as the latter had, through the urgency of it, been pulled and dragged from it before the big bird could nosedive into the sea.

The damn Japs came around once more for another run, but only once, as the Americans were dominate here and the Zero pilots knew it. Each racked an engine on their second pass and then turned and flew off. The injured nose gunner poured rounds in their direction on that second pass. Their skittishness proved the war was won; their daring proved the cost would still be very high. Many Japanese pilots would suicide now in a fight, but a lone Catalina was not worth the cost of a reasonably good pilot and a valuable Mitsubishi from the Imperial Japanese Navy's dwindling supply.

Jake had proved his worth in danger back in the string of incidents that occurred in the fall of the Philippines in '42. Now he proved his worth as a pilot nursing the Dumbo back on an engine and a half. The port engine had escaped significant damage on the Zeroes' pass, but the starboard coughed, sputtered, and slowed the intrepid crew's progress all the way home to the tender anchored just east of Guadalcanal in Iron Bottom Sound.

Skip and Chuck were both dead, and Jake understood now that some things were beyond his control. He was determined to bring them back. All of them. But now he understood, that he did not control a man's bad luck or an enemy bullet's path. He would bring them all home. But he could no longer guarantee they would all be alive.

As he looked at their faces, Skip and Chuck, whom he had not known back in the world, in the states, . . but it was as if he had . . as if he had gone to school with them, shared a huddle, gone on to college, or been rivals for the same girl, even for Sarah . . as he looked at their unrecognizable faces riddled with 7.7 millimeter machine gun rounds . . unrecognizable as who they had been, were, unrecognizable as men from the chest up . . as he looked his thoughts raged out of control and yet sensibly analytical. How did you live and work with a guy, a superior perhaps, and officer, but still a buddy on some level, and then look and they're ground beef on the butcher's stone-cold steel table? If anything came out of it, the war . . besides the patriotism that was still there . . . how could one not care for country with a Sarah back home to protect from a damn seasoned, hardened Jap soldier bent on rape . . who had maybe raped many times . . but besides that, what stood out now was death. It was all around, all the time, and it could be instant.

Command on the tender took note of the eventful flight and the ease of the auxiliary pilot's movement into the portside cockpit seat, and not a word was said beyond, "She's your ship now, Chief Pierce." The radioman had casually implied to the squadron commander, when asked about the event, that he had never seen such coolness in a man as Jake had displayed dashing to a cockpit with two dead pilots in the seats, one of which must be removed quickly, as the plane was already starting into a dive seaward. The petty officer first class mentioned further that, from the sound of it, he believed there was no way Jake should have kept either engine running long enough to get home.

"He's got a gift, sir," the radioman had said to the skipper of the squadron.

That inquisitive and informative conversation closed with the sailor's last comment, "Sir, this is my third Dumbo, and I've had my life in the hands of seven different pilots. It wasn't just the engines, you know. They'd shot the cockpit up an' the radio was out an' both wings were fullah holes . . .the control surfaces weren't workin' properly either. We really shouldn't be here. We should be in rubber rafts hopin' and prayin' for a Dumbo to pick **us** up.

Please don't transfer me nor him. Some of 'em just got a touch, you know."

The coming weeks saw routine mission after routine mission stack one upon the other, each tense, each dangerous, and none quite exactly routine.

Then there was a break and the squadron was pulled out of action to rest pilots and crewmen and to go over each plane, completely overhauling some. New systems were in play as the Navy was always trying to upgraded procedures. It was a new war being fought around the world; and especially in the big blue, and sometimes depressingly gray Pacific. No war at sea had ever been fought like this one. Fleets seldom saw or directly engaged each other. Rather, like mobile voyaging nests, they sent out their swarms of hornets and yellow jackets with deadly stings: torpedoes and bombs that could destroy and sink a whole gigantic enemy nest, a carrier. And you (not the PBYs but smaller planes) were sometimes on **their** enemy's nest (a carrier) and were their target.

Perhaps the men on the carriers felt it the most, the death, and Alvin Kernan would perhaps express it best years later in *Crossing the Line* . . that one minute you were fine, everybody was fine, and then something happened and men were dead: missed landings and such with no time to react to rescue before death appeared. Carrier landings have been described as controlled crashes after all. The ship's crews and flightdeck crews of such ships lived on the bullseye and could not fight back other than firing their, sometimes seemingly impotent, antiaircraft guns.

The submarine war was bigger in this war than in the Great War, World War I. And death came to any ship from seemingly out of nowhere that way. You knew it was there, death, lurking just below the surface. But the mind moves faster than general awareness maybe. Whenever it happened it surprised many of those involved and at great risk. What one might say overall, was that in the modern era, those close to the action on all sides, including civilians in warzones (who in fact contributed the greatest casualties) . . those people were adjusting to constantly living on the surface of a target, a dartboard. But that war was not a war of precision. The blokes in the pub weren't throwing darts, they were tossing big rotten tomatoes and potatoes.

Letters passed back and forth between the young couple, one safe and one constantly in danger.

One of hers ended with a revelation: *Jake dear, I've taken up extra duties. The volunteer campaigns for scrap metal and rubber and such have been worthwhile, but I wanted to feel as if I was contributing more. I work a few hours at the Alameda Naval Air Station in a secretarial role. You know, it's only about twelve miles from home. Dad got me through the scrutiny, and the other issue, you know, never came up. They treat me well. It's for the war effort, but I'm making a little for us too. And then on Tuesdays and Thursdays, I still help with collecting small pieces of scrap metal and rubber from people who donate. I love staying with your parent's, with Mom and Dad. But I needed to do something. The time away makes the time with them, talking and listening to records and the radio, the news and shows, all the better. It takes my mind off worrying about you too much. I must worry. It's my job, a war wife's job, but even I know that one can do it too much.*

Did it worry him. Of course. She would be around all those sailors, and he now knew sailors. Would tough and injured, but walking wounded ones with shore duty, honor another swab's wife or try to compromise her. He trusted her, but every man worried, and in lonely, actionless hours in the sweltering South Pacific islands, between engagements with death, any fellow's mind could go on a crazy trip and jealousy could arise. He had been happiest thinking of her constantly safe with his parents.

~

Sarah was happy with her job and with the volunteer work involving colleting consumable recycled material for the industries producing things for the war effort. It was going on in every city. She was conscientious and happy that she was accepted. She had secured the volunteer work on her own. Eric had set up the naval office job. He had met some of the people there when his career in distribution of institutional canned produce had brought him into contact with them. Sarah was amazed a little that her ethnicity seemed to go unnoticed by both her boss and the employees. It could happen often with respect to minority people with personality and charm such as hers, especially attractive women.

The rest of the time she could only listen to the radio for news, read the papers and magazines, walk, read novels or histories (from which she had learned so much), picnic with her parents-in-law and otherwise pass the time. But the worry wouldn't go away, as it wouldn't for thousands and thousands of other girls.

Ann saw it in her demeanor one day, already knowing it was there. He was her son; she held such worry as well.

"Sarah, honey, he'll be okay. He doesn't fly bombers or a fighter."

"I know, Mom," she replied calmly, not saying what went through her mind at the moment. Yes, Ann had caught her in a down moment as she had let the worry creep in just minutes before. Suddenly she found herself cataloging in her mind the ways he could die. She had asked after all, had requested full disclosure from him. Now, some days it seemed like too much information. But she could not tell Ann.

"Try to cheer up dear."

"I do, but we worry when anyone is away, and it is a war, Mom." She didn't want to scare the older woman, but she believed in truth and she could with clear conscious hint at it.

"It is flying mother. There are crashes here where there is no fighting. Out there he puts in a lot of hours. Maybe I'm just worried about the repetition of it."

"Jake will be back. I'm sure of it, Sarah. You two were meant for each other. God will get him home to you."

Ann knew it wasn't certain, but she believed it would end well. She had her doubts too, but what do you tell someone, someone like her sweet daughter-in-law?

"I wanted you two to have a chance . . to see it in each other despite your youth. Your mother did too. I'm sorry this war came up, sorry we put you in this terrible situation of . . of constant worry at your age."

Looking up from her seat at the kitchen table where she had been moodily sipping tea, Sarah replied, "We were meant for each other, war or no war, we put ourselves here in it, not you. Mom just put us together enough to see if something would take hold back then, and you just made sure Jake wouldn't forget about me if I was important enough to him. We did the rest."

Bending her head back down and looking forlornly into the tea mug, the young wife said quietly as if to herself, "I just don't know what I'll do if he doesn't come back."

Walking over behind the other's chair, the mother put a hand on Sarah's shoulder and said, "You'll get through it . . maybe better than us because you're young."

"I can never marry again."

Since reality was settling into this conversation, and since the older woman knew that facing things head on maybe helped best, Ann took the issue on 'head on', because that was what her generation always did, what people who had lived the Great War of 1914-18 and Great Depression always did.

"Sarah, . . if it happens, if the worst happens, that will be your choice. But you are young and smart and special. You might just find another in that long life ahead of you. And then our Jake will be a memory . . but he will be your best memory."

The girl in the chair turned with tears in her eyes, and she reached up grabbing the other's neck with both arms outstretched and pulled her down to hug. Ann bent down at the knees into a squatting position beside the chair, and the two embraced there, and both cried for some several minutes. Then as they calmed a bit, Jake's mother said, "Let's do something we can do, a positive step. I know how you pray in your room. I hear you sometimes. Let's go right down to church and pray. And let's do it every day. It's our part, our duty to help ensure safe completions of his missions."

~

Jake's Dumbo was deployed again for air sea rescue during the attempt to conquer Bougainville, the large island at the top of the Solomons and the 'Slot'. That was the bloody channel of water that went northwest to southeast down through he Solomons. The crew of the *Flying Cloud* was patrolling in search of downed American flyers and enemy movements as they often were assigned to do. There were a few Navy Grumman Hellcats flying cover at the moment, a bit of a luxury validating the increased risks.

This particular daylight patrol occurred at the beginning of the Allied assault on the enemy grip of the Bismarck Barrier, and just as they reached their assigned station, off of Bougainville, a little luck occurred. Skirting beneath the voluminous cloud cover, their Dumbo flew straight over a small fleet of two large island type fishing boats or passenger launches and what appeared to be an escorting patrol boat.

The Catalina was patrolling in a wide circle that at present found her between the Shortlands and the Treasury Islands south of the bigger Bougainville. Not wanting to push their luck by tipping off the enemy, they headed into the clouds and peeked put occasionally to observe the ships' track. The sighting was reported quickly in code, and after getting an idea of the enemy's course over an hour of observation, the crew was ordered to a different location off of Bougainville's northern coast, closer to the still dangerous enemy base at Rabaul, to watch and wait for reports of downed flyers in need of rescuing. Raids on the Japanese stronghold were slowly reducing its usefulness. There they patrolled the assigned time above Bougainville and east of Buka island.

Just as Jake was about to turn for home, swinging the PBY south along Buka's coast, Doug, a young green ensign and Jake's new copilot had darted back in the cabin to grab a thermos of coffee for them both. Zeroes and other vermin were a rare daylight sight now, what with the Navy dominant now more than ever. But the enemy was beginning to turn toward drastic suicidal measures as they had lost more and more good pilots.

The Cat was brought around by Jake to a southernly course, and the man in the starboard blister (a clear acrylic viewing bubble on each side of the plane) shouted, "Zero three o'clock low," and started working his twin .50 caliber machine guns.

The Jap was rising from off the tree treetops as it came across Buka, and its guns were blazing. The two PBYs working the area were protected by a small three plane CAP (combat air patrol) of new Grumman Hellcats, and while one circled high above on watch, the other two tore hell bent for leather toward the little demon. As they dived sharply, spraying him, the Zero swerved from the PBY and seemed bent on engaging the first of the diving Hellcats. The nimble enemy fighter, apparently controlled by a quality pilot, zoomed across the path of the Catalina, bursting into flames, debris, and nothingness just at the intersection of their courses and about forty yards ahead of the Cat's cockpit.

Jake froze as he saw the plane disappear from view, replaced by a ball of fire he must fly through. Various pieces of debris flew off in many directions.

Immobile in the instantaneous nature of it and staring, he saw one elongated small stick or tube-like object spinning as it followed a course right toward him, appeared to slowly rotate before him, perhaps God's way to adjust the minds of the heroic and allow them to be heroic. And the experienced warrior knew it was coming right at him faster than it seemed, with tremendous power and speed in fact.

It was an instant (not even a moment) in which only reflexes could be engaged, only reflexive thoughts entertained, and Jake bent over ducking and the windscreen on the left side before him shattered with a crash, clear acrylic windshield material flying and falling down and around him. The copilot, returning to the cockpit with two thermoses of coffee in hand and watching the Zero explode from just behind the two pilots' seats said, "Wow, look, what's tha...."

Recovering his position and his sharp mind having recorded everything, Jake shouted over his right shoulder, "Doug . . . Doug . . . where in the hell's Doug . . ." then looking over his shoulder, he shouted back, "Somebody check on Doug!"

Alternately looking at the sky ahead and back over his shoulder, he finally repeated louder and more urgently, "Check on Doug!"

"We have," came a voice . . "He's dead."

"Are you sure, check his pulse!" the frantic Chief Petty Officer yelled.

"No need, Skipper; it took his head off, dammit! It's a damn barrel off uh one of that damn Nip's 7.7 mm machine guns."

The radioman heard Jakes growling groaning verbal explosion, a throaty rumbling growl like a slowly angering dog, and he hollered, called loudly but without emotion, over to the plane's skipper in a firm calming way, "Stay with it Skipper, you're the only one who can get us home, now."

Talking calmly three days later, the squadron commander inquired of Jake, "You're taking Ensign Doug Leaver's death pretty hard, aren't you, Chief."

"Have the crew complained, sir?"

"No, but I can see things. I spend time here with everyone just so I can. Nothing is gained in that stuffy office aboard a big tin barge," referring to the seaplane tender.

"I see a change in both your crew and you, nothing to pull you out of the line, but you're all so quiet and serious, almost sad, right now."

"My boys must feel safe with me. I'll watch myself. I guess maybe none of us have seen a death like that 'til now, sir. I mean, sir, Skip and Chuck's were bad, but to have a guy die like that, like Doug."

"So young with so much promise."

"I keep sayin' . . to myself, you know, 'if I could of dove and peeled away to port . . if I hadn't froze'. ."

"You know Chief, those moments we freeze at such a view, something coming at us like that . . 'staring death in the face' so to speak . . they're split seconds, not the twenty or so seconds they seem. They're parts of seconds. I seriously doubt you could have changed the outcome. Your actions were reflexive, instinctual . . almost out of your conscious control. You saved you, one of our best Dumbo pilots, and you did it unselfishly. In terms of the war effort it means more. Had things turned out different, we'd have been without a pilot for a while and would have had to ground one ship. Ensign Leaver wasn't ready and you don't even carry a third pilot right now. I'm asking for one to be found and sent up here. We don't have a copilot for you right now. You're our most experienced pilot right at the moment."

~

Sarah always had lunch each day with Lenore, a girl in the naval typing pool. Lenore was very sad and lonely, but could perk up into normal moments around Sarah, who was sort of a ray of sunshine to those around her. Both young women had a man in the service, and each ached for the next letter, which sometimes seemed so long after the previous one.

Lenore was older than Sarah. Everybody was, even in a war, like all wars, manned by very young adult couples and singles. But Sarah was the stronger of the two, and when Lenore's marine went missing after Tarawa, well she almost fell completely apart.

Of course, at first, the slightly older woman could not function, taking off from work and lying in bed all day in her little apartment. Of course, that never particularly solved everything for such a woman: laying there to be close to him and because you had no will to do anything else. It was also, of course, the place where the couple most likely spent their last torrid romantically sexual moments, the girl now knowing that those had probably been the last and that if she ever enjoyed romance and sex again it would be with someone else . . and that wouldn't be the same . . it could never be quite the same. 'Missing' form a place like Betio probably meant 'killed in action'. There wasn't very much there at Tarawa to hide anything or anyone.

Sarah considered herself to be 'on duty' now more than ever, doing her share for the war, like Jake. For now, besides the volunteer work and the little office job, came the care for her friend.

The scrap metal work had energized her, as mundane as it was. She was proud of it. For, though she was never any kind of a political advocate for her people, because she had not been reservation raised, she was proud to carry a little of their share for the war effort at home and be seen doing it. If people asked her background, she told them. It wasn't for her, it was for the war and the Native American image. Maybe she felt representative because she held two native nation's blood and blended them with white as well.

This was different now, this duty to a broken war wife. And it was hard because in Lenore she saw herself, perhaps in a year or in months or in the official telegram that could replace his next letter. He had told her enough, through her insistence. Sarah knew the risks to Jake. It seemed to him ever so much worse and gory, and she couldn't know that, but she had an imaginative mind, so maybe she did.

Thus with it all around her: the worry and pain and emotions, the capable young woman plunged herself into saving Lenore's sanity for the woman's man's sake, whether he was still alive or not . . or the one that might replace him someday.

She asked time off, risking the income loss or even job loss, for what was ever so much more important was Lenore, who needed her and the job more. She went to the apartment and sat with the girl: reading in the kitchen with coffee or tea or comfortably in the living room to give the other the privacy of her bedroom of memories and still be near. She worried what her friend might do if left alone. They talked, began to go out together, and discussed what Lenore could do while awaiting news.

Sarah went so far as to sleep at Lenore's for the security of it, of what such a deeply depressed girl might do. The other was young too and had not the tools for what was happening in her life. Who did at the time? People across the planet were being slaughtered wholesale, as well as abused and raped on the same scale. Just the dead would reach over 36,000,000 civilians and 16,000,000 fighters before the dust would settle. Who on planet Earth had psychological and emotional tools to deal with that? Jake's parents were so proud of their 'daughter', and Lenore was ever so thankful for the support, even as she fought through the jealousy that Sarah had so far avoided pain such as her own. Sarah went to their employer and begged patience of the boss, and he understood, thank God. Some workers who valued it got more hours, so things were fine for the moment. Finally, Sarah got Lenore back to the volunteer work with her.

Then the two went back to work, but Sarah was not sure how long she would stay. Jake's extended stay in a war zone, as with most of the American boys, was wearing on his mother, and Sarah felt a duty and a desire to be with her surrogate mother now, doing things together to get through it.

Very capable, the young Native American woman, a quarter white and raised in a rural, mountain town, stood out at work as the beauty that she was and as a capable worker who became an office assistant to the manager. But she attracted the attention of the men of course and a couple of bad apples included. A particular conversation between two of these rough-edged sailors transpired more than once with some slight variations.

"It's getting' darker when we get off now, Jason," the rougher of the two, Al Barnes, spoke on one occasion. "That's what I'll do, catch 'er going home one night."

"She can still recognize you. You're not a killer."

"Not if I don't say nothin' an' cover my face, an' anyway, if it goes that way, I'll scare the hell outa her . . tell 'er I'll beat 'er or kill her folks if she talks. Threatenin' thur folks always works."

"I don't think your that mean."

"I don't guess I am, but I'm getting that little piece of honey brown pussy, an' that's a fact."

"Her man's in combat, and a swab like us, a brother."

"Well, I was too, and got hurt, and I'm a desk jockey now. I'm owed somethin' for it, don't you think? I'll keep her safe and warm for 'em, keep the juices flowin'. Hell, he oughta appreciate it when he gets home."

"But she's got a guy out there in the thick of it, Al."

"Listen, she's an Indian. They're all a little wild; they like it, you know."

"Yeah, you're some big expert."

"Well, yeah, I am a bit. My grandpa was around and about this Old West out here, and his grandpa, my great-great, was fur trappin' back at the end of it. He went to the last of those big rendezvous, which were orgies. Where you think they got the women? There weren't that many white gals around. Indians can't take liquor too well, they're easy. You can give 'em a couple of drinks and get anything out of 'em you want: pussy from the girls and permission for it from their daddies. He said the ol' man told him you could trade a jug of it for an old warrior's daughter . . for keeps that is. You could ride off with her before he sobered up and regretted it."

"That don't make it right. I worry about you. She's a nice girl."

Jason figured that wild things went on in old frontier days, but he didn't think it happened everywhere, all of the time, with all frontier people. And he figured some of the rugged things back then didn't fit well in modern society. Whites were rough back then and Indians were as well, but didn't that little Pocahontas girl that he learned about in school behave pretty civilized way back at the beginning of it all?

The yearly Rendezvous of fur trappers, Indians, and fur traders could be pretty wild and was in fact fueled by various types of alcoholic drinks. But like every kind of stereotyping, that did not define Sarah's ancestral sisters nor America's aborigines in general. Unfortunately, people with evil agendas always need to validate themselves and their evil, and history can usually offer something to be employed in such a way.

Lenore went back to work, and the lowliest of the men targeted her, but not openly. Male predators can be as cagey as the wild beast type, and the two or three in the office waited. Their chance would come to replace the probably dead hero in the broken young woman's bed.

One evening there were issues, supply or manpower, and work went late. Few argued. They were all too close to it to complain, close enough to feel the closeness in the cause they supported together and far enough away to feel free and safe from the battles. Fear of a West Coast invasion had waned with each American victory. Allowed to leave first, guiltily, Sarah and Lenore did.

Lenore was feeling ever so down as the days passed without word of her husband, and Sarah suggested they stop for a beer. Time passed and they talked, and the other young woman felt better. As Sarah comforted her, she clung to hope. Robert, her husband was not reported killed in action yet, still just missing.

"What's up with that?" Sarah said to her. "Have you asked?"

She spoke as they each drank a beer in the little bar just outside the base. Sarah had called home to say she would be late; there was no answer; and there were no answering machines.

The sailor who had targeted Sarah for himself had also left early. Now he watched intently from his table, as Lenore replied, "I believe, Sarah, that he is dead or alive and miss-identified. If that's true he must have been defaced. The horrible weapons they have now can destroy a man and leave him alive. I will have to live with that and accept it if he comes home. I love him. I won't let it matter, I won't."

And the girl didn't cry. She was steeling herself for it, and crying was not part of that protocol. And the brutal sailor at the back-corner table looked at the two of them as one would look at a menu, yet alive, as one might choose live lobsters in a tank.

Catching a cab, they went to Lenore's, where Sarah called again and got Jake's mom, "I called that Lenore and I were going out. I'll be there soon. If I stay with her, I will call you."

"All right dear. I'll tell your father." Turning from the phone, Sarah felt a sudden need to get home that she couldn't explain.

"Are you alright, Lenore?"

"Yes. You know I am now. We're tough. We war wives are tough. They'll write books about us you know."

"That man, the sailor with the limp, Petty Officer Al Randall. He was at the bar, and he kept staring at us. Do you have a gun?"

"Why no, Whatever for? His name is Barnes; Randall is Jason's name, his friend. Jason's much nicer."

Reaching in her purse, Sarah handed a little snub-nosed .38 to her friend, saying, "Lock the door, and don't go to sleep for a while. Don't open the door for anyone you don't know well and care about. Do you want me to stay?"

"If you think I'm suicidal about Robert, why give me a gun?"

"Are you?"

"No. He would want me to go on. And if he is . . is like that . . is disfigured, he is still Robert and will need me all the more."

Sarah looked long and hard at her new, strong friend.

"Sarah, what would it do to him if I did that. I would help the Japs destroy him if I did that. And as to his appearance, if that is the issue . . I'm not that shallow. You've taught me that. I've seen your patience for Jake and know you will accept him no matter how damaged in body, mind, and soul."

Embracing her friend, Sarah replied, "I have a bad feeling about Al tonight. He could not take his eyes off of the two of us. I'll stay if you just ask."

"I'm fine. I'm from Texas. I grew up on a ranch way out near Odessa. And I have a gun. Just keep it quiet."

"Well then. That settles that," said with a smile.

Opening her purse to return the gun, Sarah saw a piece of paper she had not seen when the gun took up so much room. Opening the unfamiliar paper folded twice, she recognized the handwriting of Jason, who worked on documents that she then typed, seeing his penmanship on a daily basis. The note simply said, '*You did not hear this from me. Watch out for Al Barnes!*'

Lenore lived in Hayward too, but it was a bit of a walk from there to the house, and Sarah loved walking in the night. It was normal for her in the mountains and she could deal with anything up there. The city was easier.

But . . she heard him. And suddenly the walk seemed a bit farther.

As Sarah walked faster, the man's feet fell faster and harder on the pavement, and her heart beat faster as well. Besides the gun, the hidden weapon the young woman possessed was her ability, several abilities in fact: speed; wiry, strong muscles; all of her natural skills and instincts of the farm, mountains, woods, and years of pushing off unwanted, untoward advances made in private, not dozens, but a few, enough.

She also had another weapon besides the gun she had almost given Lenore. Reaching in the waistband of her skirt to the small leather strap beneath that wrapped her waist, Sarah easily found the sheath that the pursuer might be surprised to discover if he assaulted her. Grasping the delicate, thin elk stag handle, she pulled out the six-inch-long spring steel hunting knife handmade for her by her father.

He made it, and her mother taught its use. As they taught its use, both insisted it remain hidden and unknown; for, if ever used, she would be hard pressed to defend herself in court as an Indian girl in a white world. They taught fear and its repression and moves no man would expect or be expected to defend in the dark with her speed. And they taught her, that if known to her assailant and in true danger, not to leave a live witness. Remembering it all, and calming herself, she knew now that she had to become the predator.

Stepping off the sidewalk to the shadows, she could visually navigate among the apartment houses in the dreary darkness of the London-like fog that rolled over across from San Pablo and San Francisco Bays. She could do that better than her pursuer, her obvious pursuer, obvious from his actions now. But she didn't see the figure pasting himself flat against the next building's side in the next narrow, black alley to her left. As big as he was, the darkness shielded him; and, as he stepped out at the last moment, Sarah stepped right into his almost massive chest as he grabbed her by both of her upper arms.

Instinctually, because that was the woman she was: the one God, nature, and family history had molded, a woman aware of her surroundings . . instinctually, the young wife exclaimed in an expressive whisper, "Dad, thank God . . there's a man . . just behind!"

Then, as he gently pushed her aside and Sarah stepped around behind him, again, instinctually knowing what to do, the father saw, even in the darkness, as the stalker drew a ball bat up that he apparently kept in the bar where he spent much of his drunken life. But in the moment it was suspended in the air before the intended stroke, Eric's rather large fist destroyed Al Barnes's face.

Grabbing his daughter-in-law's upper left arm gently with his right hand and saying not a word, Eric escorted her to the car parked at the end of the street. In the car as they drove, not a word was said until Sarah, perhaps expecting a scolding said, "I'm sorry, Dad. It was a mistake . . but I was not untrue to him."

"I know."

"Really, I was not playing around or something," said with angst and gravitating toward an emotional state, eyes slightly red and tearing a little. She imagined his controlled anger . . and she imagined her previously possible rape and murder only moments before . . . and the forever future belief by all that she had played around behind her hero husband's back while he was away defending his country and her . . that she had done that and paid dearly for it.

The father only said calmly, "I know."

"What?"

"I know you Sarah. Like you've said before, 'like a daughter'. I've got one daughter and one son who just happen to be able to be married."

"But?"

"...but you're a tired and war weary worker who stopped with a friend for a drink after work. You live with older folks and wanted a moment with a friend your age that was not just 'at work'. You just chose the wrong time and wrong tavern. And I know Lenore needs you now. You've told us."

"You were watching me? I mean like you didn't trust..."

"I was guessing, but I must be right then. I trust you. You're made of the same stuff Jake is, peas in a pod . . like brother and sister who aren't. No two were ever a better match. No, we worried that you were late, and Ann sent me down to check if you were hurt or otherwise something happened."

Sarah leaned over against him, against his arm as they drove the rest of the way, like she would have her husband, or, in this case, her real father, were he still alive.

It was still nagging at her, what her father-in-law might be thinking and not saying . . after all they had done for her, the two of them. She could never have weathered it alone, the waiting for Jake back in Paradise Ridge, with the rumors and the hollow friendships of those who half believed them as she served them over the café counter.

The older man and wiser felt it and picked up his comments and continued, "We trust you honey, your mother and me. I can figure out what happened tonight. And I know that it was probably not just your idea to stop in that tavern and that, if it was, you were helping someone deal with all of this. We know you almost like we'd raised you. You were over so much when Jake left. That was Ann's doing, she encouraged you.

You see, we were aching inside that he'd come back and you wouldn't be here. We saw it when he started working for your mom. He went there more and more and stayed longer and longer. Our son is a worker, but nobody likes it that much . . and look at all he did and wouldn't let her pay 'im. Then, we watched him when he left. He was in great pain to an extent. He hid it with the excitement of what he was doin' . . but he was gonna miss you and knew it.

For a youngster back then, Sarah you showed such character, and he couldn't stay away from you. That's why he worked so long for her. Everybody close to Jake knew how he felt about you. And that basically meant Ann and me and your mother. I think you knew too. You're too smart not to. That's why we trust you . . . that and you're a good Christian woman."

"You're powerful, Dad. What if you killed him?"

"If it's in the morning or evening paper, I'll inform the right people. They know me; it won't become an issue."

~

"Gentlemen, here's the lay of the land, and well, I guess the water too. UDT went in and looked at things, and the Marines put a commando unit ashore to scope things out and maybe stay a while. They're worried at headquarters about the people in camps. It's mostly Americans. The Filipinos are able to move around generally, and the ones the Japs catch causing trouble they just behead or shoot. We're concerned because we think these troops will go berserk as we take more and more territory. There's been a few bad reports of the damn Japs going crazy .. rapin' and burning and such."

The skipper of one of the other Dumbos, Lt. Anderson put in, "I guess it's their code of Bushido and no surrender policy. They may know they're not getting out of the Philippines like a few Japs did at Guadalcanal. The damn Imperial Navy doesn't have the resources now. We've sunk everything."

Jake added, "Far be it for me to speak kindly of a Nip right now, but I'm guessing that the ordinary Jap GI doesn't necessarily cotton to that high falootin' code of their warmongering, medieval "knights' .. the Samurai that started this mess."

"You might be a bit too kind, Jake, but otherwise, I think you've both characterized them quite well, summed up the situation pretty good. To add, I think some of those ordinary farm boys shoved into it will not handle our ass kicking well, knowing escape and surrender are both out. These Filipinos will be the worst for it, the women especially."

The commander turned to the map, "The Marines Raiders were sent in because it was believed there was no Japanese presence near the coast at that point. They were there to find out. I believe strategists wanted to slip troops in there and hit the Japs when they didn't expect it from where they didn't expect it. But they don't tell me. Not my pay grade. They tried to sneak inland, were discovered and met stiff opposition. They lost some men, realized opposition was too stiff, retired to a protected position back near the shore and need our help, a quick extraction. They managed to signal a Dumbo looking for them. That one was not there for extracting them . . to many. You're my best three pilots. Two ships should hold them, and I hate to risk three, but I'm playing it safe in order to get them all out.

We've dropped a night message for the secrecy of it. We knew exactly where they were, and a Hellcat flew in low. They have acknowledged with enough info to convince us its them and not the Japs. Unless we're somehow being tricked, it should be them. They have intelligence we need, besides saving the men. This late in the war, we want to avoid useless losses. If we can send a Dumbo in for two or three men from a downed Avenger, we can risk it for thirty-seven marines."

"I don't know, sir . . . marines? Jarheads?"

Turning with frowns toward the seeming cold insensitivity of the third PBY pilot, all three other Catalina captains present, including Jake, their three execs, and the squadron commander burst into laughter at the interservice rivalry jab. No such rivalry was stronger than that between the Navy and Marine Corp, fueled especially by the fact that the Corp was part of the U.S. Navy and, from an image standpoint, didn't particularly like that subordinate status. After all, they did the tough, dirty work ashore. The marines were the Navy's land forces, its soldiers, and they stood guard on the big ships. In wartime, small units were even on smaller Navy ships to serve as more professional landing parties than the sailors, who were less well trained for it.

The commanding officer finally commented, "Those boys have borne a big load in this war, the brunt of several landings."

Turning his head, which had been down in thought for a moment (he'd lost a brother, a marine captain at Betio) he looked from one to all of his Catalina captains and said, "We'll meet here at 0800 tomorrow and go over the plan. We'll spend hours over it if we have to. I don't want this to be a fiasco and we get those boys slaughtered, and I don't want to lose a plane if it can be avoided."

Looking at them all again a bit sternly, he said, "I expect to lose one Cat." And he let that sink in. "If the Nips are on to us, we could lose everything, all of you and the marines too. The mission is tomorrow night at 1900 hours. It'll be dark then. Of course, the return will be dark while you're in their zone of influence, but we own the air. After you're out, a couple of Black Cats will paste the whole area, with fighter escort protecting them and strafing. I'll have more information at our afternoon briefing. We're still finalizing it all. We need to make sure you fellows are safe if you go down."

At 0800 hours the following morning the briefing confirmed the details discussed the day before. Added were call letters and numbers, recognition signals, and finally escape and rescue plans should a PBY go down.

"The marines were trying to make contact with guerrillas we thought were near Ibajay. In Aklan Province. You have your maps there; Aklan, the northern tip of Panay on the northeast side is where they are (the marines) and we'll be operating. We think the resistance is strong on Panay. Tangalan is just to the east. In close you could have shallow water and the threat of debris, just forest debris, drift wood, coconut logs, and such. The beach and shallows could necessitate a long dash for those boys to the Cat.

Now, we don't have complete coordination between the Dumbos and the Raiders. We have not forced a lot of radio chatter to protect their location. We'll drop instructions before you get there and hope they follow. There will be a confirmation request via radio and instructions by radio if they do not confirm the drop.

Each of you have your sidearm. You cowboys who favor a six gun, should reconsider on this trip and take your 45 automatics. Those 1911s load quicker and have more rounds you know. We're giving you more of everything, extra pistols, lots of clips, Tommy Guns galore, survival rations, rubber rafts, medical kits, etc. There'll be a medical corpsman on each plane, codenamed 'Doc' and call him that when you need 'em."

"What's the big deal with all that, sir?" inquired the young ensign who was the copilot on PBY-114.

"We don't do this type of operation often. We've got three big planes coming into the same area close onshore and picking up multiple personnel on an enemy held island. The marines we're picking up found it too hot, and they're no pansies. There are Japs there and we do not know strength or disposition until we get those boys out to report.

Usually close in like that we're picking up a flyer or two. You boys can get in and out. And we have lost Dumbos that way too. In this operation you'll be more visible and audible with three ships, and you'll be down on the deck too long of necessity, loading those fellows.

When you're up on the step, give it all you've got, get airborne, and get the hell out of there. If you get hit and she's flyable, get as close to home as possible and safely ditch. You just have to get some little ways from Panay and you'll be in friendly territory."

The run over was a milk run, but the men on each Cat knew that was fate's ruse. As the group rendezvoused with the Hellcats, reached the proper coordinates, and prepared to land, the jungle was searched by straining eyes until the signal was blinked up by the marines. It wasn't a flickering orange signal, so it wasn't fire or a lantern. It was a modern combat flashlight. Perhaps each Dumbo crewman breathed a sigh at that. At least this would be a Twentieth Century operation.

A decision had been made to land in turn and avoid both pickup ships being caught on the water if a barrage of fire erupted. This choice necessitated longer and more involved signaling to the marines ashore. Thirty-two were still alive, and two Cats would land in sequence and load half each.

One plane could hold them all if packed in, but the loading time would be slower and might be too extended if the plane came under fire. A single Catalina in that scenario would be sluggishly heavier. Two quick landings and takeoffs could confuse the enemy if performed rapidly.

If there was an enemy presence near, they were cagey and held their fire. One plane landed quickly without receiving any incoming fire and quickly took off. The second landed, loaded, and had just shut is hatch when it was raked with machine gun fire from ashore. The heavy machine guns were just to the south along the coast and well positioned. It wasn't small arms fire. Two pickup spots might have been better, because now the first landing allowed the enemy to sight his guns to attack the second. Through Chief Pierce's mind passed the thought that the Jap commanding officer in the jungle nearby was cagey and that this was a setup.

The plane struggled in a moderate sea, and its starboard engine that was shoreward burst into flames, lighting the scene. Having hardly moved, it was almost blocking the pickup zone.

Two of the three shadowing Hellcats plastered the jungle with bombs, but they had to stay south of the area to avoid hitting the marines, and thus, their effort could not be totally effective. The enemy units engaging the brave raiders were too closely engaged with them.

Jake, at the controls of the third, extra 'flying lifeboat' started in to land and get survivors from the crashed Dumbo. As he did, the Grumman fighters roared in low again with machine guns chattering as they strafed the dark jungle below.

Jake landed further out in the bay, feeling blessed by the slight chop, and then taxied toward the wreck, trying to keep the now burning Catalina between his PBY and the place he felt the active gunfire from the jungle was the worst.

Whether the Americans had flown into a well-coordinated trap or just an accidental mess of war was unfolding, no one knew. But, with the jungle machine guns apparently silenced, the burning PBY was racked with closer small arms fire and then with the heavy machine guns again from the jungle but from another closer location that seemed to have not fired before. It would have avoided the Hellcats' fire by virtue of its closeness to the marines' defensive positions.

Loading of plane crew and marines from the seaward hatch of the wrecked Dumbo had to be quick, but was tedious and difficult, and Jake yelled over and over for an attempt to get all of them quickly, even the severely wounded.

"Let's go!" he bellowed finally and then yelled again, "Get them all!" and then, "All aboard?"

His men encouraged swimmers and sent out two rubber rafts to get as many aboard as they could. Finally, the copilot who had been back assisting screamed, "Go Go! Get her up!"

Jake taxied away from the burning plane on the seaside of it away from easy view of the shore. No mortar or other heavier fire was coming in, so he figured line of sight shooters were the main risk.

The mission commanders in the first Cat now circling safely away from any antiaircraft fire and protected by the fighter escort, inquired over the radio, "You got 'em, Jake?" . . then commanded, "Get out!"

"Get airborne. That's an order, Chief. Get out uh there. Now!"

On a southerly course like the other two planes, because that was where the wind was from, as he quickly taxied away from the wreckage, he wasn't sure what would happen because he could feel the roughness of the shoreward, starboard engine and knew the small arms fire must have laced it with holes. Well, some must be important holes because the engine ran rougher and rougher as he accelerated. Sometimes a missing engine can be bullied and forced with the power and speed of the other cylinders dragging the one that's misfiring along.

There could be no luxury of a long taxi, and Jake turned her a little away from the shore but still in the wind as best he could, still hopefully protected a little by the wreckage and fire of the crashed PBY so near the shore. He throttled the engines as safely as he dared and began the planes take off run. The damaged engine, the potential Achilles heel seemed to be like a worn-out athlete with a second wind and energized as the more numerous still structurally sound cylinders dragged the two dead ones along, broken piston particles having been knocked away by the torque of the throttling up for takeoff.

The PBY Catalina roared across the water on a southerly bearing and rose up on the step awaiting his lift off command to travel through the controls .. and, receiving them, she started to arc skyward when a heavy machine gun or antiaircraft gun hidden in the jungle and well sighted from a different location by some skilled and enterprising Japanese officer opened up with the rage of hell. Close and unnoticed, the weapon, perhaps a 20mm canon, opened the starboard side of the Dumbo like a can of sardines almost from stem to stern, sparing Jake only because the rounds began to hit just behind the cockpit and had to cross through the width of the plane. But sheered-off aluminum struck him hard, though not sharp-edged pieces.

Absorbing and flushing the shock of the sorrow instantly, like a true professional, at first Jake thought of heading for the nearest of the two supposedly abandoned islets, but he doubted the engine for the distance. Through his mind as well flashed the impossibility of remaining hidden with wounded on a small island if the Japs thought they might be there and landed in the night before rescue could come.

The decision would soon be made for him as the starboard engine began shaking and he realized it was struggling to function. Three or more cylinders were not firing, and the air flow over the gaping tear in the starboard side fuselage was not so great either. The situation made him turn and roll the Dumbo as harshly as he dared and head straight for the headland of the bulge of land described in the morning briefing.

Jake could hear the cries and moans of some of the wounded in the back. Ned the port waist gunner was injured as were two marines. The troubled engine now exploded and the starboard wing dipped. Jake compensated as best he could with rudder and flaps and, just as the engine burst into flames, the airframe gave way near the tail making the controls there useless and the tail now a hinderance. Barely in control, Jake brought her into a hard water landing near the point of the poor excuse for a peninsula. As the Cat skidded across the water toward the land but angled sideways, the tough-minded pilot realized he had no control of anything and tried to brace as the shore with a thin ribbon of beach rapidly presented itself.

Then, as more small arms rounds peppered the fuselage, the skidding flying boat hit significant submerged debris, jerked sideways, and wrenched itself up and over to port as the other engine burst into flames. Just as Jake was slammed into the instrument panel, feeling his leg wrenched and forced as well, and lost consciousness, he thought of all the extra ammunition aboard.

Would the geographical position on a point of land in the dark of night be a boon or a bust in the hours to come as the men awaited their own rescue?

"Nothing . . just a hollowness"

The first telegram, an official War Department one, said he was missing and it knocked her down. Literally knocked her down as she was standing right in front of one of the kitchen chairs and dropped right into it.

She read it over and over as anyone would, both solidifying the truth of it in one's mind as they also seek to change its truth. She went to her room, to their bed, for they had slept together there for weeks before he left. She was a strong girl, but this was the big one, the thing they all feared . . all of her family and all the girls and families across America.

She had wanted to hold it, this most recent piece of information about him, but she didn't want to be the one to tell them. She grabbed instead his latest letter, always in her apron pocket, which was really from him, had really touched his hands, and she left the telegram on the kitchen table for them, as they had been out. And she heard his mother weeping softly. Later they talked, and one need not voyeuristically listen in. It was the same things everyone said to share and console. He wasn't dead yet perhaps.

Later, days later, she went to the seashore. She drove her car there, their car. Everything was theirs now. There was no 'I' or 'me' for Sarah anymore. But what if he was taken from her just so quickly. She knew it could happen. They knew it could happen. He had mentioned it that first night after Delmonico's in her apartment. The Catholic in her said, 'til death us do part' but who would be her closest friend save Christ in heaven if she married someday again. Sarah just looked at the Bay, an arm of the Big Pacific, and she whispered, "Fight for us, Jake. Stay alive for us. I love you."

Sarah, strong as she was with inner emotional and moral fiber, went into the obvious depression: quitting her job, crying alternately while curling up in a fetal position and just lying there in bed. With the telegram and his letter clutched in her hand as she lay there and the fist that held them pressed against her breast or lips, in more lucid moments she recognized the semblance of the latter to a baby sucking its thumb.

Thoughts raged wildly through her mind: that he was surely dead because how does one go missing at sea or in a jungle and survive; that she was living with the parents of a man who no longer existed; that she would have to return to Paradise Ridge alone with her tail between her legs, a puppy whipped by life. No . . it was not about her. She missed him terribly . . ached for him, even before the news. The more she ached now . . . felt the hollow feeling if he was truly gone . . but her mind wrestled with all the implications, even her future. She had to think about something. Inner silence could be deafening.

Sarah decided that without Jake she couldn't go on; but she knew as well that she would never take her own life. And thus, there was an even more impossible state of angst.

Then, as if to relieve her near terror just a bit . . to lessen the hollow ache for him . . the second telegram, from his commanding officer, arrived within three weeks. With the defeat of the enemy in that area, the wreckage had been scrutinized and survivors were possible.

Then, with all the thoughts that news generated, the emotional ups and downs, they heard no more . . nothing . . . for week after week, month after month.

It never changed, ever.

Long, agonizing angst enveloped the young war wife, coldly embracing her, as it did so many others . . embracing with an untenable discomfort that was the antithesis of the warm embrace of the lover who may never come back, never even be found, perhaps even no longer existing, what with the way modern warfare could disintegrate its participants.

~

The morning following the fiasco rescue the night before, a fiasco that was partly successful, the squadron commander had overseen a second briefing to follow the shorter debriefing the night before. Knowing the strength of groundfire the men had faced, he would not allow an impromptu rescue of Jake's crew and survivors of the other PBY the night before. This morning would be no different.

"Gentlemen, the marine officer in charge of that incursion has fully briefed me. Lt Jacobson. A very brave man. Luckily, he said, his best noncom, Sgt, Richards is with Jake's crew and uninjured. Unless, of course, he was during the water landing or by small arms fire. We're not going back. We lost two Catalinas and can't afford to carelessly throw anymore away. Gripe at me all you like. I'm not going in there again right now.

Lt. Jacobson says the Japs probably won't defend the beaches but will fight tooth and nail inland. As we've seen lately elsewhere. Last night was probably an attempt to make us afraid to land on Panay. With the lay of the land there and the supplies on Jake's plane, including firepower, the boys may be okay. They have their crew of eight, the medical corpsman, and fourteen marines in good shape as far as we know. The wounded ones were taken off in the first plane. What we don't know is whether they have many wounded. We saw them get hit but we saw a controlled landing. They may not want to contact us because it would give their position away to the enemy and let him know there were survivors. Of course, the Japs can check the wreckage.

Now, that's it for now. No immediate rescue."

~

The second, hopeful telegram had come after attempts to reach Jake's crew were unsuccessful and might mean the capture of the men soon after going ashore. Month after month had passed as she moved through the days like a zombie or robot, doing housework and charity work, and volunteering, fighting the mourning because he wasn't dead yet. And on and on the days dragged until she was shocked from the depths of despair by a slightly longer and more personal telegram, one with just the hint of a personal touch from someone official outside the bureaucracy, someone who cared, someone who actually knew Jake:

WESTERN UNION

```
Mrs. Sarah Pierce

Re CPO Jake Pierce

Notification received survivors PBY
126. Four unidentified crewmen safe in
Panay highlands. No further
information.

My prayers with you and him

Lt Cmdr. David Shaw USN
```

Again, the silence fell, long and lingering like some bizarre level run on the rollercoaster she was unwillingly riding.

~

When the Catalina came to rest on the little wisp of beach along the shore where Jake had purposely and skillfully put it, everyone started offloading. Priority was wounded and then fighting material, followed by whatever supplies they could get before the plane flooded. The Dumbo crew, under Jake's lead went into the jungle together with the surviving marines. Of the original eighteen marines to board the second Dumbo, ten survived that crash and the forced, crash landing of Jake's plane. Of those ten, seven were unscathed or had superficial wounds. The other three had serious, survivable wounds.

On mutual agreement and Jake's deference to the ranking marine, a sergeant, the combat men advanced into the drizzly jungle as the rain appeared to increase. The equally well armed Dumbo crew of eight followed with the three ambulatory, injured marines.

The gentle rain that had been falling, began to fall harder, reducing any natural light from the sliver of moon that was in the tropical sky. And twenty minutes into the adventure it became apparent that it would become an ordeal. Perhaps staying on the shore would have been better, where the two groups of men could have awaited another Dumbo. Having realized from the fate of the original rescue that the Americans were up against more than they had bargained for, the decision had been made by the sergeant and Jake to see just how isolated and temporarily safe the little promontory that they now occupied was.

Ahead of the sailors and the three injured marines the night erupted into a fire fight, and at some point, it became obvious that the Americans were outnumbered. Soon only shouted commands in Japanese were heard and the gunfire was silenced. There were random shots here and there and only Nipponese voices. It was apparent the enemy had won the night and were executing wounded American marines.

Chief Petty Officer Jake Pierce, former adventurous California mountain boy and farmer, suddenly had the duty of his life. Weathered and honed for it now by three years of war, he was now in command and responsible for lives, as on his flying boat but out of that 'normal' environment. The wilderness in the mountain loving Jake kicked in, wrong ecosystem or not.

Whispering, he commanded, "Stay as quiet as you can and follow me. We have to reposition so we aren't where they will look. The only way is to stay along this north shore and try to get to a hiding place or get inland."

"They'll look here, Jake."

"Yeah, but it's the only way away from where they will look first, right behind the marines they just decimated. Right now, they may not know we're here. They could think the marines left us dead or injured on the *Flying Cloud*."

Harder rain blessed them and it was clear that a full blown tropical storm had enveloped the whole area. Night fighting equipped Hellcats could be heard somewhere above and nearby, but they could do nothing beyond strafing safely away from the grounded American's supposed position to keep the enemy at bay. To strafe or bomb where ground battle action was identified would risk hitting the Americans. All the Grummans could provide at the moment was the moral support of the distant drone of their engines saying, "We haven't forgotten you."

As he led them through the jungle along the coast of Aklan Province, Jake's mind processed the thought that, although his very job in the military was to save combat lives, this war often cost those lives in high numbers, and certain circumstances even sometimes dictated sacrificing those lives, even in high numbers. Would his Dumbo crew be caught in such circumstances: a needed rescue too dangerous to attempt in an area where the Navy had just lost two out of three Dumbos and their crews, 66% of its force for the mission?

Thirty or more minutes into the blind trek the group had heard no close voices or other indication of the enemy or marine survivors. Jake became more and more hopeful that they had left the enemy behind in what the briefings had characterized as rough land the enemy had discounted. Sadly, and hopefully the decimated marine force may have lured the Japanese into the secure belief that they had eliminated all of the marines and sailors except those who escaped in the first plane or died in the other two. Surely the Nipponese where angry over the bombing and strafing by the fighters and would take it out on Jake's crew if they were captured. Thoughts of Sarah kept creeping in and had to be pushed out and away. He had to focus all the more as he struggled with the opposite concern the growing feeling that they would never meet again.

At the calmest moment with the terrible possibilities within his mind all hell broke loose in a quiet unassuming way. Just as terrible but totally opposite from the overwhelming massacre of the marines an hour or so earlier Jake's crew and three wounded charges found themselves surrounded and captive. One moment in the natural quiet of a pouring rain in the night darkened South Seas jungle was followed by the soft but firm bark of a Jap command as they stood among a group of seven or eight Japs who had emerged from all sides from the dark foliage. That matched their own crew, but the Dumbo crew also had the three marines. The problem besides the enemy having the drop on them was that most of the Americans were injured in some way. Two of the three marines were in bad shape. Two of Jake's crew were in similar circumstances and the four men had hobbled along to this point. Jake was in pain with every step and did not realize yet why or the extent of his injuries. He would learn later upon reflection how adrenalin can help carry the load.

As the Japs took their weapons and hurriedly searched them in the dark then started to form them into a line Jake collapsed in dramatic pain but not so overplayed as to be obvious. It played to the audience well and as the group was marched south into the bush on a barely noticeable trail, struggling but troubled Jake brought up the rear of the line, just behind the injured, who must be carried by their comrades, and the last tough looking enemy soldier. The Jap must be tough Jake thought to ride drag alone on a herd of captives. Of course, these stragglers were injured.

"Please God, let me get them out," he whispered. "Please let me see her again. Let it pour."

Moments later, while still close enough to the coast for the tough chief and outdoorsman seasoned from youth to keep his bearings, the sky opened.

Still struggling but really mostly pretending it more, Jake scanned the scene as best he could in the darkness and pouring rain, which were working in his favor. He realized that what he had hoped for had developed, his isolation together with the last Jap.

The wily chief paused, bending over forward as if in pain, and the Jap rear guard sentry almost walked into him in the wet darkness. Then Jake abruptly turned to his own right . . spun really, to get to the man's right and, continuing to spin around toward the man and the jungle to the left of the path . . he took the big Jap into the woods and flat in the mud. It was a face on football tackle, grill-to-grill without the grills, and he took him high and from the right side to avoid becoming entangled in a wrestling match with arms as the man would perhaps shout to his friends.

As they hit the ground with the rain covering any sounds yet generated by it all, and free of the man's grasp as he had planned; Jake shoved the soldier's face in the mud. The brute was big and strong, but not exceptionally so, and Jake managed to use his feet and legs to spread the Jap's wide apart as an evil man might attempt to sexually assault a woman from behind. This restricted the Jap's control of his legs to try to rise, and unable to reach back enough to grab the American, the enemy soldier slowly succumbed to suffocation. Rising and pulling the hidden khukuri from its sheath on his inner right calf, Jake drove the knife's point into the Jap's back near the kidney, in spite of its broad spine across from the razor edge. Pulling it out he cut the soldier's soft throat for good measure. He had preserved the edge by these measures.

In the storm it seemed that the intrepid leader's plan had worked for the short column continued on. The man who had been immediately in front of Jake knew he had taken the guard out but remained in the line trusting his commander's expertise and planning. He trusted they would not be abandoned by their chief.

The commanding officer of the little Japanese squad was in the front, leading the way. The next soldier was a few yards behind, beside the first few of the captives, and the other Japanese soldiers were dispersed down the line. Because the enemy soldiers were allowing them to bring along and assist the wounded, the American's arms were not bound.

Jake followed the column through the jungle. Slowly passing them all and reaching the head, where he tracked alongside the Japanese sergeant hidden visually by the jungle and audibly by the wind and rush of heavy rain. God had surely blessed the CPO and his men and perhaps even heard his specific plea. At an opportune moment when the trail turned almost ninety degrees, putting the officer briefly out of sight of his men, Jake drove his body through the man from the jungle on the left and drove him into the mud in the bush on the opposite side. He targeted his tackle of the enemy leader from just to the back of the man's left side, so that he never knew what hit him and Jake could bury his face in the mud and mush of the wet jungle soil of formerly lush, decayed and decaying plants. Such a blatant act and surprise it was that the man could not react with any hint of defensive movement while Jake began to kneel on the officer's back and shove his head and face into the soft muddy soil, thus smothering him. Pulling the dead soldier's head out of the mush by gripping his short military cut of hair, the Navy chief twisted and broke his neck for the certainty of it.

While the assassin was still dispatching his nemesis, the column had turned the corner, and he could hear a little soft chatter in Japanese. Perhaps the Jap soldiers were confused about which way the leader had gone. They continued on as there was no branching of the hidden trail. But it was such a trail as to almost seem invisible to all but the man who had blazed it, perhaps the now dead sergeant who had been leading. There had been seven of them in the beginning, not eight. So now Jake faced five.

The tactical situation called for them to be bunched, for he knew what he was doing and how to handle this. Lola Sunny had taught him, as her mother (the original Sunny) had taught her and the Gurkha, Sanjay, had taught the mother. Maybe he should have been a Marine Raider instead of a Navy pilot. As he now frantically worked, exerting himself while remaining quiet, helped of course by the rain, he thought of Lola Sunny, his mentor in such things and a 'breed' like his three-quarters native wife.

In all of this urgent, deadly experience over the last few minutes, Jake thought he could discern the elusive trail now. And he frantically dragged the Japanese noncom's corpse along the right side of the trail and far into the bush away from their hearing. He exerted himself tremendously rushing to get ahead of them in the softer soil off of the path. Dragging it to a point up ahead, at another turn of the path, and across the road, Jake dropped the corpse and faded into the jungle on the left side. Two pauses of the concerned and confused Japanese soldiers still seeking their sergeant aided his timing, and as they continued, three bunched ahead while two guarded the walking prisoners from behind.

Reaching the body, the three soldiers in front, all bunched together as he had intended, paused, looked down at their commander and then around in the brush. Next, the ranking corporal among them knelt down to examine it as the others were supposed to be looking all around for threats. But they too were drawn to the corpse. Maybe in their confusion, they thought he may just be sick or had succumbed to some quick natural demise like a heart attack. He had no wounds. The lives of Japanese occupation soldiers had become ordeals and where stressful. It had been the situation for months even years, with Allied victories preventing resupply and offering the knowledge perhaps of ultimate defeat. Maybe for the more ordinary Nipponese soldier, some even forced into duty, the brutality their army forced upon the occupied peoples was a hard factor to face as well. Maybe some felt forced into a sort of real life morality play without having sought an acting career.

. . . And Jake burst upon them swinging wildly the well purposed and properly wielded khukuri, turning the three within seconds into butchered meat on the wet forest path.

It was done in an instant and had been expert in its execution as taught to him with a twist or two of his own added to the lessons. The storied knife of Jóhonaá, the Navajo mother, received on the desolate shores of Negros, on the Sulu Sea long ago from the brave British Gurkha officer, Lt. Sanjay, had saved people once again.

As each of the last two Japanese soldiers' attention was drawn to the melee but they could not shoot without hitting their own, each was mobbed by all the Americans, wounded and able alike, except the two more seriously wounded marines.

Coming together in a group, Jake quietly commanded, "We'll go back to the coastal trail, because they didn't take it. Thus it's at least a better than fifty-fifty chance it is safer."

He was listened to by the marines because he had the rank, and he already had the Dumbo crew's respect before this ruined mission and because they had garnered enough of what he had just done single handedly to follow him anywhere now.

One of the marines, the ranking corporal left, spoke, "We were to reach a contact in this area, a guerrilla, but we never got the chance."

"Which way?"

"South into the mountains if we stayed that long and got inland that far. That was an uncertainty in the plan."

With a whispered and urgent tone because he wanted them all away from this location quickly, Jake stated, "We can't stay here, boys, no matter how we'd like to sit here and await a rescue. Too many Japs. We'd get caught again first, or the rescue would be another failure. I know they love us boys, but they're not risking planes and men again right now. We have to get the weapons we can carry and hide the others, then leave. Let's get movin'."

~

Eventually, the same officer contacted her personally again. Rarely alone in the house, Sarah was on this occasion, as Jake's parents were nearby consoling friends who had lost a brother. Sarah reflexively jumped at the mailman's knock, wondering why he did so with no package in his hand. Instinctively, she glanced at the blue star service flag in the window indicating a son at war, praying silently that it would not soon be replaced by a gold star flag. She got up and walked to the door, opened it, nodding a silent greeting, and received a personal letter on military stationary.

She froze as the carrier nodded and turned away, perhaps not prepared to share her pain, and she looked at the envelope. She had seen a war movie or two and bravely had read a few memoirs and novels from the Great War and the current war in Europe, which, having lasted longer, had now produced them. Therefore, tenuously opening the letter, she knew some unit commanders personally wrote to notify loved ones of their son, brother, or husband's death.

> *Dear Mrs. Pierce,*
>
> *I wish I could be there to give you this news in person, but I hope you are with Jake's parents to contemplate it. I know that only a ray of hope can seem so hollow, but we are blessed to have it. We now have news from the coast watchers and Filipino guerrilla fighters that Jake was among the four (or more) survivors and was injured. We know no more other than it is believed he is still alive. Our last word was that all of them were. Somehow, I believe you two will meet soon, as this war is winding down even as it drags on. Your husband is quite a man. Considering the way he joined up in the most unusual of circumstances, he represents the best of the United States Navy. He is my friend.*
>
> Lt. Comdr. David 'Buck' Shaw, USN

And then the silence. The next period of weeks followed by months was agonizingly more bearable because of the news. Yet it became the last straw for the smart, bold, and energetic young woman. Perhaps, in some capacity, the government should have long ago put her in a uniform.

Ann came in to her daughter-in-law one afternoon as the latter was lying on her bed after numbly going through the day's motions: checking if she was needed with anything at the war support groups and then back home cleaning unenthusiastically and robotically.

Sitting on the side of the bed in the cozy little bedroom, the mother gently rubbed her 'daughter's' back in a comforting way and asked, "What are you feeling? I've never asked. I didn't want to trigger the wrong reaction at the wrong time. We really cannot avoid it though. I've been through this . . twenty-something years ago. It's our part of the job, our assignment."

For the longest time the young war wife lay there and relaxed a bit with a mother's touch.

After many a long moment of silent love between the two of them, Sarah said, "Nothing, just a hollowness."

~

Chief Petty Officer Pierce said quietly and instructively, "The signal will be when that body in the tower falls. All of you pick a target and try not to hit us three. I'll take the leader and his two buddies with Dick and Scott's help."

"Are you sure about this, Jake?"

"It doesn't look right Jonas. We've set here in this bush and watched how they've treated these women. There's not enough of a military look nor behavior about them. I know Filipinos reasonably well after those five years. These aren't guerrillas, they're bandits and we can't go around them. But they do have a radio, 'cause the antennae is in that tower. They surely control a bit of territory. If we neutralize this HQ of theirs, we face less threat."

Luckily, the small group of sailors and marines who survived the PBY crash landing had realized what was ahead of them as the approached a typical barrio town in the highlands. Apparently, the men holding it and any territory associated with it had projected their concerns and watchfulness eastward down the slopes towards greater civilization, agriculture, and the Japanese garrison troops. The enemy held the lowlands and cities on each of these islands, the developed regions, and ranged into the hills only when necessary to deter threats. They feared the guerrillas and the rough hinterland. Maybe the occupation troops were not the cutting edge in the imperial barracks, or maybe those guys were dead.

The small American squad's approach from the most wooded side of the village went unnoticed, as the marines and Jake were seasoned now by a war.

The town was a mix of unpainted, dark wooden structures and nipa houses: some just huts and some quite bigger with multiple rooms. There was no townhall, but there was a small school which seemed to also be like a community building. Any church, always a requisite in the islands, was surely in a nearby, larger municipality, though probably still quite provincially small. Beside the school, there was a small stone grotto structure with a statue of Mary in it. It was formed from those white and gray, rough, and slightly crumbly stones that appear to be made of coral skeletons. Black volcanic stones were used in the town as well. The streets and side paths were the ubiquitous dark grayish-brown, packed earth, as was the one road that led into and out of the little village.

Jake thought of the similarity of these little, faraway, rural Filipino towns to some American Indian villages back home. These were simply more Western European in appearance, perhaps like the Cherokee back east in the Appalachians and the Navajo in the Four Corners region. It was about lunchtime, and people were cooking on charcoal stoves in their homes or on occasion outside.

As if for a fiesta, a small pig was being turned over a charcoal bed in the ground near the schoolhouse. But there seemed no joy in the people, and it spoke to Jake of captivity. He had seen it that momentous and tensely sad day in Borneo, what with those cheerless captive girls forcing cheerfulness because they had too. Just like that day in Borneo, the men in this village and its women were not a match.

Moments after Jonas's second-guessing, Jake and two others approached the seven seated men in the little village square, two near the obvious leader.

As the leader started to stand, Jake said, "Oh that is not necessary sir. Please remain relaxed. We are honored to be in the presence of such brave freedom fighters helping our mutual cause, a free Philippines."

It was tactical as much as diplomatic. He could much easier kill three seated men with the khukuri than a standing one. The man complied, feeling puffed a bit with importance, and playing the game, thinking the Americans to be fooled. Jake's knife was in its sheath behind his back. That was how the Gurkhas wore them, but he had a leather sheath of Jóhonaá's making that had stood the test of time since 1902.

"Will it truly be free after we defeat these bastards, Yank?" thus, with the comment the Filipino revealed what Jake had perceived, a certain anti-Americanism.

"I hope so, 'Dong'. I live here . . did before the war. I have no problems with less government from back stateside."

It eased things immediately, and Jake saw a ray of hope that these were just rougher-edged guerrillas than he had expected and not bandits or communists like the Huks in the northern islands were becoming according to rumors.

"I see you brought us weapons and ammunition."

"We can spare little. We need some too but will help the cause."

"If you expect our help, you'll give whatever we need."

Jake was a little bit aware of some rivalries among the guerrilla bands; but most, both American and Filipino led ones, were cooperative and even acted as a unified organization. It varied between islands and even regions on individual islands. This response was clearly not cooperative or that of a true ally.

Jake inquired, "Is Miguel Llano around here?"

"Is he your contact? We do not care for him."

Looking up at the tower, Jake said, "I see you have a radio."

And, as they followed his eyes, their man in the tower overlooking the plaza took a headlong dive to the ground assisted by 1st Class Petty Officer Davis, who knew the signal would be Jake's look upward.

Utterly shocked and a bit unnerved, even in his position of strength, the leader turned angrily and was immediately killed by the broad, hard, powerful strike of the khukuri across his throat. Each of his six companions were shot by the .45 caliber sidearms of the two men on either side of Jake, and four other sailors and marines, spreading out to the sides quickly, shot every other male in the plaza with a spray of rounds from heir Thompsons. 1st Class PO Davis took out a few from his perfect perch above. The bandits were identifiable by their defensive actions.

Immediately, as per previous instruction, all the Americans flattened to the ground on their stomachs or crouched in anticipation of fire from the houses in the little nipa village.

"It is safe, Americanos," said a young woman and an older one simultaneously as they came out from the shadows of the trees where they had been lingering through it all until the lead began to fly. Both were reasonably young and not unattractive. Their dress and that of others lingering or doing chores was unremarkable and worn from over three years of depravation. The thin material was pleasantly revealing of the contours beneath.

Tentatively the men rose but remained watchful, searching every potential dark crevasse and corner.

"And you are?"

Speaking more cheerfully, the older one answered almost all questions, "We are mother and daughter. Our younger men are gone with the guerrillas or dead from the war or these bandits. They killed my husband who was our mayor. Some are off with

Miguel and the others killed by the Japanese or these poor excuses for Filipinos you have just relieved us of."

The younger one added, "We are a town of women, children, and old men only now. I hope your men have honorable intentions. We are obviously defenseless."

"We are honorable, Inday. You can count on it. My men are the best the U.S. Navy has, sailors and marines. What can we do for you? We're a bit beat up now, but not useless."

"You have done much already, cleaning our street as you have. That is quite a knife. It is Oriental like our bolos and the knives of the Moros. Allow me and I will clean it of his evil blood."

Taking the offered knife, as Jake did not want to offend her, the older woman slightly, almost imperceptibly gasped, looking up at him with widened eyes.

After a long, pregnant moment, she inquired, "You know her, the Jaguarundi?"

"She loaned it for the duration of the war. She is a lola to me, but not by blood."

"She is real? Is she as beautiful as they say?"

"She is. She seems almost like our pretty mestizas. She is half, you know. Her native side is American Indian," he said, opening his treasured photo wallet.

Moments later the three were sitting, the mother and daughter and Jake. The woman had cleaned the blade and now studied the knife, turning it over and over in her hands. The younger woman worked on Jake's arm wound from the original crash. It was healing but was a bit infected. Doc' came over and showed her how to dose the sulfa powder and pills.

When she was done with the arm, she inquired, "You said 'our' and called me 'Inday'. Are you Filipino? You don't look even part."

"I've lived here since I graduated high school back in the States and came to the South Pacific." It was a regional term the Filipinos seldom used, but Americans, especially young men used it for the adventurous sound of it.

"You have a wife here, I'll bet, though you Americans shy from that, from mixed marriages."

"No, but I came close a few times. She's American and waiting back home."

"A pretty white girl then?"

"Wrong guess again. She is as dark as you, a Native American Indian," said with a teasing smile at her failed guesses.

"Oh, like the Jaguarundi then?"

"Yes Inday."

Looking at Jake, the mother offered, "You're an interesting man, Captain…?"

"It's 'Chief Petty Officer'; I'm 'Chief Jake Pierce'."

Jake nodded to them both as a formality of introduction, and the younger woman said, "My mother is Maria Angelina Ramirez and I am Maria Pilar Elizondo, but I am widowed too now . . by the war."

She took his right hand in hers, touching the back of it to her forehead respectfully in the traditional way usually reserved for an older relative, and Jake noted her satiny soft brown skin. Perhaps it was the best way she knew to show respect. He did not offer his similarly to the mother, for she was too young and pretty looking and it would seem an insult. She held her hand out, and he thought to shake it, but then to ease the woman's obvious stress, he took it and kissed the back in the more elegant European way. She smiled.

Jake made a mental note to tell PO 1st Class Davis to talk to this girl, the daughter. In his mind, for no obvious reason other than youth, they seemed a match; and, inside, the softhearted Jake was hurting for the young widow. He saw Sarah in her. He saw Sarah in them all.

Assured that there were no more members of the bandit band, the men rested for several days and healed. All were doing well, including the two marines. For some unknown reason, after the true guerrillas were contacted, word got out eventually of only four survivors of the plane. Few of the marines had made it of course. But his crew was intact and he was going to get them home. Jake actually commanded eleven men now. With the extra medical corpsman 'Doc' included and him, they were an even dozen.

The very first night, they slept carefully, fearing betrayal. Though the mother and daughter stood out and not every woman in the village was beautiful, Filipinas in general always had for Jake a certain pleasant appeal. It was perhaps the petite delicate features and tawny brown skin. In the present scenario, pretty women just added the sense of intrigue, but his men behaved, and soon regular sentries sufficed.

Also, that first night, Jake talked to Petty Officer Davis. Regular Navy, as a young seaman, Richard had been stationed at Pearl and his wife, a waitress, died during the attack that horrible morning. She was walking to work for some early preparations for a Sunday luncheon and was strafed by a fighter with a group of civilians and sailors walking along together.

The women of the town were of average Filipino beauty, which meant of average beauty in general. They were different, smaller and brown. But the average to above average Filipina bore a pleasant face and expression that, together with voice and personality, could melt a man not concerned about color into a little puddle. The widowed daughter and her mother, amid that general description, were quite extraordinary. As much as we like to believe that looks mean nothing beyond the basic appeal they generate, the mother's appearance may have helped get her husband the mayoral job that he had held indefinitely until the bandits arrived. The towns handsomest man won the prettiest girl, and the people elected the most attractive couple to power.

"Richard. I don't know how long we're staying here. But I've got two things to say to you . . no, three: Talk to that girl there, Maria Pilar; If you feel like it after that, tell her you're comin' back when we leave; and come back when this is all over. She's a sweet, sad war widow. You're a country boy, and you said if you marry again, that's what you want. Well, you're too young to not marry, and this little town's about as country as it gets."

After a week with the pleasant villagers, during which Richard became almost inseparable from Pilar, word came from the official guerrillas, commanded in the region by Miguel Llano. Overall command on Panay rested with Col. Macario Peralta, Jr.

The Dumbo crew was ordered to remain where they were because the Japanese were not active in that sector, being too worried about the impending invasion and the struggle with the real guerrillas. The point was to allow wounds to heal and the men to be ready to fight if they were needed. Richard was happy, And the girl seemed more cheerful as well. The guerrilla headquarters commended the PBY crew and marines for the defeat of the bandits and breaking their hold on the little barrio village.

As time passed, only a week or so, the mother of the girl said, "Chief Pierce, he told my daughter he will come back after the fighting. Her heart is going to be broken again."

"I think he will if he survives it. He has nothing else, same as her."

They were eating alone under some cooling, low-hanging banana trees and she said, "There are no guarantees."

"Are there ever? The Navy may force him to go home for discharge, I have residency here, did before the war. I will try to intervene if he wants to stay. I'll hire him and tell the government he is my employee."

"I have been to some of the port cities. I have seen the casualness with which your sailors treat our girls, and few marry what you whites call 'colored' girls in the end. But they wave money around that some girls cannot imagine and ruin their lives for the future."

"Dick's not like that. He's been through what she has, too. You know that. I can't promise he will be back, Nobody can. He might not survive the war.

But, Maria, I would not have introduced him to her if I didn't trust him with her. He knows her kind of pain because he has felt it himself."

Surviving and convalescing in peace, Jake thought he might last 'til the end of it, at least in the islands.

Through all his ordeals since the crash he had borne wounds he was not aware of. Nagging pain in his right leg portended a cracked bone. Serious trauma, infection, and possible amputation had been deflected only because he had splinted it simply for the support it lended, thinking it a mere sprain. In doing so he had Doc yank it just in case. So, on a 'why not' whim, it had been properly set.

But a fairly weak and malnourished Jake Pierce had one more ordeal as the PBY crew joined the guerrillas in repelling a small unit of Japanese searching the mountains for them. These particular enemy soldiers made a sweep in the highlands, looking as always for those who refused to comply with orders to turn themselves in. One group of American refugees on Panay illustrated the enemy's attitude. Half of the little hidden village of peaceful fugitives were gold miners and their families and half were religious missionaries and religious organizational leaders with their families. After many flights in the night based on rumors of Japanese patrols (some true, some not), the religious group refused to run during the next enemy sweep and decided to peacefully surrender. They were all murdered by the Nipponese patrol that was seeking them. The beheaded adults and bayoneted children became known as the Hopevale Martyrs, after the name the larger group of miners and missionaries had given their hidden camp.

On the occasion that impacted the Dumbo crew, the enemy goals could have been one or more of several. Perhaps it was to protect their flank or to seek their own hiding place from the impending massive invading U.S. dominated Allied forces.

The combined local guerrillas had tracked the enemy's movements and chose a well defended gully below a village the Japanese had targeted. The sailors were on the frontal battleline behind barricaded embattlements and they were supported by many armed Filipinos, even some women. The weakened sailors were not the main center force, simply part of it. More experienced members of the guerrilla movement, Americans and Filipinos, commanded the center and prepared flanking attacks as part of a plan that would use the land to take the advantages of numbers of professional soldiers away from the enemy troops.

The Americans and the best of the Filipino fighters were easily the equal of the enemy they faced, some of which were less highly trained garrison troops.

Within his small command, Jake deferred for advice to the surviving marine corporal he had taken the liberty to advance to sergeant. Together the two led the defense of and held solidly a stone barricaded road far east of San Marcos, the village they had been recuperating in so pleasantly.

In the heat of the frontal assault, presented to appear to the enemy as all the Filipinos had to offer. Jake was directing fire from a group of Filipinos armed with the extra Thompson Submachine guns his crew had lugged from the plane. When they were captured weeks before near the shore the Japs had confiscated the guns and made the Americans lug them along. Thus, most were not lost in all the events that transpired. Others and ammo had been hidden and Filipinos guerrillas went back later to retrieve them.

At a point where the chief had to briefly expose himself he took a significant amount of enemy rifle fire, as well as that from one light machine gun. The latter tore across his war-battered legs, but perhaps in the heat of battle some machine gunners pan too fast. He only took three hits from just enough distance and ricocheting to take a slight edge off the damaging force. One round devastated his right calf muscle, and two did similar damage to his left thigh rebreaking his femur. A powerful, close rifle round from a charging Jap found his left shoulder and put it out of commission for the foreseeable future. Shortly after he fell back in the gully, the enemy made one of their signature banzai charges. They had the advantage in numbers, but not in strategy and tactics nor fighting skill and they fell into a simple envelopment trap.

The only problem with any such plan is that the bait, in this case the center group at the barricade has to take its blows to the very last, and Jake lay on his back with pistols drawn and his khukuri beside him. Sarah once again flashed through his mind as well as the thought of Lola Sunny's khukuri on some damn Jap officer's belt, and he gritted his teeth.

Originally a patriotic yet reluctant warrior, the nearly beaten but undefeated man now lay back, unable to rise and stand on a leg now broken for the third time since the day years prior on the Javanese woman's sloop.

Reluctantly the Guerrillas let the charge reach the barricade for the authenticity of the bait and trap, and they then came rushing in from both sides with a vengeance.

The group of Japanese facing them had chosen the trademark Nipponese banzai charge, out of desperation perhaps.

Finally, he came face to face with it . . with death and the tremendous, heavy odds of it . . . the death every frontliner and many others had faced throughout the recent years now . . the knowledge as you stood or took some other demonstrative action necessary at the moment . . . . that you were going to be horribly, viciously, ended . . and all that mattered to you would be instantly gone, you would be gone . . .

. . . a long slow fall in flames with no saving chute, or ripped to ground chuck by a chattering machine gun as you staggered and fell, tasting the rough beach sand as life left you

. . . or maybe, as Jake struggled up onto his knees . . . being ripped and gutted by a Jap bayonet, as a rifle barked some distance away and the round just happened to break his right wrist sending Lola Sunny's khukuri uselessly to the ground.

A Japanese soldier, rushing wildly up the tangled slope, appeared ten yards before him, as Jake painfully raised his .45 pistol in his left hand and pulled the trigger. The pistol was empty. His throbbing, searing left shoulder and almost useless right wrist now made changing the clip impossible with any speed; and, with arms and legs barely functioning, there was literally nothing Jake could do but attempt to dodge the bayonet now aimed right at his body from five-yard distance and closing in this rage of battle, the one time that men clearly attempted, face-to-face, to end each other's existence on the planet.

But Jake raged too, reaching back with painful arms to try to find some support, some tree or stump from which to push himself toward and into the enemy that had killed and maimed so many of his friends.

It was as if he wasn't cognizant of the bayonet or ignored it and his own impending doom . . . but then he grabbed feebly at it to try and go on . . for her . . . for there flowed instant, flashing visions, mostly filled with her . . .

But, in that suddenness of movement common of hand-to-hand combat, just as the Jap leapt the wall and Jake's usable left hand guided by a useless arm grabbed at the bayonet, Jake saw a terribly quick and forceful movement from his left that blotted out the sunlight coming through the tree foliage. And Richard, his flying body the source of the light dimming 'cloud', let the enemy know what a bayonet felt like, coming in on him from the Jap's blindside. Once he identified the darkness that he had confused with his own impending death, Jake thought it was a blow that would drive the rifle barrel through the man. Then Dick shot the still breathing man off of his bayonet with two rapid rounds.

Still kneeling arms down and looking at Dick, after having watched Sarah's calm face appear before his eyes and whispering goodbye, Jake said, "Thanks. I'd bought it."

"I owe you."

Jake fainted, and at the impromptu field hospital it was discovered he had the broken leg, two seriously abused thigh joints, one shot through the left shoulder, and a broken right wrist. Only later when x-rays would be taken at a bigger field hospital would it be discovered that he had a break from the crash that had healed badly. Given the jungle conditions, the climate, and the supply situation, his survival so far had been a blessing and in the future was not certain.

Nevertheless, weeks later, coming out of one of a few sleeps induced partly by native alcohol drink, because the guerrillas lacked morphine, the tough young adventurer and now seasoned sailor, pilot, and Navy chief woke up in an official Navy field hospital on the coast of Panay, where several of his injured crew were being seen by the doctors as well. He had a touch of malaria which had dragged him down as well, though he was apparently somewhat immune to the worst that tropical disease could do. He wasn't a beaten man; he was a worn-out man, who the war did not need at the moment. That combination, as he thought of the marines that 'he' had lost, and Steven . . wondered about Jon and Maya, perhaps in India now . . and thought about the pilots he had been unable to reach on more than one occasion . . . . that combination sent Jake a bit downward into a not unexpected depression. The slaughter of the Marine raiders at Ibajay Bay hung heavy on him for the sheer numbers of it and the bravery of them and the Corps.

~

"Mom, I'm going. I have no choice. They've forgotten him and us. Maybe he is not receiving care, proper care, I mean."

"How could you pay for the trip and your expenses, Sarah? No one does it. So many wives are hurting like you. I'm hurting like you."

"I will sell the grill, and my farm if I have to."

"You'd have nothing to go back there to."

"I don't want to."

"The government probably won't even let you. The war is not over."

"I'll find a way."

"Sarah."

"Mom, I saw the Clipper in the Bay today. It will be going west. I'm sure they brought it here for some trip out to where the boys are. They surely don't use it for anything else. They have so many planes for use here in America. It's a long-range plane, a flying boat for crossing oceans."

"Dear, it may be for celebrities or important commanders, even some congressmen."

"Well, I won't know unless I ask."

Then in a rare moment of levity, the worried young wife said, "Maybe they brought it here just to take worried wives out to look for their husbands."

The mother fell for it and looked with a jolt as she searched for a verbal comeback, as it seemed her daughter-in-law must have lost her mind under the stress of worry. Then seeing the smile, she returned it.

Sarah said, "I won't get on that plane; I know that. But I need to do something, and that is something to shoot for. I can hit the elk at five hundred yards if I'm capable of trying for one at a thousand. Maybe I'll talk someone into a job in the department that tracks lost sailors. Or maybe I'll eventually get some type of service job over there when the fighting stops . . over there where he is. We just sit at night and listen to the reports on the radio. We get the big story. I'm just worried about his story, my story."

Her father-in-law, standing at the door between the kitchen and the dining room, said, "Ladies, let's come into the living room and sort this out."

Rather than argue with their daughter-in-law like one would normally with a son or daughter, Eric decided to play along so he could play devil's advocate. He also figured correctly that whatever the girl planned in her mind at that moment was therapeutic, whether success was later achieved or not.

"How would you do it Sarah?"

"Dad, I must find out if civilian travel is available. The Pacific has been generally closed for that. I do not believe the Clippers are flying. The government still uses them though."

'Well', the older, experienced man thought, 'she's thinking it out just like I thought she would. The emotions aren't overtaking that smart little brain of hers.'

He replied, "The Clipper is cost prohibitive, Sarah."

"I'll sell my properties, as I told Mom. I don't need them. Nothing matters without him."

"And if the Clipper is not flying or any other commercial airlines? Steamers are expensive, and they won't let them sail now because of the submarines. You can get out there after the war, when they let civilians out there more easily. We can help you with money we've set aside for Jake's future, inheritance and such. You two will still have your assets then. But now, what it there's no civilian transport?"

"I plan to go to the Navy in San Francisco and seek information. Then I plan to try and get a secretarial job with some organization going there, perhaps the Red Cross going to help those poor war-ravaged Filipinos or a news service sending more people to report about the end of it when it finally comes."

"A young woman like you can be taken advantage of, Sarah. But you know that."

"I'll have my eyes open, Dad. If nothing else, civilian travel services will become more normal. I just don't want to wait that long."

Surprising both women, the father figure for the girl said, "Let us drive over there tomorrow and see what's going on now that it's getting closer to the end of it. Who knows for sure unless we go and see for ourselves?"

The father had wanted the daughter-in-law to see the difficulties for herself, and now, the next day in late morning he paid the price as they sat on a bench at the port and consoled their tearful daughter. He knew as well that she would seek a solution. The woman was made of strong stuff. But for now, she sobbed. The immensity of her purpose was soaking into her consciousness.

It was not an unusual sight. A war was on, its results still festering even as the end was in sight, and it had been causing girls to cry for almost three years now. People in civvies or in uniform passed and barely noticed while others nodded in sympathy to the two parents. No one seemed to visibly react to the differing skin tones between the older couple and the crying girl.

At some point, while she was still in tears, an officer in a crisp white uniform stood before the three and asked, "May I be of assistance."

It was a courageous offer because, assuming the young woman had just learned of a dead husband, what could he do? But, by coincidence, yet not so odd considering the historical timing, the officer worked in the personnel department dealing with the losses. The man standing before them knew that there were many kinds of cases, the lost and MIAs (missing in action) and sometimes, in a war this big, some found and lost again in the system . . or some jungle somewhere. There were lots of jungles. The Japanese, having not yet in that era left their militaristic barbarism behind, had left a trail of atrocity across East Asia from Manchuria and Korea south to Java.

The three looked up, and Jake's father explained, "Our daughter-in-law had hoped to learn something of our son somewhere in the Philippines, but there seems to be no way. Our son is injured and all information is lost to us. He seems lost in the Navy medical system."

"How so?" the officer inquired further.

"We received only notification he had been found and was wounded many months ago and then nothing more even now."

"My my. That is incredible. I know a fellow officer who can advise you if secrecy protocol allows it. His assignment is related to such cases. He is headed west into the Pacif... uh, well, I shouldn't say too much. We did not discuss his orders."

The officer stood straight and introduced himself, reaching his hand out to the father, "I am Commander Aaron G. Derickson, at your service."

As the two men shook hands, and perhaps due to the urgency of the family's concerns, he continued talking without directly greeting the two women.

"Now, what I can say is that I have just handed our records, that is copies for him of them, of all the Navy men, including Marines, in the Southwest Pacific we are aware of who are missing and seemingly shouldn't be. We want to get on this before too much time goes by. Men come in from battle sometimes and they end up on a hospital ship away from their own base or vessel. If they have memory issues or are unable to communicate for whatever reason and have no tags, no one knows who they are . . those types of snafus. There are those who might lose their dog tags. Men don't carry personnel records on them in combat. Those tags are it. The fellow I'm working with, well, just trading papers with, is going to deal with it.

I'll be meeting him within the hour. I will see if he can meet you and if he will give me any message for you if he can't. He has to leave in a few days. Could we meet back here at say, three o'clock? My office is nearby, so it would be convenient. That should give me enough time to explain your story to him after we discuss a few things about the files he has."

"Yes, and Thank you, Commander Derickson," replied Eric. Sarah looked up and nodded positively, too scared to speak. It was as if this powerful machine that was government might inconceivably be able to help her.

The three went to a nearby cafe and had a late lunch. It was one thirty in the afternoon. They spoke sparingly, the parents taking their cue from Sarah. It was the concern of them all but she was the most visibly shaken at the moment.

Just as they walked out of the little eatery's door just before three, they saw another officer crisply dressed in white standing near the bench that Sarah had occupied earlier.

Recognizing the family trio from Cmdr. Derickson's description, the well-spoken, handsome, and friendly officer held out his hand to Eric and said, "You are lucky Cmdr. Derickson stopped. Commander Gerald Phillips at your service. I know a little about cases like your son's."

The officer and Jake's father shook. The mother offered her hand followed by the still quiet Sarah, who was calming herself and trying to keep her composure. Perhaps she expected no success in this endeavor and the situation now made her afraid of messing things up.

"What is your husband's name and duty?" he asked her directly, wanting to engage Sarah immediately in this important issue involving her.

"Chief Petty Officer Jake Pierce. He flew Catalina's."

"Oh, the Black Cat's?"

"I don't think they use that name."

"They're Catalina night bombers."

"Oh no; he flew mostly rescue missions before they went down. He used the name 'Dumbo' when we talked."

"A courageous duty. In the Philippines?"

"We don't know everything, uh the secrecy, you know. Maybe, during Leyte. That's when he was lost . . uh, just after maybe. It has been suggested he is there."

"And he's been recuperating all these months?"

"Yes, we suppose, Commander. They said he was found, and then, and then . . nothing."

"The Philippines is where a lot occurred . . bigger than other terrain we've fought over. It's where one would need to be. I'm headed there shortly."

Turning back to the father-in-law, because it was the era they occupied, the officer stated in an almost official tone, yet still warm and friendly, "Sir, she's not going to find out much here. You all probably know that. The system works the same for all."

He paused looking at them all, and Eric nodded agreement with him somewhat demonstratively.

The officer had been told by the naval officer who had first met the Pierces that he had seen them earlier inquiring about the Clipper. The man had seen the girl sadly walking with her parents-in-law up from the Marine guard at the Clipper's dock where the launch that serviced the big flying boat was tied up.

Continuing to his ultimate point, Commander Gerald Phillips said, "I am willing to guess that she has proposed going out there. She will never get there on her own. I suppose you folks realize that as well. I don't see an unattached civilian young woman getting transport. They're just not going to do it."

Suddenly, looking at the red-eyed Sarah, now intently looking back at him as he spoke, Gerald asked, "Young lady, can you type?"

"Yes, of course. I took high school business classes. I can take shorthand too."

"How is your health, if I may be so bold as to ask?"

"Excellent. I am an outdoorswoman from the Sierras."

"Mrs. Pierce, Mr. and Mrs. Pierce, I have a proposal for you, for all of you. I suppose it is a bold one. If you will permit me, sir, I will employ your daughter here as my personal secretary. It will require her traveling with me. I'm headed where she needs to be, to the Philippines. I assume she might go with or without your permission. Few young women are so intent as to try it as she is. But I would like to have it, all things considered. I don't see how she could get there any other way."

All three were almost speechless at the turn of events and their luck, and Sarah's heart truly 'leapt' as described of women in many an old romance novel.

After a moment, Jake's father said, "Well of course, I suppose; but let us discuss the particulars, if you will."

"Of course, I understand."

Then, looking at Sarah, the officer offered, "Mrs. Pierce, I need a secretary with me on this tour of duty. There has been no offer of one from my superiors in the haste of this assignment. I would like to hire you, at my own expense if necessary, should the Navy fail to sanction the cost. I have the means; but I see his medals on your lapel. Perhaps we'll shame them into it. Now, if you folks will await me here for a few moments, I will go to the Clipper and check on the space for Mrs. Pierce.

Then we'll have dinner and discuss her safety and the like. Would that be alright with you folks?"

"Of course," all three said quietly; and the father inquired, "What did you have in mind?"

"I know a good old Italian owned place or two near Fisherman's Wharf. The Clipper leaves Thursday evening; so, if you are still agreeable after we talk, the ladies may need to shop for some travel clothes for Mrs. Pierce. There may be no time to go home and get back . . depending on where you folks live."

"Hayward, but she has a suitcase in the car."

"Good, but you might want to pick up some tropical things. It's eighty down there all of the time . . eighty degrees and eighty percent humidity, and the sun is bright and searing. I know a little shop that will fix her right up. The girls there understand what she'll need. Do you need an advance, Mrs. Pierce?"

"No sir."

"We'll help her with it, Commander. We'll wait here for you and then shop after we've eaten and been briefed."

"Alright then, see you back here at 'our bench' as quick as I can. No, on second thought, that shop might close early. I also have to check on clearances for Mrs. Pierce. It will all have to be done here; no time to deal with Washington. We're lucky we have a couple of days to deal with it."

Then, looking seriously and with compassion at Sarah, Commander Phillips said, "Mrs. Pierce, I will get you on board that flying boat with me if the Navy will let me. I am going to need some things from you. I don't know how we can take care of this fast enough."

"I have my passport with me, sir, and my birth certificate and high school diploma. That is literally all the documents I own except the will my mother left me and the one my dad left her. They are in a safe deposit box at our bank in Hayward. Oh, and I have our marriage license and a copy of his enlistment papers which were an impromptu thing in Singapore at the war's beginning."

"Really. It appears I'm hiring the right woman. How old is the passport?"

"It was secured by me just before the war began. When mother died a year before I graduated, I decided to clear my head with a trip once I finished school. Our business, a grill, needed me though, and people said it was becoming dangerous to travel."

"Why don't you go to the shop and I'll meet you there? Here's the address. There is a café nearby. I may be an hour or two. If this works out, Mrs. Pierce, I will need you and your documents first thing in the morning if not tonight. We'll work out the particulars at dinner. Who knows, you and I may have to put in some late hours with the FBI tonight or something. If that becomes necessary, you can come along too Mr. And Mrs. Pierce, to ease your mind under the circumstances."

He took out a little notebook and scribbled the address on a page. Then tearing it out, he handed it to Sarah. He was testing to see just how distraught she was and how well she could handle it and come out of it.

He continued, "Dresses, practical ones will be cool in that climate, but pick up some slacks and hiking boots. You'll need them if we are traipsing through what the Filipinos call the 'bundók' or we're in small planes with individual cockpit seats. Now it is easy for any cabbie to find. Just tell them your mission is for a Navy Commander. They won't drive around and fool you then. They like our business, and they're patriotic. The store can hold your purchase 'til the morning if necessary while you think about it. It's an all-purpose outfitting store. Doesn't matter how or where you're going, they've got it."

Two hours and forty minutes later, the officer walked up to the family trio standing out in front of the shop. The bags on their arms told him they had gone ahead with the purchase of some tropical attire for Sarah.

"Well, it's all set. I know the skipper of the Clipper. She's ours now, you know . . for the duration. If the passenger manifest is full by takeoff, I'll give Sarah my compartment and doze out in the lounge. We can still keep our luggage in there together. If there is room, we'll each get a compartment. There may be no private ones, and the lounges convert for communal sleeping."

Gerald had a Navy car and drove them to Fisherman's Wharf where they ate and enjoyed themselves tremendously.

Near the start of the meal, Sarah spoke at one point and said, "I cannot take your compartment, Commander."

"It is appropriate, Mrs. Pierce. What else could we do."

"I'm concerned for appearances, Commander Phillips," stated the older man.

"Look, Mr. Pierce, sir, let me level with you and get this all cleared up. My mission is to get these boys found and everyone possible accounted for. It's a big job in a mess like this, and the world and our nation have never had anything like it before. Your son is a prime example, lost in the system so it seems. Your daughter here . . I can see she's like a daughter to you . . needs to be where I am going to be to find him, because the Navy seems to think I know how to do that job.

Now sir, you know who I am and you can come down to the Clipper and verify everything tomorrow if you want. This is a way to get her impossible personal mission accomplished. It's a blessing that we met.

Also, it's a military plane, not commercial. Our rules are different than civilian. I know what can happen . . your fears and all, and I won't let it. Sarah's reputation will be fine. I'll make sure of it. If I didn't, I suppose I'd have a bonafide hero after me."

Sarah turned alternately to her parents-in-law, surrogate parents in a way, and grasping the hand of each on either side of her, said, "I'll be alright you two. Quit worrying. I'm going. This coincidence is a blessing that we met Commander Derickson who knew just the right person."

"Well, a blessing for sure, I don't know how much of a coincidence. There's only one passenger plane headed that way now, one Navy one anyway; and we both needed to be on it. Seems we were bound to run into each other. We'll switch to a ship at Pearl."

"I wonder if Pan Am will want them back after the war?" commented Sarah's father, calmer now that the issue of her going seemed settled.

"I'm not sure. They've been a great service to us, so I've been told. Even flew President Roosevelt a few times . . or at least once."

Thursday evening saw the two 'parents' tearfully and somewhat joyfully seeing their 'daughter' off to seek their son. It was a bittersweet and pregnant moment of the kind that all would remember until they died, even the officer.

"Mom and Dad, I'll be careful, and I'll write as often as I can. Maybe cables will be viable too. Working for the Navy might facilitate such things."

"We love you," was all the mother could bring herself to say at the last moment, after all the other things had been said.

Then, lastly, Jake's father said, "Find him for us if you can. But remember: be aware always . . aware of your surroundings, of any threat. Bring yourself back. That's as important as Jake."

As she turned to the boat that would take Gerald and her out to the plane, her 'father' called after her and she turned.

"I caution you so much, but you should know: I don't know a more capable woman. You are smart beyond your years. You can thank Paradise Ridge for that." And the man blew a kiss.

They watched . . the two older people did . . watched another child go into harm's way. It had become a new American tradition in the last three and a half years. They watched her ride the Navy launch with him out to the Clipper with its Navy markings now, rather than the iconic Pan Am ones . . watched them pass in through the plane's hatch across the stubby little sea wing and saw the plane's personnel load their luggage. And the older woman waxed nostalgic, remembering their late afternoon shopping trip two days prior to make sure the girl was properly prepared for the Philippine Island's steamy climate. Then they watched as the big monster Boeing 314 revved its four powerful 1,600 horsepower Wright radial engines, taxied into position in the marked channel that had been checked for debris by a safety boat, revved up again and moved slowly then deliberately forward. The big, majestic flying boat threw spray over her seawings and then rose on 'the step' to a position where only the bottom of the boat part of the hull was still clinging to the bay's water surface. Finally, they watched as the Boeing broke free and lifted off, circling back over San Francisco Bay as she climbed for altitude. The couple stood and watched until the Clipper was too small to be seen and then retired to their De Soto and headed toward home.

There were tears of course, tears of sadness, worry, and joy; for, through it all, neither of them could help but think in a pleasant way of the adventure their daughter-in-law had just embarked on . . an adventure made all the more positive because of its noble goal.

~

"Sir?"

"Come in Petty Officer Scott. My exec told me you had asked to see me about your mission and Chief Pierce."

"Yes sir. This is Petty Officer Richard Davis, sir. He was our radioman at the time."

"Well, was there some issue. I mean did anything go against regulations and such?"

"No sir; nothing like that."

"Well sailor? You boys are a fine crew. We were told no one expected you to come back from that mission. I wanna hear anything you've got to say."

"It's Chief Pierce, sir . . . well, he's a hero, sir."

"I know he led the way, I mean was in command coming back, and Davidson seriously injured. And I heard a little about you fellas fighting off a small Jap patrol and such. I don't know the details about your activities with the guerrillas."

"It was Pierce sir; it was all Pierce . . . and this," Petty Officer First class Scott said, laying the khukuri knife Jake had always carried on the Commander's desk.

Retrieving the heavy bladed weapon from the desktop, the officer turned it in his hands, feeling the antique quality of the still usable instrument . . the smooth, dark wood, the polished blade, and the razor edge. Finally, he noted the well-crafted, carved letters forming the word 'Jaguarundi'.

"Sit down and tell me what you remember. I'm told it was dark and rainy, right in the middle of that storm."

The two sailors took the chairs in front of the desk of the commanding officer of the medical unit and began, "I can't tell it all, because after the fighting started it was confused, and of course visibility was very bad. But I can tell you how it started after we were captured…"

"Captured?! No one told me that."

"Yes, sir. Just after we landed under duress, because of the storm and the engine and waded ashore, the Japs were right there. I figure a squad, about five to seven with a sergeant in charge.

They took us right then and there and took our sidearms. Jake keeps this in a leg sheath, and they didn't search him in the rain. They started us up the trail there, and, not more'n fifty yards into the woods there, the Chief turns and bulls the guy behind us into the brush. It was thick right in that spot and the rain was pouring, and we kept going 'cause we figured on getting shot otherwise an' we couldn't see Jake or what he was doin'. I don't think the other Japs even noticed.

A few minutes later, the Jap sergeant up ahead disappears, just disappeared into the wet jungle. We figured it was the Chief, but the Japs couldn't shoot without hittin' their sergeant if he was around.

Later down the trail, he slips the sergeant's body into the road to stop them. Two of the three Japs left were standing lookin' into the brush, and one held a rifle on all us. Suddenly Pierce comes out onto those others swinging this blade and making mincemeat out of 'em. Told me there's special technique and all . . told me later. They went down quick as he yelled kinda soft-like for us to run. He knew what he was doin'. But we didn't run; we took the other Japs out. I saw one of 'em's head fall back like it was hinged at the spine, one he cut with that knife."

"And your whole crew will corroborate this?"

"Yes sir, Commander. It's been on all our minds. Almost all we can talk about. Tell you what else too. He got us all up to safety in that village, and him hurt like the rest, led the plan to take down those bandits . . everything."

"Thank you for that. Is there anything you would add or change?

"No sir."

"And there is no ulterior motive here?"

"What do you mean, sir?"

"Sometimes men have an ax to grind with their superiors. Maybe your crew was not fond of the new officer that was to be assigned to the *Flying Cloud* and want to reward Jake or something like that. You had met the new guy. The change would have made Jake the exec. He told me. I'm sorry; it's the kind of question I have to ask if I want to clarify things."

"Oh no sir, this is all true. The new skipper seems like a great guy. Of course, we would rather have Jake in command though, just to be honest about it."

"Thank you, Petty Officer. I appreciate it. May I borrow this?"

"It's Chief Pierce's, sir. I'm just holding it for him. He was afraid it might grow legs in the hospital while he was on morphine or sumthin'."

"I'll see he gets it back or it comes back directly to you. Check with me in a few days."

"Thank you, Sir."

The commander went that evening to his field hospital where Jake was recuperating with quite a bit of lingering aches and pains. He visited the tough and battered chief. Jake was medicated for the pain generated by his numerous injuries and not readily alert as he might have been with less traumatic injuries. The bone breaks, burns, scrapes and cuts, and several bullet wounds had all been aggravated by time before treatment, sea water, and Jake's dramatic activities before reaching the hospital.

The commander found Jake alert enough to answer a few questions but seemingly depressed. Perhaps it was battle fatigue, more common with ground troops and combat pilots; but, if the commander knew more, he might discover if just maybe the young chief petty officer had seen enough. He resolved to look at the man's file when available.

For the moment, Commander and Doctor Richard Thomas took it slowly, "Good evening, Chief; how are you doing?"

"Not so good yet, sir. But I'll be fine. What brings this visit from the brass sir? You must have more important things than visiting me." Jake felt concerned that the 'brass' label, which had slipped out, could offend the man, but it didn't.

"You young fellas are getting it done for democracy. You're worth the time when you put it on the line like your crew. They tell me you saved them. You fighting for anybody back home son?"

"Yes sir."

"Mind telling me?"

He looked for signs in the warrior's face, as the CPO next spoke, and tried to read Jake's eyes.

"I've got a girl, sir. We were married when I was on leave in '43. And there's my parents."

"Married on leave? You must have known each other. Childhood sweethearts?"

"Sort of; she's younger than me so we actually never went out together. I was in the Pacific for five years before the war."

"That all sounds unusual."

"I was lucky she never married. Didn't know how much she liked me too. It's a crazy situation alright, but it worked out."

"Where is she now?"

"California; living with my folks. They're close."

"Sounds like God's hand. They're what we're fighting for, son. We'll get you home to her. Cheer up."

"Yes sir."

"Now, if you're up to it, I want to know about that night and the Japanese attempt to capture your crew."

"Well sir, the fire in the cockpit was put out before it burned anyone but me. The Nip's canon fire missed her vitals but a machine gun took out some of the pistons in the right engine."

"That's fine Chief Pierce, but your leaving out the fight with the Nips."

"Oh, that was nothing, sir. There was only five of 'em."

"Seven, I'm told. That you defeated singlehandedly after being relieved of your firearms and taken prisoner."

Jake looked at him straight and steady, more alert now, and it was a stare.

"I would like your version of the engagement, Chief."

"It was a group effort, sir. And I only dealt with five of them."

"Your men were not shirkers that night. That's not the issue here. They were disarmed, and were carrying your disabled men and marines or helping them walk anyway. If you're not ambulatory, the Japs kill you. And . . they followed orders during it all. Your men came to me, Chief. They're proud of you."

"What's this leading to?"

"I'd like to hear your story first."

"I had a hidden knife and overpowered the one in the rear where I managed to position myself by limping more than I needed to."

"How?"

"What?"

"How did you overpower him?"

"I knocked him into the bush and strangled him."

"Now, tell me step-by-step from there."

Jake looked at the officer again for a moment and then continued, "I went through the bush beside them unheard because of the storm. When I got to the front of the short column and we were out of sight of the others, I tackled the leader the same way, knocking him into the woods where they could not see to shoot me without risking shooting him. The darkness and violence of the storm worked in my favor. They didn't know yet, so I used his body to stop the column and then I jumped out and attacked the three waiting to see what happened, hoping my crew would deal with the last ones or would run into the brush and toward the Cat. I just managed the Japs myself due to the rain and all, sir."

"I brought your knife. Petty Officer Scott showed it to me, and I borrowed it. Do you want him to hold it, or do you want me to leave it here?"

"Whatever you feel is safe, sir."

"Our hospital staff and other personnel are trustworthy. They can lock it up if you like. You can sign it in. If you leave it with me, I could be transferred and have to remember to get it back to you. The same with Scott. Here it will follow you."

"You hold it awhile Skipper," Jake said using the familiar, casual naval term for one's commanding officer. You might find someone who can tell us more, maybe some of those British Gurkhas. I trust you'll remember me if you transfer."

"So how did you learn to use that knife and where did you get it?"

"The woman with the name on the handle gave it to me, uh . . loaned it to me. It was her mother's. She taught me the basic moves with it. It is a Nepalese Khukuri and can be dangerous if handled wrong."

"The momentum, huh?" the officer asked in meditative thought as he studied the knife and its heavy curved blade.

"A woman's knife? And that name . . that's a little panther from Central America."

"Yes sir, it is. . . . No, sir, it's not usually for women. It's carried by the Gurkha Rifles in the

British Army. They're from Nepal. They all carry them. It's a farmer's knife too."

"I've heard of them. They're fighting in Burma. I think there are a few here with a small British contingent, remnants maybe from Malaya that got attached to U.S. Forces."

"They had them in Malaya when I was there. They would go out at night through Jap lines with only that knife."

"You were there?"

"Yes sir."

"We're going to have to talk again about that, but, for now, is this *Jaguarundi* from Nepal?"

"No sir, here in the Philippines . . American sir, American Indian and white. Her mother was Navajo. That's all I can remember right now, but maybe during one of those talks. But what's this leading to, sir?"

"Probably a medal."

"I don't want it, sir. It's not important. The crew all did their jobs, and all were at risk. I've got one, sir. That's enough."

"What medal did you earn, Chief?"

Looking down a bit embarrassed, Jake replied, "The Purple Heart and Silver Star, sir."

"What for?"

"A similar action in our old Grumman Goose. We got some important officers out of the Philippines in '42 who had a lot of information."

"Where were you injured enough to be given leave back to the States?"

On that mission, sir. The plane was disabled and we had to commandeer a sloop. I commanded it because of rank and that I could sail. My legs got shot up by a Zero while steering that yacht."

"Where's your Silver Star now, Chief Pierce?"

"What do you mean? On one of my jackets."

"And the other one?"

"What . . huh. The Purpled Heart?"

"You won those medals before you went on leave. Where's the other Silver Star and Purple Heart. There's another set, isn't there . . on her lapel. She asked you for them, didn't she? That's why its important, son . . medals . . they're important for them. If they lose us, they've got to know why . . to be reminded why."

Several nights later Commander Thomas was working late on paperwork. He had served at sea on a ship big enough to have a doctor earlier in the war and had himself been wounded. He was awaiting an assignment on some new vessel somewhere on the West Coast of the United States in a shipyard half finished. For now, he was just fine: taking a break while still on the edge of it, right where the action was, or just behind it.

It was about sundown and hot yet mildly so for the tropics, and a rose glow smeared across the jungle treetops to the west, like the blood that was being let there . . that of Japanese, cornered now and raging against the Filipinos and Philippines before they died at American warrior's hands . . and that of the Filipino and Filipina who they raged against. And of course, there was American blood too.

A knock came against his office door, and the Commander said, "Come in." He had released his two or three office personnel to dinner in the mess tent.

To his surprise, and perhaps not, a Gurkha warrant officer stood before him in the doorway and saluted. Comdr. Thomas returned the salute allowing the Nepalese British soldier to release his.

"What can I do for you Warrant Officer?"

"Sir, word came to me of the unique old khukuri that you have and of your desire to learn more of it."

"Well, I appreciate your coming. I guess your commander told you. I'd left word with him indirectly. Got word to him, as it were."

"Yes, Commander. We learned of the unusual name."

"Have a seat. Yes, not a Nepali name, a small Central American wild cat . . panther-like or Jaguar-like. We have them in the south of my country too."

"I know of the knife sir. It is known to the Gurkhas and to one I am close to in particular."

"You mean the specific one? Quite the coincidence. What are the odds?"

"Sir?" inquired the stoic Gurkha, small like Southeast Asians, yet of a group literally considered then and now to be the toughest hand-to-hand, blade-to-blade fighters on the planet.

"I mean to say, if one were gambling, they would never bet any of you would have heard that old story."

"Sir, we are a small country. We have a smaller population than your great nations. Only some of us go and seek to join the British Army. Fewer of us are accepted. We are a small, proud group who know each other and our history."

"I see, and it all makes sense too. So, what can you tell me of the legend surrounding this knife and the woman."

"I know only a little. I know nothing of the woman's history except what my uncle saw and told me. He told of meeting her, an American woman, and of how her mother received a khukuri from a British Gurkha. May I see it?"

"Why yes," and the Commander reached in a desk drawer and retrieved it, handing it to him.

The brown, calm warrior sat there in his khaki uniform with his head covering (a brimmed khaki hat) on the other chair beside him. With his almond shaped Asian eyes squinted in deep concentration, he studied the implement, feeling the carved lettering in the smooth, dark antique wooden handle, then feeling the smoothness of the blade. He could not compare the two, the one in his hands with his own in the curved, softly angled, wood and leather sheath on his belt in the back. His black, thin leather veneered, carved wooden sheath was so well shaped that it seemed economically smaller than the massive blade it held.

"How does if compare to your more modern one, Warrant Officer?"

"It is the same. It is simply older. It could tell stories."

He was correct in that evaluation, for if the knife could talk, it could tell of Kathleen's survival in Luzon's highlands in the Caraballo mountains, of the struggle with a giant reptile, of Jóhonaá's battle with the Moro and her daughter's alone against the three rough deserters . . all of that before the Jaguarundi, before Kathleen was called that, before her further deeds and Jake's.

"Can we compare them side-by-side?"

"I am sorry, sir. We are not allowed to draw them without purpose."

"Is that a rule of your regiments, of the Gurkha Rifles?"

"No sir. It is our belief, our warrior belief if you will. If a blade is drawn, it must taste blood. Perhaps it seems, uh . . how do you say 'silly' to you."

"Not so," the naval officer said, half truthfully, half lying, "it may have a practical purpose as well . . unnecessary fighting. But this old khukuri? Do you know of it? You said so."

He wanted to change the course quickly to avoid any embarrassment the other might feel about the traditional belief in his eyes.

"My uncle met the woman who owned this. He said she was very beautiful with long very dark brown hair. She was part American Indian wedded to a former white officer of your Army who had fought here in the Philippines. That much she told my uncle when he met them both and they talked. Is she dead now? Is that why you have this?

"No . . uh, we do not think so. She may be in hiding in the hills of Cebu or Panay. I'm told by the man she loaned this to for the duration that she is old but looks and acts younger than her actual years."

"My uncle was in the Gurkha Rifles when they met, and it was on a ship, her ship."

"Where was this?"

"Anatolia, sir, in 1922."

"What?" said with some surprise. ". . Asia Minor, Turkey."

"Yes sir, modern Turkey and the Empire before that."

"Yes, that's right, the old Ottoman Empire crumbled and the Republic was formed. Those were dangerous times to be in the Eastern Mediterranean. I believe that was the year of the Smyrna fire."

"It was sir. It is perhaps the greatest atrocity of modern times."

"That is what all the history books say, but we'll have to see what we find in Germany and China. As you know, the Japs were out of control in Nanking in '37. What did your uncle report to you? Your English is very good Warrant Officer."

"Thank you, commander. I was raised in England much of my youth. My uncle told me that his small squad was there on the shore one of the nights of the fire, near the quay. It burned for days. Our Gurkhas were attempting to protect British interests, as there were some scholars thought to be there, but everything was too wild and uncontrollable. My uncle explained that our Gurkhas and the British they were attached to were too few in number. Reports had come out about the mass killing through the previous days, but the commander believed their uniforms and the Union Jack would protect them. My uncle reported that when the city started burning, it became too dangerous to be ashore in the night. The Turks were bent on killing Christians, the Ottoman Greeks and Armenians. They burned the Greek population out of that city, and many people ran to the shore. Such crowds in terror, in such numbers, and confined in their space is as dangerous as battle. Of course, you know our Gurkhas would have stayed and fought."

"Certainly."

"Britain was not at war with Turkey. The Gurkhas were ordered to move down the coast but there were people everywhere. Movement was not easy.

The woman and her husband and their people were there with a ship they had chartered called the *Isabella*. I believe they were there to rescue American friends who had cabled them weeks before of concerns about the troubles. It was a professor of archeology working with your Christian missionaries, I believe.

On the shore that particular night in September, in all the terror, they had brought their schooner in close, as close as possible in that depth, and they were taking children off of the beach and an old pier, a jetty with their two ship's boats. I believe the fire began on the 13th, and this was a few days later at its worst. Mothers were crying and giving them up willingly. Ashore just there or very near, the

Gurkhas were trapped and outnumbered by unfriendly, wild, irregular Turkish forces who would not honor the uniform and colors, the Bashi-bazouk. Their British commander ordered my uncle's men to go to the ship, as it was not the British's cause to fight to the death for. So, they also waded out to the *Isabella*, as they were invited with waved arms by her crew. We do not retreat that willingly, but the British commander ordered it. As the Nepalis waded past they assisted the women and children.

Turkish regulars were there to instill order, but they did not control the Bashi-bazouk, or they could not. Many Christians were killed that night and in those years sir, and women and girls were violated indiscriminately. The Muslim Turks felt the Christians were beneath them and the Bashi-bazouk were very bad men without order or honor."

"The Japs and Nazis have the same view. The rest of us aren't quite human in their eyes."

"Yes sir, Commander. Sir, on the nearest pier was an officer of some army or ethnic people with a few men he commanded. They were of a uniformed service. My uncle knew not which. The officer shouted and ordered the boats and schooner away. He had no machine gun or canon, so he fired a pistol shot. The woman, Jaguarundi, was in the rigging of the ship unnoticed, and my uncle saw her put an arrow through the officer's head. He said he saw it strike, and, unlike the soldiers, knew where to look, and he saw her.

The soldiers started to fire toward the ship, and as my uncle watched, in a blink of one's eye, she put six arrows in the chests of six men. He said it was as fast as a person could place the arrow to the string."

Commander Thomas sat wide eyed and then commented, "They call it 'nocking' the arrow. I don't know why."

"The Jaguarundi is real, sir. She is a real woman with husband and children. My uncle saw them too. She is American, but dark like your natives there; and she told him, as they cruised the Mediterranean to safety toward Suez, that her name was Kathleen. Her husband called her that, but others on the ship called her 'Sunny'. They talked. My uncle and the woman talked because he saw her knife, this knife."

"She is apparently of one of our desert tribes, the Navajo, . . that according to the man she loaned this to. And she is half white."

"At the time, the woman told my uncle that their ship would stay and try to save more people. He was posted in Suez for some time by the British because of the Great War that had ended in 1918. They were there because of the troubles that linger after a war. So, he saw her again. He told me that the British tolerated them and their small ship for some time, in spite of the old, perfectly maintained Gatling Guns it mounted, because of the humanitarian work they were doing. I believe they transported many Greeks from Ionia and Eastern Thrace to safety in Greece. But I know no details, sir."

"They must have been funded by some humanitarian organization or churches. How did they make a living?"

"You are probably correct sir, but my uncle also said that she and her husband were wealthy. The captain of the schooner and his wife, who was aboard, were Filipino. They were her friends, and she and her husband leased their ship for various adventures."

"Did you learn any more of her legendary background, the name and all that?"

"The Jaguarundi name was given by a Brazilian sea captain. She said he told her she reminded him of it. He said she was like a small brown panther after she subdued an aggressively romantic, drunken sailor in a bar in the Philippines. The Brazilian gave his pet jaguarundi to her. She had one when my uncle met her. If they live long, perhaps it was the same one."

"What?"

"Yes sir. She had it on the ship and it did not try to run. It did not try to 'jump ship' as they say," the stoic Asian of the mountains said with a slight grin.

"The jaguarundi would roam around the vessel and had its own personal hiding places. It was also quite affectionate with the woman. In danger, as in the action I described, it remained close to her, and when risk seem to come near her, it would act to defend her."

"Thank you, Warrant Officer. Is there any more that you know?"

"No sir. If I talk to my uncle through letters, I will ask more. He will be glad to know of this, of the knife's continued use and the woman's continued health, at least before this big war began."

The Searchers

The interior of the big Clipper was luxurious, its passenger cabin comfortable and well appointed. The big flying boats had been designed for comfortable travel for high paying passengers, and when commandeered by the government, there had been no reason to waste the nice appointments nor the money to get rid of them.

A heart-tugging song in a foreign language and sung by a male with a great voice struck a chord with Sarah as she seated herself with everyone else in the main lounge before takeoff near the naval base. She didn't know that it had been a signature song of Jake's adopted Philippines since before the war, Mike Velarde, Jr's. beautiful, iconic *Dahil Sa Iyo* (Because of You). The crew had secured a recording by Rogelio de la Rosa.

The other passengers were military and mostly Navy. Sarah was not the only secretary to an officer or government official. There were only three other women, a Navy WAVE, a congressman's secretary, and the congressman's daughter. No one spoke to Sarah initially other than a word and nod of greeting or an 'excuse me' here and there.

The manifest was not nearly full, allowing for ease of movement. Thus, everyone willingly congregated in the largest lounge area before takeoff, getting to know one another. There was really no traditional seating. That lounge converted into a dining room during meals. The assigned general seating areas were small lounges that converted into stateroom-like compartments for sleeping, as sofas could turn into additional beds. This had been luxury travel before the war when the Clippers were commercial. A long flight would carry small numbers of passengers who paid a lot. The well-chosen soft blues, greens, and beach sand colors served to make the long hours over the ocean neither boring nor annoying as continued, constant existence in a small space with unchanging décor can do.

It felt good to her to be in such a sort of step up in life, a chance to be with important people, knowing she was doing important things for the war effort. She controlled it, barely, but thought 'I'm on the famous Clipper!' And within she could hardly contain herself. As others began to chat and introduce themselves, Sarah savored the elements of the experience but wanted to be relaxed and appear to be normal, to belong. She opened some general informational material about the Navy that Gerald had given her and started reading, shocking him with her work ethic.

His pride in her allowed him to privately give himself a pat on the back for his employment of the woman. Then, to be sure she received respect, Commander Gerald Phillips proceeded to introduce himself and his secretary, being sure to level her up to the status of everyone else with his choice of words. Her color was of a tone that demanded interest in that era. Sadly, black Americans received the least respect, though not everywhere and everyone. Gerald knew people on the Clipper would respect her, but he figured it would be 'different' and they would want to know her background. It could be a little risky, he supposed. Native Americans, Indians, carried an enigmatic aura and reputation: exotic, historical, interestingly dangerous, and that of the noble savage, the natural man (or woman), in fact the Indian princess. But people also knew of the alcoholic, unemployed, and unindustrious men on some of the less successful reservations.

When it was more or less his turn as they all sat in the lounge area at the moment, Gerald said, "It's going to be a pleasure to travel with all of you, I'm sure. I am Commander Gerald Phillips, U.S. Navy, and this is my secretary, Mrs. Sarah Pierce. We are tasked with seeking information about our brave boys who are lost, so to speak, in the system, in a hospital perhaps with no records following them."

Respectfully, Sarah looked up as he talked, unprepared for being singled out. But he felt it necessary and continued, "Sarah is the wife of one of those boys, Chief Petty Officer Jake Pierce, USN who has received the Silver Star from early in the war. He is missing in the Philippines. To satisfy any curiosity concerning my attractive secretary, she is part American Indian, Blackfoot and Navajo. The two were childhood friends before the war."

It worked, and if there had been any previous danger of rude treatment, it had been allayed, for Sarah, the one person on the plane with no official rank, college degree, or puffed up reputation, became the only one to be greeted with a respectfully warm, light applause. It was a time when being the spouse of a hero meant everything.

The cabin took on a certain warmth, and it may have been because Gerald's words brought the group a tiny bit closer together. Sarah may have unconsciously become, in their minds, an anchor or tether to America's common roots. Of all the important people there, she was the 'commoner,' the minority, the hero's wife, the housewife, the working woman, the original native of the land. With her introduction, he had grounded them. And, within whatever self-importance and urgent duty each had, they may have sensed it.

Then, with the powering up of the engines and the easily felt liftoff from the surface of the bay and earth, a first for Sarah, a thrill surged through her.

As evening wore on, and Sarah relaxed and just leaned back with her eyes mostly closed, she assumed that she went unnoticed. The woman realized that she was surrounded by people above her on any social scale in America, and, though caught by surprise, had immediately adjusted and steeled herself for it. As music played softly in the background above the ever-present yet bearable roar of the big Wright engines that represented survival over the ocean, in Vera Lynn's recorded voice, the beautiful, classic song of their moment, *"We'll Meet Again"*. . brought Sarah to subtle, hidden tears. Across from her in facing chairs, the congressman's daughter and secretary sighed to the song's haunting message. Their men were also away. But those men were assigned safer duties. Thus, the two sensed the girl's silent, muffled sobs and sat across the aisle broken-hearted; and, without her knowing, prayed for her and Jake.

Compartments slept six people, similar to staterooms on a steamer. When people began to retire more formally than napping in a comfortable chair, the congressman's daughter and secretary invited the WAVE officer and Sarah to join them in their compartment, having learned Sarah had been added to the passenger manifest at the last minute. For the era, the offer reflected a willful challenge of the current racial standards. Bunks had privacy curtains like on railroad pullman cars. The congressman told the Navy he would not mind sharing his accommodations with brave military personnel, thus, due to his rank, Gerald shared the compartment with the legislator. The two became friends almost immediately, talking into the night sitting in comfortable chairs.

The flight terminated in Honolulu, and the two had to wait a few days as a small convoy was forming that was part of the normal supply chain for the troops fighting and preparing for the next fight, each one closer to Japan. Before the enemy had sealed off much of the Pacific, the Clipper would have gone all the way to the Philippines with refueling stops Midway, Guam, and Wake Island on the way to Manila. Now Sarah was squeezed into the tiny quarters of a junior officer on a cruiser, who gladly gave it up for the 'war effort' and the praise from his shipmates. The cruiser was part of the escort and submarine screen for the convoy. With an assignment of lesser importance and sans the Commander as a traveling companion and boss, Sarah, if on such an official voyage, would probably have been assigned to a troop ship or cargo vessel.

Through her mind, since boarding the Clipper, a surge of new experiences, one after another, bombarded her senses. She knew it would continue and wondered how Jake must have felt when he came out to the Pacific during peaceful times.

A long, often hot, tedious voyage ensued, the tedium broken by the beautiful yet eventually monotonous views and the so very rare experiences, man overboard drills, gun drills, and a list of exciting things that could occasionally break the boredom. Respectfully, Sarah dressed plainly and did not disobey orders that she was to stay off the decks except when allowed. It wasn't a cruise ship; it was a 'cruiser' (a long-range war machine). She could become a distraction the crew did not need, but one allowed during departure from Pearl and disembarkation at Tacloban, Leyte. As with the scenario of the many celebrity women who 'went to war', the officers of the big ship knew that Sarah reminded the men of why they were where they were, doing what they were doing. Over coffee, tea, fruit juices, and meals, she was able to enjoy many conversations with officers in their wardroom at times when it was not being used for official conferences, of which there were few.

Commander Phillips and Sarah found themselves based out of an office in Tacloban on Leyte as the campaign in the Philippines had shifted westward. She immediately was struck with the heat, aura and magic of the tropics and, despite the bombardments near shore and inward some distance, the rich tropical growth of palms, banana and other trees Jake had described. They seemed to embrace her. She now felt closer to him. It was just a room but was all they needed and had all they needed: a typewriter, a desk, a table, three chairs, and access to: a phone to the local offices, a radio, telegraph facilities, and a mimeograph machine (which in those days required a stencil process to duplicate papers). The latter was their era's copier and could not reproduce photographs.

Knowing that Jake was somewhere in those very islands was a tantalizing torture to the young war wife. She wanted to fly or take a launch to Panay, where she now knew he had gone missing, and run off into the hills looking for him. But she was aware of the blessings that got her there and knew she owed God, the Navy, and her country. She would now perform her duties. One of her biggest blessings was the access to the papers she now did more than 'shuffle' as the standard joke about federal employees echoes of. She had on her desk, properly categorized as to region, urgency, and alphabetical order, every paper of every man they sought, including Jake's. If still alive, he was very probably in some official medical facility on Panay, Mindoro, Negros, or the next door island of Cebu. In fact, Cebu and Panay were the most likely places, and the urge to search the smaller, closer Cebu was almost overwhelming. Sarah was Sarah however. Common sense, gratitude, faith, and duty drove her actions now, and she did not want to be this close and be sent home for poor performance and disobedience to orders. Though a civilian employee, she felt she was 'military' now. She was Navy like her husband.

Soon there was a move, and the little two person 'command' set up shop in Cebu City in a similar little office as the one in Tacloban providing similar facilities. They quickly went to work following leads in that area. The Commander wanted to follow these recent leads first as the best chance to succeed.

One morning he said to Sarah, "There's a Marine Corps colonel I want you to interview. We just found him, and he doesn't know that his family doesn't know. It will be exciting for you in that way. The personal notification. You need to ask these questions to make sure he is who we are seeking. Then notify him that he had been thought lost by his loved ones and then get a note or letter from him to them. We'll get it through for him. Then, because of his situation, if it is him, ask these questions. They're about his guerrilla missions."

"But sir, I'm not cleared ..."

"Yes, you are."

It wasn't high level secrecy work, but it was important, and the young woman felt suddenly very important, like she was really making a contribution.

"Now you've got to get to the hospital ship before she sails. Check when you land on the carrier. If the doctors have cleared him, he may be there. I don't have the name, but the *Refuge* has been on station and loading wounded for transport to Hollandia. She's made several trips. Sometimes to Guam. "I've got a TBF pilot ready to ferry you across Leyte out to the anchorage in the Gulf. Take my Jeep to the airfield. Oh, and make them secure my Jeep. Those things have a way of wandering off around here. Now, get a move on. She's loaded and ready to sail. You may have to sit in the turret or below."

The two had been there only a week and Sarah was trembling with the responsibility as she drove the Jeep, handed her authorization to those in charge at the airfield, and later walked over to the big Avenger sitting there with its engine warming. Could all this be real? Quite a few sailors, marines, and soldiers echoed the same thought at that moment, their eyes taking in the view of her. She had not had time to change and wore a dress rather than pants. In a country and city where women had not started driving, she had turned quite a few Filipino heads on the drive over.

The pilot spoke to her over the idling engine's roar, as a flight mechanic throttled it, listening carefully.

"Ma'am, there's nothing to worry about. There's nobody shooting at us. The Allies control everything east of Cebu now."

"I apologize Lieutenant Cornelson. I had no time to change to proper clothes," Sarah shouted over the roar, as she held her Panama hat on with one hand and shook his hand with the other.

"I'm sure the young men on the *Kings Mountain* won't mind when you step out on the flight deck, ma'am," the pilot, a young lieutenant, said as he smiled.

Sarah was excited and nervous, and she thought of her Jake, a pilot of slightly larger and much larger planes. She wouldn't miss this moment for the world, but she was scared.

"What are the risks, Lieutenant, if any. My husband flies, but I've only traveled on the big Clipper."

"Your husband is a pilot, ma'am? Pardon me, you are quite young . . and attractive, if I may say. You'll break some hearts out here, guys knowin' you're already married."

He helped her up on the wing and into the cockpit. She was petite and in a dress not a flight suit.

"This seat seems a bit simple, uh . . rustic, Lieutenant."

"This is a modified Avenger ma'am. She was shot up and her radio equipment shattered. They needed a taxi, so she's it. This compartment behind the pilot is usually full of impressive radio gear."

"Where does the operator sit . . I mean in a combat TBF, or is it your job?"

"Below, ma'am; he has a small bench. This baby has all her guns if we have to carry someone important to a forward area."

Looking at him seriously as she contemplated the dangers of flight, Sarah requested, "Honestly, sir?"

"Ma'am, you don't have to call me 'sir'. The biggest risk in carrier flying is the landing. The deck is too short, and we use wires across it to catch a hook on our plane's tail. If we miss, we have to keep trying, so we go around again. Taking off seems risky because of the short 'field', but this baby can handle it. The carriers have a catapult too, but we don't use 'em much. Most crashes are caused by wounded birds coming back from combat. But if anything causes you and me to end up in the drink, get unbuckled and out quick. The ones who don't are usually wounded, which we would not be. But these babies can fill up fast and drop like a rock, taking us with it. You just get out and clear of her suction, and I'll get you. I'm not having' your husband looking for my head for losing his precious wife."

He said it seriously and couched as a joke, and both came through to her. She had made the impression on him that she did on everyone she met, and he had adopted a certain sense of responsibility to get her safely to and from their destination.

He would keep the plane low for her to view things and so she wouldn't get cold without a flight jacket. The engine, warmed up now, was idling a bit quieter, but they still had to talk loudly.

As he helped buckle her in the harness, he inquired, "What does he fly?"

"A Grumman Goose at the very beginning. He was out here then and even before. Then he was flying a Dumbo when he went down."

The man, a combat pilot who could be in need of rescue someday and respected the lifesaving Dumbo crews, said, "My, my, is he . . is he . . okay, is he safe? How did you get here? Are you from the islands?" When he met her, like so many, he was totally confused as to her origins.

"We married when he came home to recuperate and retrain on Catalinas. I'm American Indian. He's lost, Lieutenant. But he's in the system, in a hospital somewhere, we think."

Checking the buckle, he had paused and listened. Lt. Cornelson inquired further, "Is he . . ?"

But she interrupted, "No, we think he is okay, in his right mind and all. He went down off Panay and was missing. Discovered later, he was with the guerrillas. Now we don't know . . nobody knows."

She said it bravely, businesslike and without emotion, and he commented, "We're waiting for clearance. A transport's comin' in. So you secured this assignment, very lucky, and . . I'm guessing resourceful of you. Here, put on this headgear and radio. We will be able to communicate with each other." And in a very respectful manner, because he couldn't kiss her, the young officer said, "Excuse me," reached across her body and seat, gently took her right hand, and kissed the back of it. Then he stepped up the wing to his forward cockpit.

The Grumman TBF Avenger torpedo bomber was a marvelous design of its day. Sarah tensed and became ever so much more excited than on any roller coaster or Ferris wheel ride, and the big single Wright Cyclone radial engine revved up its 1,900 horsepower to a tremendous roar. It was 300 more hp than each of the four Wright's that hung on the wing of the Clipper and it lifted the TBF off with an impressive performance, the young pilot full of the emotional element of his mission. Across the channel and the Leyte Jungle they flew, low enough to avoid the need of a warming flight suit.

Looking out of the canopy, the excited woman could see the world from above but close enough, and the roar of the engine engulfed her being. She could not begin to see directly below or even nearly so due to the fat body of the TBF Avenger, a big torpedo bomber that was able to hold the torpedo within a bomb bay for a more aerodynamic flight. Unlike such planes earlier in the war, the plane could carry a crew of three, with the bubble turret gunner and combination radioman, ventral tail gunner, bombardier, besides the pilot.

Approaching the *USS Kings Mountain,* cruising in Leyte Gulf in order to launch planes into the wind, Sarah remembered that a carrier landing had been described by the lieutenant as like a crash that is in control of the pilot. Looking forward past him as they made their approach, she saw the urgent wave off from the Landing Signals Officer and felt the rolling turn as the big engine roared and hauled the heavy plane to the left and skyward at an extreme angle. She was getting the full experience, and the show wasn't over. Lt. Cornelson was not waved off for a wrong approach but for another reason.

Climbing and circling slowly as he positioned the Avenger for her view, he said, "Can you take it, ma'am? You're an adventurous woman. You want to see this wounded bird come in?"

"Yes."

As they tracked so as to almost hover, she saw the plane come in, a Hellcat fighter. It must have been patrolling in an area that was not quite safe and due to location and the pilot's injuries, he found himself here over the Gulf looking for a carrier, any carrier. The plane was coming in slow and smoking from the engine. She guessed that his control was poor because she could see the rudder was shot up. She knew the basics of flying from her years of avid reading.

The Hellcat made a pretty good approach but was wobbly, and Sarah saw the smoking, flaming engine make a small burst on one side as if a cylinder had exploded. It appeared from above, as Lt. Cornelson flew low for her to see better, that the plane came in low, and the landing gear immediately collapsed. The fighter skidded on its belly down the deck at an angle and then turned sideways and burst into flames. Sarah saw the flight deck crew rush to each duty, some fighting the fire as others rushed to pull the pilot from the inferno that seemed now to engulf it. Her hand was to her mouth and she was crying . . crying for them all, for almost three years' worth of them . . heroic deeds and men, one of them hers. The pilots got the glory, but the young war wife now marveled at the courage of the flightdeck crew, as she saw one, who must have not been in protective garments, drop on the deck and roll to smother his burning clothing.

Through her radio, the voice of the flight controller came from the big carrier's island tower, "Lt., let us get the deck clear." And Sarah watched as the ship turned, the men on the deck wrestled the plane with the help of a tractor to the starboard side, and then the tractor shoved the very expensive wreckage into the sea.

"In a moment, Lieutenant, we've debris to clear and arrester cables to check."

Sarah said in her mouthpiece, "Thank you Lieutenant. I'm sorry I cried if you heard it. We need to know what you men face. Thank you." and she thought of Jake.

As he had described it, she now watched and caught a glimpse of the Landing Signals Officer and saw him wave wing position and height instructions with his paddles, one in each hand. Then she saw the signal to land . . and . . with a rush of excitement and adrenalin within her (as if she were part of the complicated systems of the flying marvel) the big carrier bomber touched with the soft jolt of a plane in the hands of a good, if not yet battle-scarred pilot. She was just able to see the signal of a good landing and then felt the cable pull abruptly against the hook and the machine she was in.

With assistance from a flight deck crewman, Sarah stepped off onto the wing, was assisted down by the next two flight deck crewman to reach the plane and stepped on to the big flat flight deck. All the while she tried to control her navy-blue skirt; and, with all the urge to do the opposite, the young men who were currently her handlers, true gentlemen, assisted. She was living a dream few girls her age or any age could even contemplate. Or, if their men were based on such ships, maybe many secretly contemplated but could never hope to experience it.

"Miss, it's dangerous here. Have you been around airports?"

"Not much."

"Wait here for your escort. You could walk into a spinning propeller here real easy."

"Thank you, sailor," addressing him that way because she saw no rank on his working uniform.

A flight deck was a dangerous place; but, given that the recent drama of the crash-landing and the TBF's routine landing had ended action on this ship's deck for the moment, the men who now immediately froze at the sight of Sarah could be forgiven their brief inattention to their work.

The civilian, given this rare chance to be close to the extreme danger and ever-present death of this war, stood for a split second looking straight ahead toward the sea and the hospital ship, standing offshore majestically white in the bright sunshine with the bright red crosses marking her. She was a complete hospital and even carried a complete portable field hospital aboard. Then Sarah looked toward where the wrecked fighter plane had been.

She had decided that, since she was not in the Navy, but she was 'of the Navy', an official Navy employee out with the fleet, she would at least appear similar to them. It was an act and decision based on respect. She was not trying to be what later eras would call a 'wannabe'.

Wearing a knee length dark navy-blue dress with a white baby (Peter Pan) collar, a white Panama hat with a broad navy-blue band, and white canvas boat shoes, the girl stood taking in the scene for a moment wanting to remember it forever. Strong winds across the big, flat deck at sea forced her left hand to clamp the hat on, blew her long dark tresses out to leeward dramatically and wistfully, and tugged, lifted, and flapped her dress around, as she fought with her free arm held down to control it. Finally, she grabbed the cloth of the skirt together and held it. Then there was the appearance of a stateside girl with the unusual, beautiful, brown skin of the local Filipina girls, . . . and the men could be forgiven, for even the officers on the bridge and elsewhere hung-over rails and stared.

Finally, the silence was broken by a single, clear wolf whistle, as every ship had at least one whistler stronger than the others and courageous enough to use it when he shouldn't.

Over the loud speaker was heard, "Belay that sailor. The lady knows our opinion of her. The silence speaks for itself." and that bit of wit from the brass was met with a cheer.

The one in command of the flight deck walked up to her and said, "Ma'am, what brings you here?"

He noted her youth. She was now twenty-one. And no Navy man would miss Jake's medals on her left breast. Where it had been fine back home, in her current role, it might be pushing the envelope a bit. If so, it was unintentional on her part. What with what it told about her husband and the impression the girl made on all she met, the issue was ignored by all.

No planes were preparing for flight so they could hear each other as they talked.

"I'm to be taken to the *Refuge,* sir. I'm with the Navy Department's mission to find Missing in Action personnel and specifically men found but lost in the bureaucracy or in uncertain circumstances. I've a Marine colonel to interview there, sir."

"It will be a pleasure and an honor. Your duty is noble. I only wish I could be your escort. They are always sight to behold with the glistening white paint, the red crosses, and succor they bring. Those torn up guys are most happy to see the nurses of course. Steel yourself miss. You'll see some sad things and sad men. You'll receive some wolf whistles too. Don't hold it against them."

"It is 'Mrs.', sir. I won't be offended."

Then exhibiting that serious yet open maturity, she joked with him, "You know, sir. We women like to look at you fellas too but imagine how inappropriate the whistles would seem."

He looked at the petite girl walking beside him to the big ship's island, skillfully controlling her skirt and hat as she walked. Their eyes met and the two broke into a smile and then a laugh at her joke based on truth.

"Is your husband out here?"

"A chief petty officer, a missing Dumbo pilot, but we know he survived and was with the Guerrillas." He nodded and opened the hatch (door) to the shade of the superstructure and led the way to the wardroom and coffee.

An hour later after meeting several important officers in the chain of command on the ship and getting to see the bridge from which the ship was controlled and commanded, the young secretary, now elevated to assistant, was on the ship's launch headed for the hospital ship. The woman understood that she wasn't important; but, like everyone else out there, the duty was. And she sensed it once more when the big carrier, underway to operate planes, was brought to a dead stop just so this little wisp of an American woman could board a naval launch safely in order to do her duty. Now, after experiencing her reception at each stop of importance, the woman was armed with the knowledge that she was a bit of a celebrity. Obviously, it was not because of Hollywood fame or glamorous looks or being some congressman's daughter. No . . She just shouldn't be there, wasn't expected to be there, . . and she was doing good work respected by these warriors of her country, these men she revered so, and . . she was a sight for their sore, battle burned eyes . . she was, in not a derogatory sense, what culture would later call 'eye candy' . . not the glamorous kind but the 'girl next door I left back home' kind . . the kind they really longed for. She represented 'why they were there'_ the reason. I suppose as well, since she bore her origins so obviously, easily, and pleasantly, she also elevated her Indian people and other tawny peoples in these sailors and marines' minds.

Aboard the hospital ship Sarah presented her credentials to the officer standing beside the marine guard at the top of the ship's ladder. She was escorted down the ship outboard of the superstructure and avoided the expected encounter with the many patients in the small crowded wards.

The colonel, who had been presumed lost in the Philippines at the war's beginning, was in and office fabricated out of a small storage compartment where he was writing a report. He had been rescued during the conquest of the islands and had valuable information. Sarah's interest was mostly information to give to his family, and immediate information of a military nature to return to her boss to be passed on to people in command. If his report was ready, she could bring it too. She actually had such clearance. First and foremost, as news of the man's safety was very recent, Sarah was there to find out just who he was and if he was the officer her boss thought he was, a positive identification, as it were.

Knocking on the side of the ship's bulkhead beside the open hatch (door from the outside deck), Sarah requested, "Permission to enter, sir?"

Turning, the war weathered and weary officer looked surprised and a bit confused. Perhaps her well thought out fashion choice was the reason, and he said pleasantly but with the gruff tone of the man he had become in the jungles and mountains of Cebu and Panay, "Miss, uh, ma'am, Yes, enter. Are you a nurse, Inday?"

Puzzled for a brief moment then remembering Jake's occasional use of the Filipino feminine pet name for her, Sarah said, "No sir, I'm from the States, from the Navy Department. I'm here to get information to send to your family and to confirm your survival for them."

"You're very young."

"I have a husband lost out here. I was determined to get here."

He was a get-to-the-point battle scarred warrior and survivor. He saw the Silver Star and Purple Heart now. He would appreciate straight talk even from this wisp of a girl, and she knew it.

"Resourceful, no doubt. I hope it cost you no compromise."

"No sir, blessings and luck. I met my boss, Commander Phillips, as I was trying to wrangle a way. He needed a secretary. All very honorable but thank you for your concern."

His inference had been abrupt, almost rude, and she chose not to be offended. His words echoed truths: white or brown, she shouldn't have been able to get where she now was, and some people naturally assumed lower standards of darker peoples. She had no reason to blame him for that. He did not create the current American culture of social beliefs that had seen a long development, and she had at least sensed in him a genuine concerned for her.

The tough marine officer, who had just spent the entire war up to that point in the rugged world of the guerrilla fighters of the wildest of lands, looked at Sarah long and hard, taking the measure of the girl as he had many a fellow fighter among the small, brown, brave people that inhabited these islands. Some were petite Filipinas who he would watch go out in the night to slice a Jap officer from ear to ear or nearly cut their head of by strangling them with piano wire.

"Did you find him?"

"No, but there is hope. He ended up among those in your line of work. I pray he survived it."

He saw her cross, and a Catholic himself by coincidence, he commented, "He has been among those so strong in our faith, if that is a comfort, Inday." The word of female endearment came easy to him having been there in the islands so long.

He stood and reached in the corner for a folding chair for her, and sitting, she said wistfully, "Jake calls me that."

"He's been here then?"

"Yes, for some five years after high school."

"And you?"

"Northern California, Blackfoot mostly. He came back on leave and to heal and woo me."

There was a long pause and both were in thought and looking at each other.

"You'll find him, 'Day," he consoled her finally. "Well, what do you need from me. I've written a letter to my wife. I suppose you can get it off quicker than I can. Have you seen any of this? It's so hard to express it to them."

"A fighter crashed in flames just before us on that carrier over there. My first close view of the dangers my husband told me of."

"You were on the TBF then?"

"Yes sir."

Sarah asked him several questions. Some were couched to reveal any deceit. A man could go off to war and want to come back as someone else; and, to see if they could have, she and Phillips had no recent photos of most of the men they sought. The talk became more cordial and he asked a nurse if he was free to escort his visitor to the officer's mess. He had been medically cleared except for his malnutrition which wasn't acute and was improving. There over ice tea the woman renewed his knowledge of home. His only information to that point had come from a Filipino couple, Attorney and Doctora Taboada, who he met when he moved across to Cebu. Hiding in the mountains they had an old car radio, which would of course only receive.

At one point the marine said, "I knew of your husband's rescue mission, and of the marines who were lost. I wanted to blame him until I learned the boys were brought safely down on the beach, what

355

beach there was, but went the wrong way into the jungle. That wasn't his fault. The Marine commander was in charge of that. They couldn't have known. The intelligence was just bad. Your man is a hero for bringing his men and those few wounded Leathernecks back from hell. I left for Cebu before he came up in my area and I missed him. I believe he fought with our men and I am pretty sure he survived it. I would probably have heard if Navy personnel were in the casualties' lists. I hope that helps. Nothing is ever sure about these things. I won't lie to you about it, 'Day."

Outside his small office later, the interview over, the officer placed a hand on her shoulder and said, "Savor this, Inday. You have a rare seat at the biggest show on earth right now. Not even many Navy waves are out here. For a young woman, you are blessed. Savor it."

They shook hands warmly and she took her leave.

The little impromptu office the ship's captain had offered was near the fantail. And later he stood outside of it at the rail watching her board the launch at the foot of the ship's ladder. Sarah was the kind of girl many a man's eyes followed longingly.

The same TBF pilot waited to return Sara to Cebu City. Helped aboard the big bomber up the wing, Sarah nestled into the makeshift passenger's seat again, aware of the eyes of her many fans and the many waves. She hurt for those men and their girls back home and knew the boys on those big flattops lived with danger whether they saw battle or not. As she waved back and blew a kiss or two, her eyes grew moist and red and stung and burned.

As big as the *Kings Mountain* was, Sarah realized it was steaming faster. The big ship was maintaining a combat air patrol off to the northwest above Leyte, and it had to cruise to make launching easier. Sarah felt the slight pitch to port and the acceleration as the ship turned into the wind, and the big Wright Cyclone began to roar. She saw the lieutenant lean to look down, and, following his gaze, saw a crewman on the deck signal take off. The TBF rolled forward slowly, then ever faster, dipped off the deck, and finished with a roaring climb for altitude, as she looked back to see the flat deck disappear behind and below her. Then she absorbed the visual experience of the return across Leyte.

All Sarah could think to say after landing at the field in Cebu and receiving his help disembarking was, "Thank you. Thank you so much, Lieutenant Cornelson, I will pray for you and your missions."

She reported to Commander Phillips and turned over everything she had including the marine colonel's mail for home. She was given free rein for a few days to follow various leads that were potentially helpful in the search in that area for Jake and a couple of other men. It was thought that, though lost on Panay, Jake could have been transferred to Cebu without any identification. One informative note stood out as she read it and her eyes widened. She would check it out the first thing in the morning.

It was just one of many clues concerning men in the Central Philippines who were missing but presumed not dead, to turn the common phrase a more pleasant way. The marine officer whom she had interviewed had spent the war in the region, the beautiful Visayan Islands, when he could not get out. He had been instrumental in the guerilla campaign and had mentioned the couple. Sarah made all the inquires she could, for Jake and his crew of course, but for them all, four other brave Americans, two more sailors, another marine and an army captain, whose name she had received from the U.S. Army. The energetic, resourceful, and meticulous woman had hit the ground running when the little two-person detail had landed, and her superior was amazed at the luck in their meeting back home. First of all, what stood out most was her lack of favoritism.

After one day settling in and making sure the two-person team, augmented by an additional yeoman, could be very mobile, the girl poured herself into paper work. Commander Phillips had been pleased that such a young woman with such a personal mission showed no discomfort with turning womanly and motherly and arranging the team's equipment so as to be able to move on a moment's notice without leaving anything important behind. For that brief time, she was more steward and valet than secretary. Then she turned to the nuts and bolts of the job. Perhaps inheriting one's own business at eighteen was a boon and had been her training ground.

Late the second night, when they were still in tents, he came to hers to see why the light was still on, as it was really early in the wee hours of the third morning. Thinking her asleep with the light on, a Coleman lantern that could cause a fire if unattended, Phillips peaked in discreetly to see her pouring over records, copies of old messages, and old radio conversation transcripts that, thankfully some personnel had thought to retain.

"Sarah, you won't find him the first few days. This will take time and patience, and you need rest to stay fresh enough to think these things through."

Turning, she paused, looking clueless for a moment, then said, "Huh . . what . . oh, well, it's just that this is a good lead. He could be right here mere miles from us."

They were still in Leyte at the time, and the Commander seemed shocked and said, "Sarah, you're getting too emotional now that you're here. Jake's trials were nowhere near here; he couldn't be here."

"Oh . . not Jake, that Army captain. He almost has to be here; and, with all the evidence, he must be dead or very incapacitated. Something in all this tells me he had or has a memory loss. Speed in our work may be urgent, the 'order of the day' so to speak", she finished with military terminology.

Gerald just stood a moment and looked at her, amazed at this woman so close to the goal of finding her lost man or answering why she would never be able to, and yet she was losing sleep pouring over records to save another who might or might not be in greater need. He replied, "I'm proud of you. I chose well, or perhaps God did for me, but get some rest."

The search for each man in the region dragged on and was both tedious and initially unrewarding. It could have been so demoralizing for the youngest member of the team were the general experience not so new, exotic, and exciting.

PARADISE RIDGE DISPATCH   May 19, 1945
LOCAL GIRL GOES TO WAR

Paradise Ridge's youth continue to serve our little community and our nation. The latest, Sarah Willowood Pierce, having left the grill and our stomachs in the good hands of Eloise Sanderson and gone off in marriage with one of our favorite sons, Chief Petty Officer Jake Pierce, has now dared to face this great conflagration as few young women in America can. She joins metaphorically the military and Red Cross nurses in a way. Concerned, as we all are, about the lack of news about her missing husband, the young Paradise

Ridge woman we all remember as being so capable and resourceful has secured a job with the Navy and is off searching for missing men who may yet still be alive and still in harm's way.

According to her parents-in-law with whom she had been living, Sarah sought out help and discovered that others were 'found' yet somehow still missing, just like her Jake. It seems to be a complicated situation more confusing than a man just being missing on a mission or on a battlefield. By luck or the grace of God, the young woman and Jake's parents encountered an officer on that exact mission and in need of a secretary. Well, a graduate of Mrs. Orinach's business classes at Paradise Ridge High, Sarah was just what the situation called for.

Pray for the best of Paradise Ridge youth as they face danger: Jake, missing now for many months but thought to be alive with the jungle guerrilla movement in the Philippine highlands; Darrell Robinson, just off to the Pacific as an aircraft mechanic aboard a carrier; Darrel's older brother, David, killed in action flying in North Africa; and Sarah, going closer to the dangers of this war than any women save our nation's brave combat nurses and a few journalists.

Mr. and Mrs. Pierce ask your prayers for them all and for Sarah especially now, as they have learned through letters that she is near the combat. Only recently, according to Eric Pierce, his daughter-in-law, while being transported in a carrier-based Navy bomber from one island location to another to do her job, landed on a carrier [name withheld] just after a brave, wounded fighter pilot had crash landed on the deck. Our local beauty is within the grasp of the beast.

Some local boys from the class of 1943 have finished advanced training and have joined the fleet, and two are soldiers. They are all listed below.

She knew them all, so Eloise Sanderson laid the paper down on the counter and just sat on the stool and nursed her still too hot coffee. She was confused. Happy now with the grill and her long-distance friendship with Sarah, she was still jealous of Jake, Sarah, and her

Darrell all off to see the world. She wondered if the latter would want to settle here when he got back or would take her out into the broader world. She would sit in these slow moments in the afternoons and daydream of going and visiting the other couple in the tropics and maybe staying forever.

The bell rang and the door opened as three of the old group from high school strolled in. Eloise had graduated with Sarah; some of the girls that made up her close friends were a year behind. The grill was technically closed for business between two and four-thirty in the afternoon, but Eloise left the door open for friends to drop by.

After the casual greetings the sarcasm she had expected for weeks reared its head. But Eloise had grown up now and it would not bite very hard. Helping the situation was the fact that, among them, she had been and still was one of the popular girls, one of the most popular. Now that love and a war had settled and matured her, she could not become very damaged by the cruel strafing from a few outdated 'pilots'. The main issue with them, she knew, though not yet addressed through cruel jokes, was her romance with Darrell, Paradise Ridge's lovable bad boy.

"Well, you're workin' for an 'Injun' now. How's that working out?"

It was Ellen, and Jerri chimed in immediately, "You guys could have some great parties in that apartment if she was still here. I mean she knows so many fellas."

"That's cruel. You all know Sarah's okay. We didn't treat her right."

None of it could phase her, the garbage the two were trying to playfully sling around, as Delana just watched and listened. Eloise was now the adult in the room. The center of their click in youth because of her beauty, brains, and personality, she now needed to work and face life; and, through Darrell, Sarah had offered a job and a business partnership. The other three (from mining and lumbering families) were a bit more well off and could lazily play while living at home and waiting to marry. That could be a dangerous game if no offers came. The local boys off to war might not return, and Paradise Ridge was not yet the tourist destination it was destined to become on some small scale when nature loving outdoors people would discover it.

"You know your guy just threatened his brothers to clear her name," Jerri continued.

"No, I don't. I'm on the inside on this. I know the truth. I trust, my guy."

"Paradise Ridge's finest, pillar of the community."

"Hoodlum," added Ellen.

Eloise didn't reply. Truth was the proper counter to crude comments, but it must be measured by letting some of the cruel words slide and be ignored.

"So, what's he doing in the Navy now? I don't see them using a lot of motorcycles," Jerri continued to bait.

Darrell actually had become quite the entrepreneur with a good motorcycle garage that also serviced small engines and occasionally automobiles when work was slow or someone was in need. He started with nothing but a full toolbox and an old structure somewhere between a large shed and a small garage. Now, between that and Eloise's share of profits from the grill, the two would begin marriage in good financial shape.

"He is an aircraft mechanic on one of those big carriers. I'm worried. I believe he is near Japan and they have those suicide bombers now."

Her face was serious and intense, and being women and not really stupid, just shallow, the two taunting girls became quiet for just a brief moment.

"Well, if your guys don't make it, you and your new gal friend can share that apartment and just cuddle up together . . and of course, party."

All eyes turned to Jerri as the words left her lips. It was as if some pagan god of stupid had entered the room and her.

Within an instant Eloise had unleashed a strong, solid, stinging slap across the speaker's face. Stunned and clueless as to what to do . . maybe realizing she had crossed a line and feeling nakedly exposed, Jerri turned in tears for the door. Eloise followed.

While the other two surprisingly, respectfully remained inside, the grill owner-manager caught up with her friend and tormentor a few steps up the road. The other was clearly intent on not returning.

Eloise grabbed Jerri's arm and spun her, the latter glaring back at her as they came face to face.

Eloise took Jerri by the upper arms and said, "I'm sorry, I'm sorry, but you shouldn't have and neither should I. But that hurt, Jerri. They might not come back. Don't you get it? This game is for keeps. I mean really, for some of them, depending on their duties, the odds are against them coming back . . . and then to make those sex jokes. Me and Sarah together? . . and then with a bunch of men? Grow up, Jerri. I'm your friend and Sarah should be. We may be widows when this is over, Sarah and me. Hell, we may be widows now. I'm two years out of high school and I may be a widow. If it happens, I'll need you. There is . . sometimes such a numbness even now, just thinking about it too much. If it really happens, my life will be so hollow and empty. Sarah may need me, and to be strong for her, I'll need you. You've got to grow up for me."

She pulled Jerri close and hugged her, and the two cried for quite some long moments. As they broke apart, she looked in Jerri's eyes again and said, "The papers say the Japs are getting desperate. They're crashing their planes into our ships, you know . . suicide. Their good pilots are dead I guess, so they crash into our big aircraft carriers," she added, her eyes welling up again. The youthful, creamy white face twisting in pain and the tears starting to flow, Eloise embraced Jerri again and sobbed softly, and still easily understandable through the tears, she said, "Darrell is on one of them. The Japs crash them to blow them up and destroy all the planes with just the loss of one of their own. He's a mechanic, Jerri . . he can't shoot back."

The two longtime friends embraced again tightly and cried together. Then as they slowly stood back and smiled at each other, Eloise handed her friend the newspaper she had been reading earlier and had grabbed from the counter. It was still folded to the news of locals in the war zones.

When the girls left each other, Eloise decided, she would grab the bull by the horns and write a letter to them all, to all three. God had given them a second chance: two couples, two slightly older guys who shared an unusual friendship and two slightly younger gals much the same . . and all three old hometown friends who, on some basic level she couldn't quite grasp, were really quite close.

She would tell them in the next letter, almost a duplicate to the three, that she and Darrell should consider visiting them in the Philippines, if the other two remained there after the war. Furthermore, she wanted to see if she and Darrell liked it enough to stay.

Later, back at the grill alone, the woman just sat and drank her coffee and thought. Eloise was a strong girl, and in Sarah's shoes then, would have performed as heroically, for such a job was heroic. Nevertheless, having processed such joyless thoughts and joyful dreams of the future, she came back to the reality of the present in her mind and, remembering where she guessed Darrell was now in the enormous Pacific Ocean and the news daily riddled with reports of Jap kamikazes, she put her head down on her folded arms and cried some more. It was part of a war wife's job.

~

"Sarah! Grab your gear, I mean your fatigues. We're taking a flight."

"Where? Is it a lead on someone?"

"No. We're going on one of those rescue missions like your husband did."

"What, really! On a Dumbo?"

"That's all they use now, maybe the occasional Goose in a pinch."

"He flew that too. You know, when he got hurt."

"Really . . a real flyboy. Well, let's go. You can tell me those stories later."

Some minutes later the two were at the water ready to be ferried out to a PBY sitting on its belly in the water near her tender and among other Catalinas. She noticed no names or art work on the flying boats, no cartoon characters or paintings of beautiful babes in swimsuits. Sarah deduced that the name on her husband's Catalina was rare.

It was dusk, and within another minute, the Commander was in a small argument with the pilot, a lieutenant and the plane's captain.

"Commander, it's just not regulation, not just that she's a woman, but a civilian."

"When you offered this flight experience, you said I could bring my assistant. We're only a two-person unit under my command. I answer directly to the Navy Department. What could be the problem?"

"That you didn't tell me she was a twenty-year-old girl."

"I'm twenty-one and a married woman. Married to a Dumbo pilot lost out here."

"I'm sorry Miss . . uh . . Ma'am, but we won't find him tonight. It doesn't work that way."

Looking at the somewhat young officer with a sarcastic smile, Sarah replied, "Really, lieutenant, did you really think I expected that?"

"Lieutenant, Sarah is a uniquely capable woman."

"This isn't a milk run. I mean it is in a way. But every time we go up, every time a Hellcat takes off from a carrier or comes in, . . every time, men are tense. There's too much death out here. It's not always guns and combat. It being secured here in the Philippines doesn't end the risk."

"I'm used to risk."

He looked at her, and her boss put in, "The flight out was dangerous, Lieutenant."

Sarah added, "Sir, I won't disturb your crew or become hysterical in a crisis. I know danger and procedure. I'm a hunter . . have been since a kid. I've been alone in the woods and mountains for several days many times."

Looking back to her, he couldn't help inquiring, "What are you?" He quickly sensed the rudeness of it and felt bad.

"Blackfoot, Navajo, and white," the woman calmly replied.

"It's my butt if something goes wrong tonight."

"I'll take the heat. I have the rank, and I'll tell anyone who asks that this is training for my assistant. Civilian or not I have a right to train her. Her husband is a missing decorated hero who flew Cats."

"Yes sir. That might be enough. Okay, you two. Let's go."

Sara felt exhilarated as the plane rose on the step, clinging briefly to the water of the Visayan Sea before rising into the deep indigo Philippine sky, turning dark red in the West, and soaring across northern Leyte and Samar. Flying through the evening charged her with excitement and knowing this was what Jake did just charged it up more. She withheld it openly. She was only an observer, but she was on duty, she was a professional now. Her job was to learn and experience when she wasn't looking for lost warriors. If there was an emergency this night, she would find another role to play.

She was shocked at the interior of the plane. Her only reference was the luxurious Clipper and the small passenger's cockpit in the Avenger. She discounted the latter because it was only intended for fighting and there was no room to consider comfort beyond the basic kind.

The Catalina was bigger and she knew it ferried men sometimes and rescued them often. But there were no comforts. This one didn't even have seats except at the crew positions. There were little portable ones pulled out for her and Gerald. Pieces of gear of all kinds were secured here and there, which Sarah assumed were proper places, as the Navy had a place and a rule about everything. Jake had said it was because men could easily get hurt or killed on ships. But what surprised her the most was that no decorative panels covered the planes mechanical components that passed through the compartment, which was essentially one big compartment taking up most of the ship. Tubing and cables, joints, pipes, and various connections seemed everywhere. She knew control originated with the pilot and copilot in the cockpit up front. So, she guessed that such control was passed through some of these mechanical things around her and on back to the tail, wings, and up above to the two roaring engines. She knew about the control surfaces from common sense, and even what to call them from her husband's stories. Finding herself in his world now, but without his guidance, Sarah was afraid to touch anything.

Just as everything appeared routine, which was not routine for the young woman who was savoring every moment, word came over the radio of a downed TBF possibly within their patrol area. The plane was on a routine night patrol in the northern Philippines and developed electrical problems off Cape Engaño. Its carrier was cruising in the Philippine Sea north by west of Polillo Island; and, since the Avenger could overshoot without navigation equipment at night, the PBY was a possible lifeboat in the southern range of its fuel supply.

The hours passed and her own tension rose as if she were part of the Dumbo crew, which in a broader sense she and Gerald were. Having flown in an Avenger, there was a connection for the woman there as well. She watched the Catalina crew's professionalism and fought the urge to try to peer out the port or starboard bubble. These men were trained, and she wasn't and she knew it. She would be in their way and might cost the lives of the men in the sea below.

Through her mind the thoughts ran, 'This is what Jake did.' He had been on both sides of it, rescuer and lost pilot, lost and not yet found.

The engines droned on and the search was fruitless, and she hoped the men had found their ship, or another, or had been found by another Dumbo crew.

The flight back was quiet at first, somber. Closer to the tender there was quiet talk without any levity of course, and the men weren't totally silent as they deplaned from their mission. They had work to do to stand down from it anyway. But they felt it and she knew it. She wanted to say something but knew not what. It would have seemed arrogant anyway. Who was she after all? 'It's not like I'm Lana Turner or Betty Grable or someone,' she thought to herself.

Hoping none blamed her, the bad luck of a woman in a man's world, Sarah stepped with Gerald into the small launch by the hatch of the plane and turned to say goodbye to the crewman who helped her into it.

"Thank you, Petty Officer. And thank you for the experience. My husband flew Dumbos. This meant something to me. You are brave men."

The sailor, a young petty officer third class, nodded and said, "You're welcome ma'am."

Somehow, saying it to just one of them privately seemed to mean more.

With a certain imaginative ability, the young woman reflected as she sat in the little launch as it pulled toward shore and the outline of the low-setting water bird became more indistinct in the haze of early dawn as they pulled away from it.

There were the beginnings of the rose glow of morning off to the east across the water, just at the planet's rim, and she remembered her husband joking on early morning walks that the sun was hull down over the horizon. She thought it such a quaint naval term. But then weren't they all?

'How did I become a part of this?' the woman thought. 'Thank God I am a part of this.'

Staring at the dull, yet beautiful yellow, rose, and gray sky slowly developing, Sarah wondered at all of them . . these young men and women, of which she was now one . . how their lives had changed, some just a year or so out of school, many off a farm they thought they would never leave . . now dying horrible sometimes lonely deaths, like drowning in the night somewhere between Cape Engaño and Polillo Island around the world from home in the Philippine Sea. But they were also winning the greatest war ever fought . . a bunch of teenagers and twenty something year olds, and the old guys and gals in their thirties: sinking expensive giant enemy aircraft carriers and destroying armies, and nurses stealing broken men from the gaping maw of death. Just kids . . doing that.

And she had her small part looking for the lost and almost forgotten.

Some weeks later, Sarah walked up to the Filipino couple, who adding to the confused, incongruous nature of this war, of any war, were building a nipa hut in the middle of a city. Something about them, of their demeanor, seemed to not speak of the farmer or the peasant. But she already knew that. She had sought them out. Maybe it was their speech that she picked up on as she approached. Maybe it was how they carried themselves as they worked and perhaps their possessions. These two were the people Sarah was looking for. There were few belongings but telling ones: a doctor's bag, a tool kit, ...

As she came nearer, quite near, the woman noticed her more than she had before and said in the dialect of Cebu and its region, Cebuano, "Good afternoon, Inday."

Sarah did not look very traditionally Filipino, but because of the many ethnic varieties in the islands and the mixing of everything else in the coastal areas, Spanish, English, American, Indians from Southern Asia . . . a dark-skinned person like her would more likely be considered to belong than not.

Surprising herself with all she had picked up and learned, the American Navy employee replied in smooth Cebuano, "Good afternoon to you as well, Inday. May I be of assistance?"

"It is quite alright; your dress is too fine for the work. But thank you."

Sarah said, "You are welcome. I am seeking Attorney and Doctora Taboada. I want …" and then she seemed to search for words.

Her linguistic struggle was a bit obvious and the woman said in English, making her own guess about the one to whom she spoke, "You are not a Visayan speaker, Inday?"

Laughing softly and cheerfully with her warm smile, Sarah said, "I am not Filipino; I am American . . mostly Blackfoot and Navajo Indian." She thought in this way to get the origins questions out of the way so the woman would not feel awkward in having to wonder or inquire.

The couple both seemed a bit surprised with that and impressed in the way one is when they meet someone of a race or ethnicity that history, literature, and the cinema had elevated to near mythical and legendary status. Sarah's overall native people were comparable in history and legend to the Muslim Moros of the Southern Philippines, the warriors that Jóhonaá had fought with the very same khukuri Sarah's husband might still possess if she could find him.

Sarah offered her hand to the woman and said, "I am Sarah Pierce. I work for the U.S. Navy searching for missing sailors and soldiers, ones we know are alive but have lost track of."

By now the man had stopped his work and was listening with interest, and the woman, taking Sarah's hand, replied, "I am Doctora Natividad Taboada and this is my husband, Attorney Jose Taboada. We have returned from the hills and are making a temporary home here until we can build better."

They shook hands gently in a womanly way and Sarah offered her hand to Jose, who took it of course as they gently shook hands as well. The two Filipinos were older than her but of her generation and probably a little older than Jake. The woman was a medical school graduate after all.

"I have been blessed to be able to come here and see your country. My husband lived here in Cebu before the war. He is a Navy flyer and among those I now seek."

"I am so sorry to hear that, Inday," still using the native word for a young woman or a woman friend of any age, as Sarah had readily responded to it.

"What do you know of him, of his situation?" the husband inquired.

"Thank you for your concern. I was blessed to get this job by pure chance. Few women in my place can be out here with the war still raging not far off. I feel I am working for them too. We know he survived a crash and was on Panay for some time. The guerrillas hid him and he may have even served with them. We are uncertain of his survival, but there is thankfully no news of his death. I thought he might try to get back to Cebu. He will be concerned for his friends here. He has not seen them since the war began."

As she spoke, she could be professional about it now, having too often considered the worst outcome in her mind. She had not accepted it but had come to terms on some level that she might already be a widow. It was the tremendous sensory experience of the trip on every level and the tremendous duty she served that helped her survive and function emotionally at the current time. And the two Filipinos could discern the slight redness and wetness that had developed in Sarah's eyes as the last information had been delivered. But they needed to ask it; maybe they could be helpful with information from Cebu's hills.

The attorney continued, "You said he lived here; what is his name, . . you are 'Pierce'?"

"He is now Chief Petty Officer Jake Pierce."

"I have met him. I am from Cebu, originally from Badian in the mountains. My wife is from Mambajao off Northern Mindanao. We were at Santo Tomas University in Manila before the war. I did not know Jake well, but we know each other well enough to call each other by our first names. We met at a function or two. We are near the same age and he was not the type of American to frequent those bars at the docks. My family has shipped with the O'Brians before, as well. Jake is a fine man. People told me of his sailing skills and how quickly he learned to be a pilot. He really loves the Philippines and Filipinos. If he can, he will survive for you. If anyone can, he can. I believe he is tough."

Sarah felt no need to press with questions. These were the two people the marine colonel had spoken of, and they were professionals. If they had information about Jake, they would surely have volunteered it.

In that very vein of thought the woman said, "Some of them are probably safe. You can tell him that when you see him. We saw Kathleen Allison and her husband once. I believe they survived it though I have not seen them in a year or more. We saw Rosario O'Brian more recently."

Jose added, "We were near Badian, and that is near where we saw them. When you and Jake are together, look there first, unless they are already down from the hills."

"If … When I find him, we will come to see you again, Attorney, Doctora. I would like to hear about your experience in the hills if they are not too painful."

"Sarah, Sarah, Sarah . . . !" she heard her name called over the characteristic metallic grinding drone of a Willys MB Jeep and recognized Yeoman, Petty Officer 2nd Class Randall Oliver. Even in their dreams, the sound of ubiquitous little vehicle would live on for those who were around it during the war.

Turning she saw him pulling up as the Jeep threw a bit of dust.

"Yes. What's wrong, Randall?"

"You have to hurry! We've found him!"

Registering shock with an open mouth and wide eyes, Sarah looked at him, then jerked her head back to the couple with the same expression, as Randall still continued to speak, "You have to hurry!"

Turning back to him as the Jeep sat right there now and the engine idled, the Yeoman continued, "We have to hurry. You have to get to Leyte. We found him on the hospital ship *Refuge*. She's departing for Hollandia or Guam this evening. I don't know which."

"I thought she left already."

"She's back. They're pretty quick. She's been back and she's loaded again. Hurry, Get in!"

Turning back to the couple both smiled happily.

"Tell me," she said urgently but under self-control turning back to Randall.

"While we drive. Get in"

Sarah looked anxiously to the Filipino couple as she reached to grab the window frame with her left hand to get into the vehicle, and the two of them shooed her away, the husband saying, "Go . . Go . . Inday. You must hurry. Be safe."

Thru it all the young Filipino doctora listened with interest and contemplated the excitement of such duty on the big hospital ships, of which the United States operated thirty-nine in various theaters during the current conflict.

Driving fast, the yeoman filled Sarah in, "I don't know where you'll be goin'. Just grab all your gear fast. She picks up wounded and then shuttles them to hospitals at those two places, Guam or Hollandia and Seeadler Harbor. All the while the doctors on board work on the serious cases at sea. The Commander got one of the officers of the ship on the radio. He pleaded with him. Told him all you and Jake have been through. His captain can't and won't hold the ship; but he'll take you aboard and find room if we get you there. They said they'd shove you in a storage cabinet if they had to after the skipper told the officer you were petite. We're tryin' to line up a *Kingfisher* or *Avenger* or somethin' . . anything with two seats to fly you over."

Back at the office, Sarah learned the *Refuge* was going to Hollandia in New Guinea and perhaps on to Seeadler Harbor, Manus, in the Admiralty

Islands. That was a regular shuttle run for the ship, taking wounded out of the bloody jungle battlefields of the Central Philippines as the Americans and Japanese contested the Visayan Islands, particularly, Mindoro. As with other hospital ships on station in combat zones, the *Refuge* shuttle service cycled as fast she could fill her wards; and, with active surgeries at sea, could bring the wounded to military hospitals to the South and return to Leyte Gulf for more wounded men. For her, such duty would last as long as needed, as long as brave wounded men were brought to her motherly arms, her wards.

The float plane was a different experience than the TBF had been. Perched a bit high above its big pontoon-like float, the *Vought OS2U Kingfisher*, a work horse of the Pacific war was unusual, stately in a strange sort of way, and efficient in its role, underpowered engine aside. The leaner body allowed even a slightly short person like Sarah to see more downward when looking below. With both it and the Avenger there was the issue of the wing blocking some viewing angles. Again, she had an accommodating pilot who tried to make the experience meaningful and educational.

But Sarah's nerves had a new experience to contemplate before she would observe anything from the air this time. The seaplane was a cruiser plane, and Sarah was now sitting in it on the catapult near the stern of a large American warship sitting at anchor out in the Camotes Sea just north of Cebu Strait, waiting to be literally 'shot' off into the sky.

The engine revved up and the plane shot off of its catapult pushing her back in the seat where she was held momentarily as the Kingfisher climbed. Being catapulted and once again flying across Leyte with a U.S. Navy pilot was another experience to savor, but it was soon over and found the pretty civilian Navy secretary in yet another Navy launch being ferried the few yards from the seaplane to the hospital ship where her war battered husband was supposed to now be, finally 'found'.

The *USS Refuge AH-11* was so big and white as the seaplane came in for a thrilling landing near her anchorage in San Pedro Bay at the north end of the gulf. The large red cross and stripe on her side seemed to radiate in the golden Philippine sun. The whole scene whispered to her, "Peace, peace has almost come to the world." And under the bright blue sky, Sarah looked up at the marine sentry at the top of the metal steps that the Navy called a ladder even when it was stairs or steps.

She had a self-assurance that had always been in her but, being so young, needed drawing out, and it had been encouraged all the more by the naval officer that had been her boss these many weeks. Pay wasn't certain as there had not been time to make everything official, and the Navy could possibly ask later why a sailor or WAVE had not been used for the purpose. But her expenses were paid and she had made it to her destination for free. She thought if any issue was made of it officially, Gerald would pull the 'hero card' with respect to her husband. She also had learned that Gerald had significant wealth and could absorb any expenses she might cause, even if the Navy charged her air fare. She made a point to not be extravagant, but Gerald gave her expense money quite freely. Of course, she wasn't naïve after the childhood she had experienced back in Paradise Ridge, so she wondered about any ulterior motive. But the officer had been a perfect gentleman in spite of the many opportunities he had been given by their circumstances and the leverage he would have had over her. For him, it was his contribution beyond his actual naval career. He had seen some action, but not like Jake.

From the launch looking up she took the measure quickly of the ship's ladder attached to the white hull, parallel to it. Angled for a reasonably normal stair climb it was really a type of metal stairs like an aluminum step ladder. Holding the narrow chain rail tightly with her right hand, the petite young woman confidently climbed up the long, steep, thickly painted ladder to the top and, turning toward the officer of the deck who was standing there beside the marine guard, said, "I'm the assistant of Commander Phillips, Gerald C. Phillips. Permission to come aboard?" With the request she offered her credentials.

Sara was expected, and the officer beside the sentry was obviously at the top of the ladder so conveniently because his attention had been drawn by the Kingfisher's landing. He nodded and answered her in the affirmative, "Permission granted."

Turning to the officer she then held the credentials out again and said, "Lieutenant, we have learned my missing husband is aboard. I have not known for sure of his location in seven months, only that he was probably alive and somewhere in the Navy's medical system. I wonder if I might see him?"

The woman had assured herself that she could remain composed when this moment came, when she was finally this close, but the moment she spoke, her eyes dampened and burned. The officer saw it, with the accompanying redness.

Sarah added in a professional manner, "The assignment of my superior's small command is actually to seek men such as my husband whose locations' have been unknown though they were not officially considered missing in action. My visit is personal yet official."

The man stared at her only a moment. Most men meeting Sarah stared a moment at least, and then there was her surprising request for him to contemplate. It was like a new captain coming aboard to take command and saying, 'Oh, I hear my brother is the exec on this ship and my son's the chief cook.' Then the young lieutenant said, "Why of course ma'am. Give me a moment."

Within five minutes, Sarah was being escorted by a sailor to the main office section that handled the hospital operations on the ship, as opposed to the navigation and steaming duties. As the sailor guided her down the deck to the hatch into the superstructure, she observed 'swabs' (sailors) doing just that: swabbing the deck in several places.

She looked around and studied the stains and darkened water, and the sailor said, "We just embarked a full complement of wounded ma'am."

As the two of them continued to the passageway, the young woman turned and looked at him with one of those subtle, shocked, blank, and questioning stares one wears when they are processing something ominous, and he simply stated with a word, "Blood, ma'am,"

He opened the hatch and gentlemanly allowed her to go first. And, as she stepped through and followed his verbal directions from behind her, a chill had gone up her spine and she seemed weak and cardboard-like as she walked, like a paper doll.

Glancing back, the girl inquired, "How many did you embark, sailor?"

"Six hundred and thirty, ma'am."

Sarah turned her face forward, feeling weak in the knees, and seemed as if she had to think about each step as she continued down the passageway. Otherwise she might collapse.

A moment later in an office, looking down at the nurse seated behind the desk, she repeated the exact words about Jake she had said topside at the ladder, using the full name of her true love, Chief Petty Officer Jake Pierce USNR.

The desk nurse was a bit confused. Sarah was civilian, in no uniform, and had come around the world to see her combat wounded lover. Not too many of the thousands of women in the current world conflagration had done that or even could if they wanted. What made this one so special?

Perhaps there was professional resentment at a blatant, unusual request_ no paperwork presented yet, a civilian in their tense stressful world, and her obvious ethnic minority status. Perhaps she could be, in the nurse's mind, of some Negro mix that showed less normal features for that group . . so, there was that, as little as it should have mattered.

A more commanding appearing nurse came over to stand behind the desk and said, "I did not catch all that. How did you say you got all the way out here, honey?" She was probably the head nurse on duty and certainly an officer. Most nurses were.

Remembering Jake's paperwork, she now presented them saying, "I came on the Clipper and a cruiser with Commander Gerald C. Phillips, as his secretary. He is charged with seeking missing injured and such, the bureaucracy you know. It must have been horrible for you ladies out here, you're heroes too . . heroines."

Sarah hoped it did not seem like 'brownnosing'. She really meant it. Jake had told her what it could be like and she couldn't imagine how these nurses could do their jobs.

"Well, seeking your loved one, how did you luck out with the job as his assistant, Mrs.?"

She was getting anxious and it showed. Jake was here, right here on this ship! The doctor leaning on the filing cabinet in the back saw it, but he let it go for a bit longer.

"The Commander was called too fast to secure an assistant and met me as I was seeking passage. I guess I passed the interview."

"I suppose you did," the head nurse said with a slight smile that Sarah could not recognize as friendly or an expression of disdain full of innuendo.

Then the same woman inquired. "Your last name again?"

"Pierce, Chief Petty Officer Pierce's wife." Sarah still replied with control but she knew she was about to lose it.

The head nurse and her subordinate were not being cruel, just careful and a bit surprised, and perhaps irritated with such an interruption into their world where they were charged with holding men's bodies and lives together . . a world where they could barely hold it together themselves sometimes. And maybe, as much as they knew the women at home hurt . . they knew that those women could barely imagine what they had seen and done out here . . and then here comes this little young thing barely old enough to be married to check up on them. So young? . . How could she be the wife of a chief petty officer?

And as those thoughts went through their minds and hers, the head nurse noticed the medals on Sarah's lapel, obviously her husband's.

Just then the doctor pulled his tired body, somewhat rested now, lazily from the filing cabinet and inquired, "Pierce, CPO Pierce . . ?"

It was almost rhetorical, and before Sarah could answer, the man said to the head nurse who was still standing behind the desk, "Her lapel, Captain . . that's a Silver Star."

"Yes sir."

"He's the one just down the passage toward the stern on this deck…"

"I know sir. He has a Navy Cross pinned to his pillow. I think she passes muster. Let's let the hero see his gal and vice versa."

"That's what we're here for," the younger nurse at the desk added . . to put 'em back together, the guys and the couples."

As the head nurse said, "Come on, honey," grabbing Sarah by the left arm near the elbow, the other one added, "We just don't usually get to see it, the final resolution like this."

It was soaking into both angels of mercy . . 'Florence Nightingales' as they were in the toughest of times for their noblest of professions . . that they were being blessed with the rare chance to see the end result of their work. That normally did not happen where they worked here, now in the far Pacific and previously off the coasts of Africa and Normandy.

Walking briskly down the hall beside Sarah, the supervising nurse inquired, "Are you a tough cookie, honey?"

Looking to the side and a bit up at the taller woman with an equally inquisitive expression and a crinkled brow as the two women walked, Sarah said, "Yes, I suppose I am. I'm here aren't I?"

"Well, it's good you are. He's gonna need you. He's in some kind of unhappy mood. Most of 'em are when they come back . . come out here to us. But his is different. It's not shell shock exactly with him. He's depressed, honey."

She spoke with a strong but not overwhelming Southern Accent, Tennessee perhaps. Sarah wasn't sure. The woman stopped, turning and took the younger girl's hands both in hers.

"He may think he was never gonna see you again, and you can't think it bad of him."

"Why would I do that?"

"Well, let's go see your guy. Then he'll know."

Walking briskly now and trying to prepare Sarah, the woman continued, "Honey, you can't know where they've been. None of us can."

And hearing that, Sarah looked up at her inquisitively again.

"Mentally, you can't know where they've been mentally. Each has inhabited, for a time, their own private hell, I guess each one personal and different. We can't blame 'em for anything. If one grabbed a rifle and shot us all right now, it wouldn't be his fault." And with the last she turned as they walked and glanced into Sarah's brown eyes.

They continued walking, and the nurse added more information, "He is whole but in some strong pain still . . and scarred. By the way, where are you from . . uh, what are you?"

"California, Navajo and Blackfoot, mostly the latter, and some white."

"Blackfoot? Interesting. We'll have some long talks over a lot of coffee . . or bourbon. California? Were you the minority there where you lived."

The two had been walking down the ship aft along the deck passageway at the rail. Now they stepped into a ward that led to where Jake and few patients were in a smaller compartment to themselves. The nurse now led Sarah down the center space of a ward with beds full of recuperating warriors along each side. The beds were parallel with the narrow passage down the center of the compartment between them. The bunk style beds were close, Indicating how packed it was with men injured enough to be transported to hospitals. The men lay or sat up in their beds, and a chorus of strong wolf whistles filled the ward. Yet somehow it seemed very respectful. There were a few solos to this accompanying background of whistles as many of them invited her to come see them personally or hold their hand. It was not crass as such war roughened ordinary men had become; it was all very respectful in a crude way. They were ordinary American guys after all. And a few Aussies and perhaps a New Zealander or two. The tawny tone of her seemed to matter little in a negative way. Those who had fought and earned their wounds in these Philippine Islands, and any Anzacs who had been in Malaya, were desensitized to the color issue and now admiring of the café latte girls of South East Asia and the East Indies.

As the nurse and the young wounded warrior's wife had reached the door at the end of the ward, Sarah's head went down and her face noticeably reddened, and then she stopped and turned back to the room and said, "I hope to talk to each of you and thank you very much. Thank you for everything . . everything you have done for our . . your country."

There were tears in her eyes, and she did not know where that courage came from within her, but the ward erupted in not loud but warm applause and a few more whistles.

They must have seen how she carried herself with the unusual maturity of someone who had grown up normal but fast . . no, not fast . . early, for she had done the work and bore the concerns of an adult from an early age. It was in her. It was in her mother and from her . . put there by her mother from memories of the old ways, the subsistence life in the mountains and on the plains . . remnants of that…

The nurse, picking up on the young woman's words and trusting the truth in them, said to them all, "Sarah will honor her promise, I'm sure. Now she must go see her recuperating husband. Some of you know Chief Pierce."

A voice from one of the beds said clearly and without disdain or jealousy, "Lucky Chief Pierce."

Walking to the back corner where Jake's bed was behind a screen, Sarah became concerned, and turned with an inquisitive expression and started to speak. The nurse, in anticipation, explained, "He's had a respiratory infection. We're protecting the other boys. I'll not make you wear a mask. I doubt it would stay on very long. I think he's over it now anyway."

Anxiously, the war weathered and so lonely sailor's wife stepped around the screen and stood at the foot of the bed. Seeing him sleeping, she was trembling, not knowing what to do . . all she wanted to do was climb in that bed, grab him in a tremendous hug and never let go.

Sarah thought the nurse had left them but knowing not whether she could wake him for medical reasons and bursting with love and emotion inside, she glanced, and the woman was right outside, where she could only see Sarah, and nodded her head.

Quietly . . still trembling, the lover crept up the side of the bed between him and the cloth screen stretched between a steel frame.

Through the screen she heard the nurse's voice, "I'll go now. He doesn't need sleep. He needs you. That's his therapy now."

With that teasing nature she had adopted early in their brief time together as two adults, Sarah said, "Chief Pierce your wife is here to see you."

Softly touching his forehead with the fingertips of her left hand, leaning over closer to his face and right ear, as he lay on his left side with his face toward the opposite bulkhead, she said it again, "Chief Pierce your wife is here to see you. Darling, I'm here."

Turning a bit startled, but not in a jerk, quickly but not roughly, Jake looked at her. His eyes focused and he jumped up to a sitting position.

Her hand slipped from his forehead and she reached to embrace Jake just as he turned to her and grasped her to him and she ended up sitting in the bed as he pulled her to him and her body rotated around from the force of it and into him. It was all very non-regulation as the woman ended up half sitting half laying across the bed, her upper body leaning across it into her husband's arms. Her back was toward the small, confined area's entrance between the screen's edge and the stern bulkhead.

But the nurse didn't notice; she was gone.

Both, now embracing tightly and softly, strongly cried. At some point they had to look into each other's face and eyes, which they had only briefly seen . . and each leaned back only enough to do so and then they shared a long, deeply loving kiss as they embraced again.

"We haven't heard anything about you for months. They said you were found and then nothing."

"How did you get here?"

"I work for a Commander. We search for those like you who are lost in the field hospitals and elsewhere, found and lost again in the bureaucracy."

They had been embracing ever so closely and tightly as any two lovers would have in the same situation. He leaned back, still holding her but more loosely, and looked at her. And it was blank perhaps, yet searching . . as if he was taking the measure of the woman he had married . . to be out here, to have forced it and found a way. How many others could have . . would have even tried.

"I'm sorry Sarah. To put you through this. It must seem I'd forgotten you…"

"Not at all, and it was a labor of love."

"…But I just got here and sent a letter as soon as I could. Maybe you passed it over the Pacific. Nothing would have gotten out anywhere else I was."

There was a momentary pause as they still stared into each other's eyes and then they embraced again, with the face and head of each beside the other's looking past them. It was the conundrum of such emotionally charged moments: you could not both hug so tightly and look at your lover at the same time and you wanted to.

"I've missed you so much. I need you so much."

"I'm here. I wish I could have been here."

At that moment, a big plane roared over the harbor a bit low, and he instinctively looked up. Both were quiet.

She saw his hollow sad look; and, when he looked at her, he noticed and said after a moment, "There's a strange beauty in it, you know. I hope you never get to know . . a big one like that. When a big one breaks up . . you know really high and it's so peaceful and the sky is clear and blue with big puffy cumulus clouds . . and they all fall so floaty and gracefully. If it burns, they usually burn . . there's a certain horrible beauty in that too."

She was tearful now as she took his head in both her hands and arms and held it against her breast, whispering, "I'm sorry Jake, I'm so sorry." It's all she knew to say and she held the tears as best she could. She had to be strong for him.

He was still teary eyed just ever so slightly. He must be strong for her. But he had lost so many friends now.

But then the woman said, "You'll tell me all of it. It's how to heal from it. Not now . . someday, and we'll cry together."

He looked at her, perhaps to see if she was so shallow to just want the stories he could hardly bare to speak of, and her soft brown eyes met his, and Sarah said, "I learned it from my mother when my dad had that bad accident. You remember. They wouldn't let me see. But she told me everything later. To help me heal."

"Are you ready for more travel?"

"Of course, That's all I've been doing. We need to see your parents, but they may want to come here, since they know you may want to settle here again."

"Well, let's wait on that then . . see if they are willing to come. We have to conserve money. I wanna see 'em of course."

"What did you mean, 'travel'? They haven't cleared you for release yet. And you are still in the Navy, Chief," his wife teased.

"Trincomalee. I've gotta find Jon and Maya."

"Where?"

"Trincomalee. It's in Ceylon off India. Their ship was headed there, but the Jap Navy was too, and the Germans had U-boats in the Indian Ocean back then."

"I remember. What a pretty name. We'll find them Jake. I know we will."

"It's a beautiful port they say . . one of the most beautiful natural harbors in the world. That's what they say anyway. The rest of the family is in Darwin or somewhere and in the hills of Cebu or Panay."

"Panay seems safer, so big." Her comment revealing her observational skills, being only briefly in the islands. "I met a Filipino couple, Jake. An attorney and his wife who is a doctora. They said they had seen your Lola Sunny and Rosario O'Brian in the mountains of Cebu."

"Lola's is surely a woman I want you to meet . . if she survived. She was healthy the last time I saw her."

"I remember."

"What?"

"The stories in the cabin . . on our honeymoon."

Somehow two chairs were discovered and dragged in for the two sweethearts to sit arm-in-arm, side-by-side, and she asked him, "How did you get here and why did we never know it? Do you know? Did you know that when I heard a few hours ago that you were aboard the *Refuge*, we knew nothing about what happened to you after you were with the guerrillas?"

"Oh Sarah . . I'm so sorry. My Go… I . . I guess it is because I had no papers. That happens with everyone brought into field hospitals and aboard these hospital ships. We have our tags and that's it. I lost mine in the jungle.

The guerrillas were able to get control of Panay after the Leyte landings, so the Army and Marines didn't get into there quickly to find us. They weren't needed. I was wounded again and had a lot of responsibilities . . you know, for my crew. I didn't forget you. You were on my mind almost constantly. When I reached here, I became a bit depressed. I don't know where any of the guys are now from my crew. I hoped the field hospital would handle my recovery, but they insist on sending me to a big one in New Guinea. That captain, the nurse, she went through my wallet asking me all about you. I think she thought I was about to lose it . . you know all that's happened and the men."

And as he looked pleadingly into her eyes for understanding, his love replied, "Chief Pierce, you did your duty. Without that, you may not have made it back and this moment might never have happened. Don't you ever apologize to me for anything you've done, . . had to do in this war. You're all heroes, every one of you."

And she stared back a moment with her chair turned a little toward him as his was to hers, and she held his hands and he held hers and she said, "But you're *my* hero."

Later, a nurse came by and insisted nicely that Sarah leave for Jake to rest. Walking down the passage she approached the desk that she had before and asked for Capt. Lewis.

"She's right behind you ma'am," responded the RN lieutenant at the station now.

Turning, Sarah came face to face with the woman who said, "I'm off duty, would you join me for what these Filipinos call 'merienda'?"

"Certainly," the surprised younger woman replied. "Thank you."

The two went to the nurses' mess and had coffee and cake. The ship was not yet underway, but when I weighed anchor soon, all refreshments and meals were provided aboard her. The nurses had their own facilities, which being a woman, Sarah was invited to use.

Small talk ensued for a brief moment, and then obviously went to their shared interest, Sarah's romantically, the nurse's professionally and a bit emotionally.

Unabashedly, the Captain said, "You have quite a man there. You know that, don't you?"

"Oh, my yes."

There was a pause, and Sarah continued, "He is feeling it hard. I'm sure many are . . all maybe."

"There will be long healing for many, not their bodies, their …"

"I know," Sarah interrupted. "I see it in him. Not a weakness, a scar . . scars."

The nurse looked at her and studied the young face a moment, and replied, "Well, I can see he's in good hands. I think a lot off gals in your shoes are just wondering when they can go out on the town and . . well, you know, get back to business in the bedroom."

"I guess each one misses something, and some of those girls put their longings before his, or think he just misses what she does. I know these guys lost friends and shared horrible things. You know."

"Tell me about it. We go through some psychological trauma too."

"I saw them mopping the deck. Uh 'swabbing' it. Capt. Lewis, I want to thank you," Sarah said as she toyed with some cake with her fork.

"For what? I . . we all just do our duty."

"He told me what your talks have meant to him. I'm sure you didn't have the time. Surely it added to your workload. I don't know how those pictures survived it . . all he went through, but the way you apparently kept talking about us, Jake and me . . .

well, asking him over and over to tell you more about the girl in the photos . . . he survived because of that. He's so devastated about it all. I might have arrived here to visit a grave, were it not for you."

"He told you all of that in your hour visit?"

"We communicate well. We were meant for each other. He left Paradise Ridge, where we both grew up, when he graduated high school and I was only thirteen, just to get away because of my youth. He came back when I was nineteen to see if I cared. . . . . . I did."

"Wow, what a story. He didn't tell me all of it."

The nurse paused, and quietly, seriously said, "They think their girls, however much they love' 'em, will find someone else…"

"I would never…"

"Honey, no one plans too, but that is part of the story of this war . . 'specially young girls like you . . they get hungry, pardon me; I'm sorry, It just happens…"

"Captain…"

"Mrs. Pierce, I have to read the 'Dear John' letters to them, the ones whose eyes are bandaged. I read four to those boys, those mangled partial boys . . off the coast near Naples and off Africa, . . Oran at Algeria. Oh, and there was one off Wales. We anchored off the coast at Milford Haven. Sounds like a town back home, doesn't it? . . I mean already out of harm's way and heading home, and she'd dumped him. And there was one more at Belfast, six in all. They were not whole anymore and knew they could never win another. At least your guy is complete."

There were tears in the nurse's eyes, and she continued as Sarah just took it in, took in the story that was one of the many that characterized this war and any war.

"He's a lucky man . . your Jake. You were not only true to him but came out here."

"We're from the same small town."

"And?"

"Everyone 'liked' me . . They liked my coffee. We owned a grill. No one wanted to date me except Jake, and he knew I was too young at the time. He came back later, the first time he was injured and on a long leave."

"Oh, we have to talk. How romantic. I can relate to your experience. I moved from Knoxville to Michigan. Everyone loved the Southern girl's cute accent, but no one dated me 'til college."

"And…?"

"I've a handsome Doctor somewhere in Europe saving widows and orphans of the enemy and their victims. We have two darling kids with my parents right now. I didn't hear from him for the longest after the Italian landings . . Anzio, but Doc Bryant, our CO said they would have notified me if he was one in that terrible attack. Later he wrote."

"I heard about it. That attack was horrible."

"I received a letter today from his CO. Chuck's okay but they were deep in it and he somehow couldn't get mail out. The CO mentioned liberating camps of some kind in Belgium and Germany, civilian prison camps, and the medical staff being overwhelmed. At least they're not in combat now. I should hear from him any day now."

Jake could not be released just yet, not until he was seen in the hospital in Hollandia. Then the particulars of his future had to be worked out since transports ships took many home to the states, and Jake had matriculated into the Navy, the college of life, there where they now were, in the Far East.

So, in the evening when the *Refuge* weighed anchor, Jake was bound for New Guinea and Sarah was allowed to stay without sleeping in a cabinet.

War compressed time, and in the five day voyage to Hollandia, the staff in Jake's immediate department got to know the out-of-place visitor, and nothing was ever said about her color or her being there. Many learned of her duty with the Commander, which she still attended to, handling some correspondence she had brought with her mostly.

Some also knew her husband's story. Surely none could miss the three medals on her lapel, knowing where they came from. Perhaps the scuttlebutt got around that he was a Dumbo jockey and won those saving other young men. She was treated with respect. Surely there was a bond between Dumbo pilots and hospital ship personnel during that war.

Sarah and the nurses she had met the first day she arrived on the ship had lunch, coffee, tea, calamansi juice, or any combination of them together quite often.

"So, you and Jake won't go home yet?" Jane Lewis inquired.

"Not if his parents come out. We might not move back at all."

"Why? After all this, home should be comforting for him."

"This is home too. You know some of it. He's got some roots out here now, and I haven't had my life adventure yet . . well, except for this."

"I'm afraid for what he will find. That's partly why I hoped you two would go back stateside."

"He is definitely worried about his employers and their friends here."

"You be with him every step of the way. He will need that."

Sarah nodded almost imperceptibly.

And, with the times and less privacy rules, the wounded men could be discussed more feely. Those heroes were, after all, the whole reason all the women were there.

They were on deck for the air and sitting in deck chairs. Turning to the younger one of the two nurses, Sarah said, "Lieutenant, do you see that guy sitting over near the rail? Don't look!" whispered strongly.

"'Clark Gable'? Yeah, I know him. I can't tell if he's stuffy or not. Another hero they say."

"A raid to release some prisoners or something like that, among other things, someone told me. Oh, it was him. I asked," said with an almost imperceptible chuckle.

"Bragging, is he?"

"No. He's actually quite humble. I did ask. You told me that most of them won't talk about it. He was willing, that's all."

"Why did you bring him up?"

"Jake asked me to talk to him. Seems they are friends or the closest thing to it for Jake, except for you two . . I mean now. Jake's real sociable back in the real world. He may be worried about him. He saw some kids die."

"And?"

"Well the Captain there, with his Gable looks and similar charm, thinks you and I are close friends."

"We are now. We're so much alike," the nurse said with a chuckle.

To Sarah's furrowed, funny inquisitive expression, Carolyn replied, "You're young, naturally 'tanned', pretty, happily married, etcetera; I'm older, blushingly pink, reasonably attractive, widowed . . . see like identical twins."

Sarah smiled whimsically and knowingly, with the cute, crooked smile that turned up more on one side.

Then she said, "Wait . . you're a widow, Lieutenant? When? The war?"

"Pearl Harbor. It's why I'm here, I suppose. When I saw his mangled body, I had to get close to it. I mean to this, the war. It was the only way I could deal with it. I was a hospital nurse in Honolulu, and he was Navy. Here was this big war, and I had a place in it, I mean as a nurse, and it had already taken my life partner. The only way to honor him and feel a part of it was to get close to it, to get out into it. So here I am."

"I'm so sorry, Carolyn," Sarah said and reached her right hand across the table to grasp the other's. Then all three leaned back in their chairs and sipped calamansi juice made with the lemoncitos they had brought from the Philippines.

Jane said, "I have talked with him a lot like I did with your husband. I couldn't read him as well though. He might have more complicated problems, or he may have before this war. We don't know all their backgrounds you know. . . He's an enigma."

"Well, enigma or not, one thing is no mystery," Put in Sarah. "All he wants to talk about is Carolyn."

Carolyn replied to the thought of it, "I'm a professional; we all are. If he's around somehow when we stand-down and disembark the last time, I'll have a drink with him. I have to move forward."

"I worry about them. Some die in suspicious ways out in combat," commented Jane.

"You mean like suicide," inquired Sarah and Carolyn in concert.

The nurse nodded.

Later, walking to his room, Sara thought about it, and realized Jake would never do that. He loved her and his parents, and he was Catholic.

But she knew also that suicidal people were not in their right minds usually and not in control. She must be strong for Jake. He had lost too many whom he had tasked himself to bring back. His search for some of them now would be therapeutic, and courageous, a continuation of duty.

Turning into his room, Sarah saw Jake sitting on the side of the bed. A pretty nurse was beside him with her right hand across his back and his left in her left. He was looking down, and, being taller, as she was standing, she was looking down at him in a caring concerned way.

It startled the wife ever so briefly, but she barely missed a step. Her subconscious mind reminded her that images in real life, like snapshots, never tell the whole story. Her husband's health was the duty of these women after all; and, at the moment, his health problems were partially emotional.

Approaching them, Sarah saw the nurse look up and maybe display the slightest hint of startled embarrassment.

Then as if to explain and also display her professionalism, the young Naval officer said, "He's just learned from another patient that he's lost a close friend, Mrs. Pierce. I hope you don't…"

"Of course not, Lieutenant," Sarah said as she took Jake's offered right hand, and simultaneously gave the young officer a look of genuine thanks and respect. A smile was shared between them.

She had learned each of their names, and it was only the second day at sea. They were caring for her man in a very personal way after all. They had been doing that before she could get there, and it must be psychologically and emotionally hard on them. Jake still had trouble walking, having suffered multiple breaks or cracks involving his femur, tibia and fibula bones over three years; and he did not have full use of his left arm, the shoulder having been devastated by the rifle round in the fighting in support of the guerrillas.

Sarah, a young woman out of her more regionally cloistered world and pressed by her own self into the final moments of the great event of the era, one of the greatest events in history, revealed, with everything she did, a composure and intelligence that secretly surprised all who encountered her.

"It's Buck, Sarah," Jake said. "The one you said wrote to you. The one who recruited me. He was back in Indonesia and his plane went down in flames. I guess he could have survived. He's got a wife and two girls waiting in Sydney."

He wasn't tearful, he was somewhat stoic about it now.

Sarah sat beside him on the bed, and taking both of his hands in hers, she said. "We'll talk all about it over these next few days. That's on the route to Ceylon, you know."

Looking up at her with a wry smile and misunderstanding her meaning, Jake said, "Many a story. The pain will fade a little with time. The best memories are the ones we remember the most." He knew that, since their honeymoon, telling each other stories was one of their best shared things.

"Let's talk about what's next, Jake."

She had seen his open wallet as she had sat down beside him. It had managed to survive all Jake's trials and was laying open on a bedside hospital stand with a glass of water beside it.

"What do you want, Honey? I can't go home yet. There are so many I don't know about. I'm military. It's my duty to find them. I lost some. I don't know what to do about that."

"You have done your best, Jake. I can't imagine anyone doing better. I doubt any man out here with responsibilities has been perfect. War is chaos," the young wife added, revealing once again depth of understanding of the struggle the whole world was engaged in.

He coughed a bit more than normal, and dutifully the wife stood up off the bed and stepped over to retrieve the water glass. As she did she glanced at the wallet and saw Jon O'Brian's picture. In the other, facing side of the open wallet was a small paper with the words:

Of those whom you gave me, I lost not one.
John 18: 9

Sarah handed him the water and watched him drink. And, after a pause, while looking at her husband with a peaceful loving gaze, she said calmly and softly, "No one could have done this, Jake." and she held the wallet out to him in her other hand.

He took it and looked at it, and his wife continued, "This is war. Christ did not put his disciples in actual physical combat. Maybe, . . just maybe, if every mission was a Dumbo run . . as dangerous as they are, maybe everyone comes back. I've been on one, you know."

His head raised somewhat slowly but with eyes full of unspoken surprise.

"That mission, Jake? Your last one . . They told me about it. That was a combat mission . . one of the most dangerous . . "

Their eyes were locked now and Sarah took his head in her hands, one palm cradling each side. He had gone to the storied South Pacific seven years ago, to the world of Cook, Magellan, and Gaugin, of Stevenson, Fr. Damián and Raffles . . gone there for adventure and to wait for her to grow up . . . . he had found death and sorrow and had grown up ever so much more traumatically, had found a war and been in the center of the tempest, and now he bore the weight of it . . .

"Jake, my love, just say to yourself, over and over . . . . like a prayer if you must, these words from Mathew, 'Well done, my good and faithful servant' . . just say that." She paused and added, "You won't be the only one."

They were alone in the room, and standing, he took her in his arms and kissed her. Then leaning back, he said. "I'm being released and either discharged from the Navy or being put on standby if they think I can be useful out here. They know I consider myself a Philippine resident for now. A personnel yeoman came by today, and I told him you were here and working as a civilian Navy employee for your Commander and why. He seemed surprised and impressed. Maybe they'll attach me to your small command. It could make sense with my knowledge of the islands. But you know the Navy. Logic in such things is not their strong suit."

They looked at each other and sort of nodded agreement, and he spoke again, "If they discharge me or I have a long leave…"

She interrupted and finished his sentence, "…we can perhaps see to your other duties together. I will check with my boss about my status and his needs. He relieved me to come here."

"My duties?"

"I said you needn't feel to blame . . to feel guilt. I didn't say you couldn't care or feel a responsibility to find them."

Looking in her eyes, he could tell she was serious, as, at that moment, to her he appeared perhaps a bit curiously inquisitive.

"Jake . . Honey, what did you think I would want to do? We'll look for them together. So, where do we begin . . Cebu, Panay, or Trincomalee?"

Quality fiction is imagined reality

Regions of Events in the Novel Outside the United States: The Philippines & The East Indies bearing names during the Colonial Period at the Beginning of the Second World War.

Cities or harbors are indicated with a dot or the point of a directional line.

The top of Australia is seen, and New Zealand would be to the right and below it. Knowing that these Dutch East Indies seen here were almost completely conquered by the Japanese, as well as British Malaya, Singapore, and Borneo, one can easily grasp the fear in Australians and New Zealanders. With their men at war in other theaters as part of the forces of the United Kingdom, the people at home were concerned to a greater degree than what might be considered normal.

The Java sea, shown here, was the location of a devastating naval defeat of the Allies at the hands of the Japanese. This terrified the people of Australia even more, as did the bombing of Darwin.

Map of the Philippines ………….. page 415

Map of the East Indies ………….. page 416

The Philippines

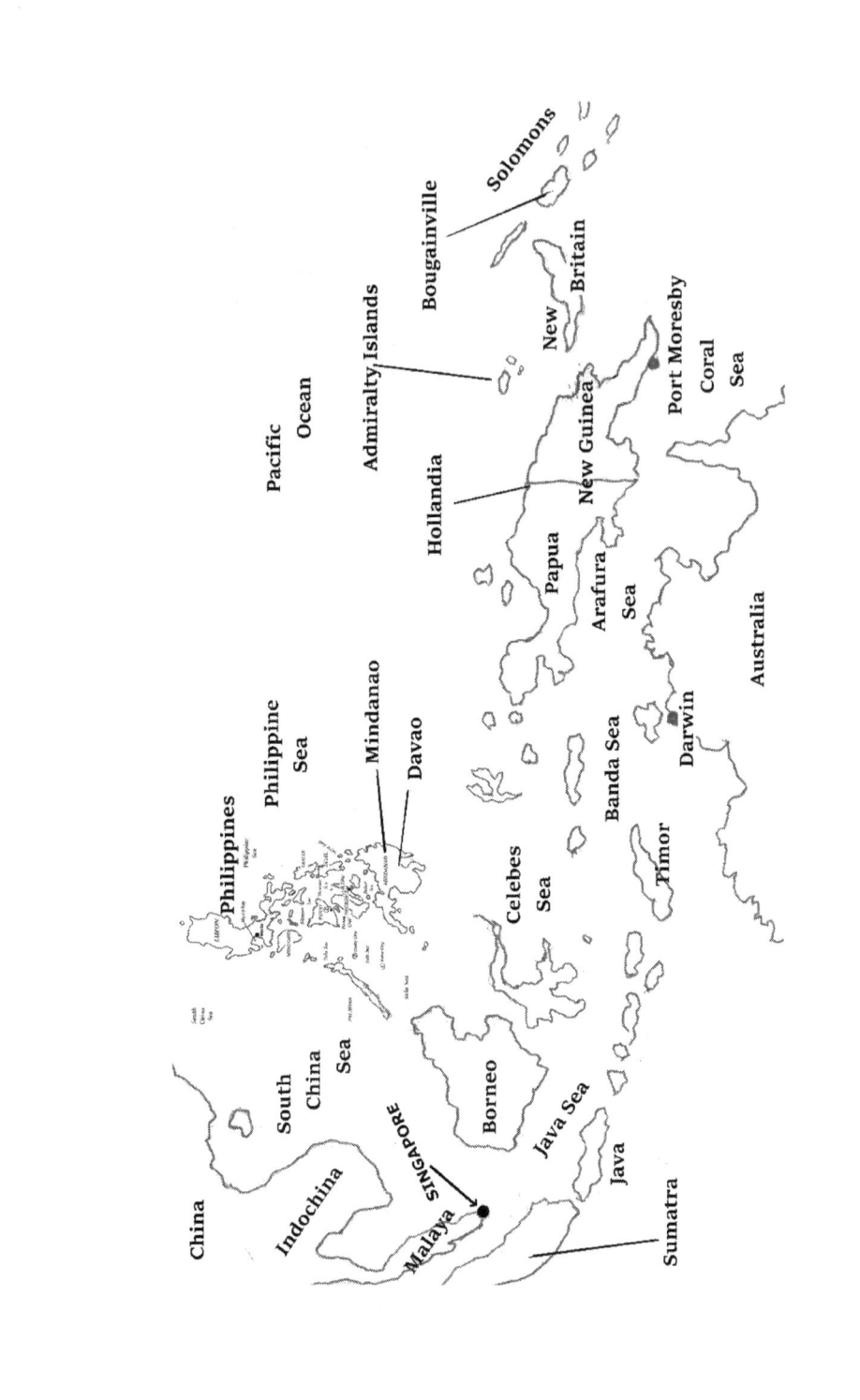

Made in the USA
Columbia, SC
22 May 2022